BREACH
of
TRUST

BREACH
of
TRUST

BONNIE MACDOUGAL

POCKET BOOKS
New York   London   Toronto   Sydney   Tokyo   Singapore

POCKET BOOKS, a division of Simon & Schuster Inc.
1230 Avenue of the Americas, New York, NY 10020

MacDougal, Bonnie.
    Breach of trust / Bonnie MacDougal.
        p.   cm.
    ISBN 0-671-53720-2
    I. Title.
PS3563.A2917B74   1996   96-15059
813'.54—dc20   CIP

First Pocket Books hardcover printing October 1996

10 9 8 7 6 5 4 3 2 1

For my husband,
Robert Kistler

*Nothing is easier than self-deceit.
For what each man wishes, that he also
believes to be true.*

—Demosthenes

PART 1

PLEADING

1

HEADS TURNED AND PATHS CLEARED WHEN DAN CASELLA ENTERED
a room. Jenny had witnessed it before, in courtrooms and conference rooms alike, but her ballet class was an unexpected venue. .
The pianist faltered and stopped, and in the sudden silence, one
last dissonant chord still rang. Monsieur duBret spun a perfect
pirouette on his sixty-year-old toes and drew his brows together in
a furious glare at the intrusion. Jenny froze, almost spellbound at
Dan's manifestation then and there, but the lithe bodies of the
other dancers stirred at his approach, and the line at the barre
fluttered apart like a windblown curtain.

Dan walked past them as if it were nothing more than a deposition he interrupted, and bore down on Jenny. She was bent low
to the floor in a grand plié; her grace evaporated, and she straightened like a leggy colt first finding its feet. She was suddenly horribly aware of her sweat-ringed leotard and the ponytail trailing
limply down her back.

Leslie's head popped up in the mirror, and she made a face at
Jenny, her eyes and mouth going round in an exaggerated panto-
mime of the question "Is that *him?!*"

Jenny shook her head, although it was.

"Jennifer, I need you," Dan said in his hushed attorney-
confidential voice.

Hers was not to question why; Dan was her supervising partner.
"I'll go and change," she offered.

"There's no time. Just put something on and meet me out front."

She nodded and started at once for the dressing room.

"What eez thees?" the ballet master barked.

"I'm sorry, monsieur," Jenny said, breaking her flight beside
him. "I have an emergency at the office."

"You meez too much work at ze barre!"

"Because she's got too much work at ze other bar!" Leslie hooted
from the end of the line.

He turned his glare on Leslie, and Jenny seized her chance to
flee.

"See ya later, litigator!" Leslie called.

Jenny hurried into the curtained stall of the dressing room, pulled off her toe shoes and leg warmers, and pulled on her gray suit jacket and pleated skirt. No time to change, Dan had said, and she took him at his word. She stuffed the toe shoes into her ballet bag, pulled her dress pumps out of her briefcase, and dashed out in under five minutes.

Dan stood waiting, his hands in his overcoat pockets, at ease there in the musty old vestibule of the arts building as he was everywhere. A stream of women brushed past him with raised brows and salacious smiles, some of them dancers, some of them instrumental students from upstairs, all of them enticed by the incongruity of this darkly handsome, dangerous-edged man all done up as a Philadelphia lawyer.

"What is it?" she asked as she shrugged into her coat and hurried through the door he held open for her.

"New case," he said. "A crisis."

It was cold on the street and twilight dark. The January days were growing longer, but not enough to notice. Jenny did a breathless half-skip to keep up with Dan's long-legged strides up Broad Street.

"Who's the client?" she asked first. Not even two years out of law school, and already she knew to ask that first: no point in learning the facts before fixing the perspective.

"Harding & McMann."

Harding & McMann wasn't a client, it was a competitor, another major Philadelphia law firm even bluer-chipped than their own Foster, Bell, & McNeil. If Harding & McMann needed a lawyer, it had two hundred of its own to call upon. Why Dan?

"What's the crisis?" she asked instead.

"They caught one of their lawyers dipping into the till."

"Stealing from the firm?"

"Worse." The traffic light at Chestnut was red, and Dan paused at the corner. "He was stealing from a client."

The light changed, and he plunged across the street.

"Now what?" she asked, hurrying after.

"Now he wants to spill his guts." Dan turned and gave her his first and last smile of the evening. "And we need to be there to catch them."

*　　*　　*

4

Harding & McMann's clients were upper management and old money, and so the firm occupied the upper floors of an old office building in a once-grand block of Broad Street. The other big law firms had moved to the new office towers on Market West, but H&M stuck fast to South Broad. The firm had more than a hundred-year history there, its partners maintained; there were traditions to be preserved, not to mention a substantial equity interest in the joint venture that owned the building. A block away stood the statue of William Penn, an austere English Quaker perched unhappily atop the ornate French Empire architecture of City Hall.

The lobby was locked when they arrived, but the guard had been alerted. Dan spoke his name into the intercom, the lock buzzed free, and they stepped into the elevator to the twentieth floor. Jenny gave him a sidelong glance as he ran his fingers through his crisp black hair and straightened his glasses. They were tortoiseshell today. Dan changed glasses the way he changed ties, with the result that they were never a part of him. Whenever he went without, his face was still unmistakably his own.

In the polished brass of the elevator doors, Jenny could see her own face, devoid of makeup and therefore also unmistakably her own, thin and oval, the eyes too light-colored and too deep-set, her too-high forehead not at all disguised by the long brown hair pulled straight back into a ponytail. She dropped her gaze to the floor, but not soon enough to miss the reflection of her legs, clad in smudged pink tights.

The elevator doors opened, and a tall, blond, balding man sprang from a chair in the reception area.

"Dan." His relief was audible.

"Charlie," Dan said with a handshake but no smile. "Is he still here?"

"Still holding court in the conference room."

This must be Charles Duncan, Jenny realized, the managing partner of Harding & McMann. He wore shirtsleeves, a tie at half-mast, and a deep furrow across his brow.

"Charlie, this is my associate, Jennifer Lodge. Charlie Duncan."

Duncan gave a distracted nod in her direction and turned to lead them down the corridor. All the offices were in after-hours darkness, but at the end of the corridor a light flashed on and off like a storm warning. A door opened and the light shone again from inside the room as a woman emerged, middle-aged, wearing a crushed blouse barely tucked into a creased skirt. She brandished an empty coffeepot. "Coats," she said, her voice too tired for the inflection of a question mark.

Their coats were surrendered, and the woman swayed around a corner as Duncan ushered them into the conference room.

Every Philadelphia law firm worth its timesheets had one grand conference room dedicated to important ceremonies and other occasions when it was necessary to impress. This was Harding & McMann's. The ceiling was twelve feet high and coffered; the walls were paneled in some rich-grained wood from the rain forest and hung with portraits of the founding fathers in garb and facial hair that bespoke the nineteenth century; and the table was thirty seamless feet of burnished wood, necessarily built where it stood.

That table was ringed with men in shirtsleeves who could have formed the receiving line at a meeting of a Distinguished Philadelphia Lawyers club. This, Jenny surmised, must be the executive committee of Harding & McMann. Affirmative action had not trespassed here; to a man they were white and over the age of forty-five. But they looked less distinguished now, in rumpled shirts with five-o'clock shadows creeping up from their collars.

Dan was crisp by contrast, and the partners brightened at his entrance as if he brought a fresh set of facts with him.

"Dan, good to see you."

"Thanks for coming on such short notice."

A white-haired man sat near one end of the conference table with his shoulders hunched and his head bowed as if the weight of guilt were heavy upon him. The eyes of the executive committee seemed to touch him and skitter away.

A younger man stood against the wall at the other end of the room. He was slim and blond and fine-boned, and although he was also weary-eyed and shirt-sleeved, he looked fresher by twenty years than his colleagues. There was a tension to his stance, and one that Jenny knew well. He was on hyper-alert, the muscles stretched tight beneath the white cotton of his shirt, coiled to spring at the bidding of anyone and everyone who might beckon. An associate, then, in a room full of his bosses, maybe none of them officially so, but each of them having a full vote when his own partnership election came up. He looked past Dan to Jenny, and his face lit up a second before he suppressed a grin at her curious ensemble, and in that second his eyes warmed to a hazy blue.

Fellow lowly associate, Jenny recognized, and the spark of kinship was almost worth her flush of embarrassment.

"Dan, this is Tucker Podsworth, chairman of our estates department," Duncan said.

The white-haired man rose and Dan shook his hand, with more courtesy than Jenny thought a thief deserved. She gave him only a curt nod.

The woman who took their coats returned with a fresh pot of coffee. She set it on the credenza and took a seat at the foot of the table. A steno pad lay before her, the top page covered with angry black doodles. Jenny took a seat at midtable and pulled from her briefcase the yellow pad she never traveled far without.

"So," Duncan asked Dan, "how do you want to begin?"

Dan took off his suit coat and hung it carefully over the back of his chair before he sat at the head of the table. Jenny had never seen him sit anywhere else. She had once watched him take the head of the table with a disarming apology—"I just want to be sure I can see everyone"—then watched him wrest control of the meeting while everyone else was too dazzled to notice. He was only thirty-seven, young in lawyer years, and except for the vigilant associate, was the youngest man in the room. Yet even here, with a former federal judge in attendance, there was no question who was in command.

"I want Scott to begin," Dan said, and he turned to fix his gaze on the young blond man standing against the wall. "At the beginning."

With a jolt, Jenny realized that the attentive associate was the thief, not the old man wearing the mantle of guilt. She threw him a startled look and he flushed pink; it was the curse of the fair-skinned that they could never hide their shame. She looked down at her legal pad. Only Dan kept his gaze on Scott. Everyone else preferred to watch Dan—a natural enough reaction, to watch the man who might rescue them, rather than the man who might have ruined them.

The thief straightened from his post against the wall. "I have a client . . ." he began, then stopped to clear his throat. "Or should I say 'had'?"

There was an appalled silence, and Jenny stole a glance at him through her lashes. He met her eyes, and she thought she saw a glimmer of something in the way he held her gaze, pleading, perhaps, for somewhere to look other than the backs of his bosses and the face of his inquisitor.

"Go on," Dan said.

"I was counsel for a trust created under the will of the late Elizabeth Mason Chapman."

The names registered. The Masons and the Chapmans were two of Philadelphia's oldest and most blue-blooded families. Each had founded itself on something industrial in the 1800s, branched into banking, and now concerned itself principally with charities and horses.

"Who's the beneficiary of the trust?"

"It pays fixed income for life to the widower, Reese Chapman, additional income at the trustee's discretion to their daughter Catherine, the corpus to Catherine when Reese dies."

"Who's the trustee?"

"Mrs. Chapman's brother, Curtis Mason. Uncle Curt brought the trust to me."

"Uncle?" Dan cut in.

"No, we're not related." His attention wandered to Jenny. "He and Father are old friends. Went to Lawrenceville together."

Frowns flickered around the conference table. This was the kind of background Harding & McMann thrived on—someone whose father went to prep school with a Mason, who moved in the right circles and could be counted on to bring in the right kind of business, and who, if not brilliant, was at least safe and reliable. Seemingly. Frowns deepened.

"Uncle Curt retired as chairman of Macoal Corporation last year. He started spending winters in Palm Beach and summers in Bar Harbor, and he needed someone to take day-to-day control of the trust. So I did more than just draw up instruments. I started handling the investments, and I made the disbursements."

"He gave you a power of attorney?"

Scott said simply, "He gave me the checkbook."

Jenny's eyes shot to Dan, but he never gave anything away. "Go on," he said.

"I wrote the checks. Twenty thousand a month to Reese Chapman, per the terms of the trust. Varying amounts to Catherine, as requested. As needed, to pay taxes and accountants' fees. To pay our own fees, as a matter of fact."

Charlie Duncan blanched and ducked his head to hide it.

"How'd you sign the checks?"

"Curtis G. Mason, Trustee."

"Did Mason know what you were doing?"

"He knew *that* much."

"What didn't he know?"

Scott stopped and drew a breath. "He didn't know I started writing checks to cash and depositing them into my own bank account."

Jenny stared at him, but Dan didn't miss a beat. "How long and how much?" he asked.

"Started about four months ago. Roughly two million dollars."

Those were the kind of numbers people like the Masons and Chapmans dealt in; nobody would bother robbing them for a few thousand dollars. But what for? Jenny wondered. Student loans, BMW payments, even a recreational drug habit wouldn't amount to a fraction of that.

But Dan wasn't interested in the why until he understood the how. "What bank did you write the checks on?"

"Not a bank, a brokerage—Connolly and Company. The trust assets were held there, in an account with check-writing privileges."

"Who got the account statements? And the canceled checks?"

"Curtis G. Mason, care of me."

Dan let a silence pass before he asked his next question. It came conversationally, as if he were merely curious. "How'd you get caught?"

Scott lifted his chin toward Tucker Podsworth, who squared his shoulders and cleared his throat.

"Purely by accident, I'm afraid," he said in a voice as self-consciously patrician as his name. "I was looking for a file in Scott's office. He'd left the trust checkbook open on his desk, with a check already made out to cash and signed Curtis Mason."

"How'd you know it wasn't legitimate?"

"The ink was still wet. And I spoke with Curt in Palm Beach this morning."

Dan turned back to Scott and gave him a long look of silent appraisal.

"You're right," Scott admitted. "Careless. I deserved to be caught."

"Or wanted to be."

The tension in his body gave way and he uncoiled from the wall in a burst of agitation. "No! No—you see, I was going to pay it all back. If I had time to finish—"

"Finish what?"

"Uncle Curt's investments."

"The trust investments, you mean."

"No. Uncle Curt's personal investments. That's where the two million went. Seed money for Uncle Curt's investments."

Dan looked at Jenny, and down the length of the table she could feel the charge he sent out, the electric thrill that there might be a defense here after all.

"Back up," Dan said. "The money went into your own bank account."

"For starters. But then I wrote checks on that account—counter-checks so my name wasn't printed on them. And I signed them with a signature *nobody* could decipher. Then I deposited them into Uncle Curt's brokerage account."

"Why?"

Scott flashed a lopsided grin, one Jenny would have found charming under different circumstances. "I like to play the market. I'm good at it, I really am. But I never had enough capital. I won't until Grandmother's trust kicks in when I'm thirty-five. So I'd make up phantom portfolios, you know? And track how an investment would have performed if I'd actually bought it. I was a millionaire a couple times over, on paper.

"Uncle Curt was complaining that his broker didn't deliver, and I showed him my numbers, and, man, was he impressed. He said, 'How about doing that for me? Direct my trades, deal with my broker, and see what kind of results you can get.' He said, 'The broker gets the commissions, but tell you what—I'll pay you for your time like you're doing legal work, and if you deliver, there'll be a nice cash bonus for you.'

"I said fine, but the truth is I would've done it for nothing. It was my chance to play for real, and if Uncle Curt got all the profits— hey, he was always sending me business, talking me up—I figured it was a fair exchange.

"He put a hundred thousand into his brokerage account, gave me a trading authorization, and told me to have at it."

"Who's the broker?" Dan asked.

"Brian Kearney. Connolly and Company."

"Same guy who had the trust account?"

Scott nodded, impatient to tell the rest of his story. "So I opened a new file, Mason Investment Advice, and logged all my time against it. I went heavy into options. I needed a quick turnaround to show Uncle Curt some fast results. The broker said I was too far out, but you have to be aggressive to win this game."

"You lost it all," Dan said.

"Nope," Scott said. "In one month, the account value was two hundred thousand. I'd doubled his investment!

"But then the market turned on me. All the positions went south, and I couldn't keep up with them fast enough. Uncle Curt kept calling. 'How're we doing today?' I didn't have the balls to tell him the truth. No reason for him to know—it'll turn around. So I said, 'Great, you made fifty thou yesterday on those IBM puts.'

"It snowballed. At the end of three months, the account was zeroed and Uncle Curt thought he had two million dollars."

Dan gave Jenny a look that said *This is important, get it down.* "He thought he had a two-*thousand*-percent return on his money in three months?"

Scott nodded, both earnest and matter-of-fact. "That's what I told him. And he trusted me."

"So you dipped into the trust account to make it good."

"It was just sitting there," he said. "A ten-million-dollar corpus. Reese Chapman's only getting twenty thousand a month, and Catherine doesn't ask for much. The corpus won't be distributed until Chapman dies, and he's only fifty something. Nobody would miss it. So, yeah, I robbed Catherine to pay Curt."

"And Mason had no idea."

"Of course not."

"Where'd he think the check deposits were coming from?"

"I told him it was income. Trading profits."

"Are you still directing his trades?"

"Yep. And I'm turning it around."

"What's Mason's account balance today?"

"Roughly one point seven five million. I'm up fifty thousand since last month."

"You're *up?*" Dan said in the razor-sharp voice he saved for moments like this. "Let's see—you're missing two million from the trust, you lost Mason's hundred grand, and his balance is two fifty less than what you told him it is. Sounds to me like you're *down* two point three five."

He drew blood. The color left Scott's face, and his back slumped against the wall. "Yeah," he mumbled.

2

THE NIGHT WENT BLACK OUTSIDE, AND THE LONG STRING OF LIGHTS that formed the commuter traffic on the Schuylkill Expressway dwindled to solitary flashes. Jenny's watch was stuffed in a toe shoe in her ballet bag, but she guessed it was after ten. The coffee no one had helped themselves to burned acrid on the credenza, its fumes alone keeping them awake. The woman who had brought it moved to a secretarial station outside, where she was typing Jenny's notes into a statement that Dan might or might not allow Scott to sign.

Now that the big picture was in focus, Dan was filling in the details. What checks were written when? What deposits made when? What trades ordered? What conversations with the broker? What conversations with Mason? Files were retrieved from Scott's office one floor down and spread out over the table. Dan pored over them, reconstructing the paper trail, shooting staccato questions at Scott when the path wasn't marked.

Scott was eager to help. "No, this came first," he said, reordering the chronology of the papers. "See this entry? That's when I did it." Dan posed questions from an hour before and watched carefully to see that he got the same answer. Scott noticed but answered anyway. *Hey, no resentment; just doing your job. I understand.*

The why of it plagued Jenny. Fellow lowly associate, erstwhile kindred spirit—why would he throw it all away before it even arrived? Like her, he'd suffered through law school and surely some of the yawing self-doubt that went with it. He'd endured an apprenticeship like her own, with a firm that regarded associates as fungible nonentities, worth two thousand billable hours a year, ever in the shadow of partners with little interest in grooming others to share their limelight. And since she now knew he was thirty-two, she also knew he was almost through his apprenticeship and on the brink of transmogrification into partner—i.e., real lawyer, a goal that was still unfathomable years away for Jenny. To forfeit all that was incomprehensible.

But the mystery was over for everyone else. The executive committee members dispersed through the corridors, and their voices could be heard in a buzz of conversations outside. Jenny's stomach rumbled inside her leotard, and she faintly recalled the salad at noon that had been its last visitor.

The whine of the printer stopped, and the secretary reappeared in the conference room with a sheaf of papers. Without a glance, Dan handed them to Jenny, who at last began to earn her fees. Focus on the firm's actions or inactions, knowledge or ignorance, Dan had instructed her, and so the statement read: "No one at Harding & McMann participated . . ."; "I acted alone and without the knowledge of anyone . . ."; "I took the following steps to conceal my activities from the firm."

Typed below the signature line at the bottom of the last page was his name, Scott Bartlett Sterling.

Jenny's jaw dropped, and she looked up and around the room until she found him staring at himself in the black mirror of the window. Scott the thief was Scott *Sterling?* She *knew* that name. For much of the past year, Leslie had schemed at fixing her up with her fiancé's college buddy, a lawyer named Scott Sterling. Bruce and Leslie were convinced Scott and Jenny were perfect for each other, but she'd resisted the idea and nothing had come of it. Still, she'd heard enough about him to fill a small file. His family was old Philadelphia, and his father was some kind of corporate bigwig. He'd been married to a capricious heiress who dumped him for a polo player. There was a child somewhere, whom he seldom got to see.

He saw her reflection in the glass as she watched him, and she looked away in embarrassment, wondering if her name rang the same bell with him, if he'd been reciprocally pestered by his friend Bruce. She gathered up her papers and escaped into the corridor.

Twenty minutes later, the revised statement came out of the printer, and the group shuffled back into the conference room. Their five-o'clock shadows were now full-fledged stubble that rose almost to meet the bags drooping under their eyes.

"Read through this," Dan said to Scott, placing the pages before him. "Let me know if it's accurate."

No one spoke as Scott read the statement. Someone in the room wore an old-fashioned watch that ticked the seconds. The ticks sounded more loudly with each passing minute.

At last Scott looked up, his expression more sober than before. "Yes, it's all true," he said, but there was something in his voice, perhaps audible only to Jenny, that said, no, it couldn't possibly be.

"Scott."

The change in Dan's voice might have been too subtle for anyone else to notice, but Jenny heard it and knew what it meant. No more inquisition. Now he wanted cooperation.

"I think I speak for everyone around this table when I say you've really gone the distance in what you did here tonight," Dan said. "Any other guy might have clammed up and left the firm to flounder in the dark. You've made my job a hell of a lot easier, and you've put your firm in a much more tenable position than it would have been otherwise. I appreciate it, and I know everyone in the room feels the same."

No one else looked appreciative, and if Scott had only glanced at their faces, he would have seen the lie. But he kept his eager-to-please face turned to Dan.

"I want to do the right thing," he said. "It's my mess, and I should clean it up."

Dan stood up and reached into the breast pocket of his coat where it still hung on the back of his chair. He pulled out his pen and handed it to Scott.

All the eyes that had refused to touch Scott for the last several hours now forgot their squeamishness and homed in. Scott's posture altered in that instant from ever-alert to a strange self-importance. *Got your attention now, don't I?* he seemed to say.

Dan leaned over him and pointed to the signature line on the last of the pages. Scott's eyes moved down the page and his fingers gripped Dan's pen.

But suddenly his head came up and his eyes sought Jenny. There was no self-importance now. She saw only trepidation. And then something else—a plea for help.

No, she thought, horrified. *Don't look to me for guidance. Don't you realize I'm on the other side?*

But his eyes beseeched her, *What should I do? I'm out of my league here.*

Dan followed the line of Scott's vision, his gaze ending at Jenny. He straightened and gave her the same steady look as Scott. But there was no question in Dan's eyes. It was an order.

Jenny let a ghost of an encouraging smile come to her lips, and she inclined her head a fraction of an inch.

It was all Scott was waiting for. He signed his name with a flourish.

Pent-up breath was released around the table.

"Initial each page, too?" Scott said, the voice of a lawyer who'd presided over hundreds of will signings. Without waiting for an answer, he scrawled his initials on the corner of each page.

"We won't keep you," Dan said. "Let me walk you to the elevator."

Scott's eyes skirted the table as he rose, but he didn't press his luck with farewells.

Chairs groaned as two-hundred-pound weights sank back deeply. Tension blew out like a sighing breeze through the room.

"You were right, Charlie," one of the men said, his palm massaging his beard stubble. "Casella's good. I'd never have believed he'd pull that off."

"We're damn lucky to get him," another voice spoke.

"But even Dan Casella can't save our asses on this one."

The last remark came in the sonorous tones of Judge Moore, and Jenny felt a sinking dread that it must be true.

Dan returned, brushing his hands together as if he'd just taken out the garbage. He lifted his chin at Charlie Duncan, and Duncan cleared his throat. "Maggie?"

The secretary looked up, drained.

"We won't need you anymore tonight. Get yourself a cab home."

She climbed out of her chair, and Dan closed the door behind her and turned back to the men around the table.

"What next?" Duncan asked.

"Fire him."

Jenny flinched, though clearly it had to be done.

"All in favor?" Duncan said, and the hands went up around the table.

Dan remained on his feet. "I'll draft the termination letter for your signature, Charlie. Have it hand-delivered to him at home tomorrow."

"What if he comes to work tomorrow?" Tucker Podsworth wondered.

No one seemed to doubt he was capable of it. "Give him the letter," Dan said. "If he wants to clear out his office, let him, but somebody stay with him and look over everything he packs. If he gives you any trouble, call me."

"Tucker, you're elected," Duncan said, and Podsworth sighed.

"Station somebody outside his office," Dan said. "Keep it sealed off until we can go through everything in there. Get into his computer and back out every piece of data he put into it.

"Charlie, tomorrow morning you and I call Curtis Mason. Tucker, what's the law on beneficiaries? Do we have an obligation to notify Reese Chapman and his daughter? Or the right?"

Podsworth delayed in answering so long Jenny thought he'd lost the question. "In a situation like this," he intoned at last, "where there seems rather clear evidence of a breach of fiduciary duty on the part of Mason, I'd say, yes, we have a right and a duty to notify Chapman of what's happened."

"What about the daughter?"

Another pause before Podsworth shook his head. "Notice to her father ought to suffice."

"Okay. Tomorrow we put in calls to Mason and Chapman, tell them what's happened and ask them to come in—separately—to discuss it. Judge Moore, can you sit in with us?"

The judge nodded. Aging partners brought in as figureheads knew their duty.

Dan braced his hands on the chairback. "Next, we call the district attorney."

A murmur of objection sounded. "Surely that's not necessary?" one of them, John Warrington, said.

Dan turned on him. "Does anyone here doubt a crime's been committed?" He waited, but no one dared to. "Does anyone volunteer for obstruction of justice? Or accessory after the fact?"

Warrington shook his head.

"If it helps," Dan offered, "I'll make that call alone." Silence carried the vote.

"Last item for tonight. A press release, explaining what you've discovered and what steps you're taking to remedy the problem."

"No," several protested, while others shook their heads emphatically.

"You want Mason to get there first, and put his own spin on it?"

"He won't do that," Podsworth said. "He's one of us."

Dan released the chairback and thrust his hands in his pockets. "One of you who happened to let two million dollars of trust money trickle into his own account? He's got no choice but to get to the press first."

"Dan, we can't afford to go public with this," Duncan said. "Half our trust clients will yank their business out of here within a week."

"Any of our clients will," Warrington cut in, "if they think they can't trust their own lawyers."

"And what will they think when they read Mason's version?"

Duncan shrugged. "We can only hope they'll think he's some crank, and that it's his word against ours."

Dan waited, unhappy with the verdict and weighing his chances on appeal. "You're the client," he said finally.

Exhausted good-nights were exchanged as he shrugged into his coat and left the room, Jenny in his wake.

3

DAN WAS SILENT DURING THE LONG ELEVATOR PLUNGE TO THE ground. Jenny had seen him thus preoccupied with battles a dozen times, planning his next campaign, oblivious to all else. He'd been her supervising partner for all of her six months at the firm, but still she felt no more at ease with him than she had the first day she was summoned to his office. She was reluctant to interrupt his thoughts, even to inquire what he wanted of her next.

But he came alert when they emerged into the cold night air. "Where's your car, Jennifer?" he asked. "I'll walk you there."

His gallantry always disconcerted her. "I took the train," she said, shaking her head. "I'll just go down to the station at the next corner."

"It's one A.M. The trains stopped running at midnight."

"Oh." *Time flies,* she thought better of quipping.

"Come on. I'll drive you," he said.

"No," she protested. "You can't. I mean—I live way out in Radnor."

"Come on," he repeated and walked on.

She hesitated, afraid to risk his displeasure by objecting further, afraid she'd already earned it by causing him to drive out to the Main Line suburbs in the middle of the night when he lived no more than ten blocks from here. But after a moment, she trotted to catch up and fell into silent step beside him. The empty streets were bathed in amber lights and sepia shadows, and there was a bone-deep chill in the air.

His was the last car left on the firm's floor of the garage. It was black and crouched low and sleek, ready to spring into motion like the jungle cat it was named for. Jenny slid into the passenger seat, clutching her purse, her briefcase, and her ballet bag on her lap like some kind of Yuppie bag lady. It was even colder in the car, and she huddled inside her coat.

"I knew I'd need you tonight," Dan said. "But I never guessed how much." He switched on the ignition but the illumination of the dashboard lights on his face gave her no clue of what he could mean.

"All I did was draft the statement," she said.

"There wouldn't *be* a statement if it weren't for you." He backed out of the parking space and started down the ramp. "Didn't you see what happened back there? He wasn't going to sign. He finally remembered he's a lawyer, for Chrissake. But he looked to you. And you gave him the push."

"I thought you were signaling me to," Jenny said, as if that absolved her.

"I was." They'd reached street level and Dan pulled out onto Market Street. "Once I saw that connection, I made the most of it."

Connection, she thought, and debated telling him of Leslie's matchmaking, and her almost-acquaintance with Scott Sterling. But it seemed trivial in light of the night's revelations and the problems that lay ahead. Only a fool would bring up such a thing at a time like this, and Jenny couldn't bear to look foolish to Dan.

"What will you do with the statement?" she asked him. "Will you give it to the DA?"

He shook his head. "It's strictly for H&M's protection."

Protection from what? Jenny was missing something.

In the firm's orientation program last fall, one of the senior partners delivered what he styled as *The Best Advice You'll Ever Hear:* "No question is ever more stupid than not asking it. *Ask.*"

But that advice was easier to nod at than to act on. Jenny tried forming the words "I don't get it," but the most she could muster was, "I'm not sure I fully understand the exposure here." She winced at herself, not only an idiot, but a tentative idiot. "I mean, the money was misappropriated, but it's not lost. It's almost all in Mason's own account."

"You think he'll just put it back where it came from?"

"He has to. It's not his."

"Isn't it? If his so-called investment advisor had delivered what he promised, Mason would have two million dollars today. Sterling didn't funnel off the trust money just for the hell of it. He did it to cover up his losses on the options trading."

"You mean H&M could be liable not only for the two million stolen from the trust, but also for the two million in trading profits that never even existed?"

"For starters."

19

"But Sterling isn't a broker. How could H&M be liable for his private dealings with Mason?"

"That's it," Dan said, pleased that her mind had found the tracks of his own. "But Mason was smart. He had Sterling open a new file. Mason Investment Advice. A good cover for his claim that this business was all within the scope of representation."

"You don't think Mason engineered this?"

"Who else benefited?"

"H&M, through its billings," Jenny shot back.

Dan's brows lifted, and she stammered, "I mean, maybe somebody—"

"No—" he cut her off. "You're right. They were profiting from it; they should have been supervising it."

As his gaze returned to the highway, Jenny was reminded of two events in their brief history. One occurred a few months before: in an offhand comment that undoubtedly left his memory the moment he uttered it, Dan had said, "You know, you'd be a hell of a lawyer if you'd learn to stick up for yourself."

The other went back to her first assignment with him. He'd just won a big antitrust trial, appeal had been taken, and Jenny, fresh from a court of appeals clerkship, was dispatched to his office.

"I want you to go through the trial record," he'd told her as she diligently took notes. "Figure out what all the issues on appeal will be. Do the research. Then give me a good first draft"—Jenny was already nodding, knowing what was next—"of the other side's brief."

She'd looked up with a jolt.

"I don't know what to say in my brief until I know what they'll say in theirs," he'd explained. "Oh, and Jennifer," he'd added as she started to leave, "write it like you mean it."

Good lessons, both of them. A young lawyer could learn a lot from Dan Casella, which was why so many of Jenny's fellow associates envied her assignments.

He took the exit off the expressway, and turned left and left again at her directions. A fog was sinking into the hollows of the back roads. "What's your street?" he asked her.

"Coventry Road. Turn here and it's about two miles down."

The well-kept suburban houses gave way to open countryside. A four-foot-high fieldstone wall appeared on the right and ran along the roadside for a hundred yards, until Jenny said, "Turn right at the crest of this hill."

Dan slowed and turned, and the car passed between a pair of stone pillars that once held an iron gate to block the lane. Nothing but deep woods appeared through the fog ahead.

"What *is* this place?" he finally asked.

"It's the old Dundee estate. I live in the carriage house."

"Dundee? The Heritage Cereal people?"

"Yes. Turn left here where the road forks."

The headlights swept like search beacons over weed-choked fields and dense stands of trees before they finally came to rest on an old building. It was shingle-sided and wrapped around a courtyard like a squared-off horseshoe, and it looked more like a barn than a house. The car dipped as the tires hit the cobblestones in the courtyard. The wings on either side each held two garage bays while the center section was a dormered two-story house built around a massive central chimney.

"Quite a place," Dan remarked.

"It's drafty and the roof leaks, but I like it."

"You live here alone?"

The question meant nothing. Young lawyers in center city firms typically didn't live in remote carriage houses in the country, that was all.

"No." But then she rushed on, "I have a housemate, my friend Leslie—" Even that was too ambiguous, so she tacked on, "A friend from dance class."

"And a few pets, too," Dan observed.

The big yellow dog Jenny had been feeding for a month stood by the door, his tail swaying from side to side in tentative welcome, while the two cats snaked in and around his legs.

"No, they're just strays." Jenny gathered up her purse, her briefcase, and her dance bag and worked a hand free to pull the door open. "Thanks for the ride."

When she reached the door, Dan lowered the window and called after her. "Hey, Jennifer."

"Yes?" She turned back, her eyes blinded by his headlights but all ears for another assignment.

"I never knew you were a dancer."

The window closed, and the car looped around the courtyard and was gone.

4

Dan's hand worked the gearshift and his foot the accelerator until he had the Jaguar up to sixty. The road was narrow and winding, but at this hour it was all his. The countryside blurred past him in black shapes swirling through white fog against the gray night. He twisted his shoulders, trying to shake some of the tautness out of his neck. Christ, what a night. H&M was going to take a hit, big time, but everyone in that room expected him to pull something out of the hat and save their collective ass. So what was his next move? Search desperately for something in the hat, or convince his client there was no hat?

A dark shape streaked through his headlights, and he slammed his foot to the metal. The tires screeched to a stop and the engine stalled. Six feet ahead a deer stood frozen and trembling on the road.

Dan caught his breath. Wisps of fog drifted in an eerie glow around the deer. He sounded the horn, and the deer trembled more violently, but still didn't move. He remembered then that light immobilized deer, and he pushed the headlights off. When he turned them on again, they stared blindly at an empty road.

He had a dizzying sense of disorientation. The Main Line was foreign turf for him, but it was more than that. There was a sense of unreality about this place—the mist, the deer, Jennifer's otherworldly house. For a second he felt as if he'd lost his place. He turned the ignition and the roar of the engine brought him back. He pointed the car for home.

Dan's high-rise condominium was a few blocks south of the federal courthouse where he'd spent the start of his career prosecuting drug dealers and politicians. His fortunes had improved since he left the government, but instead of moving out of the building, he moved up. Now he owned a small penthouse—a penthouse because that was the best—small because a bed and a bath were still all he needed in a home.

The lighting in the apartment was a cool white to go with the minimalist look for which the decorator had charged him the maximum price. He hit the switch and the lights washed over the pewter-gray leather of the furniture. The cleaning lady must have been in today—the place reeked of lemon and Lysol.

The red light was flashing by the phone in the hallway. Dan hung up his topcoat and pulled off his tie and suit coat. His glasses came off, too. He didn't need them—the lenses had a barely perceptible prescription—but he'd learned that most people didn't automatically attribute intelligence to a man with an Italian surname and vaguely Mediterranean features. The glasses helped.

He pushed the message button on the answering machine and turned up the volume so he could listen from the kitchen. He swung open the refrigerator door; a six-pack of beer and a carton of leftover Chinese stared back.

"Dan," a voice purred on the machine as he opened a beer, "I've been thinking about you. It's been such a long time. Why don't you come over sometime? 'Bye."

Dan took a swig and mumbled a curse on all women who refused to identify themselves on answering machines. He went back to push the replay button when the second message began.

"Danny, it's Teresa," said his sister, one voice he didn't need to have identified, even when it was strained with anxiety. "You hear from Tony? It's after midnight, and he's not home yet. We had some trouble with him before he went out, and Mom's worried sick. Give us a call, huh?"

He grabbed the phone and dialed before the message ended. Teresa answered on the first ring. "Tony?"

"Jesus." Dan raised his wrist. It was nearly two. "He's not home yet?"

"It's Danny." He could hear his mother sobbing in the background. "What should we do, Dan? Call the cops?"

"No." His brother was only fourteen, but he'd already had enough near-misses with the police to last a lifetime. "Don't do anything. I'll be right there."

*   *   *

23

It was twenty blocks south and a world away to the tightly packed Perma-Stone rowhouses of Gasker Avenue. Halfway there, Dan realized he should have taken a cab, because he'd never find a place to park. This was a neighborhood where old men sat in lawn chairs all day to save parking spaces for their sons when they came home from work. Nobody was saving a space for Dan.

The lights were blazing at his mother's house, but he had to circle the block and turn back onto Broad before he found fifteen feet of vacant curb. He was in his shirtsleeves, and the cold bit into his arms as he ran the last few blocks and up the white marble steps that his mother kept polished to a gleam. Teresa's face was at the window. She let the sheers fall when she saw it was Dan, and stepped over to open the door. She was wearing her coat.

"Any sign of him?"

She shook her head. Their mother Mary sat in a corner of the couch, wearing a floral-print bathrobe that made her fade into the cabbage-rose slipcovers.

"What happened?" Dan asked, and at the edge in his voice Mary rocked forward, clutching her arms over her abdomen. Tony had come too late in her life; she'd been overwhelmed by him since his birth.

Teresa flopped down on the couch, her coat still buttoned. "He blew up. I told him to stay home tonight for once—we never know where he is or who he's with; he's turned Mom into a nervous wreck—and he blew up."

She lifted her hand and pushed a wisp of dark hair out of her eyes. A purple circle stained her cheekbone, the imprint of a fist.

A gorge of anger rose in Dan's throat. "I'll kill him," he choked. He spun on his heel and burst out of the house.

"Danny, no," Mary cried behind him, but Teresa said nothing and he kept on running, down the marble steps and along the pavement to the end of the block. The cold didn't touch him now. A hot mist of fury steamed his eyes, and he stopped at the corner and blinked to clear his vision.

This was his old turf, the neighborhood he could once map out blindfolded in his sleep. Now it felt like enemy territory. Every other house on the block was in darkness, and the streetlights made shadows that lurked in the doorways. He used to prowl

24

these streets, invulnerable, the immortal youth, but now it seemed they were landmined with danger.

A van turned off Broad and advanced at a crawl down the block. It was dark, with blacked-out windows along the sides and back. It passed his mother's house and drifted to a stop at the far corner. Dan started back, keeping to the shadow line against the houses. The dome light came on inside the van and shone on three men across the front seat. Some words were exchanged, low and guttural, before the back door swung open and a dark shape climbed out on the pavement. The face that passed under the streetlight belonged to Tony.

"Hey!" Dan shouted.

At the sound of Dan's voice, the door slammed and the van turned the corner and was gone.

Tony froze on the sidewalk. He was a muscular boy, and from a distance, dressed as he was in a motorcycle jacket and combat boots, he passed for an older punk than he was. But close up, he was still a smooth-cheeked boy with a head of silky black curls and bright dark eyes. Those eyes were shifting right and left, looking for escape or formulating an alibi, but Dan reached him before there was time for either. He grabbed the front of his jacket in two fistfuls.

"What's going on? Who were those guys? Do you know what time it is?"

"Nobody," Tony said, choosing his question. "They gave me a ride, that's all."

"Ride from where? Where the hell've you been?"

"Lemme go." The boy brought his arms up and broke free, and Dan grabbed him to hold him back. There was a hard metal lump inside his jacket.

"What's this?" Dan said, reaching for it.

"Keep your fucking hands off me!"

Dan twisted Tony's arm behind his back and worked a hand into the pocket. He pulled out a gun.

"Jesus Christ," he breathed.

"No! Give me that; it's not mine!"

It was the real thing, a .38-caliber revolver, heavy, cold, and lethal. He checked the cylinder and the chamber and was only marginally relieved to find them empty. He jammed the gun into his belt, and when Tony made a dive for it, Dan cracked him on the jaw. The boy cried out.

The door flew open, and their mother stood silhouetted on the threshold. If there was one thing she'd drummed into them as children, it was that decent people didn't conduct their personal business on the street. Dan collared Tony and dragged him into the house.

"Danny, he's home now; it'll be all right," Mary said, clutching at his arm.

Teresa stood silent, her bruise reproaching him from across the room.

Tony tore loose and bolted up the stairs. Dan shook his mother's hand away and followed after him, taking the stairs two at a time. He arrived panting on the third-floor landing just as Tony's door was closing, and a second later, the lock sounded. But Dan remembered those locks. He raised his foot and kicked the door in with a crash.

Tony was at the window, struggling to raise the sash high enough to scramble through. Dan remembered those windows, too, and knew he'd never get this one open in time to escape.

"I warned you," he said. "I told you, anything like this happened again, I'd beat the crap out of you."

Tony gave up on the window and turned to fight. "Did she call you?" he screamed. "That cunt—"

Dan unbuckled his belt and whipped it off. Tony tried a fake around him, but Dan grabbed him in a headlock under one arm and gave him a half a dozen licks across the rear before he set him free.

The hot mist was gone, but the steam of Dan's rage was still heavy in the room. Tony dove for his bed and pulled himself into a huddle in the corner. Dan threaded his belt back on, but let it hang unbuckled, an unspoken threat of resumption. The women's murmurs sounded in the hall, and he yanked the door open. Mary took a step into the room, glanced once at Dan, then rushed to Tony's side. Tony turned blindly to her, and she cradled his head, rocking him as he cried. "Hush. Hush, my baby," she crooned.

Dan looked at Teresa. She rolled her eyes.

"Get away from me!" Tony screamed, and gave his mother a shove that sent her sprawling backward across the bed.

"That does it!" Dan grabbed Tony's arm and jerked him to his feet.

"No, Danny," Teresa said quietly. "That's enough."

"It's not enough," he said, though his hands dropped to his sides.

Tony sank to the edge of his bed. A trickle of blood ran from one corner of his mouth. He looked smaller than he was, like the little boy who'd once been everyone's pet.

Teresa helped Mary to her feet, and they both stared uncertainly at Dan.

"Yeah. What now?" he muttered. He raked his fingers through his hair, and spun out of the room.

In the hallway, he sagged against the cracked plaster wall. For five years, he'd been meaning to spackle and paint these walls. While he was at it, he ought to wire a new ceiling fixture so it wouldn't look so gloomy coming up the stairs. His mother and Teresa had enough gloom in their lives without living with bad light, too.

"Yeah, what now?" he repeated to himself.

A few minutes later, he stepped back into the room. The women still hovered, waiting for Dan to steer their course. Tony was holding a tissue to his lip and watching Dan through his lashes.

"Teresa, get me a suitcase," he said. "A big one. Mom, give me a hand here." He opened the top drawer of the dresser. Underwear, socks, *Hustler* magazine.

"Danny, what are you thinking?" Teresa said.

"He's moving out," Dan said. "He's coming with me."

"No!" Tony shrieked.

"Shut up," Dan said, wheeling on him. "Not another word out of you."

"He'll be a good boy," Mary said. "Won't you, Tony? Tell Danny you'll be good."

"Come on," Teresa scoffed. "You can't do this. You work twelve hours a day. You travel all over the country. Who's gonna look after him if he lives with you?"

"Who's gonna look after you two if he lives here?"

"We can take care of ourselves."

"Oh, yeah?" When Dan reached out to finger the bruise on her cheekbone, she flinched and brushed his hand away. He pulled the gun from his waistband and held it in front of her face. "You wanna see if next time he uses this?"

Mary gasped. "He would never—"

"Get a suitcase," Dan said, and Teresa left at once.

Dan pulled the car into his underground space, reserved for him not by an old man in a lawn chair but by a number that matched an account into which he paid a hundred dollars a month. He put the gun into the glove compartment and locked it. Clutching Tony's arm in one hand and his suitcase in the other, he pulled him out of the car and into the elevator. He pushed the Stop button at the lobby floor.

"Morning, Al," he called to the security guard.

The black man looked up from his newspaper and his eyes moved from Dan to Tony.

"This is my brother. He's gonna live with me for a while."

"How do," the guard said, his expression carefully blank.

"Do me a favor," Dan went on. "You ever see him leave my apartment without me, you call the cops first and me second."

"You got it, Mr. Casella."

No one had slept in the spare room since one of Dan's old prosecutor buddies came to town on assignment last summer and wanted to pocket his per diem. He was damned if he was going to make up the bed now. The kid could sleep on the mattress for all he cared. But when he pulled back the spread, he found there were sheets on it, courtesy of the cleaning lady, he supposed, or maybe that redhead he dated for a week last month who wanted to move in and play house.

"Get into bed," Dan said.

"Can I take a leak first?" Tony jeered. "Or you want me to pee all over your fancy sheets?"

Dan jerked his head toward the bathroom and watched him stalk into it and slam the door.

God, he was tired. He stood at the window and tried to stretch out his spine and rub some of the stiffness out of his neck. The view from here stretched south, all the way past the stadiums. He could almost make out his old neighborhood; he could clearly remember how badly he'd wanted out of it. And now he'd brought the worst of it home with him. The ignorance, the violence, the unthinking rages, all rolled up into one fourteen-year-old boy.

Tony came out of the bathroom and sullenly kicked off his clothes. One side of his lower lip was swollen, and Dan knew he should get some ice for it, but he couldn't make himself move. Tony slid under the covers and turned on his side with his back hunched toward Dan. "I got school, you know," he said, his voice muffled against the pillow.

"You're through at that school," Dan said. "The nuns've had their chance with you." One more chore for tomorrow—scout out a new school for Tony.

"So what happens to me? Don't I even get to know?"

"Vince retires from the navy next year." The plan came to Dan as he spoke, but it sounded good. His older brother had escaped family responsibilities for nineteen years. Let him take his turn. "Until then, you're staying with me."

"You *think.*"

Dan lunged for him and thrust him onto his back. "Let me tell you something, wise guy," he warned, looming large over his face. "You try to run away, you won't even make it to the river. I used to be a fed, remember? I got more friends at the Bureau than you can count. One call from me, and they'll be all over you. And they won't do it nice, like I did tonight."

Tony's expression gave nothing away. It was impossible to tell whether he was scared or scornful. The streets had done that to Dan, too. The first lesson you learned was build up your armor.

He left the room and picked up the warm beer he'd started two hours earlier. It was four o'clock. In five or six hours, he'd be at Harding & McMann, placing the calls to Curtis Mason and Reese Chapman, inviting them to make his life hell for the next two years. The thought of Scott Sterling made him wearier still. Another bad boy, but if he was telling the truth, one with no armor at all.

He went to the window in the dining room and leaned his forehead against the cool glass. A squad car was at the corner of Sixth Street, flashing blue and red lights on a knot of people huddled around it. For all he knew they were looking for Tony. God only knew where he'd been all night, and what he'd done.

The thought of the gun made Dan sick. He *should* take it to the police, have the registration traced, and get a fix on what kind of trouble Tony was in. But he knew that what he *would* do was throw it in the river first chance he got.

He looked in the bedroom a half-hour later. Tony was sprawled across the bed on his stomach. The covers had twisted away, and Dan pulled them up. The boy stirred and made a sound between a groan and a whimper but didn't wake.

The resemblance between Dan and Tony was so strong Dan could see it himself. People routinely mistook them for father and son, and there'd been fleeting moments when Dan was amused by that, long ago when Tony was a winning little boy and seemed like a gift their father had left behind, instead of a drain on all their energy and emotion.

There wasn't a day in Tony's life that Dan's feelings for him hadn't been tinged with resentment and plagued with guilt. Dan was twenty-three when he was born, in his first year of law school and on the brink of the world. His plans were laid; the scholarships and loans were all in place. He'd worked hard, but the payoff was close.

Until one night outside Lancaster, his father collapsed over the steering wheel of his rig, took out a mile of barbed-wire fence, ran up an embankment, and landed upside down in the middle of Route 30. The autopsy showed a mild heart attack, one he easily could have survived if he hadn't been decapitated in the wreck.

After the funeral guests were gone, their mother gathered them together and wept out the news that she and her husband had been so far keeping to themselves: in six months, she would have another baby.

Vince was already career navy, and never thought to give it up to come home and support the unexpected little brother. Dan had lined up the part-time jobs he needed to support himself until he finished school, but there was no room in his plans for his mother to quit work and have another baby.

It fell to Teresa, a senior in high school with plans of her own. She withdrew her college application, got a job as a secretary for a funeral director around the corner, and devoted her income and her life to her mother and Tony. She'd been the beauty of South Philadelphia, and bright enough to do anything she wanted. Now she was thirty-three, with a pinched face and rounded shoulders and a job that was death in every sense of the word. All for the sake of this punk. No, not true. All so Vince could sail and Dan could soar.

He went back to the dining-room window and looked down on the street. The squad car was gone, but the huddle of people remained, rehashing whatever event had brought the police earlier. A car cornered Washington Square too fast, and its headlights caught the people in a guilty pose, like a search beacon on fleeing felons. The scene reminded him of the deer he'd caught in his headlights on the back road in Radnor last night.

Unexpectedly, his thoughts flashed on Jennifer Lodge. He knew her as a hard-working, bright young lawyer, but he hadn't failed to notice that she was also quietly beautiful, with her glossy brown hair, the clear blue eyes, the fluid way she moved her body. He'd never known she danced, but wasn't surprised when one of the other associates directed him to the studio to find her. How incredibly graceful she'd seemed when his eyes found her in the room. She was swept low to the floor like a willow tree in a gentle breeze. And when he came closer, she'd been like something wild, like that doe, coiled for flight. What a beauty she was. A Dundee, apparently, or at least connected to them. And living in a house all out of time and place to anything he'd ever known.

Dan cast a look over his shoulder to the room where his worthless double slumbered.

Out of your league, Casella, he chided himself, and tossed back the dregs of his beer.

5

THERE WAS A PHOTOGRAPH OF A LITTLE GIRL ON SCOTT STERLING'S desk, a chubby toddler with hair like fine-spun silk and the bubble of a laugh just bursting on her lips. Jenny's eyes kept wandering back to it as she worked her way through the drawers of the desk. The camera had caught the child on the beach, with her arms outflung and her sun-kissed face raised up for more. It was a face that could bring tears to the eyes of any childless woman approaching thirty.

Jenny knew from the tax returns in the bottom left-hand drawer that the little girl was Amanda Bennington Sterling, now not quite three. She knew from the papers in the file labeled Sterling, Scott—Domestic, that her mother was Valerie Bennington Sterling Ross and lived in Florida. She knew from the American Express bills that Sterling flew down to see his little girl once a month. Were those expenses somehow a factor in what he'd done? Jenny added the bills to the stack of documents to be photocopied.

She'd spent the morning picking through the flotsam of his life. Tucker Podsworth and his crew had already been through all the Chapman Trust files and Mason Securities Advice files and were now reviewing Sterling's remaining files for other "irregularities." The bank and brokerage statements, the canceled checks from his bank account, the trade confirmations from Connolly and Company—all had been carted to a conference room down the hall, where a team of auditors was tracing the flow of money. The only things left in Sterling's office were his personal effects, and it was to these Dan had pointed Jenny.

She paged through his calendar and his timesheets, his form files and his Rolodex. He had the expected numbers for the Register of Wills and the clerk of the Orphans' Court for Philadelphia and the four outlying counties. He had neatly typed cards for Curtis Mason (home), Curtis Mason (FLA), and Curtis Mason (ME). He organized his pens by color and point size, but left another drawer full of pretzel crumbs and candy wrappers.

The same drawer held an old-fashioned gold pocket watch etched with an elaborate coat of arms featuring a rampant stallion in one quadrant and a dove bearing an olive branch in another. There was another photograph here, of a boy of about twelve on horseback, outfitted the proper English way in hard hat and jodhpurs and gleaming knee-high boots. The fine-boned features were the first clue, but the lopsided grin was the giveaway: Scott Sterling as a boy equestrian.

At the back of the drawer were scraps of paper with cryptic scrawls of letters and numbers that might have been stock trades. Jenny added them to the stack for photocopying. A full-size sheet of paper was crumpled and tossed into the back of the drawer. She laid it on the blotter and spread out the creases. It was a memo from Charles Duncan and Tucker Podsworth to Scott Sterling, dated last November, "Re: Annual Performance Evaluation."

Suddenly her scalp crawled. She'd never violated anyone's privacy as much as she was violating Sterling's at that moment. His work was slipshod, according to the evaluation; his billable hours were low; his clients found him unreliable. His chances of being elected to partnership were slim to nonexistent.

The memo was certainly no secret to Harding & McMann, but only Jenny knew that Sterling's reaction had been to ball it up and hurl it into his junk drawer.

She thought of how it would feel to receive such a memo, and the horror was more than she could imagine. But this much she knew: she'd want to receive it in privacy, with no one ever to witness her shame.

She couldn't bring herself to add the memo to the stack of evidence against Sterling. The creases in the paper seemed the grossest self-incrimination, and something he had the right to be protected from. She crumpled it up again and placed it back in the drawer for him to reclaim when he cleaned out his desk.

If he ever did. Jenny hesitated for only a second before she snatched the memo out of the drawer and stuffed it into her skirt pocket.

The desk phone rang, and Jenny gave a guilty start before she picked it up.

"Jennifer," Dan said, before she could wonder how to answer. He and Charlie Duncan were across town meeting with H&M's liability carrier, which had wasted no time in denying insurance coverage for Scott Sterling's intentional wrongdoing. "See if Sterling has a number for Mason in Florida."

"He does," Jenny said, thumbing through the Rolodex. "Done at the insurance company?"

"They're done with us. It was a waste of time."

"Here." She read him the telephone number.

"Finding anything?" he asked.

"Not really."

"Looks like we're all wasting our time," he said before he hung up.

"Exactly," she said to no one.

33

Absently, she held the phone in her hand while her mind wandered a thousand miles away—until an angry buzzing on the line roused her and she hung it up.

"Ssssh."

Jenny bolted upright in the chair. Scott Sterling stood in the doorway with his finger pressed to his lips.

"I'm not supposed to be here," he whispered. He was in a business suit and perfectly groomed, his golden hair brushed and gleaming.

She hurried to her feet. "It's your office."

"Not anymore." He patted his breast pocket and something crackled inside. "I've just been *terminated*. Interesting word, huh?"

She inched out from behind his desk. "Do you want me to call anyone?"

He shook his head. "I just need to get something out of my desk."

He pulled the junk drawer open, and Jenny felt the memo burn hot in her pocket.

"Here it is." He reached into the drawer and pulled out the pocket watch. "It's my good-luck piece," he said. "And something tells me I'm going to need it." He gave a rueful glance to the pretzel crumbs before he closed the drawer and headed for the corridor. "Sorry about the mess."

He tossed the watch into the air and it winked gold in the light before he caught it and slipped it into his pocket.

It was almost seven before Dan called her again.

"Can you come up?"

She'd been his associate for six months and still he didn't remember that her office was two floors above his. She picked up her file—a two-page inventory of the contents of Sterling's desk and a ten-page outline of her afternoon's research on attorney-client relations, securities fraud, breach of trust, conversion, and unjust enrichment—every issue she could anticipate he might ask her about.

Dan was on the phone when she arrived and he waved her into a chair. His office was a sterile place, all polished chrome and black leather, and not a photograph to be found. But it occupied a prime location, with six windows looking out on the art museum—clear testimony to his stature in the firm.

"Who's this? Bobby?" He dropped his voice and swiveled his chair a quarter-turn away. "Listen, do me a favor? Send out for some food and have it delivered to my apartment. I don't know. Hoagie, chips. Maybe a chocolate shake. I'll settle up tonight. Thanks, Bobby. Appreciate it."

Not even a business call, Jenny thought, trying to work up irritation. *Ordering a snack for a lazy lover while he keeps me waiting. And one with a monstrous appetite besides.*

Dan hung up and turned back to his desk. "Sorry," he said. He was wearing steel-rimmed glasses today, and the frames were too thin to hide the dark circles of fatigue under his eyes.

"Let's see." He shuffled through the papers on his desk. "I met with the DA this afternoon."

Jenny had been puzzling through that question since the night before. She put her notes down and leaned forward in her chair. "If this is a case of securities fraud, doesn't it belong with the U.S. Attorney?"

"It would if it were. And if we reported it to the feds, we'd be as good as stipulating that it is."

She saw his point and instantly regretted the question. "Yes, of course," she murmured.

"It wasn't securities fraud," Dan insisted, his voice rising. "It was a diversion of funds. And that's it."

"Yes," Jenny repeated, her own voice rising to match his. "I understand."

He pulled off his glasses and massaged the bridge of his nose. "Sorry," he said. His eyes were opaque and impenetrable to her, like black ice on a frozen pond. After a moment he said, "Where'd you go to school, Jennifer?"

Her comment was even stupider than she thought. Now he was questioning her credentials.

"Penn."

"No, I mean high school."

"The Alexander School," she said, baffled.

"Alexander. That's here in Center City, isn't it?"

"Yes. On the Parkway."

"Good school, you think?"

"Very good."

Dan replaced his glasses. Without explanation, he picked up his notes again. "Charlie and I put in the calls to Mason and Chapman this morning. Mason's flying up from Florida in the morning. We're meeting with Chapman at ten, and Mason at two."

"How'd they react to the news?"

"Chapman was confused. He didn't know which trust we were talking about. Jeez, imagine having so many trust funds you can't keep them straight. He didn't know who Scott Sterling was, and he suggested we contact the trustee."

"And Mason?"

"Exact quote?" Dan picked up his notes: " 'That money's my trading profits. I don't care where it came from. And besides, you owe me more.' "

Jenny's eyes went wide.

Dan tossed the paper onto his desk. "We're in for a fight," he said.

6

THERE WAS SNOW IN THE FORECAST, AND WHEN JENNY DROVE HOME from the train station that night, the air was so cold it pierced her flesh like shards of ice. It was two miles from the station to the Dundee place, and there wasn't enough time for her car to warm up before she was home. Her shivers came like convulsions.

She found the animals huddled on the slate doorstep, cats curled up against the dog, primeval grudges forgotten in the quest for warmth. The dog gave her a mournful look as she rattled her keys, and his tail beat disconsolately on the slates. She unlocked the door and swung it open.

"In you go."

The cats streaked past her, too savvy to question their good fortune, but the dog turned up an astonished, hopeful look. "You, too," she said. He skulked through the doorway and looked up at her again. "Yes, I really mean it," she laughed. Only when she closed the door behind her could he accept that it was true and venture all the way in.

The first floor of the carriage house was one enormous room with a huge double-sided fireplace rising like a spinal cord through the middle of it. The kitchen was crammed against the rear wall to the left under the stairs, and in front of it was the dining room, consisting of four mismatched chairs and an oak slab table Jenny had found at a flea market. On the other side of the room a sofa draped with patchwork quilts huddled before a dying fire on the hearth. One good piece of furniture stood like a shrine against the front wall: an antique armoire that was Leslie's and would leave when she did in April.

Jenny stoked the fire and started for the stairs when a blast of music trumpeted from beyond the dining room. It was Léo Delibes ballet music, Leslie's not-so-subtle signal that Jenny was late for barre.

"I'm coming!" she called, and to the animals she coaxed in a whisper, "Come on, this way—atta boy," until she had them safely herded into the garage bay used for storage, before Leslie could see them and squeal at the horror of four-footed creatures in the house. Whatever heat the storeroom held was somewhere up in the rafters, but it was warmer than outside, and the animals still looked grateful. She closed them in and hurried upstairs.

Three doors opened off the second-floor landing: Jenny's room, Leslie's, and their single bath. She pulled off her clothes as she ran to her room and threw them across her brass bed. Another horror for Leslie: she worked as a department-store buyer of designer fashions and treated clothes with a reverence most people reserved for great works of art. Jenny pulled her door shut to spare her the sight and trotted downstairs in a leotard and tights.

A door from the dining room led into the other garage bay, and she found Leslie waiting there by the woodstove in the corner.

"What eez thees?" Leslie cried in perfect mimicry of their balletmaster. She was a tiny woman with a mop of black curls and a lively sparkle that just saved her from waifdom. "Eight-feefteen, mademoiselle!"

"Par-done!" Jenny dropped a mock curtsy and skipped to her place at the barre.

It was a room once meant for fine brougham carriages, then for

Packards and Bentleys all the way up to Mercedes, but a few years ago the progression came to a crashing halt. Now the Dundees were gone, their manor house razed, and this garage bay lovingly converted by Jenny into a ballet studio. The old concrete floor still showed around the perimeter, but the center was covered by a free-standing dance floor she bought from a party rental company going out of business. She'd hung plate-glass mirror on three walls and mounted a barre on the fourth.

Like throwing money away, Greg had said while he stood and watched her work with his arms crossed disapprovingly over his chest. Greg was the one who found the carriage house. He'd been hired to do the soil engineering tests for the land use plans that eventually would lead to the Estates at Dundee, a Luxury Home Community, and he cajoled the builder into renting the place to them until it was slated for demolition. Six months later Jenny came home from work to find the lease, Greg's house keys, and a one-word note—"Sorry." She carried a lot of regrets about Greg, but she never regretted building the studio. Already it had outlasted her engagement.

"*Battement tendu*," she called out, grasping the barre, and started the slide of her working leg to the front, the side, the rear. In the mirror, she watched Leslie follow her lead. Although Leslie had the perfect petite, flat-chested ballerina's body, her dance career was recent; Jenny was the serious student. She checked her own form in the mirror. She was too tall and full-breasted for the ballet, but she was satisfied with her carriage.

"Come on, give!" Leslie said.

"*Tendu jeté.*"

"Jenny! Was that him?"

"Who?"

"Was that the famous Dan Casella? And what did he want you for?"

"Work, what else?"

"He's gorgeous!" Leslie could safely make such a declaration. Her wedding was three months away, and Bruce knew he was adored.

"*Grand battement jeté*," Jenny said. Her muscles were warming now and limber enough for her to raise her leg straight up to waist height, to the front, the side, and the back.

"Your mom called last night," Leslie said, mimicking her movements. "She said don't bother to call her back. I gave her all your news."

"I don't have any news. Besides, she only calls to talk to you. Otherwise she'd call me at the office."

"She had this weird idea you'd be home by ten o'clock. She hasn't figured out yet that the office is your real home."

"Not true. *Port de bras.*" Jenny's arm swept the way as she bent her torso over to the front, then the back.

"But who can blame you? With a gorgeous guy like Casella to share quarters with."

Jenny tried to ignore that, but upside down between her legs, Leslie made a face at her, and both of them dissolved into giggles.

A sweep of headlights was reflected in the mirror, and a car door slammed in the courtyard. "There's Bruce!" Leslie exclaimed, as if he didn't arrive every evening at this hour. "Gotta go!"

"I'm telling Monsieur duBret," Jenny called after her.

"Tattletale," Leslie hurled back.

Alone, Jenny finished at the barre, then laced on her toe shoes and changed the CD to Fauré's *Pavane.* She moved to the center of the floor, and as the stately lyrical music of the violin filled the studio, she danced freely, in movements from old performances and new inventions. She let her mind wander as she danced, into places she usually kept if from, where nothing was too much to hope for and dreams almost always came true—away from this place, where it seemed to be her fate to be forever longing for things beyond any hope of fulfillment.

Like ballet. It was her passion from the time she was five years old, but by puberty there was no chance of a dance career. She should have stopped then. She should stop now—she was twenty-seven years old, for heaven's sake. Baryshnikov wasn't likely to come down and recruit her for his corps de ballet—but somehow the disappointment had become addictive, like a tongue that can't stop probing a cavity. She'd become addicted to the pain of longing for things that could never be.

Leslie and Bruce were snuggling before the fire when Jenny came back into the main house. "Hello," she called and kept her eyes averted as she crossed the room.

"Hi, Jenny," Bruce called.

For half a second on the stairs, she wondered if she should tell Bruce about his friend Scott Sterling and his troubles. It wouldn't hurt; it would be public knowledge before long. But she held her tongue, and not only because she still took her oath of confidentiality seriously. Bruce, she knew, would call Scott at once, and somehow she hated for Scott to think she was gossiping about him.

Jenny's blue suit lay on the bed where she'd tossed it an hour before. Something crunched as she hung up her skirt, and when she slipped her hand into its pocket, she found the memo she'd filched from Sterling's desk. Her cheeks burned with an echo of guilt, and she hurried to toss it in the wastebasket.

7

THE MORNING SKY HUNG HEAVY WITH SNOW CLOUDS. DAN STUDIED it through the schoolroom window and wondered if Mason's plane would make it in from Florida. If not, their afternoon meeting would have to carry over until Monday, giving Dan more time to sort through the facts and get a fix on what had really happened between Mason and Sterling. But it would also give Mason more time to line up his lawyer and his story. A wash, then.

He looked at his watch. Nine-fifteen. If he were kept waiting any longer, he'd miss the ten-o'clock with Reese Chapman. No, he wouldn't. He'd miss the interview first, and the Alexander School could find some other sap to pay its exorbitant tuition.

Tony paced beside him. They'd both spurned the seats in the classroom, Dan because he was not about to be relegated to a pupil's desk, and Tony because he was too restless to sit still. Tony's tie was badly knotted—Dan had made a botch of tying a Windsor backward—and his hair needed cutting. But it didn't matter how well he might have been groomed—nothing but a fist would wipe the surly look off his face.

"I'm sorry to have kept you." Those were words that sounded sincere only when delivered breathlessly, but the woman simply strolled into the room, not a hair out of place in her dark-blond pageboy. She was dressed in Main Line matron chic—boiled-wool jacket, plaid skirt, flat shoes.

"I appreciate your seeing us on such short notice," Dan said. He crossed the room and gave her a solid handshake. Behind him, Tony slouched against the windowsill. "I'm Dan Casella. You must be Abby Greenley. How are you today?"

Dan had wooed women and courted clients for years. The skills were transferrable. He held out one of the student chairs for her, preempting her chance to settle behind the teacher's desk. He stayed on his feet.

"Have you had a chance to look over my brother's application?"

The woman gave a cool nod and started to sort through her file. Dan preempted her again.

"Then you know he's had nine years of parochial school, that his standardized test scores are way above average, but his grades have been pretty darn dismal. Miss Greenley, Tony needs a new academic environment. And he needs it now, before it's too late for him."

It was a fair opening statement, but he'd lost the jury. Her eyes weren't steady on Dan where they belonged. She was gazing across the room at Tony.

"Tony, would you come and sit down here, please?" she said.

Tony scowled. Dan walked the length of the room in an effort to pull her attention back to him.

"There's something else you should know about Tony," he said. "Our father died before he was born. He hasn't had a strong male presence in his life. That was my omission, but it's one I'm trying to make up for now. Tony's recently come to live with me. We've still got some kinks to work out in our relationship. If you sense any tension here, that's what it's all about. But we're determined to get through it, and the right school could make all the difference."

"Tony," she said. "Do you want to come to Alexander?"

He straightened from the sill and looked her in the eye. "No," he said and walked out of the room.

The woman finally gave her attention to Dan. She looked at him and shook her head.

Dan smiled. "Would you excuse me for just a minute?"

He reached Tony at the end of the hall and grabbed him by his shirtfront and hoisted him up against the cinder-block walls. "You go back in there and you give the right answers," he rasped against his ear. "You hear me?"

Tony's shuttered eyes showed nothing, but he gave a nod. Dan marched him back to the classroom, dropping his arm as they cleared the doorway.

"I mean yes," Tony said immediately.

"Sudden change of heart?" the woman asked.

He shrugged. "I just said no to piss off my brother. You know, we got some kinks to work out." He shot a sly look at Dan. "The truth is I've been wanting my whole life to come to—to— What's this place called again?"

Dan gave up the façade. He turned an openly beseeching look at the admissions officer. "I hope you'll excuse him," he said, without much hope at all.

The woman closed her file, rose from her seat, and walked past Dan. " 'This isn't a reform school, Mr. Casella.' "

" 'This isn't a reform school, Mr. Casella,' " Dan repeated bitterly as he hauled Tony into the elevator at his apartment building. The woman was insufferably condescending, and that infuriated him as much as Tony's smart-assed sabotage of the interview.

"You think you won, huh?" he said, wrestling with the key and wrenching his apartment door open. "Well, here's your prize, wise guy." He gave Tony a push into the apartment. "You get an indefinite stay in my apartment, with no time off for bad behavior. Have fun." He slammed the door shut and spun on his heel back to the elevator.

By the time Dan parked his car in Center City, the snow clouds had sunk lower and a cold wind had whipped up and was blasting down the north–south streets. It was a two-block walk from the garage to Harding & McMann, and the wind blew so hard it stung his cheeks red.

He arrived at the building with only five minutes to spare. The single elevator at lobby level was shut down for vacuuming. He punched the call button and flipped open his briefcase, rifling through his papers for his notes. They weren't there.

Another elevator arrived, and as he ran for it, his briefcase popped open and his papers spilled out over the lobby floor. A pounding began in his temples as he bent to pick them up. He managed to smooth his hair in the elevator, but everything else felt rough and out of place as the doors opened on Harding & McMann.

Jennifer Lodge was waiting for him in the reception area. "Chapman hasn't arrived yet," she told him in a low voice. "Mr. Duncan and Judge Moore just went into the conference room. I brought your notes."

She radiated a calmness that instantly relaxed him. "What would I do without you?" Dan murmured.

Jennifer lowered her eyes. He felt himself drawn again to her deep, quiet beauty, and it was with a wrench that he remembered she was from a world he couldn't get into for love or money.

Charlie Duncan was as ashen as he was Wednesday night, and he looked as if he hadn't slept in the thirty-six hours since then. Dan gave his shoulder a quick squeeze as he came in the room, and circled past him to shake hands with Judge Moore.

"Appreciate your joining us, Judge."

Judge Moore had sat on the federal district court before he left the bench to appease his second wife's love of money. Dan had cut his teeth as a trial lawyer in front of him, and even though he now knew him for a fool, he never lost his respect for him. He recalled a blistering lecture Judge Moore once gave him on the workings of the hearsay rule; Dan thought he was wrong then, and he knew it now. Still, Moore had taught him a valuable lesson: a lawyer's job was to convince the judge he was wrong without exposing him for an idiot. It was a delicate art.

"Any word from the auditors?" Duncan asked.

"Preliminary report: every penny went into Mason's account at Connolly," Dan said.

"Does that help?"

Dan sat down at the head of the conference table, and Jennifer took a seat near the other end. "It makes it a whole lot cleaner," Dan said. "At least Sterling didn't profit from any of this. On the other hand, he ran through a small fortune. Our boys tell me his trades were so bad he couldn't have done any worse if he were *trying* to lose money."

Jennifer's expression sharpened at that remark, and Dan wondered why. He felt his thoughts drifting toward her again, like the needle of a compass finding its way north.

"Let's review the game plan," he said, turning abruptly to the two men. "The trust is out two million and some change. Mason's account is holding one point seven five. Our opening bid: if Mason pays his account value over to the trust, Harding & McMann will make up the difference in principal, plus absorb all the lost time value. Agreed?"

"That's it," Duncan nodded.

Dan reached for a legal pad and began to sketch out the facts as he would present them to Chapman. Charlie Duncan's fingers drummed a nervous beat on the table. Only Judge Moore seemed immune to the tension; he sat with all the patience instilled by long years on the bench.

At last the intercom buzzed. "Mr. Chapman and another gentleman are here, Mr. Duncan. Shall I send them in?"

"Please."

"Got himself a lawyer," Dan said, and stood up to face the door.

It opened, and a scowling man shouldered his way into the room.

"Curt!" Duncan said. "We weren't expecting you until this afternoon."

"Reese told me what you boys were up to," Mason said. He beckoned to the man in his shadow. "Divide and conquer, eh?"

"Not at all, Mr. Mason," Dan said. "We're glad you could make it here so quickly. Much better for us all to sit down at the same time. I'm Dan Casella."

He held out his hand.

Mason's eyes narrowed. He was a tall and powerfully built man with thinning gray hair receding from a high forehead. His teeth flashed white in a deep bronze tan as his lips pulled back in a semblance of a smile. He took Dan's hand in a hard grip.

"So you're Casella," he said. "I asked around about you. You're a street fighter, they tell me."

Dan felt the sting of the insult. "Oh, I do most of my fighting in the courtroom these days," he said. "Mr. Chapman?" He reached around Mason to hold out his hand to the man behind him.

Chapman was younger, thinner, softer, with a pair of horn-rimmed glasses slipping down his nose. A lock of graying brown hair fell over his brow and a white silk scarf was draped jauntily around his neck, as if he were an airborne aviator or on his way to the opera. "How do you do," he said in an Anglicized accent.

Charlie Duncan and Judge Moore had met them both before, under happier circumstances, acknowledged in murmurs as they shook hands across the table.

"My associate, Jennifer Lodge," Dan said.

Mason ignored her, but Chapman walked down the length of the table to shake hands with her, then took a chair at her end of the table, effectively removing himself from the fray.

The conference room door opened, and Duncan's secretary Maggie backed her way into the room with a tray holding a silver coffee service and a plate of elegant cookies.

"Well," Dan said when everyone was seated and served, "you know the worst already: Scott Sterling diverted two million dollars from the trust. We're here today to figure out the fastest, fairest way to get that money back into the trust."

Mason shot out of his seat. "If that's what we're here to talk about, I'm leaving!"

Charlie Duncan stumbled to his feet, his face more ashen than ever. "Wait, Curt—" he began.

Dan leaned back, his gears clicking into place. He glanced down the table. Judge Moore looked bored, Jennifer looked expectant, and Reese Chapman looked strangely amused.

"What do *you* want to talk about?" Dan asked. "Your trading profits?"

"You got it," Mason fired back.

"Then sit down and talk."

Mason gave him a hard look, smoothed back his hair with both hands, and took his seat again. Dan leaned back farther still, his fingertips forming a bridge in front of him, a posture of deliberate cockiness. He gave a slight nod to Jennifer to take notes, but she was already poised.

"Scott told me he was making money in my account," Mason said. "He quoted me buy and sell prices over the telephone. He kept a running tab of my profits. I believed him. I trusted him. He was my lawyer. I paid Harding & McMann for his services. I expected him to deliver what he promised. And now I expect Harding & McMann to deliver what he promised."

"And exactly what was that?" Dan asked.

Mason pulled a sheet of paper from his breast pocket and slowly and deliberately unfolded it. "As of Monday, the balance in my account should have been two point one million. It turns out there's only one point seven five. You owe me the difference."

"Let me get this straight," Dan said. "You want to keep the two million that belongs to the trust, plus recover another three hundred and fifty thousand from Harding & McMann?"

"You're damn right I do," Mason said, snapping at the mockery he heard in Dan's tone.

"And what about the trust losses?"

"Harding & McMann'd better pay those, too."

Dan turned to face Chapman. "You go along with this, Mr. Chapman?"

Chapman cleared his throat, and his voice sounded in elegant contrast to the harsh echo of Mason's demands. "Not my say, really," he said. "Curt's the trustee. I'm only an income beneficiary, and rather a small one at that."

"Your daughter's the one with the biggest stake, isn't she?"

"Oh, yes. But Curt's always looked after Catherine's interests. I'm sure he will this time, too."

Dan watched Mason's eyes as he looked at Chapman. They were hooded, but the lids didn't droop enough to hide the contempt he had for his brother-in-law.

Dan jotted down the figures Mason had demanded. "How do you happen to know what the actual account balance was on Monday?"

"It says so right on the account statement," Mason said scornfully.

"The same statements your broker sent you every month since you opened the account?"

Mason set his jaw. "Scott told me there was a computer error in the statements. But he was keeping an accurate tally of the account, and he verified it every day with the broker."

"The broker tell you that?"

"Scott told me that!" Mason thundered.

"And you believed him?"

"Ask Scott! He'll tell you I believed him!"

"Scott can't know that," Dan said. "Only you know what you believed and what you didn't believe."

Mason stared at him. "What are you suggesting?" he demanded. "That I fooled Scott into thinking he had me fooled? Good God, try peddling that one to a jury."

"Let's not go talking about juries," Duncan broke in. "There has to be some reasonable solution we can work out."

"Maybe," Mason said, glowering. "Send your hired thug out of the room, and maybe you and I can get this settled."

Dan raised both arms in an attitude of surrender. "Hey, far be it from me to stand in the way. Charlie, Judge Moore, you want to go it alone?"

"I think not," the judge pronounced. "Stay where you are, Dan. Curt, give us your bottom line."

Mason looked pleased, as if he'd broken through a final barrier. "Two million for the trust, plus three hundred and fifty thousand for me."

"Bottom line?" Duncan said. "Curt, that's every penny you're claiming from us. There's no room to move up from there."

"Ha," Mason sneered. "There's punitive damages. I've been learning a lot about punitives in the last twenty-four hours."

"Then you know how often punitives are awarded against trustees who breach their fiduciary duties," Dan said.

"I didn't breach anything."

"You let Sterling have unchecked access to monies that were in your care and keeping."

"Those monies were in the care and keeping of Harding & McMann, one of the most respected law firms in the city. Besides," Mason added with a short laugh, "who's gonna sue me for breach of trust? Reese? Catherine? Not on your life."

The intercom buzzed again. Charlie Duncan snapped an irritated "What?" at the speaker phone.

"Mr. Duncan, there's a gentleman out here who says he's to join your meeting in progress."

Now Mason leaned back in his chair and folded his hands on his chest.

"Who?" Duncan asked, his face a blank.

There was a whispered discussion before the receptionist's voice came back. "A Mr. Robert Perlman," she replied.

A slow grin spread over Curt Mason's face. "See that?" he said to Dan. "I got a street fighter of my own."

"Stop this meeting right now," Bob Perlman said before he was even through the door. "You've got some nerve, Casella, meeting with parties without their counsel present."

Perlman had more girth and less hair since their days together at the U.S. Attorney's office, but he continued to photograph well, and Dan kept up with his career in the newspapers. His cases ran the gamut from murder to mergers to matrimony, and his clients had only one thing in common: notoriety.

"Turn down the flame, Bob," Dan said. "Nobody told us you were retained."

"The meeting's over," Perlman said. "And if anything damaging was said in this room, I'll move to exclude it under Rule 408."

"Damaging?" Dan asked ingenuously. "You mean like Mr. Mason knew to the penny how much money was going from the trust into his own account? You mean like Mr. Mason told Sterling to do it?"

Perlman shot a quick look to Mason to assure himself it was a joke. "Very funny, Casella," he said. "Well, see if this makes you laugh."

He plopped a manila envelope on the table in front of Dan, and handed another envelope to Charlie Duncan.

"You've been served," Perlman said.

"With what?"

"A complaint. Curtis Mason, trustee, and Curtis Mason, individually, versus Harding & McMann and Scott Sterling. Securities fraud, breach of fiduciary duty, conversion, and common law fraud."

"What, no antitrust conspiracy?" Dan asked.

"Keep laughing, big guy," Perlman said. "Your client's gonna be crying all the way home from the bank."

"What's the claim?" Charlie Duncan asked in a whisper.

"Five million compensatory. Ten million punitive."

"Good Lord," Judge Moore said.

"Come on, Bob," Dan said. "Sit down. Have a cookie. You know this thing has to settle, and we might as well do it today."

"You heard the demand," Mason said. Perlman waved him silent, but Mason ignored him. "Two point three five, or we go for emotional distress and punitives."

"Come on," Dan said to Perlman. "How d'you think you're gonna get punitives?"

Perlman gave the room a broad and humorless smile. "Well, Danny boy, it just so happens I know something you don't know."

"Want to share it?"

"We got Sterling on tape," he said. "Curt, Reese, let's go. Gentlemen, see you in court."

8

THE LONG-THREATENED SNOW STARTED TO FALL AT MIDDAY, AND BY late afternoon, the offices of Foster, Bell, & McNeil were all but deserted; the coalescence of a snowstorm and a Friday afternoon was enough to drive even the longest lingerers home. By the time Jenny finished drafting a request for production of the tape recordings, her secretary was gone. She typed it herself, then loitered outside the men's room to ambush one of the messengers as he came out zipping his fly. Grudgingly, he agreed to make a hand-delivery to Perlman's office.

Dan was staring out his window at the eddies of snow when she arrived at his office. Nothing that morning had gone according to plan. When Mason barged into the meeting, they'd lost any chance to woodshed Chapman. When he brought in Perlman, they'd lost any chance of avoiding litigation. Dan could handle surprises like that, but the revelation of the tape recordings seemed to rattle him.

"I've done a request," Jenny said. "It's being served right now."

"He's got thirty days to serve a response. It could be another sixty before we actually get the tapes."

He turned from the window, and she was surprised to see he wasn't brooding at all. The adrenaline was pumping, his mind was working, and she felt herself catching his excitement.

"Here, sit down." To her astonishment, he pointed to his desk chair. "I want you to make a phone call. We'll put it on the speaker, but don't tell him I'm in the room."

"Tell who?"

"Scott Sterling. Here's his home number."

She perched on the edge of the chair. "What do I say?"

"Tell him what Perlman said. Ask him what he knows about any tape recordings."

"Dan, maybe you should—"

"No. He'll talk to you."

Jenny dialed the number. Dan circled his desk and remained on his feet opposite her. The phone rang once, then again, three times, then four. "I guess he's not—" she began.

"Hello," Sterling's voice sounded through the speaker.

Dan gave her a nod.

"Mr. Sterling, my name is Jennifer Lodge. I'm an associate at Foster, Bell. We met—"

"Sure. The ballerina."

"Yes," she said with a shaky laugh. "We represent Harding & McMann—"

"Yeah, I know. Hey, your voice sounds like you're in a concert hall. Why don't you take me off the squawk box?"

Jenny looked to Dan. He shrugged.

She picked up the receiver and put it to her ear. "Can you hear me better now?"

"Much," he said in a voice suddenly intimate.

"I'm sorry to bother you," she said. "But we had a meeting this morning with Mr. Mason's attorney, and he said something that has our curiosity aroused." She felt satisfied with the casualness of that last part and looked to Dan for approval. He nodded it to her.

"Uncle Curt's lawyer? Which one?"

"Robert Perlman."

"Perlman? You mean that criminal guy? Since when is he Uncle Curt's lawyer?"

"Since yesterday, I gather."

"Jeez."

"He said they have you on tape. Any idea what he's talking about?"

There was a long silence. Dan circled around the desk and put his ear next to Jenny's.

When Sterling's response finally came, it was an explosion. "God! Are you saying he recorded me?"

Jenny could hear Dan breathing beside her, so close she could smell the snow and the wind in his hair. "I take it you weren't aware that you were being recorded?"

"No! I mean, why would he do that? What was it, our phone calls? Or was it when I went to his house?"

"We don't know. We're trying to get copies. But meanwhile, any guess what's on the tapes?"

"I can't believe he'd do that. I mean, we all know I deserved to be trapped like a skunk, but Uncle Curt didn't know that."

Jenny's eyes met Dan's. "Maybe he did," she said. "Maybe he didn't trust you as much as you thought he did."

Dan's lips parted in a smile, and Jenny felt the snow melt and the wind stop and the storm give way to sunshine.

"I can't believe it," Scott muttered. "Well, whatever he has, whenever he taped it, it'll be the same old song and dance." His voice went into an exuberant pitch as he mimicked himself. " 'Uncle Curt, guess what you did on the PLA puts yesterday? You're up another ten grand! You bet I'll keep doing it, just as long as I can.' " His tone went flat again. "That's what you're gonna hear."

Dan straightened and crossed the office to the windows.

"I see," Jenny said, unable to keep the disappointment from her voice. "Well, thanks for . . . thanks for . . . Thank you."

She hung up and stared at Dan's back, knowing this was only more bad news. But when he turned from the window he was smiling.

"Jennifer, that was great," he said warmly. "You got him starting to doubt his own story. By the time he sits in front of a jury, he'll wonder how he ever could have thought Mason believed him. Maybe he'll start to remember all the hints Mason dropped about using the trust money to fund his portfolio. Maybe he'll realize he was Mason's victim and not vice versa."

"Is that what you think?"

He rolled up his shirt sleeves. "It's one of the things I think. Come on, let's get to work."

Late in the afternoon they moved to a conference room. Copies of Perlman's complaint were spread out on the table, along with Dan's notes, Jenny's notes, and the auditor's preliminary report. Volumes of the U.S. Code were laid open on the table, turned to the pages of the statutes Perlman was claiming under. Dan was pacing, his Dictaphone to his mouth, stream-of-consciousness words forming themselves into a strategic planning memorandum.

"Find out if Mason paid his quarterly taxes yet. Doubtful—these guys always go out on extension. But if he paid, did he include his so-called trading profits? The brokerage had to send him a 1099 at year end, and it sure didn't show any profits. What did he think when he saw that? Computer glitch there, too? Get a copy of the 1099 from Connolly. Get Mason's correspondence with his tax accountant. Subpoena the accountant's files. They might've had conversations about what he had to report. Jennifer, find out if there's any recent authority on accountant-client privilege in Pennsylvania."

Her head came up when he spoke her name, but he was speaking to her as if she were reading the memo and not as if she were in the room with him. She got up and went into the corridor.

Night had pulled a black veil over the windows, and she couldn't tell whether the snow was still falling. It was after seven, and the cookies at the ten-o'clock meeting were the last things they'd eaten. She went to her office and called out for a pizza.

There was a message on her voice mail from Leslie, recorded at six-fifteen. "Hi! I hope you're already on your way home, but if you're not, don't try it now—it's awful out there! I'm staying at Bruce's tonight. See you whenever we get shoveled out."

The pizza delivery man was crusted with snow when he arrived in the elevator lobby a half-hour later. "Helluva night to be making deliveries," he grumbled. "Roads are a bitch."

Dan was still on his feet with the Dictaphone when she returned to the conference room. She cleared a space on the table and opened the pizza box. The aroma of marinara sauce filled the room. Dan reached for a slice and bit into it.

"Mason's credibility is crucial. Talk to Charlie about hiring a private detective to do a full field investigation. Where does he spend his time and money, and with whom? Does he owe anybody? Is he vulnerable to blackmail? Be sure the entire investigation is conducted under our direction so it's cloaked as attorney work product."

Dan stopped, wolfed down the slice of pizza, then picked up the Dictaphone again.

"Our response to the complaint is due in twenty days," he said.

"Jennifer, draft a motion to dismiss for lack of federal jurisdiction. H&M isn't a broker-dealer, isn't a seller of securities, and isn't otherwise subject to the securities laws. The only federal causes of action pleaded are under the securities acts. If those acts don't apply as a matter of law, then federal jurisdiction falls. If we can kick it into state court, Perlman's looking at three years until trial, and he'll have to talk settlement."

Dan bit into another slice of pizza, and there was a moment's silence while he chewed. "But chances are we lose that motion," he conceded. "If Sterling's fraud was in connection with the purchase and sale of securities, and it was, at least in the broadest sense, then Perlman can probably make it stick in federal court."

Jenny cleaned up the remains of the pizza, disposed of the box and napkins, and returned to the conference room with a soda for each of them. Dan studied his notes in silence while he drained the can.

"Memorandum to file," he started dictating again. "Re: what really happened.

"Theory one: Just what it looks like. Sterling started playing the stock market for Mason, got in over his head, and couldn't stomach telling Mason the truth. So he lied. Little lies at first. Harmless, he thought, forgotten as soon as he had a few good trades to compensate. But the good trades never came. The lie took on a life of its own, and the only way out was to raid the trust.

"Theory two," he continued. "Same as one, except that Mason knows what's going on. He gets the brokerage statements, he knows when trades are really taking place and when Sterling is lying to him. He's known Sterling since he was a kid; he knows he craves approval like a junkie. He knows Scotty has to lie about profits so old Uncle Curt will still think highly of him. But he lets him lie, he pretends to fall for it, because he knows Scotty wants to make it right. He also knows there's an easy way Sterling can get the money to make it right, because he's the one who gave him the checkbooks."

Jennifer was following closely and making notes of her own. Beside each theory she made two columns headed Pro and Con. Beside theory one, she noted as pro: "Both victim and perpetrator swear it's what happened." As con: "It can't be." Beside theory two, pro: "Scott's telling the truth as he sees it; Mason's the liar." Con: "How do we ever prove it?"

"Theory three," Dan continued. "Same as two, except the idea of looting the trust was Mason's from the start. He caught Sterling with his pants down, and he threatened him with exposure, disbarment, the works, if Sterling didn't make it good. Sterling said he couldn't raise that kind of money. Mason said, 'You know where you can get it.' "

Jenny wrote, pro: "Mason's a liar." Con: "So is Scott."

"And finally, theory four," Dan said. "There's something else going on here that doesn't have a thing to do with the trust money or Mason's trading account. Somebody's out to ruin Scott Sterling? Or Scott Sterling's out to ruin Harding & McMann?

"Betty, separate memo to the file. Speak to Charlie about a full field on Sterling, too."

Dan clicked off the Dictaphone and stood silent in the middle of the conference room, his unfocused gaze landing somewhere on the carpet in front of him.

Jenny gazed at him. Despite the late hour and the long day, he was vibrant, pulsing with intelligence, and so handsome it made her eyes sting to look at him.

But still she looked. She stared at his hair where it went into crisp curls at the back of his neck and at his shoulders stretching out the smooth white cotton of his shirt. Her eyes traced the square line of his jaw to the cleft of his chin and up to the lush curve of his lips. And stayed there.

Dan's head came up and his eyes focused. "Jennifer," he said in surprise. "Have you been here all along?"

"Yes," she said softly, watching his lips move as if she were in a trance. *All along.*

Suddenly she went stiff with horror. He *saw.* Her face held all the longing of an unrequited lover, and this time he *saw.*

She jumped to her feet and shuffled her papers together in a flurry, stacking pages in a pretense of order and stuffing them into file folders, shutting books with a slam. She could feel Dan watching her, but she dared not look up.

"I'm sorry, I didn't realize," he said. "I guess I got kind of caught up here. I never meant to keep you so late, especially on a Friday night. I hope I didn't ruin your plans."

"I didn't have any plans." Jenny held the volumes of the U.S. Code to her chest like a shield. "I'll go reshelve these," she said.

"Leave them. Betty can do it Monday."

"It's no—"

"Jennifer, leave them," he repeated, and this time laid a hand on her arm that sent a shiver through her body. "Come on, let me drive you home."

"It's only ten o'clock," she said. "The trains are still running."

"But it's snowing. You know SEPTA shuts down for a drizzle." He leaned close and for a moment, Jenny forgot to breathe.

"I won't take no for an answer," he said.

The wipers beat a maddening cadence across the windshield as they drove out of the city. The snow crossed the headlights in a dense curtain from the north, and a few inches blanketed the shoulders of the road. Traffic on the expressway was light, but the road surface was slick and Dan drove slowly. They did not speak. Once as they passed a car in a tailspin, Dan breathed, "Whew." If that was a word, it was the only one spoken between them until they came to the St. Davids exit.

The trip was already endless, and it would only get worse if they tried to navigate the back roads to Coventry Road. The expressway was black and shiny with melted snow; the moment they left it, the roads turned white, with only two brown ruts to mark the cars that had passed before them.

"Dan, stop here," Jenny blurted on the exit ramp. "We'll never make it through."

He turned to her and laughed. "Stop here and do what? Camp out until the snowplow comes?"

"You get back on the expressway," she insisted. "I'll make my way home from here."

"Jennifer, it's three or four miles to your house. What are you going to do, walk?" He took his eyes from the road and let them run down her legs, stopping at her high-heeled shoes. "I don't think so."

The wipers continued to beat out a steady rhythm as the interminable drive continued. They survived the first steep hill, but one of the tires went into a spin on the next one. Jenny clenched her hands so tightly her fingers went numb. Dan backed the car up a few feet and tried it again. The tire spun again, this time with an angry whir. He backed up a second time, wrenched the steering wheel and approached the hill on the diagonal. Finally they crossed the spot without spinning.

Dan straightened the wheels, and they continued slowly up the hill. They passed a car marooned in the ditch on the side of the road. Jenny peered through a circle in her fogged window, searching for passengers, but saw instead the footprints in the snow leading off to safety.

No car had ventured down Coventry Road in the last hour, and there were no ruts to follow. The snow crunched under the tires, a satisfying sound that made Jenny imagine they had traction. But as the stone pillars came in sight, the Jaguar fishtailed and went into a spin that sent them reeling across the road. Jenny let out a gasp as Dan wrestled with the wheel, and they went spinning and sliding from one side to the other until at last the car came to rest only inches from the ditch along the side of the road.

Dan blew out his breath again, then put the car in gear and slowly pressed on the accelerator. They moved forward and continued that slow, careful pull until at last they turned into the courtyard.

Jenny's relief was short-lived. She was home safe, but Dan had an impossible trip ahead of him. She didn't know what to do. If they were only colleagues, she could invite him inside. If he were only her boss, she could call for help or give him some coffee while they waited for the plow. But tonight she'd let her guard down and destroyed all chance of normal behavior between them.

He switched off the ignition, and her eyes flew to his face.

"I'm afraid you're stuck with me for a while," he said.

"Please come in," she murmured while her heart pounded so hard she could hear the blood rushing in her ears.

She switched on the lights, hung up their coats, showed him to a chair in the living room, and turned on the television for a weather update. She let the animals out of the storeroom and plopped their food into three bowls on the kitchen floor. She turned up the thermostat, and the oil burner cranked on with a grumble.

"Okay if I build a fire?" Dan called from the other side of the fireplace.

"Fine."

The animals finished lapping at their bowls and Jenny opened the back door for them. She turned on the floodlights and watched the cats pick their way gingerly across the patio. The snow was still falling, and it blanketed the wrought-iron chairs like dust sheets over the furniture in an empty house.

Dan was crouched at the hearth with his shirtsleeves rolled up despite the chill. Jenny laid the morning newspaper beside him for kindling. Her eyes skittered away from the thick black hair on his forearms.

"Where's your roommate?" he asked.

"She got snowed in at her boyfriend's place tonight."

"What a shame," he said in a voice she didn't know.

The animals were at the door again; Jenny let them in and herded them into the storeroom. She closed the door and pretended to turn her attention to the television. The weatherman was droning that the storm center might move out to sea, or it might stay where it was and dump as much as twenty inches over the Delaware Valley.

Dan had the fire blazing, and he settled back on his haunches, dusting off his hands with satisfaction. He let his gaze move through the room. "This is some place," he said. "How'd you ever find it?"

"A friend of mine found it."

"Boyfriend?"

She hesitated. "Fiancé."

His eyebrows lifted. "What happened to him?"

Jenny shook her head. "He turned out to have other interests."

"Like what?" he said, grinning. "Stamp collecting? Or cannibalism?"

"Other women."

His grin faded. "What a fool," he said slowly.

She turned away and cleared her throat. "Can I get you some coffee or something?"

Dan climbed to his feet. "I could really use a drink after that drive we had. You too, I bet."

"I'm afraid all I have is wine."

"Sounds good."

Her legs seemed too weak to cross the room to the kitchen. She found a bottle of cabernet sauvignon and struggled to get the corkscrew started, but she fumbled and it fell to the counter with a clatter.

Dan moved behind her and his hand came down over her wrist. "Let me."

He opened the wine and filled two glasses, then motioned her to the fireside. Jenny sank to the rug by the hearth and tucked her feet under the folds of her skirt. He sat down beside her and handed her a glass.

"Here's to the storm," he said.

The wine shone a rich red in the fire's glow. She held her glass still for a toasting click, but she was so bewildered by his words that her first sip became a gulp that half drained the glass.

Dan pulled off his glasses and laid them behind him on the floor. When he turned back to Jenny, his face had changed. His eyes were no longer opaque and impenetrable; they were alive and sparking with desire.

Her vision blurred, but she felt his hand on her neck, slipped under her ponytail, his fingertips warm from the fire. They barely touched her skin, yet a tingle spread wildly down her spine. He slid a finger into the hairband and slowly pulled it off until her hair spilled out over her shoulders. He reached around the nape of her neck to the bone of her jaw and with firmer pressure, he turned her face and lifted it toward his own.

"Jennifer," he breathed before he bent his head and pressed his lips to hers.

Her heart clutched with disbelief, but slowly she forgot that this could never happen and remembered only how she craved him. The kiss deepened and she pressed herself hard against him. The longing welled up inside her and came out in a sob against his mouth.

Dan pulled back and caught her face between his hands. "Stop me if you don't want this," he whispered.

Want this? her mind echoed. This was all she wanted, from the moment she first saw him till the end of time.

"Yes," she said on a sigh.

He bent his head and kissed her again.

The heat from the fire spread like a slow, thick liquid over the hearth and into the room. His hands were on her face and her hair, then her buttons. Her clothes shed like old skin from her body, and a new, naked skin emerged. His emerged as well, and slid against the length of hers, a delicious sensation of skin against skin. They wrapped themselves up in each other and rolled together on the hearth rug. The fire burned hot, and Jenny felt herself glowing. She lay on her back, then opened her legs and pulled him in with a cry.

He moved with unhurried pleasure, taking his time, pausing to kiss and nibble and stroke. He levered back to thrust with long slow strokes, and she forced her eyes open to watch, but the sight was as unreal as the fantasies that played behind her eyelids. In time, it didn't matter, because her eyes hazed over and her breath came out in labored gasps. The strokes came harder and faster, and so did her breath, until she arched up against him with a muffled gasp.

The fire crackled beside them and that was the only sound in the room until Dan released a long, shuddering groan and rolled to the rug beside her. He pulled her to him and tucked her head into the hollow of his neck. His chest hair crunched against her cheek, and his breathing lifted her up and down like the rocking of a boat.

Outside the snow fell deeper and thicker, covering his car until it was nothing but a dim white phantom in her driveway.

9

CURTIS MASON WAS AN ANGRY MAN. HE WAS SUPPOSED TO BE ON A golf course today, in a foursome that included Gerry Ford. Instead, he was snowbound in a musty house with nothing in the refrigerator. The maid claimed she couldn't get a train out to Devon, and the restaurant that had catered their last three parties had the gall to declare an emergency closing. Goddamn that boy, he wished he'd never laid eyes on him.

Otto had to be walked. He'd put if off all day, but it had to be done. Blizzard or not, you didn't let a champion Rottweiler go without exercise. He called the Brewer boy next door to do it—he meant to pay handsomely—but the boy's mother said that he had a cold, she didn't want him going out in the storm. What did she think she'd gain from that kind of coddling? Another Scott Sterling, that's what, soft and spineless to the core.

He snapped the leash on Otto's collar and seethed more. When he got the news from Charlie Duncan yesterday morning, the first thing he did was call Edgar Sterling. It was *his* boy's mess; it seemed only right that he clean it up. Ed heard him out, then politely kissed him off. Mason couldn't believe it. He called back three times, and each time was told, "Mr. Sterling is unavailable." Goddamn him.

Mason was out of sorts, out of patience, and out of ideas. It looked like they'd have to do it Perlman's way, though God knew the newspapers would have a field day. The PR man at Macoal was playing spin doctor, but it would take a whirlpool of spins for Mason to come through this without looking like a dupe, at best. Which was why goddamned Reese Chapman sailed through the meetings yesterday looking like the cat that swallowed the canary.

Otto growled and lunged at the leash, eager to be on his way. Mason jerked the leash back with one hand and clamped his hat down tightly on his head with the other. When he pulled the door open, a dune of snow drifted into the hall. Dorrie would have a fit about that, too, like the fit she had yesterday when she had realized she had to let Bob Perlman into her living room. "I don't understand why Dickinson Barlow can't handle it," she complained. Dorrie lived in a little dream world full of teas and good works. She didn't have a clue how vulnerable he was.

It was almost dark outside; he should have left sooner, but who remembered such things when the sun was still shining in Palm Beach? He waded to the street through snow deeper than his Wellington boots were high. If the Brewer kid couldn't go out to walk the dog, there wasn't a snowball's chance in hell that he'd be allowed to shovel the walk tomorrow. Mason tried to remember if there were any other kids in the neighborhood, but drew a blank. He'd have to ask Dorrie; she kept lists full of trivial details like that.

The driving snow and wind stung his face. It was eighty-five in Palm Beach today, and clear skies. Goddamn that Harding & Mc-

Mann. Why couldn't they wait until spring to make their big discovery?

Otto was no Saint Bernard, but those powerful shoulders and legs plowed a path that Mason could more or less follow through the snow. Not a soul was out on either side of the street. Everyone else was south, he figured—where he'd be if it weren't for that goddamned boy.

Otto lifted his leg high and squirted a yellow stream against a drift of snow.

"Atta boy, Otto," Mason said.

Otto had won Best of Breed two years running, and Mason thought he had a good shot at Best of Show next time around. His stud fees were going through the ceiling. He was a dog worth having—not like those little froufrou numbers their friends had down in Florida. Jesus Christ, it was bad enough you had to put up with fags in the human population—why would anyone want to have a fairy dog?

Otto pulled him across the street and into the park. The wind was blowing so hard now that their trail was fast disappearing behind them. A bicycle path cut down the hill and through the woods, and Otto pulled that way. "Not much farther now, boy," he called, but Otto kept on barreling.

The light grew dimmer and Mason's stomach growled. What the hell were they supposed to do about dinner? Nobody was going to deliver and there wasn't even a TV dinner in the freezer. The pantry was full of canned goods, but Dorrie hadn't cooked a meal in ten years. They might have to go next door and beg for hospitality from that Brewer woman with the sniveling brat.

A crack sounded from the woods, and the air creased beside his ear.

"Wha—!" he bellowed, spinning.

Otto braced his legs and started barking furiously in all directions.

"Who's there?" Mason shouted.

The woods were full of shadows, and he couldn't make out a goddamned thing. The wind howled all around him, and he started to wonder if he'd only imagined a gunshot. Maybe it was nothing more than a dead limb snapping off a tree. He'd felt a bullet whiz past his head, though—he was sure of it.

"Home, Otto!" he said.

But Otto held himself firmly braced and a tug on the leash didn't budge him.

"Come on, boy, let's go," he said, jerking again.

A second crack sounded, and this time Otto did move, up into the air with a yelp. He landed back on the snow, his head lolling to the side while a puddle of blood formed beneath him.

Mason dove to the ground and flung his arms over his head as Otto's whimpers faded into silence.

10

IN THE LIGHT OF EARLY DAWN, DAN SLIPPED OUT OF JENNIFER'S BED and stole down the stairs to the kitchen. He found the telephone and punched the numbers on the keypad. It rang three times, then a fourth, before the answering machine clicked on.

"Tony, pick up the phone," Dan said. "I know you're there, because if you're not, you're in one hell of a lot of trouble."

The only response was the whir of the reels spinning in the machine.

No reason to panic. It was five-fifty by the clock on the stove. Tony was probably asleep in his room with the door closed, and if he didn't hear the phone ring, he wasn't going to wake at the sound of Dan's voice on the machine. Especially when Dan had to whisper, with his hand cupped around the mouthpiece so that Jennifer would sleep on peacefully upstairs.

He hung up and redialed. The phone again rang the obligatory four times. "Tony, god damn—"

"Dan?" Tony's voice came on as the machine shut off.

"Tony! Where were you?"

"In bed. Where are you?"

"Listen, I got stranded in this storm. I'm holed up out in the 'burbs."

"Oh."

Tony's voice was as expressionless as ever, yet Dan imagined he heard a forlorn note. "Are you okay? Do you need anything?"

"I'm okay."

"There's plenty of food in the fridge."

"I said I'm okay."

"Well, hang in there. I'll be home as soon as the roads are clear."

"Yeah, right," Tony said, with an edge.

Dan felt a pang of guilt, but he didn't answer to anybody, least of all to the unspoken questions of a fourteen-year-old. Like, why'd it take you until six A.M. to call? Why are you whispering? Why'd you go out to the suburbs in the middle of a blizzard anyway?

"Listen up," Dan said. "Don't you even think about leaving that apartment. I already called the desk, and they're primed for you."

The line clicked, and the dial tone buzzed in his ear.

Cursing softly, Dan hung up the phone and crept up the stairs.

"Where were you?" Jennifer mumbled sleepily when he slipped back under the comforter beside her.

"Sorry," he whispered. "I didn't mean to wake you."

"Is anything wrong?"

"No." He pressed his body along the length of hers. "In fact," he said huskily, "I'd say things are just about perfect."

His hands went to her breasts and his face burrowed against her neck. She smelled fresh-washed, of good ordinary soap. A hundred differences separated Jennifer from the women he'd known before, but this one now stood out. She didn't have a cloying artificial scent or the heavy muskiness of sex that some women exuded naturally. She just smelled clean.

Still, she was wet for him when he reached between her legs. He pressed her to her back, and she raised her knees and guided him in. He thrust up high against her, and her breath sucked in with a little hiss. She didn't speak—no dirty talk, no exhortations—but soft moans sounded in his ear as her pelvis rocked hard against his. This time she came with him, explosively, and with a throaty cry he could scarcely believe came from Jennifer Lodge.

When he woke again, the sun was bright through the window, the bed was empty beside him, and the aroma of coffee floated up from the kitchen. He pulled on his clothes and went downstairs. Jennifer was standing at the stove in an ivory velvet robe.

"Hi," she said in a voice so shy he might have thought they'd never met.

"Hi, yourself," he said, spinning her from the stove. He opened her robe and found her breasts and her mouth at the same time.

"Oh," she gasped, breathless when they parted. "The pancakes." She turned and flipped them, her robe still hanging open.

"A bare-breasted short-order cook," he said appreciatively. "I think this idea could catch on."

She clutched the lapels together and knotted the sash again.

"Don't cover up on my account," he said, and when she swatted at him with the pancake turner, he knew the shyness was over.

They sat at the oaken table with their chairs pulled together, and all through the coffee and pancakes and slices of melon, their eyes kept straying to each other, and their hands and mouths followed. He'd been through the first flush of a relationship before; he knew it was always this way, so caught up in each other, like a drug they couldn't get enough of. And he knew it always seemed different, every time, no matter how many times it had happened before. But this time it really *did* seem different, and it had to be because Jennifer was different, from another world all out of time and place from what he was used to.

"Tell me about your family," he said.

She smiled and shrugged and flipped her hair over her shoulder, where he captured it and wrapped it around his fingers. "Well, I have an older sister, Meg. She's married to an English professor, and they have two little boys. My mother lives with them now, in Madison, Wisconsin."

"And your dad?"

"He died four years ago."

"I'm sorry." After a minute he said, "He never got to see you finish law school."

She turned toward him, astonished. "Yes! That's the hardest part. He would have been so proud if only he could have lived that long. How did you guess?"

"I've got the same regret. My dad died just before I started law school."

"He would have been proud, too, I bet," Jennifer said. "Not just of law school. Of everything you've become."

Dan nodded at the compliment, though he had little confidence it was true. He couldn't remember his father ever using the word *lawyer* in a sentence that did not also include the word *crook*. He was telling lawyer jokes years before they became the rage.

"What did your dad do?" he asked.

"He worked for a bank."

Dan imagined that must rank high among understatements. Chances were he headed the board of directors and spent his days moving millions of dollars from one ledger column to another. But the mystery of the Dundee connection still remained.

"So how come you stayed here with the rest of your family off in Wisconsin?" he asked. It was the kind of loaded question he specialized in.

But the answer wasn't the one he expected. "Well, I was already in law school here, and then—" A shadow crossed her face, and she stopped and bit her lip.

"And then what?" he teased, lifting her chin. But when she shook her head and looked away, he realized what had happened next. "Oh. The fiancé."

She pushed her plate away and picked up her coffee cup. "Greg," she said finally. "He had a job lined up here, so I stayed, too."

Dan didn't know what to say. Yeah, some guys can be real jerks? His loss is Philadelphia's gain?

But in the end Jennifer saved him. "Let's go out and play in the snow," she said suddenly, her face aglow.

"Play in the snow?" he repeated skeptically. "What's that? Some kind of WASP mating ritual?"

"We'll go sledding, or build a snowman. Come on!" She laughed, then jumped up and ran upstairs.

Dan cleared the table and decided he'd pass. Kids from South Philly didn't go in big for sledding and snowman-building. But five minutes later, Jennifer skipped down in blue jeans that fit tightly over the swell of her bottom, with her long brown hair bounding loose on her shoulders and her fresh-scrubbed face shining down at him, and he decided it was never too late to learn a new sport.

*   *   *

The snow was shin-high in the courtyard without a hint of where the lane was buried. The sun shone through the snow clouds, and it caught the flakes in a prism and sent sparkles of light through the air. Jennifer scooped up a handful of snow and started to roll it in a path from the front door, and by the time she reached her mailbox, the snowball was the size of a boulder. They rolled the middle ball together, and Dan lifted it into place and started the third.

"I'll be right back," Jennifer promised, disappearing into the house.

He mounted the head, and in a few minutes she returned with a basket from which she pulled two sticks of stovewood. "Here's his arms," she said, and Dan dutifully stuck them in place. "His eyes," and two bottle caps followed. "And his nose and mouth," she said, handing him a melon rind and a carrot.

"There," he said. "Done."

"Not so fast, pardner."

Dan watched askance as she draped a white scarf around the neck, molded a rakish lock of hair over the forehead, and balanced Dan's discarded glasses over the carrot.

"There," she said. "It's Reese Chapman."

An astonished laugh burst out of him before he grabbed her in a cold, damp hug and swung her in a circle so fast and hard her feet flew out from under her.

They had a snowball battle, and when Dan hit her smack on the rear, she squealed and ran around to the back of the carriage house. Expecting an ambush, he circled the other way. At first he couldn't see her and he almost turned back. But then the sun hit her where she lay, flat on her back, her arms and legs flung wide, making an angel in the snow. He crept up beside her and lowered himself in the snow. Her eyes were closed, and the falling flakes gathered on her lashes and brows. He kissed each eye, then her lips.

"Careful," she sighed. "We'll melt all the snow, and then I won't have you trapped anymore."

He almost answered that she could trap him anytime.

*   *   *

66

That night they dined by the light of tall white candles on a cloth of snowy damask. They sat across from each other this time, even this small separation building up the tension for what would follow. Jennifer served a meal of veal chops with wild rice and snow peas and a bottle of pinot noir, and as he ate Dan decided that next weekend they'd eat at his place, with the lights out and all of the city lying before them.

When dinner was done, they stood a moment at the back door and watched the steady, silent fall of the snow on the patio. He put his arms around her and she settled back against his chest as they watched the snow collect in the edges of the muntins, making each pane of glass a framed painting of a winter landscape. The backyard was ringed with evergreens black in the night and so dense not even a flicker of nearby lights shone through. They could have been miles from anywhere, alone in a snowstorm.

"Beautiful, isn't it?" she murmured.

"Mmmm."

He nuzzled her neck and nudged her toward the sofa, where they slowly undressed each other in the firelight. "Have any music?" he asked.

"Mmmm, that would be nice," she said, and reluctantly she pulled her hands away from him and rose from the sofa. "Don't go away."

"Where're you going?"

"The CD player's in the studio. I have to—"

"Studio?"

"My ballet studio."

He stood up. "Show me."

They wrapped themselves in the quilts off the sofa and she led him to the door of the studio and hit the lights.

Dan walked in and turned slowly and watched his reflection revolve through the room. Jennifer switched on the CD player and as music filled the room, she added some logs to the woodstove in the corner. When she turned around, he was beside her, and he bent his head to brush his lips close to her ear. "Got any candles?"

He lit some and set them around the perimeter of the room. When he turned off the overhead light, the mirrors caught the light of the candles in a thousand sparkling pinpoints. Jenny stood watching him with the quilt clutched around her shoulders. He dropped his quilt to the floor and stood naked before her, and she went hot again, too weak to resist when he peeled the quilt from her fingers and let it slide down the length of her body. He dropped back to the pile of quilts and pulled her down on top of him. She found her place and lowered herself with a moan.

The lush strains of Rachmaninov crashed over them like the surf, and the candles glowed like a sky full of stars. Dan could see Jennifer's reflection in all directions—every one of them was different, and none of them was the girl he thought he knew.

11

DAN DROVE BACK INTO THE CITY SUNDAY AFTERNOON AFTER THE plows finally cleared Coventry Road. The message light was flashing on the answering machine when he opened his door, and he wondered if Jennifer had called. He took a look around. The place was strewn with discarded clothes and food wrappers, but was otherwise intact. Tony was sprawled on the couch, MTV blaring.

"I'm home."

"Duh," Tony said without turning.

Dan bent to pick up a wet bath towel from the floor. The weight of the snow he'd shoveled that morning suddenly announced itself across his shoulders and down his back, and he straightened with a grimace. He tossed the towel in the bathroom and came back to hit the play button on the machine.

"Daniel Casella," a woman's voice began in clipped tones. "My name is Liz Nofert. I'm a business reporter for the *Inquirer*. I understand you may be representing the Harding & McMann firm in connection with a lawsuit filed Friday. I'd like to ask you some questions."

She recited her number but her tone gave no indication she actually expected a return call. Dan wondered which way she would report it. Daniel Casella was unavailable for comment? Or Daniel Casella did not return telephone calls on the subject? Either way, there was nothing he could do about it. His instructions were clear—no press.

The machine played on. Another woman's voice, this one pouty. "Dan, it's Lisa again." Lisa, he remembered, slapping his forehead. She was the unidentified caller the other night. "I wish you'd call me sometime."

Another message, another woman. "Mr. Casella, this is Abby Greenley from The Alexander School. The admissions committee conferred over the weekend and has decided to allow your brother to matriculate at Alexander on a trial basis. He may register and begin classes tomorrow at eight."

Dan gave a hoot and pushed the rewind button. "Tony!" he called. "Get out here and listen to this."

When Tony shuffled into the hall, Dan replayed the message. The distastefulness of her task was patent in the woman's voice. It was a defeat for her, which meant a victory for Dan.

"You're in!" he said, clapping Tony on the back.

But Tony jerked away from his touch. "I'm not going!" he shouted. "Fuck it! I'm not going!" He spun on his heel and walked away.

"Hold it right there."

Tony headed for his room. Dan caught up before he got the door closed, and Tony turned and charged. His head rammed into Dan's chest, and one fist went into his stomach and the other hit him high on the side. The air left Dan's lungs in a rush. He staggered backward into the hall, and his head banged hard against the wall. Tony drove into him, his fists flailing and choked screams strangling out of his throat.

"God damn it, stop!" Dan shouted.

He dropped his arms around Tony in the fierce embrace of a wrestling hold. Tony struggled to break free, and Dan squeezed harder. He was a big kid, and a strong one, but Dan still had six inches and forty pounds on him. He gave him a shake. "Quit it, Tony! Quit it!"

Tony's face was hidden against Dan's chest, but Dan could tell by the racking in his shoulders when his screams turned to sobs. He gave him another shake. "Do I have to beat some sense into you, or are we gonna sit down and talk about this?"

"I don't care what you do to me! I'm not going."

A lump was rising on the back of Dan's skull. Now he had a headache to go with the backache, and probably some bruised ribs as well.

"Come on," he said when he could speak without gasping. "Sit down over here."

He seized Tony's wrists, steered him to his bed, and pushed him onto it. Tony rolled away from him and buried his face into the pillow. Dan stretched out beside him, his aching shoulders leaning uncomfortably against the headboard. He fingered the back of his head and found the lump, swelling but not bleeding.

"So tell me what's so awful about Alexander that you'd rather take a beating than go there."

"I hate it," Tony said into his pillow.

"Why?"

"I don't need a reason."

"Nope. And if you don't have one, I don't have to listen to it."

"I'm not like them!"

"I don't see why not," Dan said. "You're smart, you're good-looking, you'll probably beat their athletes all to hell in every sport they've got."

"They're rich kids," he ground out.

"Yeah, well, you've got a brother with some bucks."

There was a long silence before Tony advanced his next argument. "I wanna stay with my friends."

"Nope. Nonnegotiable."

Another silence followed. Dan's eyes moved across the antiseptic decor of the room. Gray carpeting, white walls, silver miniblinds at the windows, white laminate desk and dresser. Maybe it was time to redecorate, on his own this time, without professional decorators. This room could use some color. Jennifer's house held a motley collection of cast-off furniture in mismatched colors, but it all came together with a warmth and vibrancy that was missing here.

"What's your favorite color?" Dan asked suddenly.

Tony rolled over. "Huh?"

"Your favorite color. Got one?"

"I don't know. Blue."

"Blue sounds good." Maybe a navy blue, with a little red thrown in. Dan propped up on one elbow. "Listen, Tony—you heard what the lady said on the phone. Trial basis. You try Alexander and see how you like it."

Tony made a face. "I don't think that's what they mean."

"What else *could* they mean?" Dan said, wide-eyed. "Come on, what d'you say?"

"Do I have a choice?"

"Absolutely. You can go happy or go sore."

Tony rolled his eyes, disgusted. "Can I just go?"

"Deal."

Tony fell asleep that night as effortlessly as a little boy, their fight and his hysteria over the new school all but forgotten. But Dan couldn't forget, and he sat up brooding long into the night. Tony's rages were a frightening thing. Where did the line fall, he wondered, between normal adolescent tantrums and something worse?

He knew what his father would say if he'd lived to see what his posthumous baby had become: "All that kid needs is a good kick in the butt." But Dan hadn't built any shrines to his father. He had been an imperfect father to the three older kids; there was no reason to expect wisdom from him where Tony was concerned.

And he knew what some of his partners would do if any of them ever encountered this kind of trouble. Put the kid in therapy: a thousand dollars a month assuages a lot of guilt and doesn't take five minutes away from the practice. But Dan was finished with hiring professionals to do things he ought to do himself.

He slid into bed, his aching back straining to find a comfortable position on the mattress. He thought again of Jennifer, living like a princess in a fairy-tale world. Incredible to think a girl like her was besotted with a guy like him, but he'd seen it for himself Friday night when he pulled out of his reverie and found her staring at him with the shine of tears in her eyes.

The adoration of a beautiful girl was an intoxicating thing. Off and on all day, he'd fantasized about having her up to the apartment, showing her the view, introducing her to Tony, the three of them sitting down to dinner together. When the call came out of the blue from Alexander and he knew he'd beaten the odds and gotten Tony in—for about thirty seconds, he'd felt like anything was possible. Until Tony went ballistic.

He must have been dreaming to think he could bring Jennifer into this life, he thought as he finally forced himself to sleep.

12

JENNY STEPPED OUT OF THE SHOWER MONDAY MORNING AND blushed at the sight of her own body in the mirror. It was twenty-four hours since Dan last made love to her, yet she remained hot and weak and aroused by the mere brush of the towel over her skin. It was the first time she'd ever had sex with no expressions of love or plans of marriage, but she didn't care. It was the first time she'd done it with no concern for contraception, but she didn't care about that either, and it was pure luck that Dan had handled it. She knew there was no returning to what she'd been before, his bright young egoless associate, secretly adoring him—but she didn't care.

Jenny returned to her room to get dressed for work, and she picked a navy blue suit and white cotton shirt out of her closet. But impulsively, she put the shirt back and pulled out a white silk blouse. Today she wanted to feel silk against her skin.

She bought the morning paper at the train station. The front page was full of snowstorm stories, but the headline on the first page of the business section was what caught her eye.

Law Firm Sued for Theft of Millions

Curtis Mason, former CEO of Macoal Corporation, filed suit Friday against Harding & McMann, a prominent Center City law firm. The suit claims that $2,000,000 was stolen from a family trust fund managed by attorney Scott Sterling. Mason also alleges that Sterling defrauded him personally of $350,000.

Charles Duncan, managing partner of Harding & McMann, confirmed that improprieties had been discovered in Sterling's handling of certain monies, and stated that Sterling's employment with the firm had been terminated.

Daniel Casella, counsel for Harding & McMann, could not be reached for comment.

Jenny felt a blush spread over her cheeks but read on:

Sterling, reached at his parents' home in Gladwyne, made the following statement: "I deeply regret my actions and all of the losses for which I am responsible. I only hope I can begin to make reparation to all those who have suffered."

Further down the page Sterling's background was sketched. Episcopal Academy, Williams College, Cornell Law School, followed by a successful if undistinguished practice in estates and trusts at Harding & McMann. Son of Edgar Sterling, president of Phoenix Pharmaceutical Company, who refused comment.

The article continued:

In an apparently unrelated development, Curtis Mason reported that shots were fired at him Saturday evening while walking his dog in Laurelwood Park near his home in Devon. Although Mason was unharmed, his dog, a champion Rottweiler, was killed by a single rifle shot. Police attribute the incident to a random shooting by an unknown assailant.

Dan read the same article at his desk when he arrived at the office that morning. He was relieved at the gentle treatment he'd gotten—"could not be reached" was better than "was unavailable" and a clear favorite over "did not return calls."

But his relief was short-lived. Sterling's abject apology—in print—was the last thing Dan needed to make out a case that Sterling was victim, not perpetrator. He threw down the newspaper in disgust.

The day might come when he'd have to accept Sterling's story at face value. If it were true, there was a lesson in it: don't promise more than you can deliver and you never have to face the awful moment of truth Sterling had shied away from. The lesson for Dan: don't promise Charlie Duncan he's got a good defense and you'll never have to let him down.

Or maybe a different lesson: don't promise anything to Jennifer and you'll never have to hurt her.

He needed to see her. He got up from his desk and strode past his secretary's questioning look. But he soon had to return.

73

"What floor's Jennifer Lodge on?"

"Forty-two," Betty replied.

He saw her write Jennifer's name on her message pad, keeping tabs on his every movement like the good secretary she was.

Jim Feldman was passing through the lobby of forty-two when Dan got off the elevator.

"Dan, got a minute?" Without breaking stride, Feldman ushered him into his office and closed the door.

"Only a minute," Dan said. "What's up?"

Feldman was chairman of Foster, Bell, and liked to style himself a working executive. He toiled in shirtsleeves all day and kept a deliberately cluttered office. No mere figurehead here, he liked to project. He perched on the edge of a one-foot clearing on his desk, crossed his ankle over his knee, and leaned conspiratorially toward Dan.

"Ken's leaving."

"Stively?" Ken Stively was their partner, a few years senior to Dan. A friend, he thought.

"He's going to Jackson, Rieders."

"How come?"

"They made him a deal we couldn't begin to match."

Then how could Jackson, Rieders afford him, Dan wondered, before the answer came to him. "He's taking Tramco?"

"He *thinks* he is. But you've logged almost as much time on Tramco matters as he has the past couple of years, and you've got a better record. You've made some real friends up there."

"Christ," Dan muttered as realization struck. "You want me to battle Ken over a client?"

"This client is worth three million in annual billings," Feldman said, eyebrows raised. "Worth fighting for, don't you think?"

"I'm an old government lawyer. I never got into this rainmaking business."

"Bullshit." Feldman got up and stalked around his desk. "Come on, Dan. Help us out here. Tramco's pretty important to our bottom line. We'll all feel the pinch if we lose." When Dan remained unmoved, Feldman added, "And we wouldn't expect you to do it for nothing. We'll take a look at your percentage."

Dan's head came up. "How close a look?"

Now that he had his interest, Feldman turned coy. "Tell you

what. Come to the executive committee meeting at five. We'll
sharpen our pencils."

"Better bring a box of them."

Ken couldn't complain, Dan decided as he wandered the corridor looking for Jennifer's office. It was all business as usual in this
new game the law profession had become. If he had to enter a
beauty contest against Stively, he'd run to win. He'd go up to
Hartford and make a pitch to Tramco, court the general counsel,
and angle for a meeting with the CEO. He'd put together a good
presentation. Lots of legwork on Tramco itself, plus a complete
rundown on everything Foster, Bell had done for it without Kenneth Stively.

Jennifer could pull that information together and sketch out a
speech. Maybe he should take her along to Hartford. Clients liked
to see deep staffing at lower levels and cheaper rates. And Jennifer
made a good appearance even if she didn't know how to sell
herself. In fact, he thought with a grin, Jennifer made a *great* appearance.

He stopped his thoughts abruptly. He was fucking her now, for
Chrissake. He couldn't sign her up for new projects—he couldn't
work with her at all anymore. The firm had rules about these
things, and Dan had his own, even tougher. Appearances mattered. Vulnerabilities showed. Jennifer was completely artless.
There was no way she could play out the charade.

His fears were confirmed the moment he stepped into her office
and she looked up from her work. Her eyes widened, her cheeks
flushed, and a little pulse hammered in her throat. Dan closed the
door and bent to press his lips against that pulse. It raced even
more wildly.

"Missed you," he murmured.

"Missed you, too," she whispered as she lifted her face to kiss
him.

He cleared a space to sit down on her desk. One of the papers he
brushed aside was a clipping from the *Inquirer.* "You saw the
article."

"What do you think?"

"They've got nobody to blame but themselves. We could've
had this story out our way Friday morning. Maybe then Sterling

would've thought about it for thirty seconds before he started shooting off his mouth."

"He makes himself sound pretty bad."

"He's on self-destruct. I only hope his old man gets him a lawyer fast enough to muzzle him before it gets any worse."

"Mmmm. So, what do you want me to work on today?"

Dan gave her a lazy grin and slowly raised her from her chair until she leaned against him between his open knees. "Let me think. What do I want from you today?"

She laughed and happily received his kiss, then pulled back, serious again. "Should I start on the motion to dismiss? Or do you think the research on accountant-client privilege should be done first?"

He smoothed her hair where the silky tendrils at her temples escaped the ponytail. "Tell you what. Let's put everything on hold until I have a chance to sit down with Charlie. They've got a couple hundred lawyers over there who might have some ideas of their own."

"Then what should I work on?"

"I don't think I have anything for you right now," Dan said after a moment. "Call Jim. See what he has."

Going to Jim Feldman for work assignments was something the associates did only as a last resort, because it put them at the mercy of any random assignment floating through the firm, and everyone knew the floaters were usually the dogs. "Okay," she said.

"Hey." He tilted her chin up and gave her another kiss. "What are you doing for dinner tonight?"

She winced. "I have ballet. I could skip it, though."

His memory of her swept low to the floor danced in his mind. "No, I don't want you to do that."

"It's not until seven. Maybe an early dinner?"

"I have a meeting at five. Tomorrow night okay?"

"Tomorrow night's wonderful."

"It's a date, then."

He pulled the door shut when he left so she could compose herself. Jennifer had a beautiful face, but it betrayed every thought and feeling she had. And it would betray him, too, if he wasn't careful.

13

THE MEMBERS OF HARDING & McMANN'S EXECUTIVE COMMITTEE behaved like open wounds after Monday's headlines, and Dan found them starting to fester on Tuesday. The agenda called for him to brief them on the status of the case, but most of them used the meeting as a forum for sniping at Charlie Duncan, or at Tucker Podsworth, who was conveniently out of the room, or at Dan.

"I got twelve calls yesterday," John Warrington complained. "Good clients, big clients, all wanting to know what the hell is going on."

The others nodded. They'd been fending off those calls, too.

"This has got to end, and end fast."

That comment came from a tax lawyer. Dan fixed him with his cross-examination stare. "How, exactly?"

"That's what we hired you to figure out."

"If anybody sees grounds for a 12(b)(6) dismissal, let me know," Dan said. "Otherwise, there's only one way to end this fast. Pay Mason what he wants."

"Maybe that's what we need to do," Warrington said.

"We've got some defenses," Charlie Duncan reminded them.

"But how good are they?" the tax man said. "Are we going to end up paying Mason what he wants along with Casella's bills, too?"

"Give us a ballpark, Dan," Warrington said. "What are our odds of winning?"

"Find yourself another bookmaker, John," Dan said. "I gave up laying odds when I got my law degree."

"But you must have some feeling—"

"That's all I have," Dan cut him off. "A feeling. A gut instinct that there's more to this than Scott Sterling's little confession. But all we've seen so far is the tip of the iceberg. If that tip scares you, then pay up and be done with it. But if you want to know what's holding the iceberg up, defend the case the way it ought to be defended."

Dan moved his gaze to each man around the table until he got a reluctant nod from each.

*   *   *

Later, Tucker Podsworth made an appearance, after all but Duncan had gone.

"We've put it together as best we can," he told Dan. "Bear in mind that we were not involved in Mrs. Chapman's estate plan, we did not draft her will, and we had nothing to do with the administration of her estate."

"Just tell me what you do know."

"Mrs. Chapman was of course a Mason, and thus a substantial shareholder in the Macoal Corporation. As you know, the Mason family founded that company, originally as the Mason Coal Company. Today it's a regional energy conglomerate and is still controlled by the Masons."

"Privately held?"

"Public, but the family has a lock on the majority interest. It's widely dispersed through the family, however. The Masons are something like the duPonts—rather prolific. But they've always stayed well in line with one another, thanks to Curt's stewardship. You may recall when that corporate raider fellow—what was his name?"

"Jack Stengel?"

"That's it. When he launched his hostile takeover effort last year? The analysts thought he'd be successful, but the family utterly closed ranks."

"So how did Mrs. Chapman fit into the Macoal picture?"

"Oh, well. You see, Doody didn't marry until the age of forty." Dan hid a grin at the nickname, but Podsworth didn't notice. "The family assumed she never would marry, and probably for that reason she came into a disproportionate amount of the family wealth, including the single largest holding in Macoal."

"More than brother Curt?"

"Oh, a good deal more. Then, of course, she surprised everyone by marrying Reese Chapman."

"Money of his own?"

"Very little. None, really."

"So why'd Doody marry him?"

"He was twenty-five to her forty, and I'm told he had some appeal in his youth."

78

Dan cracked a smile. "You're telling me Chapman was a gigolo?"

"Good Lord, no," Podsworth said. "The Chapmans are a fine old Philadelphia family. At any rate, whatever brought them together, they did marry, and probably surprised everyone even more by producing a daughter, Catherine."

"How old is she?"

"Late twenties, I should think."

"Where's she today?"

"I'm not certain. She married a German prince—"

"So she's got plenty of money," Dan said hopefully.

"An impoverished German prince," Podsworth said, shaking his head. "Most of them are, you know. At any rate, I'm told the marriage is foundering, and she may be coming home to stay."

"Okay, fast forward," Dan said. "Doody dies. Walk me through the will."

"Very straightforward. A number of charitable bequests. Everything else into a residuary trust. Curt was named as trustee. Reese was guaranteed income of twenty thousand a month. The balance of the income to be paid to Catherine at the trustee's discretion, and the corpus to Catherine when Reese dies."

"This is a kick in the teeth to Chapman, right?"

Podsworth leaned back and laced his fingers over his paunch. "I don't know that I'd characterize it that way. But Chapman does receive far less than his elective share."

"What's that?"

"A surviving spouse can elect to take against the will. He could have filed the election and gotten a third of the estate."

"Could he still?"

"The time's past. The election has to be filed within six months of the date of probate."

"So why didn't he file it?"

"He may be happy with the will for all we know. The money's being preserved for his daughter, after all."

"But Doody could have named Chapman as trustee. She picked her brother over her husband."

"Her brother ran a Fortune 500 company for a dozen years. Reese Chapman never held a job in his life."

Dan laughed. "But he's still not a gigolo, huh?"

Podsworth ignored him. "Or he could have waived his right of election. It *can* be waived—before marriage, after marriage, before death, after death."

Dan turned to Duncan. "Mason must have some dirt on Chapman."

"Must you look for unsavory details everywhere?" Podsworth objected. "These are upstanding people."

"Upstanding people who're suing you for fifteen million dollars."

Podsworth climbed to his feet with a disgusted shake of his head. "I assure you *I* don't know anything about any dirt."

"Well, Tucker," Dan said, rising to take his leave as well. "I guess that's what you hired me for."

"There's a message from Mr. Feldman," Betty said when Dan returned to his office after the meeting.

Jim Feldman preferred the country lanes of hand-scrawled notes to the electronic messages of the information superhighway. Lying on Dan's chair where he couldn't miss it without sitting on it was a memo reading, "Dinner at Morton's tonight at 8 to map out the Tramco campaign. You, me, Ray, Joe, and Elliott." The signature was a scrawl of his initials.

Dan had his own dinner plans, and he picked up the phone to tell him so, but he hung up before he finished dialing. He'd emerged from last night's executive committee meeting with a deal that could net him another fifty thousand the first year depending upon the level of Tramco collections. He already drew more money from the firm than he'd ever dreamed of, but there were new things to think of now. Tony's tuition, for one—another three years of high school and college after that. He'd like to buy a house down the shore for his mother and sister, a place where Teresa could relax, maybe meet a guy. The Tramco bonus could come in handy.

Besides, he thought, picking up the phone and dialing a different number, *this is exactly the kind of mess that comes with office affairs*, and that he was determined to avoid.

"Jennifer Lodge," she answered, in her crisp lawyer-to-the-world voice.

"Hi."

"Hi," she said, melting at once into the other voice he now knew, all soft and sweet and sexy.

"Listen, about tonight. I'm sorry, I got a command performance with Feldman. Can I take a rain check?"

"Oh," she said in a new voice, this one disappointed. "Sure."

"Tomorrow night?"

"I have ballet."

No offer to skip this time, he noted. "Late supper after class?"

"Okay."

"Great. 'Bye," he said and pushed the intercom. "Betty, call Feldman and confirm."

14

NIGHT FELL OVER THE CITY, AND THE PLATE-GLASS WINDOWS THAT lined the perimeter of the Foster, Bell offices became black mirrors reflecting back the harsh fluorescent light and the young lawyers like Jenny who lingered in it. Most of them networked through the halls or swapped stories by the soda machine while they pretended to log a few more hours on their timesheets, but Jenny toiled on with case reporters spread out over her desk and the computer screen glowing blue beside her.

She was writing an article for law review submission, and she worked on it sporadically, whenever she had no client work to preempt it. The subject was sexual harassment in the workplace, inspired by a pro bono case she'd handled in a law school clinical program. It was a clear case of harassment, but a difficult case to prove because the supervisor covered his tracks so well: for every refusal to perform a sexual act, another negative comment went into the woman's personnel file. By the time she complained about him, she had a work record so poor no one would take her seriously. Jenny won the case, but only after she tracked down the woman who held the job before her client and who'd been the victim of the same supervisor.

"Hey," called a voice from the doorway, and she looked up to find Rick Mancill, fellow associate and resident pig. "Want to chip in on Chinese? Or do you have some kind of hot date tonight?''

Jenny gave him a level stare. "Shrimp lo mein."

"Oooh, the lady joins us," he said, walking away.

A half-hour later, he buzzed her to come to the conference room down the hall, and she was happy to find Sharon Fista and Brad Martin also there, serving themselves from cardboard boxes on the teak tabletop.

"Anybody got any good gossip?" Rick said, chewing with his mouth open.

Sharon and Brad exchanged a quick look and shook their heads.

"I'll bet you do," Rick said to Jenny, leering. "Hanging around Casella all the time. I mean, the man's like a walking tabloid."

"What's that supposed to mean?" Jenny looked across the table at Sharon and Brad, and again she thought she saw a furtive current of something pass between them. "What?" she asked them.

"Oh, you know." Sharon shrugged. "He's got a reputation."

"For what?"

"Fucking and firing!" Rick cackled.

"Get out—"

Brad leaned forward. "There *was* that paralegal. What was her name?"

"The one on the bank fraud case?" Sharon said.

"Yeah. Wasn't she one—"

"Right. And then her officemate—"

"People, people," Rick crowed. "I got the full scoop—don't bother trying to piece odds and ends together."

He wagged his eyebrows at Jenny and waited for her to ask. Instead she picked up her plate and rose from the table. "I'd better get back to work now."

Rick's voice followed her out into the deserted corridor. "He screwed four different paralegals and fired them when he was done with them. They're all at Lassiter & Conway now. I got *names!*"

Jenny dumped her plate in the trash and went back to her computer. The screen saver was on, and she stared at images of tropical fish swimming through blue waters.

During the weekend she'd made a pact with herself that she wouldn't worry about where this thing with Dan was going but would simply enjoy it as long as it lasted. Here it was Tuesday, and she'd broken the pact already. He'd left Sunday morning in the wake of the snowplows, even though nothing was calling him home and they could have finished the day together. He begged off Monday night and now canceled Tuesday night. She didn't understand any of it, but she was worrying about all of it.

She hit a key and the screen of print reappeared. She read through the last few paragraphs of her article. Everything she'd written so far in the article was with a clear image of the man in her clinical case as the typical harasser.

He fired them when he was done with them, Rick had said.

It wasn't true; she wasn't worried. Rick Mancill was a swine, and jealous of anyone with more looks and talent than he had, which constituted most of the population.

Jenny turned off her computer at ten and was buttoning up her coat for the commute home when another voice spoke from her doorway.

"Drive you home?"

Her heart felt close to bursting with the rush of happiness she felt. She moved across the office and into Dan's arms.

"Does that mean yes?" he murmured when their mouths broke apart.

"Mmmm."

He took her briefcase from her as they walked to the elevator lobby. "Get much work done tonight?"

"Not a lick," she laughed. "No concentration. What about you?"

"You have to stay focused, Jennifer," he chided her. "You can't let your feelings ruin your concentration."

He was lecturing her, but she didn't mind; she was accustomed to receiving his lectures. "I guess that means your evening was a success," she said, still smiling up at him.

"Too soon to tell."

The Jaguar was in its customary spot in the garage. Dan started the engine, then turned to put his arms around her. "I like to warm her up," he whispered before his mouth covered hers.

"The car, or me?" she said breathlessly when they parted.

"Hold that thought."

Patches of unplowed snow still lay on the side streets. Dan maneuvered around them and finally hit the smooth pavement of the expressway and shifted into overdrive. His right hand now free, he moved it purposefully to Jennifer's thigh.

"Your fiancé," he said suddenly. "Was he the only one before me?"

Jenny gaped at him. "Was I that bad?"

"Jennifer! No!" He laughed, and his fingers pressed into her thigh. "But you know the first rule of cross-examination. Ask a question the right way, and you might get the answer you want."

"Cross-examination? Is that what this is?"

"Cross-examination," he expounded. " 'The art of asking questions to win.' "

"You left out a part. It's the art of asking questions of an adverse witness. I'm not adverse."

"Are you on my side?" Dan said. "I hope so."

"Of course I am." Her fingers found his and they laced together and held. "But tell me—why is that the answer you wanted?"

He gave her a sheepish grin. "You found me out: I'm an old-fashioned guy. I hope you don't find that disgusting."

"I find it charming. Sexist maybe, but charming."

"But how come? A beautiful girl like you—why weren't there a dozen guys ahead of me?"

"I loved a boy from afar all through my teens. I wouldn't go out with anyone else, and he never knew."

"He was a fool not to notice and do something about it."

"Then you were a fool, too," Jenny teased. "It took you six months to notice."

"You're right," he said heavily. "I'm a fool."

Her eyes flew to his face at the change in his voice. He gave her a glance and cleared his throat.

"Jennifer, the other night—I didn't plan what happened. I didn't even see it coming. If I had, I might have paced things differently. I guess what I'm trying to say is, my timing's all screwed up."

"I don't know what you mean."

"My life's a little complicated right now."

Jenny's right hand clutched at the edge of her seat. She managed to choke out, "Is there someone else?"

"No." Brake lights flashed on ahead of them. Dan's gaze darted to the rear-view mirror, and his hand pulled free of hers to downshift. "The thing is, I've got my kid brother living with me for a while."

Relief coursed through her. "Dan! How nice! How old is he? Can I meet him?"

"Fourteen. And the whole situation isn't very nice at all."

"Oh."

"The point is that my time's not really my own. If it were, I'd probably move right into your brass bed."

That was all she needed to hear. She placed her hand over his on top of the gearshift lever. "I understand," she said. "We'll just have to make time when we can."

He turned to gaze at her, his eyes tender and warm.

"Hey, my exit!" she laughed, and he wrenched his attention back to the road and spun the wheel onto the ramp.

"Could you take me to my car?" she asked. "It's at the Radnor train station."

"Sure."

Hers was the only car left in the lot when Dan pulled up next to it. A fresh dusting of snow covered the roof and windows. He reached for his scraper. "I'll clear it off for you. Why don't you get it warmed up?"

She cranked the ignition while Dan swept the snow off. A thin sheet of ice coated the windshield, and she turned on the defroster. He pulled her out of the car and into his arms.

She threaded her arms inside his overcoat and snuggled close. "Is this the part where I get to quiz you about all the women in your past?"

"No, this is the part where I get to kiss you."

He bent his head and pressed his lips against hers. A streetlight shone down on them and traffic sounded out on the highway, but she knew they were alone in the parking lot, two solitary cars hazy in the fog of their own exhaust.

"I think the ice is melted," Jenny said.

"Mmmm. And pretty much gone to boiling."

"Can you come home with me tonight?"

"I wish I could."

"Soon, I hope."

"Me, too." His mouth moved against hers. "God, real soon."

They stood and kissed between the two sputtering cars until a cold wind blew up off the snow and drove them apart.

15

BY FRIDAY MORNING, THE SKIES WERE CLEAR AND THE SUN WAS shining bright enough for Dan to need his sunglasses as he drove Tony to school. Day five at The Alexander School, and so far, so good. Tony got up mostly on time every morning, got out of the car without incident, and returned to the apartment and called Dan as instructed every afternoon. Twice he'd even brought books home.

Dan stopped at a red light and gave Tony an appraising look. He carried his books in a beat-up backpack, wore padded hightop sneakers and Dan's old ski jacket, and looked like every other kid who climbed out of the cars at the line-up in front of the school. *Except better-looking,* Dan thought smugly, and was amazed to realize he could ever feel smug about anything where Tony was concerned.

"The deal's still on, isn't it?" Tony said when the light turned green.

"What deal?" Dan said, distracted by the traffic.

"Come on!" Tony protested. "You promised!"

"Yeah, okay," Dan said. "You get through today without any trouble and you can spend tonight at Mom's."

Tony slumped back, relieved that he didn't have to fight for it. He had no idea how much Dan was counting on the night off. Tonight he was bringing Jennifer home. He'd changed his sheets, stocked up on wine, and bought some food. One thing or another had kept them apart all week. He was damned if Tony was going to get in the way tonight.

"Wait a minute," Dan said when Tony started to scramble out of the car in front of the school. "Let's go over the ground rules. School ends, you go straight to the subway and then straight to Mom's. Got your token?"

"Got it."

"Call me when you get there."

"Right."

"Inside the house by ten tonight. And that means you stay inside, continuously, until, say, seven tomorrow morning. Got it?"

"Jeez, Dan, you talk like a lawyer."

"If you spell things out, there's no room for misunderstandings. No booze or dope—"

"I *told* you, I don't do—"

"And I'll pick you up around noon tomorrow."

"Okay." Tony jumped out onto the sidewalk.

"One more thing," Dan called, and Tony stuck his head back in the window, a pained expression on his face. "Have a good time."

Dan gave him a smile, and Tony didn't know what to do with it. He broke into a run for the school.

"Mr. Casella," the receptionist whispered as Dan stepped off the elevator. "This gentleman's been waiting to see you."

Dan's practice didn't cater to drop-in visitors. The whisper gave him a chance to avoid this one if he wanted; a barely perceptible jerk of her head told him which gentleman she meant.

A dark, burly man about Dan's age was seated in the reception area beside an untouched issue of the *Wall Street Journal*. After five years as a prosecutor, Dan recognized a cop when he saw one, even one dressed up in his best suit. What he didn't expect was that the cop would recognize him as easily. As soon as their eyes met, the man was on his feet, his hand in his breast pocket.

"Mr. Casella, Detective Michael diMaio, Philadelphia Police Department. How ya doin' today?" He flipped his badge open, held it out for a count of three, and pocketed it again. "Wonder if you could spare a few minutes to talk about that matter you reported to the DA last week."

Dan gave an irritated glance at his watch. "A few," he said. "Come on back."

He led the way to his office and watched diMaio follow out of the corner of his eye. He was shorter and squatter than Dan, but light on his feet, like a boxer. Dan picked up the contents of his In box and waved the detective into his office. "This is the Sterling case, I take it?" he said, pointing him into a chair.

"Yes, sir."

"Who's heading up the investigation?"

"You're looking at him."

Dan tossed his mail aside. "I told them to assign an assistant DA to run this one."

DiMaio shrugged. "I go where they tell me."

"This is a complex case," Dan said, his voice rising. "There's a lot more to this than meets the eye."

DiMaio leaned back and gave Dan a considered smile. "Whatsa matter, Mr. Casella? Afraid I'm just another dumb wop?"

Dan would have laughed at that if the stakes weren't so high. "No offense, Detective. But this case needs a lawyer in charge."

"The DA's got this funny idea that the lawyers oughta be lawyering, and the investigators oughta be investigating. Screwy, huh?" Dan started to cut in, but diMaio kept on talking. "If it makes you feel better, I've been doing white-collar crime for five years.

"And if that don't do the trick," he went on, "I'll tell you this: the easiest thing for me to do is to swallow Sterling's story whole, book him for fraud and larceny, and get another quick notch on my gun. But I don't get off on the easy cases anymore, Mr. Casella. You reported Sterling because you had to, but your case depends on him being more clean than dirty. Maybe my case does, too. Who knows? I got an open mind."

Dan looked at him, impressed. "More open than mine, obviously. I apologize. It's just that a lot of cops would've written this one off as a simple embezzlement."

"Already it don't look simple. You heard about Mason's dog?"

"I thought that was just a drive-by shooting."

DiMaio shrugged. "Who knows? All they got is a dead dog with a slug in him. The tracks were covered over with snow by the time anybody looked for them. But it's got my curiosity aroused. Maybe it's a random hit, or maybe the sniper's a friend of Mason's, trying to send him a little message. And maybe it's got something to do with some missing money."

"What can I do to help?"

"Share information, for starters."

"You got it," Dan said. "Anything that's not privileged or work product."

"Auditors' workpapers?"

"That's work product."

"We're off to a bad start."

Dan stood and walked to the window where he could just make out the detective's reflection in the glass. DiMaio was smart; he knew he was being watched, and his face showed nothing but an amused smile. The face was familiar to Dan; he'd grown up with a dozen or more like it—heavy southern Italian features tempered by a light dose of American cross-breeding. It was a face many of his boyhood friends and enemies shared. Always better to find it on a friend.

Dan turned from the window. "Maybe we can work out a trade."

"What do I got that you don't?"

"Subpoena power."

"I'm listening."

"If I pointed you in the direction of some evidence, would you share it with me?"

DiMaio considered the proposal for half a second. "If I get the workpapers as part of the deal."

"Done."

"Go ahead and point me, then."

"Mason has tape recordings of his conversations with Sterling."

DiMaio gave a long, low whistle.

"I've served a request for production, but it'll be a long time before I actually get my hands on the tapes."

"The anticipation's killing you, huh?"

"I don't like to run down any more blind alleys than I have to."

DiMaio flipped open his notepad. "Perlman got 'em, you think?"

"Probably, but serve Mason, too. They might play it cute otherwise." Dan's intercom buzzed but he ignored it.

"I'll bring 'em 'round to you next week."

Dan extended his hand. "I'll have the auditors' papers ready for you then."

DiMaio stood up and they shook on it.

Betty appeared in the doorway. "I'm sorry to interrupt, Mr. Casella, but The Alexander School is on the line. They say it's an emergency."

The color drained from Dan's face. He leaned over his desk and punched the button on his phone. "Dan Casella," he barked into the speaker.

"Paul Stover, Mr. Casella, headmaster at Alexander. I'm afraid there's been an accident, and your brother's been hurt. He's been taken to the emergency room at Jefferson."

"What kind of accident? How was he hurt?"

"Some kind of fight, apparently. We're not sure of the details."

Dan squeezed his eyes shut against the headache that suddenly pounded in his temples. "Thanks for calling," he said and punched the button again.

When he opened his eyes, Mike diMaio was standing next to him. "Come on," he said. "I got my car right out front."

Dan shook his head. "I've got my own."

"But I can park where I want, and you can't. Come on."

Twenty minutes later, Dan burst through the double doors of the emergency room, scarcely aware of diMaio on his heels. He ran up to the nurse at the duty station. "I'm Dan Casella."

"Stacy," she called to another nurse in the corridor. "The boy's father is here. Take him back, will you?"

Dan didn't bother to correct her. He followed the second nurse through another set of double doors, then another, and through a room and behind a curtain, where Tony reclined on a gurney.

No blood, no sign of broken bones. Dan's relief was instantly surpassed by his fury.

"Goddamn it," he said through clenched teeth. "You couldn't get through one lousy week without screwing up. You had to pick a fight with somebody, just for the hell of it."

"It wasn't my fault!" Tony cried. His voice shook, and it was then Dan noticed the clammy whiteness of his skin. "I was just standing there—a guy comes up and mugs me. I didn't do anything!"

Dan seized both his hands and looked at the knuckles. They weren't split, grazed, or even red. He winced. Tony stared back, vindicated, defiant.

A man in hospital greens stepped between them. "I'm Dr. Goldstein. You the brother?"

"Yeah."

"He's taken a few hard body punches. We're gonna take him down to x-ray and see what we got in there."

"Yeah, okay."

"Stacy, take a history till we get back."

"Mr. Casella, will you have a seat over here?" the nurse said, beckoning to him.

Mike diMaio clapped a hand on his shoulder. "I'll be back. Take it easy."

Tony wasn't covered on Dan's Blue Cross, and Dan didn't know what he was allergic to, or what childhood diseases he'd had. A pretty worthless excuse for a guardian, all around. "Who *would* know?" the nurse asked, exasperated. His mother, but he was damned if he'd call her. They left it that he'd pay cash, and they could assume whatever they wanted to on the history.

He spent an hour flipping through the pages of several *People* magazines in the waiting room before he remembered Jennifer. A young black woman was holding a marathon conversation on the only telephone in sight. Dan stood behind her, jingling the change in his pocket. She turned once, lifted her eyebrows at him, and wheeled back to launch into the next phase of the conversation.

Jennifer was at her desk when he finally got through. She picked up on the first ring, and he knew she'd been waiting for his call. "Jennifer, I'm sorry," he said immediately.

"What?" she asked, knowing already.

"Something's come up. I have to call off tonight. I'm sorry."

"What happened?"

What could he tell her? People didn't get mugged in Jennifer's world, and they didn't have street punks for little brothers, and if they did, they took a hell of a lot better care of them than this.

"Family trouble," he said finally.

"Your brother?"

"Yeah. Listen, can I call you tomorrow?"

"I'll be at home."

"Talk to you then."

Mike diMaio was behind him when he hung up. "The kid's story checks out," he said. "He was mugged."

Dan turned around, stunned. "How do you know?"

"I went down to the school, asked around. A dozen kids saw it. Your brother was hangin' out in the schoolyard, guy comes up to him, white guy, not a kid. They have words, guy gives him three or four killer punches in the gut, kid falls over, guy takes off."

"Jesus," Dan breathed. Fourteen years on the streets and Tony never got hurt until his first week at an exclusive private school.

The doctor appeared beside them. "We got two cracked ribs," he said. "Organs seem okay; no sign of fluid in the lungs, but there might be internal bleeding. You have to watch for dizziness and chills."

"Cracked ribs?" Dan repeated.

"We taped him up," the doctor said. "He'll be in some pain for a few days. We'll get you something for it and you can take him home. You have your car here?"

"Yeah," Mike answered for him.

"Thanks," Dan said. The sun was setting and Mike stood at his living room window to watch the southwestern sky turn pink and orange. "I don't know how I would have managed to get him home on my own."

"Glad I could help."

"You off duty?"

"Yeah," Mike said. "And I'll have whatever you're having."

Dan pulled two beers out of the refrigerator and tossed one to Mike. "Schoolyard muggings seem a little far afield for a white-collar investigator."

Mike shrugged. "You know how it is. Somebody you know gets hurt, you want to find out why."

"But you don't know Tony."

Mike took a pull on his beer. "Turns out I do."

The bottle froze on the way to Dan's mouth. "What?"

"Nothin' serious," Mike said. "A few months back I ran across a bunch of kids raisin' hell. Your brother was the one I caught. I took him home. Met your sister—Teresa, is it? End of story."

"What kind of hell?"

"Kid stuff. I told you, nothin' serious. So how long's he been livin' with you?"

Dan blew out his breath. "Nine days." He barked a short laugh. "Nine days of one crisis after another." He sat down and put his feet up on the glass coffee table. "But I guess I can't hold this one against him. It's not his fault some guy decides to mug him."

Mike gave him a long look before he spoke again. "There's only one funny thing about it," he said. "The kids at the school? They swear your brother and this guy knew each other."

Dan's bottle hit the table as his feet hit the floor. He went down the hall and threw open the bedroom door. Tony was dozing, but his eyes flashed open on Dan and shifted suspiciously to Mike behind him.

"Tony, who was the guy who punched you?" Dan said.

The boy's eyes widened. "How should I know?"

"The witnesses say you knew him."

"You were having some kind of argument with him," Mike added.

"Sure, we were arguing." Tony shifted his weight under the covers and winced with the effort. "He wanted my money and I said no."

"The truth, Tony," Dan said.

"All right, I told him to fuck off. Maybe that's why he decked me. He didn't like my mouth."

Mike was moving behind Dan, and Tony's eyes followed him as he picked up Tony's clothes from the chair by the window. "I noticed your wallet was still in your pants pocket." He pulled it out and tossed it to Dan.

Dan flipped it open. Tony's student I.D. and seventeen dollars lay inside. He threw it onto Tony's chest. "What's going on?"

"What is this?" Tony complained. "I get mugged, and you bring some cop in to hassle me about it? I'm the one who got hurt, remember?"

"Why didn't he take your money if that was what he was after?"

"I had twenty bucks loose in my coat pocket. That's what he saw, and that's what he took."

Dan and Mike exchanged a long look before Mike nodded. "Coulda been."

"Sorry," Dan mumbled. "Need anything?"

"Just let me sleep." Tony closed his eyes to shut them out.

"My fault," Mike said in the hall. "I always got questions, but they ain't always good ones."

"Forget it. If we didn't fight about that, we'd fight about something else."

Mike found his coat and shrugged it on. "Still, you're doin' the right thing. Keepin' him here with you, I mean."

"What do you know about it?" Dan said wearily.

"I know your sister's a lovely lady, and she shouldn't have to deal with this crap."

Dan's eyes darted to Mike's left hand. Mike saw it and laughed. "I'm single."

"Just checking," Dan said. "The last thing Teresa needs is a married man sniffing around."

"I hear you," Mike said. "Well, thanks for the beer. I'll be talking to you next week. Charge up the batteries on your tape player."

Dan stuck out his hand. "Good meeting you."

Saturday morning, Dan stepped softly into Tony's room. He was asleep, and his head lay against the pillow in a nest of black curls. "Hey," Dan said softly. "Time for your medicine."

He slipped his hand under the boy's neck to raise him off the pillow. Tony nodded sleepily and opened his mouth to receive the pill. Dan held a glass of water to his lips and let him take a few sips.

"I'm sorry you missed your Friday night at home. Maybe next week."

"No big deal," he mumbled.

"Want some breakfast?"

"I just wanna sleep."

"I have to get my car. You be all right for a while?"

"I just wanna sleep," the boy repeated, fading fast.

Dan walked to Center City and got his car out of the parking garage, but when he pulled out onto the street, he turned west instead of east, and headed for the expressway.

It was only eight when he rang Jennifer's doorbell. He rang it again, and after a few minutes, she threw the door open. *Little innocent*, he thought, *opening the door to anybody*. She was wearing an old blue bathrobe, her hair was tousled, and her eyes were puffy. She blinked when she saw it was Dan, and her face lit up like a summer morning.

Dan pulled her into his arms. Despite everything, he thought, burrowing his face into her neck, he had to get her into his life. And the first step was to get her out of the firm.

16

JENNY ARRIVED EARLY AT WORK MONDAY MORNING, AND SHE SET-tled into her chair and gazed around the two-windowed room. For the past six months she'd spent most of her waking hours here, and already it felt like home. Her diplomas and bar certificates hung on one wall, and her favorite Degas print on another. The chair was at just the right height to the desk, and when she sat in it she felt like the last piece of the puzzle, fitting perfectly to complete the picture.

She swiveled in her chair and looked to her In box. It was still empty. Although Dan had spent much of the weekend with her, he didn't discuss work once. She didn't understand. He'd broken off their Friday-night plans, then showed up Saturday morning so early her bed was still warm when they fell into it. He left at noon, but was back at six to take her to dinner at a country inn near Chadds Ford, miles from anyone who might recognize them. He arrived unexpectedly at dusk on Sunday, and when she met him at the door, he grabbed her hand without a word and pulled her up the stairs and into bed. He left her again before the sweat dried on their bodies.

But more baffling was the fact that for the first time in six months Dan had no work for her. She wanted to believe he was being gallant in some sweet, old-fashioned way, but there was nothing gallant about fobbing her off on Feldman. Was this the price she was supposed to pay for sleeping with him? It wasn't one she'd bargained for. She loved him powerfully, she had for months, but she loved her work, too, and she never imagined that one would be the price for the other.

Jenny might not have any claim to his time, she might not have control over his comings and goings, but she was determined to exercise some control over her work. On Friday, she'd finished the last stray project on her list. Today she either had to get an assignment from Jim Feldman or spend the hours staring at an empty timesheet. Unless— She'd thought of a new approach to the *respondeat superior* question in the H&M case, and whether Dan liked it or not, she was going to spend the rest of the day in the library finding case law support for her theory.

She got a fresh legal pad out of her desk drawer, but her file of H&M research notes wasn't on the credenza where she thought she'd left it. She went into the corridor to search through the bank of file drawers, and when she bent over, a wolf whistle sounded behind her. She threw a hot glare over her shoulder. Rick Mancill stood smirking behind her.

"Not funny," she said, straightening.

"Not meant to be," he replied. "Hey, you hear the news about Ken Stively?"

"No, what?"

"He's leaving. Defecting to Jackson, Rieders. Big-bucks deal."

"Really?" Jenny thought of Sharon Fista, who worked almost exclusively for Ken. "What's going to happen to Sharon?"

"She goes with him. Package deal. Brad Martin, too."

"Brad? What's his connection to Ken?"

"None, but he's done a lot of work for Tramco, and Tramco is Ken's ticket out of here."

"Too bad. I worked on a few cases for Tramco myself."

"Watch out," Rick said, leering. "Ken may want you, too."

Jenny turned her back on him and went to her secretary's desk. "Celeste, have you seen my research files on Harding & McMann? I can't seem to put my hands on them."

"Oh, Betty came and got them last week."

Jenny went blank. "Who?"

"You know. Mr. Casella's secretary."

17

DAN STOOD OUTSIDE THE BALLET STUDIO THAT NIGHT, STAMPING HIS feet against the creep of the cold and breathing puffs of fog into the night air. Jennifer's classmates were straggling out of the building in pairs and trios, but there was no sign of her. He should have buzzed her in the office to make sure she was going to class tonight, but he wanted to avoid office contacts now. Jennifer was part of his private life, and he needed to keep her well away from his professional life. Tonight he would tell her why.

"Excuse me?" he called out to a young woman prancing down the stairs. She hoisted her ballet bag over her shoulder and came toward him with a smile. "I'm waiting for Jennifer Lodge. Do you know her?"

"Sure. She's putting in some overtime. Go on in. Last door on the right."

Dan looked at his watch. He had to be home by ten to give Tony his pain pill. He couldn't waste any more time standing on the sidewalk. He went up the stairs and through the heavy wooden door.

The hallway inside was in darkness, but a light glowed at the end of the hall, and the faint strains of violin music sounded. He went to the last door and slipped through it into the dim vestibule.

Jennifer was alone on the gleaming oak floor. A violin was singing a single prolonged note, and her body was stretched into a pose as lyrically beautiful as the music. Her left leg was in the air, her toes pointed upward, while the long line of her torso slanted downward and her fingertips swept the floor amid the gleaming strands of her hair.

Abruptly the music changed, and Jennifer moved with it. Dan shrank back into the shadows and watched her bound across the dance floor. The exaggerated poses and stylized affectations of the ballet lent her an attitude of haughtiness she didn't possess. She struck a pose—her arms rounded over her head, her chin lifted and her head cocked—and held it for a flickering instant before she leapt into motion again.

He sucked in his breath. The Jennifer he knew was modest and demure, nothing like this woman with the disdainful carriage. The arrogance on her features didn't belong to the girl he was falling in love with. She was only performing, like an actress playing a role, but it struck him that this could be Jennifer's second self, the one he could fall in love with next. He grew hard watching her.

The music ended. Jennifer broke her pose, shook out her arms and neck, and reached for a towel on the table beside the tape deck. She turned, mopping her brow, as Dan stepped out of the shadows.

"That was incredible," he said huskily.

She started, and blushed, his shy little Jennifer again.

"I was hoping we could have a drink before your train."

But maybe not so shy after all. She lifted her chin and spoke firmly. "Yes. I want to talk to you about my work."

"Okay."

"I'll hurry and change."

She disappeared through the door to the women's dressing room while Dan stood listening to the silence of the building and feeling the beat of the pulse in his groin. A minute later, he followed her.

The dressing room held rows of open stalls, all of them empty but the one where Jennifer stood with her leotard peeled down to her waist. She spun at the sound of his footsteps, and her breasts bounced softly with the movement.

A lump grew in Dan's throat, as hard as the one in his pants. He'd seen them before, devoted much attention to them already, but they looked different—*she* looked different, like some lush and primeval creature, an ancient goddess of sex.

He reached her in three strides. Her voice caught in her throat as he seized her, and he froze, waiting for her reaction, until at last her muscles went soft and he knew she was yielding to him. His hands found the bunches of her leotard at her waist and he peeled it down to the floor and pulled her down after it.

"Do you think anybody heard?" he asked her later. They lay together on the black and white linoleum, Jennifer gloriously naked, Dan with his pants around his ankles.

She gave him a smile he didn't recognize, a knowing, powerful smile. "Do you care?"

"Not if you don't."

She stretched, her arms reaching above her head and her toes uncurling. "I'd better get dressed." She pushed his arms away when he reached for her again. "My train leaves in twenty minutes."

"Christ," he muttered.

"I know," she said. "Dan, we have to sit down and talk. I need to work."

He lay on his back and watched her pull her clothes on. What an idiot he was. All the carefully phrased statements he'd prepared for tonight would have to wait. They had to talk sometime, and soon, but there was always too little time and too much lust.

He was a worse idiot than that, too, he realized next. For the first time in ten years, he'd forgotten a condom. He debated whether he should apologize, or maybe make a bad joke about unbridled passion, but in the end he was too ashamed to say anything. He climbed to his feet and pulled his clothes together.

"Why do you?" he asked suddenly.

"What?"

"Need to work."

"Same reason anybody does. Food on the table and a roof overhead."

"Come on."

"Come on what?"

"A WASP princess usually has a trust fund sitting someplace. Like Catherine Chapman."

"A WASP princess?" She laughed. "Is that what you think I am?"

"Aren't you?"

"My father was an accountant and my mother was a nurse. They were the first college graduates on either side of the family. Believe me, I come from good working-class stock."

"Then what's your connection to the Dundees?"

"None, except that I rent their old carriage house."

"You went to The Alexander School," he pointed out, as if he'd caught a witness in a contradiction.

"Only for high school. And only because my parents worked hard and saved their money. And raised me to do the same."

A week ago Dan thought her connection to the Dundees defined everything about her. Funny how little difference it made now to learn the connection didn't exist.

"So you're not a trust-fund baby?" He grabbed her in a playful embrace. "Now I have to decide if you hold any other attraction for me."

She pretended to wrestle away, but changed her mind and caught him close for another kiss.

He walked her the five blocks to the station and below ground to the platform to wait for her train with the rest of the late commuter crowd. This was dangerous territory; any number of Foster,

Bell lawyers could be waiting to board the 9:15 Paoli local. Dan and Jennifer stood apart, touching only with their eyes.

But when the train pulled into the station, he pulled her into his arms and gave her a long kiss before she boarded. In a few days, their affair would be nobody's business but their own.

18

"Uncle Curt!" sounded Scott Sterling's voice. "Wait till you hear this! Got a pencil? IBM, up three and three-eighths. Bell Atlantic, up two and a quarter. Reebok, up four. Microzen—"

"What the bloody hell is that?" Mason cut in.

"New issue. High-tech. Stick with me on that one, Uncle Curt, it's going places. Up five and a half. You're like King Midas these days—it's gold, all of it!"

"Listen, it's time I liquidated part of this portfolio. Start looking for some good sells."

"Bad time to sell," Sterling said. "Bad. We're not even to the crest of the hill yet. You'll regret it forever if you cash out any positions now."

"Do I have any options contracts coming due?"

Sterling's voice hesitated. "I think so. Let me check on that and call you back. How's the sailing today?"

"Couldn't be better. Wind was perfect. Dorrie sends her love, by the way."

"Same for me. I'll call you back at the end of the day."

Six months out of the complex relationship between Curtis Mason and Scott Sterling was reduced to this—two-minute sound bites contained on a single cassette tape. Dan stared at the tape player on the conference table, his notes forgotten.

"Scotty," began the next bite.

"Uncle Curt, how's it—"

"What the hell is going on with these idiots at Connolly? Why can't their computer spit out a statement that bears any resemblance to my actual account?"

"It's a zoo over there," Sterling said. "I've talked to a dozen guys with the same problem. They've got a glitch in their system, and each account affected has to be traced through by hand. And they won't hire the extra help to do it. But they've acknowledged the errors, Uncle Curt; we're all squared away there."

"What if the IRS calls me in for an audit? Am I supposed to show them this garbage? I'm gonna call these idiots myself and—"

"No, let me, Uncle Curt. If I don't straighten it out myself, you know how it'll be—they won't take me seriously the next time there's trouble. I'll sit down with Kearney. We'll get it fixed if I have to do the key-punching myself."

A click signaled the end of the conversation. The next one began.

"Scotty, my boy. What's the good news?"

"Hi. Listen, I've got someone in my office. Can I call you back in ten minutes?" Another click. "Uncle Curt, sorry to keep you waiting. I didn't want to spill this news to anyone but you. You cleared thirty-five thou on the IBM puts!"

"Outstanding, my boy! Well done!"

Another click. "Scotty. Anything going on in the trust I need to know about?"

"Not a thing. It just hums along on its own. Spitting out those monthly checks to Reese Chapman."

"Send me the Macoal proxies as soon as they arrive. Shareholders' meeting coming up."

"You got it."

The cassette finally reached its end. Dan pushed the off button on the player and picked up his notes again. The tape opened a Pandora's box of new issues to chase after. He blew out his breath and reached for his dictaphone.

"Betty, memo to"—who? Not Jennifer anymore, though he would have valued her insight—"the file. Ed O'Reilly had a case a few years back involving doctored tapes. Find out who his expert was; have him listen to this." But he harbored little hope there; the tape sounded like genuine Sterling.

"There's some question about the legality of taping telephone conversations. Depends on what law governs—maybe federal, but maybe state. Pennsylvania, Florida, Maine, or wherever else Mason was calling from. Research it. Mason would look pretty sleazy to the jury if it turns out he was violating a wiretap statute.

"Third point. Jury argument. If Mason trusted Sterling so much, why's he secretly recording their conversations?"

Dan pushed away from the table and got to his feet. The fourth point he wouldn't bother dictating: Scott Sterling could charm the birds out of the trees; he had Mason eating out of his hand.

Betty's voice came over the intercom. "Detective diMaio is here, Mr. Casella."

"I'll be right there."

Mike was admiring the view when Dan strode into his office. He turned from the window with a grin. "You got the catbird seat everywhere you go, doncha?"

"I don't much feel like it after listening to that tape." Dan sat down at his desk. "Thanks for the quick delivery, by the way."

"Thanks for the tip." Mike sat down and gave him a sly look. "Tell me, you hear anything funny on the tape?"

"Yeah, Sterling never answers a question if Mason calls him. He always has to get back to him."

"I heard it, too."

"So what's Scotty boy doing between phone calls?" Dan said. "Whipping out the *Wall Street Journal* and a calculator? Doing a line of coke to help him sell the lie?"

"Could be nothing. Maybe he keeps his notes in the file cabinet out in the hall and he has to go get 'em."

"Maybe," Dan said. "But the night he confessed, we found all the Mason Investment Advice files in his own desk drawer."

"*Inn*eresting," Mike said, pronouncing the word in four syllables. "I stumbled over somethin' else inneresting, too. Anything you wanna trade?"

"Will you take an IOU?"

"I ain't runnin' a credit operation here. Tell you what, though, I'll trade you some information for dinner."

Dan's eyebrows went up. "You want to have dinner with me, Mike? And here I wasn't even sure you liked me."

"You and your sister Teresa. You can bring a date, too. Pick a night."

Dan's laughter died. "You move fast, diMaio."

"Hey," Mike complained, his chin jutting out. "If I was so damn fast, I wouldn'ta waited all this time to try and get a date with her.

And I sure as hell wouldn't be asking her brother to come along and chaperon."

Dan's face stayed tight while he considered the idea. Maybe Teresa would enjoy a night out, whether she went for Mike or not. And it might not be too soon to take Jennifer out publicly, even introduce her to his sister.

"All right, you're on," he said. "But you pay for your own damn dinner. Now, what do you got?"

Mike leaned back, grinning with satisfaction. "I went lookin' for some black marks on Uncle Curt's record. No," he said, holding up both hands to ward off the spark of excitement in Dan's eyes. "I didn't find a thing. He's one mean son of a bitch, but he's clean."

"What's the scoop, then?"

"His brother-in-law."

"Reese Chapman?"

"Seems he likes boys."

"You're kidding."

"It was hushed up pretty well," Mike said. "But there was an incident a while back."

Dan gave a caustic laugh. "So that's what Mason has on him. That's why Chapman didn't file a will contest when Doody died. And that's why he won't sue Mason for breach of trust now."

"I figure it that way, too."

Dan rose from his chair and stalked the length of his office, his hands thrust deep in his pockets. "Christ, these people. Doesn't it burn you up?" Mike shook his head, not following. "I mean, they're the aristocracy, right? They're supposed to be so much better than the rest of us? And what are they really? Chicken hawks and blackmailers."

"You got a little chip on your shoulder there, buddy."

"Come on," Dan said, wheeling. "Doesn't it bug the hell out of you? What makes them so special? Why're they any better than us?"

"Us?" Mike laughed. "Let me tell you something, Dan. Except that your name's Casella, you got a helluva lot more in common with Curtis Mason than you do with me. To me and my kind, you're the them."

Dan shook his head dismissively, but his brain spun a few times at the notion. He'd always aimed to rise above his origins, there was no escaping that, but he shrank from the thought that he'd defected to the Masons' side of the world. He wondered what Jennifer saw when she looked at him—a diMaio or a Mason? Was she slumming or climbing, or was he? He hoped there was nothing hierarchical in their relationship. But of course there was: he was her boss, and that would be there between them as long as she stayed with the firm.

Dan leaned on the intercom buzzer. "Betty, do you have that package ready for Detective diMaio?"

"Be right there," she said.

"The auditors' workpapers," Dan explained, as Betty staggered in with the file box. "Bear in mind, this is all preliminary. Everything has to be triple cross-checked before these boys sign off on anything."

"Thanks," Mike said, hoisting the box out of Betty's arms. "I like a man who pays his debts early. Oh," he added, pulling an envelope out of his breast pocket. "I got something else for you."

Dan opened the flap. A black and white police mug shot slipped out.

"I took the book over to The Alexander School yesterday," Mike said. "Most of the kids fingered this guy as Tony's mugger."

Dan studied the face in the photograph. The man looked to be in his early twenties, greasy-haired, straggly-bearded, with a fixed vacancy in his eyes that chilled Dan's blood. "This is the guy who beat up my little brother?"

"Probably not," Mike said. "But do me a favor. Show it to Tony. See what his reaction is."

"Who is he?"

"Small-time hood name of Joey Ricci. Maybe trying to graduate to big-time hood."

"By mugging schoolboys for their lunch money?"

"Ain'tcha heard?" Mike grumbled, hefting the box of papers onto his shoulder. "There's a recession going on."

A radio station was blaring rap music from all the speakers in Dan's state-of-the-art five-thousand-dollar sound system when he arrived home that night. He picked his way across a floor strewn with clothing and littered with junk-food boxes, found the shelf that held the tuner, and punched the power button off.

"Hi," Tony said, and Dan saw him lying amid the debris, his back on the floor, his legs in the seat of the armchair, last month's *Playboy* on his chest.

"You look like you're feeling better."

"You kidding? I've been stuck in this position all day. Couldn't move." He grinned. "Just waiting for you to come home and rescue me."

Dan pulled him to his feet. This time he noticed only a slight twinge cross Tony's face.

"Feel up to school tomorrow?" he asked, sweeping up the laundry and litter on the floor.

Tony gave him a calculating look. "What're my chances of milking another couple sick days out of this?"

Dan pretended to give it some thought. "Slim to none."

"All right," he shrugged. "Tomorrow I'm back."

Dan went into the kitchen to dump the trash into the compactor. "Hey, I almost forgot. C'mere a minute." Tony stuck his head around the kitchen door, and Dan pulled the mug shot from his pocket. "Take a look at this. You know this guy?"

Tony's face went blank as he peered at the picture. "Nope," he said finally. "Who is he?"

"Detective diMaio thought he might be your mugger."

"Nah. If he looked like that, I mighta been scared."

"Next time, be scared," Dan snapped. "Twenty bucks isn't worth two cracked ribs."

"Right. Next time I hold out for fifty per."

Dan was geared to launch into a lecture about self-preservation, or smart-assed backtalk, or even household cleanliness, but Tony stood before him wearing such a silly little-boy grin that Dan gave him a swift, hard hug instead. "Just be careful, okay?"

Tony's surprise slowly gave way to a look of shy pleasure. "Okay," he said.

19

THE CALL CAME AT LAST THURSDAY MORNING. "JENNIFER, CAN YOU come up?" She closed her eyes and sagged against the back of her chair. Dan wasn't cutting her out of the case, he wasn't getting her reassigned, he still needed her.

"I'll be right there."

She went to the ladies' room and stared at herself in the mirror while she waited for her pulse to slow. She was wearing a severe man-tailored charcoal gray suit with a stark white blouse. It was a no-nonsense look, perfect for today. She was more than a paralegal. She was one of the top members of her law school class, she'd held a prestigious federal appellate clerkship, and she'd been heavily and persistently recruited by Foster, Bell and half a dozen other big firms. She was a valuable asset to the firm in general and to Dan Casella in particular.

Buoyed by those thoughts, she took the elevator and arrived at his office door. "Go right in; they're expecting you," Betty said.

She gave Betty a puzzled frown as she opened the door. Dan rose from behind his desk with a smile. Shirtsleeves, she noted, and horn-rimmed glasses, a studious look today, but one that could never conceal his heart-breaking handsomeness from her.

"Here she is now," he said.

Another man stood, and Jenny's eyes darted in confusion toward him. He was silver-haired and silver-suited, with the bland good looks of a politician, and she knew she'd seen him somewhere before.

"Jennifer, this is Stan Lassiter. Stan was my boss when he was U.S. Attorney. Stan, Jennifer Lodge."

"A pleasure," he said, moving toward her with a broad smile and his hand outstretched.

"How do you do?"

"Have a seat. Make yourselves comfortable."

Dan was expansive, as if hosting a gala reception. Lassiter returned to his chair and beamed at Jenny like she was a favorite niece graduating from high school. She sat down beside him and turned a questioning look to Dan.

"Stan heads up his own firm now."

"Lassiter & Conway?" The name shot bulletholes in her cortex; according to Rick Mancill, that was the graveyard for Dan's discarded lovers.

"It's the most up and coming firm in town," Dan said.

"We're a litigation firm, first and foremost," Lassiter said. "We represent quality clients in significant lawsuits. And we've got some of the best young talent around."

There was a break in the dialogue, a cue for Jenny to utter some response. "Yes, I've heard good things."

"I've heard good things about you, too," Lassiter said, pulling a leg up across his knee. "Dan showed me your résumé. Magna cum laude from Mount Holyoke, articles editor on the *Penn Law Review*, court of appeals clerkship. You might have tried for a Supreme Court clerkship after your stint with Judge Lodner."

It was clear to her now. She was being interviewed for a new job under Dan's watchful eye. She held back the burning rush of tears. She mustn't cry, not with Lassiter staring at her. Better to be angry than to cry.

"I considered it," she said. "But I was too eager to get started on my career here." She directed her next remark at Dan. "You see, it was a long-time goal of mine to join Foster, Bell, & McNeil."

Lassiter sent an uneasy glance to Dan and cleared his throat. "This is a fine firm, of course. But you know, the opportunities are often greater for a younger lawyer at a younger firm like ours."

Jenny kept her hands folded in her lap. Her gaze stayed forward, on Dan. "I've always believed that the greatest opportunity is to be the apprentice of a more experienced lawyer," she said. "Someone with incredible talent of his own. Someone a young lawyer could really respect. And trust."

Dan's eyes dropped, and he spun a quarter-turn away from her. *There*, she thought, with a stab of satisfaction. She'd made him squirm.

"That's exactly the kind of relationship we thrive on in our firm," Lassiter was saying.

"I understand you have an excellent support staff," Jenny said, gaining momentum.

"Yes, indeed."

"Your paralegals in particular," she said. "I hear they're first-rate."

Dan shot out of his chair. "Stan, I can't thank you enough for coming over," he said, walking briskly around his desk. "Let me walk you to the elevator."

Lassiter gave him a confused look and climbed to his feet. "Nice meeting you, Miss—um—I'm sorry?"

Jennifer smiled up at him. "The names are so hard to remember, aren't they?" she said. "Like they say, you need a scorecard."

"Stan, I won't keep you," Dan urged, his hand at his elbow to usher him out. He glanced back at Jennifer, who sat frozen with fury in the chair, and pulled the door closed when he left.

"That was my fault," he said, flushed with embarrassment as he led Lassiter to the elevator. "I should have cleared it with her first. I hope you won't hold this against her."

"I won't hold it against *her*," Lassiter said. The elevator doors opened, and he stepped on and turned back to stab a finger at Dan. "But I've got some advice for you, Casella. Get your goddamned life in order!"

The doors snapped shut, and Dan stared at them, knowing he'd botched it. Jennifer was furious, and he hadn't even seen it coming. The girl whose emotions he thought so transparent sat through the interview, cool and composed to the end, and he had no idea she was eviscerating him until his guts were lying on the desk.

He tried to formulate an apology on the way to his office, but it rang like a closing argument in a weak case—a plea to ignore the facts and give points for sincerity. She was still frozen in his client chair when he returned.

"I handled that badly," he said, pressing his back against the door to close it. "I'm sorry."

Her eyes were steely blue when she turned to him. "Are there good ways to handle these things?"

"I should have told you, I know. But I wanted to make sure it was a go with Stan before I got your hopes up."

"My hopes up?" she repeated, her voice alien in its sarcasm.

"Hey, a lot of people would be happy to end up at Lassiter & Conway."

She gave an abrupt laugh. "A lot of people, like maybe your four paralegals?"

"You've been listening to gossip."

"You've been fueling it!"

"It's not true. Well, only with one. We had a thing and it ended mutually. She didn't feel comfortable working here anymore, so I sent her over to Stan. She liked it so much she talked three of her friends here into following her. The gossips put one and three together and decided I'd slept with all of them. But it only happened once."

"Wrong," she said coldly. "It happened twice."

"Jennifer." Dan went down on one knee beside her chair. "We can't work together *and* sleep together. That's the bottom line. If you have any interest in *us,* you have to leave the firm."

She jumped to her feet. "*I* have to leave!"

He got up and grabbed for her hand, but she snatched it away and backed out of his reach.

"Why me? Why don't you leave?"

"I can't leave," he said, exasperated. "I have seven years invested in this place. Seven years to your six months. I've got clients. I'm a partner, for Chrissake."

"Ken Stively's a partner. He's leaving."

"Sure, for business reasons."

"Ah!" she cried. "It's worth it for business, but not for love."

"Jennifer—" he warned.

"Business before love. Is that today's lecture?" she mocked.

"I never said love," he retorted.

Jennifer went back a step as if a gale-force wind blew her. Dan bit his lip but it was too late—the words were out.

A knock sounded on the door, and Betty opened it wide enough to present a nervous eye through the crack. "Mr. Casella? Mr. Feldman says they're waiting for you in the forty-first-floor conference room."

"Damn." He'd forgotten the scheduled bull session on the Tramco campaign. "Tell him I'll be right there." He shrugged into his suit coat and tightened his tie. At the doorway he turned and locked eyes with Jennifer. "Wait here."

* * *

Jenny waited, until he was gone and the door closed behind him, before she folded her arms on his desk and put her head down and let herself cry in hard, noiseless sobs.

It was over, fewer than two weeks after it began. Her once-in-a-lifetime love affair was nothing but a passing diversion for Dan. Of course he didn't love her; he'd never said so. What a fool she was to try to put those words in his mouth. She'd thought it was too much to hope for, that the man for whom heads turned and paths cleared might clear a path for her, and it turned out she was right. She'd amused him for a time, but now he was done with her; he had someone else. He wanted her out of the way, so far out of the way that he didn't even mind losing her as a lawyer if that's what it took to get rid of her as a lover. She'd been dumped before. God knows she knew how it felt, but this time she'd been spectacularly dumped, because she'd lost her job, too.

For a moment she let herself consider Dan's alibi, that he only wanted her at Lassiter & Conway so they could continue their affair. But even if it were true, it didn't matter. He had no right to treat her like chattel, to be moved about at his convenience, regardless of his motive.

But the alibi couldn't be true, tolerable or not, she thought with a fresh ache. The evidence was too much to the contrary: the four paralegals, the broken dates and lame excuses, the brother he never talked about or allowed her to meet. There had to be someone else, probably lots of someones. The truth was what came out spontaneously when he blurted, "I never said love."

In time, Jenny sat up and wiped her eyes dry. It was no use dwelling on Dan and what he'd done wrong. He was out of her life now, and nothing he did would ever affect her again. But she had herself to live with for a long time yet—she needed to take a close look at all that she'd done wrong.

For a second time in two years, she'd been dumped. It had to be more than just a run of bad luck. It was something about her. She was too compliant, so eager to please that no one ever felt any need to please her. And it was something about the men she was drawn to. Though Greg was only a shadow of Dan, the same light hit them both and made Jenny see them as masterful and in control, when in truth they were simply selfish and controlling.

Never again. If ever she let another man come into her life, it would be because he was eager to please her. Never again would she be drawn to a man who had to be master of all he surveyed. A quiet man, humble and safe—that was the only kind she would ever consider.

She stood up and straightened her skirt and moved her thoughts to the next question: her career, or what was left of it. Her ambition was stoked high when she first came to Foster, Bell, & McNeil, but not high enough to keep it from burning out the moment she fell in love with Dan Casella. She needed to light a new match, and this time, keep the fire fueled.

What were her options? Go with Lassiter & Conway? Never, no matter if they were the best firm in town. Stay at Foster, Bell and get herself assigned to another supervising partner? People would speculate about that, and rumors would fly, launched by slugs like Rick Mancill. She might be able to weather that storm, but she knew she'd never survive the first day she found herself alone in an elevator with Dan Casella.

There was another option, trendy these days, and one with which she had some expertise. She could file an EEOC complaint, charging Casella and vicariously the firm with sexual harassment.

The lawyer in her felt a surge of excitement at that prospect, but it died almost at once. The facts were not with her. She'd been a willing participant in their sexual relationship—God, more than willing. An unhappy love affair did not amount to sexual harassment, and in any event she hadn't been fired, not in any legal sense.

But it was more than that. She didn't want to play the role of victim. She'd played that part for too long. Now it was time to be the victor. And suddenly she knew how.

Jenny left Dan's office and took the stairs up one flight and walked down the corridor to the corner office. Kenneth P. Stively, the nameplate read. She wiped her eyes, squared her shoulders, and lifted her fist to knock.

20

D<small>AN WAS RELIEVED TO FIND</small> J<small>ENNY GONE WHEN HE RETURNED TO HIS</small> office an hour later. A day for her to cool off and she'd be reasonable, he felt certain.

Friday morning he called her office.

"She hasn't come in today, Mr. Casella," her secretary reported. "In fact, I haven't heard from her since yesterday morning. I've been wondering what to do. Should I call Mr. Feldman?"

"No," Dan said quickly. "Jeez, I just remembered. She's working on a project for me. I know where to track her down."

"I've got quite a few messages for her—"

"I'll remind her to call in."

By Monday morning Jennifer had neither called nor put in an appearance at the office, and every time Dan called her at home he got the answering machine. That was fine at first; it was easier for him to apologize to a silent listener than to a seething voice. But by Monday he was getting tired of the whole charade.

He dialed her number one more time from his desk, and this time when the machine answered, he cursed. "Jennifer, goddamn it, pick up the phone. We have to talk."

There was only silence. "This isn't cute anymore, Jennifer," he warned. "Call me."

He hung up the phone as Jim Feldman strode into his office without knocking. "What do you know about this?" he barked and laid the *Daily News* dead center on the desk blotter.

It was folded to the "Heard Around Town" rumor-mill column. Today's headline read S<small>TIVELY DEFECTS FROM FOSTER FIRM</small>.

"So? We knew this was coming."

"Read it."

Dan leaned back in his chair and scanned the column. It summarized some of Ken's significant cases and estimated the amount of his portable billings. Feldman was quoted as refusing comment at this time.

"Yeah, so?"

"To the end," Feldman said, his forefinger jabbing the page.

Stively takes with him the representation of Hartford-based Tramco, Inc., with an annual legal budget estimated at three million dollars. Accompanying him in the move across town are Foster, Bell associates Sharon Fista, Bradford Martin, and Jennifer Lodge.

Dan sat up straight and read it again, but the words didn't change. He pulled off his glasses and passed his hand over his eyes. "I don't know anything," he muttered to Feldman. "At all."

PART 2

DISCOVERY

1

"THERE."

Leslie made a final adjustment to Jenny's collar and stepped back to survey the results.

A new woman stared out of the full-length mirror. Her hair was chin-length now, and smooth and rounded like a helmet. Her suit was a soft wool turquoise by Escada. Thanks to discounts and extended credit arranged by Leslie, Jenny now owned a dozen such designer suits and dresses. The colors were brighter, the skirts were shorter, and the heels were higher. No more dark man-tailored suits for her. From now on, she would dress as if the terms *feminine* and *successful* were not mutually exclusive.

Leslie gazed at her and chewed her lower lip.

"What's wrong?" Jenny asked, pivoting to check the back.

"Nothing. It's just that I—I feel like I don't know you anymore."

Jenny stared at her reflection, and the woman who stared back was poised and self-assured and perhaps just a bit disdainful. "Good," she said.

Leslie perched in Jenny's window seat and wrapped her night-gown around her ankles. "It's a great look for the first day on the job, anyway."

It had to be, Jenny mused. Her career almost sustained its death blow at Foster, Bell, and it was only through lucky timing that she'd been able to grab Ken Stively's coattails on his way out the door to Jackson, Rieders. She needed to get off to a good start and stay there.

The sound of a diesel engine grinding gears came from the lane. "What's that?" Leslie twisted around to look out the window.

Jenny leaned over her to see. A truck labored up the hill past their courtyard with a long green and white construction trailer behind it. "I guess the builder's finally ready to break ground."

"Oh, what a shame," Leslie sighed. They crossed the room and watched from the rear dormer as the truck climbed up the lane through the grove and across the open lawns that surrounded the site where the manor house once stood. "That means they'll be tearing this place down before long."

Jenny looked around her but felt little regret. Much as she loved the funny old house, it had to go the way of her girlish ponytail and severe suits, jettisoned into a past from which she was determined to steam away.

She reached for her bag and briefcase. "I'd better get going."

Leslie flopped onto the bed. The alarm clock displayed the time as six-thirty A.M. Her eyes rolled to the ceiling, but she held her tongue. "Don't forget your ballet bag," she called as Jenny started out of the room. "Class tonight."

Jenny turned back. "I forgot to tell you," she said.

"What?"

"I dropped out of class."

"*What?*" Leslie sat straight up in the middle of the bed.

"I don't have time for it anymore."

"But, Jenny—you *love* to dance."

"I love to sleep late, too, but I can't have everything."

Leslie's eyes narrowed. "This is more than just starting a new job at a new firm, isn't it? Does this have something to do with Dan Casella?"

"Nobody would ask an ambitious man a question like that," Jenny retorted. "Leslie, I want to succeed at Jackson, Rieders. And that's all."

She hurried outside to her car. She was driving into the city today, and every day from now on. No longer would she be dependent upon train schedules or charitable drivers. From now on nothing would interfere with or distract her from her work.

Arthur Lessin was the chairman of the litigation department at Jackson, Rieders, and the third stop on Jenny's orientation schedule. He rose from behind his desk with a smile to greet her as she came into his office. His face was haggard and his shoulders stooped—twenty years of keeping the lid on a major litigation practice had taken their toll.

"Everything's backward these days," he said. "We used to meet a young lawyer and then make an offer. Now it's the other way around."

Jenny surmised that she was third on his schedule this morning, too, behind Sharon Fista and Brad Martin.

"Not really in my case," she said. "I interviewed here when I was in law school. You made me an offer then."

That piqued his interest and, she saw, gave him some reassurance. She wasn't merely part of Ken's package deal, but someone worthy of the firm in her own right.

"And you turned us down?" he asked, feigning hurt. "Well, I guess it's like they say—good things come to those who wait."

"I'll do my best to prove that's true."

"Good. Here's what we have in mind for you. Of course you'll work with Ken on any major Tramco cases. At the moment, though, there's nothing big in the works. So we're putting you on the RTC team."

"Savings and loan fraud?"

"Right. RTC's the receiver of a failed S&L called Collier Financial. We've brought suit against the former officers and directors and the outside accountants. It's a massive piece of litigation. We had to rent space across town just to accommodate all the documents."

"How many other lawyers on the team?"

"You make fifteen."

Jenny knew what this meant, and her heart sank. For the next two years, she'd be working in a warehouse with a handful of other young associates and paralegals, reviewing documents and creating indices, the tedium broken only by occasional troop inspections by the senior lawyers who would actually try the case.

"All right," she said.

He didn't expect enthusiasm and wasn't disappointed when she showed none. "There's one other thing I have to ask you to do first. And let me apologize in advance."

Jenny waited, wondering what could be worse than what he'd already asked.

"We've got a client, a software systems design firm called Intellitech."

The name was familiar to her. "Isn't that Gordon St. James's company?"

Lessin acknowledged it with a grimace. Gordon St. James was something of a minor celebrity in Philadelphia. In the sixties, he was a prominent student radical at Penn; he led marches, organized sit-ins, and wrote a best-selling book about how to overturn the establishment. Fifteen years later he founded his own software company and wrote another book about how to exploit the establishment.

"We represent Intellitech in a suit against a former employee who defected to the competition."

"In breach of a covenant not to compete?" This was something else St. James was famous for—locking in his employees with contracts that prohibited them from working for any other company in the industry for two years after they left Intellitech. The result was that few people could afford to leave.

"The case is being run by one of our labor litigators, Bill Moran, and he's doing a fine job. But St. James has some kind of bug up his ass, pardon my French. He thinks he needs a woman lawyer, because the defendant's a woman. He insisted on interviewing every woman in the department, but nobody suited him. He called after he saw the press release about Ken. Now he wants to interview you and Sharon."

"Fine."

"Obviously, there's no way either of you could be expected to step in and try a case of this magnitude," Lessin said. "In fact, nobody could at this point—there's an April tenth trial date. But we have to humor the guy."

"Fine," Jenny repeated.

"Sharon's going out there today, and he asked to see you tomorrow at two." He scribbled on a notepad and tore the page off. "Here's the address."

"What should I do to prepare?"

Lessin shook his head. "Don't waste any more time than you have to."

Jenny spent the balance of the morning settling into her new office. Her assigned secretary was a middle-aged woman named Marilyn, whom she would be sharing with the partner in the larger office next door. He was Walter Boenning, an old-time general practitioner who gave her a warm welcome, but who she could tell instantly was not among the power players at Jackson, Rieders.

That afternoon she went in search of Bill Moran. She found him with his feet on his desk and his Dictaphone to his mouth.

"Excuse me," she said, tapping on the open door.

He looked up and stopped dictating, but did not alter his posture.

"I'm Jennifer Lodge, new on board today."

"Fresh meat, huh?"

She gave him the benefit of the doubt and ignored the remark. "I'm scheduled to meet with Gordon St. James tomorrow."

He leaned back so far in the chair he looked like he was waiting for his teeth to be cleaned. "Yeah, so?"

"I'd like to take a look at the file before I go."

"Didn't Artie tell you this is just a beauty contest?" he said, disgusted. "All you have to do is walk down the runway."

Jenny knew the term *beauty contest* was often used to describe clients' auditions of lawyers, but there was something odious in the way this man said it.

"I'm going out there to talk, not to walk," she said. "And I want to know what I'm talking about."

"This is a straightforward restrictive covenant case," he ground out. "Probably my thirtieth. I'm not about to be second-guessed on it by a first-day associate. So you just find yourself something else to talk to Gordy about."

At nine o'clock, Bill Moran's office was in darkness, and so was his secretary's station and the file room behind it. Jenny slipped inside and closed the door before she hit the light switch. She started with the top drawer of the first file cabinet and saw that every client name on every folder began with the letter A. No trick to breaking this code. She moved closer to the center of the bank of cabinets and found the drawer holding H, I, and J. There it was: *Intellitech Systems, Inc. v. Cynthia Lehmann.* She pulled out the first pleadings binder and hefted it to the work table.

Cynthia Lehmann was thirty years old, had a finance degree from Wharton, and had served as a product manager for Intellitech. Her specialty was analyzing the financial operations of banks and customizing software systems to suit their needs. She was so highly regarded that she'd been under serious consideration for a vice-presidency. But the job went to an older man, and shortly thereafter she tendered her resignation. She surfaced a few weeks later working as product manager for Plex Systems, and calling on the same clients she'd cultivated for Intellitech.

Jenny opened Cynthia Lehmann's personnel file. Her photograph looked up from the table. She was a striking brunette with soft brown eyes and a warm smile. Her handwritten resignation letter lay in the file, too. Jenny read through it once for what it said, then again for what it didn't say.

At eleven o'clock she put the file away. She knew enough to know she didn't need to know any more.

2

INTELLITECH HEADQUARTERS WAS IN AN OFFICE PARK ON THE ROUTE 202 corridor, where all the new high-tech companies had planted themselves, in a windowless black granite building looming over a man-made lake. Jenny was directed through the center core of the building to a glass elevator that looked out over a thousand workstations on its route to the top.

She passed through a door marking the executive suite, and suddenly the windowless building was nothing but windows, in the shape of a prism pointing skyward. The floor here was white marble, and the furniture white leather. The effect was blinding.

"This way, please." The receptionist beckoned, and Jenny blinked away the glare and walked past her into St. James's office.

Instantly the light went dim, and she was in a windowless room again, an enormous one lit only by a desk lamp and the lights in the giant aquariums that lined the walls. It took a moment for her eyes to adjust, and when they did, the outline of a man stood before her.

"I'm Gordon St. James." There was amusement in his voice, and Jenny was amused, too, that a major corporate executive would engage in such parlor tricks with his guests.

"Jennifer Lodge. May I compliment you on your design?"

"You're interested in architecture?"

"Actually I was referring to your lighting design. It's amazing, what you do to your visitors' pupils in the space of a minute. I imagine it gives you a real home-court advantage."

His teeth flashed white in the shadow. "You make me feel so transparent."

"Impossible, in a room with no light to pass through you."

He moved behind her and pressed a button on the wall. Soft lights washed over the ceiling and spotlights shone down on the floor. She turned for a better look at him.

Her image of a software designer was a chubby man with shaggy hair wearing corduroys. But St. James was slightly built, wore a European-cut suit, and had a ponytail and a carefully cultivated beard stubble.

"Now I can see you're completely opaque," Jenny said.

"I pray I stay that way. Come and sit down."

He led her to a pair of club chairs facing a couch, all covered in a deep teal leather. Jenny took one of the chairs, and he positioned himself in the middle of the couch, crossed his legs and spread his arms wide over the seatback.

"I suppose I should tell you something about the case."

"I've been through the file."

"Do you have any experience with the issue in this case? Non-compete covenants?"

Jenny watched a brightly striped tiger fish swim close to the glass in the aquarium. "That's strange," she said after a moment. "I thought the issue in this case was sexual harassment."

St. James allowed a smirk. "What makes you say that?"

"Cynthia Lehmann's defense is that circumstances forced her out of the company, that she had no choice but to leave. That's a pretty vague position. There's a certain coyness to her restraint. I had the feeling when I read her resignation letter and again when I read her answer to the complaint that she doesn't say more because you already know the rest. But there's nothing in her personnel file to suggest she was forced out. So I wonder—what will she testify was her reason for leaving? I think it must be sex. And so do you, don't you, Mr. St. James? That's why you want a woman to try this case."

He gave an enigmatic smile, reached for a cigarette from an onyx box on the table, and lit it. "Let's imagine for a moment that's it," he said, after a deep inhalation. "Do you have any experience with *that* issue?"

"I do. And for the other side."

"Ah. Can you switch sides and tell me what kind of defense you'd put on in this case?"

"Let's hear the charges."

He leaned forward and tapped his cigarette against a marble dish. "Imagine she says something like I pressured her into a sexual relationship, she thought her job was riding on it, we had an affair, it ended, and she felt she couldn't stay here any longer. What if she says that?"

"Will she bring in anyone to corroborate?"

"No, not a chance."

"It's her word against yours?"

"Count on it."

"Then I've heard her word. What's yours?"

He considered his answer while he drew again on the cigarette. "What if I said it never happened, I never touched her, she's delusional?"

"Then I'd say she's not delusional, she's deliberately fabricating a story designed to embarrass you and avoid her noncompete restrictions."

"Hmmm. And what if I said it *did* happen?" He watched her slyly, hoping to trip her up, or better yet, shock her.

"Then I'd say—even better."

He blinked, off his guard.

"What's your marital situation?" she asked.

"Separated."

"When? Before, after?"

"I don't know. I'd have to look at the charge accounts to figure out whether Andrea was home then. We've been separated on and off most of our marriage."

"Cynthia Lehmann knew that?"

"Of course."

"Then this is what I'd day: Cynthia Lehmann is a talented and ambitious young woman who worked hard to get a good position here, but she wasn't content with it. She had her eye on a vice-presidency. She considered herself the best-qualified person for the position, but she lacked about ten years' experience.

"She knew that your marriage was troubled, your wife came and went as she pleased, you felt uncertain and adrift and lonely. An affair with you was her ticket to the vice-presidency. She's an attractive and exciting young woman. She romanced you, she seduced you, you fell in love with her. But when the time came to fill the position, you gave it to someone with better credentials.

"Cynthia was furious. She stole your customer list and went to work for your competition, where she plans to achieve not only the career success you wouldn't give her but personal revenge against you."

Gordon St. James stared at her long after the echo of her voice faded into air. Jenny lifted her chin and held his gaze as her nails dug into her palms.

He ground out his cigarette and picked up the phone and dialed. "Art Lessin," he said, and her nails dug deeper. He watched her while he waited for the call to go through.

"Art, call off the womanhunt," he said. "I've found my lawyer."

He smiled at Jenny, and her hands went limp with relief.

"I don't care how old she is, you give her whatever support she needs," St. James barked into the phone. "You give her anything she wants. What do you want?" he said to Jenny, and hit the speaker button.

"I want Bill Moran off the case," she said without hesitation. "And I want two associates of my choosing to assist."

"Got that, Art?"

"I got it."

St. James hit the button and the line went dead.

"You know, it's amazing," he said to Jenny. "The way you described it? That's exactly how it happened."

5

AT FIVE O'CLOCK, BETTY STUCK HER HEAD IN DAN'S OFFICE AND pointed to her watch.

"Sorry," Dan said into the telephone. "I've got a conference call coming in. Let's wrap this up tomorrow—how's that?" He pinned the phone between his chin and shoulder and used both hands to sweep the top of his desk into his briefcase. "Ten? Let me check." He flipped his calendar with one hand while he stuck the other into the sleeve of his coat. "No good, I'm in court then. Let's make it early—say eight o'clock? Good. Talk to you then."

By the time he hung up, he was packed and ready to go. " 'Night," he called on his way out.

Betty looked up from her desk with a smile. She was amused at the sudden role reversal that had her lingering at work later than her boss, and pleased, too. "Tell him I said good luck tomorrow."

"You bet."

Outside, the air was cool but the April sky was bright. The spring had come so suddenly it still felt new. People leaving their offices at the end of the day still felt moved to say, "Can you believe how bright it is?"

The usual cluster of lacrosse parents was waiting outside the locker room. "Practice over?" Dan asked the woman beside him when he joined the crowd.

She turned on an inviting smile. "Yes, but I think the coach is giving them a pep talk for tomorrow's game."

From her carefully styled auburn hair and even more carefully applied makeup, he guessed she was divorced; middle-aged married women rarely took such pains with their appearances on a weeknight.

"Don't tell me one of them belongs to you," she said, her green eyes betraying her curiosity. "You're too young to have a teenager."

He was grateful for the compliment. More parents than he liked to count routinely mistook him for a peer. "One of them's my brother," he said. "Which one is your brother?"

"Oh, you!" She laughed, slapping his arm in delight.

She held the evening paper folded in her hand, and Dan turned his head sideways to read the headline: THE SAINT AND THE CYNNER: COURTROOM ROCKS.

"What's that all about?" he asked.

"That hot new sex trial," she said. "Aren't you following it? The woman executive sleeping her way up the corporate ladder?" Her gaze went bold. "As if she needed an excuse, right?"

Dan gave her the grin she was waiting for. A few months ago this little flirtation would have led to something. But not anymore.

A divorced mother came with baggage, and the last thing he needed was another complicated woman.

The locker-room doors burst open and the boys spilled out like a litter of pups scrambling out of a basket. Tony shoved his way through the crowd, lowered his head, and charged for Dan's belly. Dan feinted left, tackled him around the middle, hoisted him on one shoulder, and spun twice before he deposited him, laughing, back on his feet.

Tony pulled his baseball cap on backward, and they fell into step together to the car. An easy affection had grown between them the last couple months. Tony's high-spirited companionship gave Dan more pleasure than he ever would have believed.

"How'd it go today?"

"Great! We're gonna whip some major butt tomorrow. Think you'll make it?"

"I wouldn't miss it."

After dinner, they cleared the table and spread their papers out. Dan never used to leave the office before his day's work was done, but now it was his routine to come home early and work late. It was a new feeling for him to crawl through the trenches of paper warfare in his own dining room. His perspective was starting to change. Questions that once seemed of life-and-death urgency were starting to fade beside more important questions, like how was Tony's day at school?

At a quarter to ten, after two hours of alternating between furious writing and long vacant stares, Tony stacked his papers together and handed them to Dan. The subject of his report was Congressional term limits, and the analysis was surprisingly good. Dan felt himself swelling with pride, but knew he had to be careful. If he were too lavish in his praise, Tony would be embarrassed or suspicious; if he didn't give the paper its due, Tony would be hurt. It was a tricky business, walking the fine line of adolescence.

"Good job," Dan said. "You got me convinced." He hit it right; Tony was pleased. "Tell you what—why don't you go through it again for spelling, and I'll have Betty type it up tomorrow."

"Spelling?" Tony scowled and snatched the pages back.

Dan laughed. In the space of a second he'd fallen over the line and made Tony mad. He got up from the table and clapped the boy on the shoulder as he passed behind him to the TV. He switched on the local news and went to the kitchen for a beer. When he came back, the news story was a feature on income tax and the April 15 filing deadline, and Dan scribbled a note to call his accountant and make sure he was on top of things.

"Here." Tony handed up his report.

Dan heard the word *trial* and his head swiveled toward the screen as Jennifer Lodge appeared on the screen. The lid of his briefcase slammed shut on his fingers. He didn't notice. He moved toward the TV and stopped dead.

Jennifer was crossing the courthouse plaza toward the cab stand.

"Tempers ran high today during the cross-examination of defendant Cynthia Lehmann," the voiceover said.

It was Jennifer, but he could hardly believe it. Her hair was short, and the coral-colored suit more sophisticated than anything he'd seen her in before. Her bearing was different, and her demeanor. A different Jennifer, her second self, the one he thought he would love next.

"Intellitech counsel Jennifer Lodge hit hard with questions about Lehmann's career ambitions, her desire to obtain a vice-presidency at the company, and her anger when another candidate was chosen. Lodge claims that Lehmann initiated an affair with Intellitech chairman Gordon St. James for the sole purpose of gaining a promotion."

The camera cut to a dark-haired woman walking out of the courthouse beside her lawyer. "Lehmann adamantly denied that charge, and today the debate continued even after court was adjourned."

On screen the dark-haired woman broke away from the restraining hand of her lawyer and charged up to Jennifer on the pavement. What followed was a cameraman's dream.

"What kind of a woman are you," she shouted at Jennifer, "to do something like this to another woman?"

Jennifer's response came in a low voice, but the microphone caught it and broadcast it to a million listeners. "You may use your sex in the workplace, Ms. Lehmann, but I leave mine at home."

It was a perfect sound bite, and one that would be repeated with every story aired on the case.

Jennifer turned and climbed into the cab, and as he watched

her go, Dan felt a sudden dizzying sense of disorientation, like he'd felt the night he almost hit the deer, a sense that he'd somehow lost his place. He spun around to make sure Tony was still where he'd left him.

Tony was watching him, curious.

"She used to work for me," Dan mumbled.

The boy grinned. "Looks like you should've held on to her."

4

THURSDAY MORNING, DAN HOPED TO SLIP INTO THE COURTROOM unnoticed, but Art Lessin stood at the door like a sentinel.

"Dan, how are you?" Lessin said, reaching to shake hands.

"Art." Dan started to go in, but stopped and turned back. "I gotta tell you, you have some weird ideas about associate training over at your shop."

Lessin's haggard face went blank. "What are you talking about?"

"A major jury trial for a brand-new associate? What d'you call that? Baptism by fire?"

"Who, Jennifer?" The blankness dissolved. "Oh, yeah, she's one of yours, isn't she?"

Dan gave a curt nod.

"Then I should ask you about *your* training program. Her second day on the job, she stole the case away from Bill Moran."

"Jennifer *Lodge?*" Dan blurted, but Lessin had already turned to speak to someone else.

Dan took a seat in the back of the courtroom and was soon lost in a sea of spectators. In the first row on plaintiff's side sat Gordon St. James, alone. Dan couldn't guess whether Jennifer had deliberately placed him there instead of with her at counsel table, but the effect was exactly right. He was a lonely man, without female companionship, even from his own lawyer.

Jennifer emerged from chambers and a buzz went through the courtroom as she was sighted by the crowd. She was dressed in a soft butter-yellow suit, breaking every dark-suit rule ever drummed into trial lawyers. Her minions followed in her wake, and he was stunned to see Brad Martin among them. Brad was four years senior to Jennifer, yet here he was, carrying her bags and looking grateful for the opportunity.

The evidence was in, and this morning the attorneys would present closing arguments. The judge went through the usual preliminaries, then ceded the floor to plaintiff.

Jennifer rose from counsel table and walked slowly to the jury box.

"We live in a world where success doesn't come easily," she began. Her voice was soft but clear, like the color of her suit.

"If you want to be a doctor, you have to go to college, then to medical school, then do an internship, then a residency. Then after you finally get a paying job, you spend the next ten years paying off all your school loans."

She stood motionless before the jury, an island of stillness in the sea of the courtroom. Her posture was ballet perfect, and quietly assured.

"Or say you want to be a union carpenter. You have to wait for an opening in an apprenticeship program, and put in your time doing all the back-breaking work the journeymen won't touch, then wait for your union card, then wait your turn to get hired on the good crews.

"If you want to be a company executive, you work your way up to department head, then division manager, and so on until you know that company inside out.

"How many of us wouldn't want to skip over all those years of hard work and waiting? Wouldn't it be wonderful if you could just pick up a little remote-control like you have for your VCR and push the fast-forward button and skip past all the years of toil and drudgery?"

Jennifer turned, her first grand gesture, and fixed her eyes on the defendant.

"That's what Cynthia Lehmann wanted to do. She's a bright and talented woman. She's highly regarded by her colleagues and her clients alike. At the age of thirty, she was already a product manager for Intellitech. In another ten years, with hard work and diligence, she might have become a company executive.

"But she didn't want to wait another ten years. She didn't want to do her internship and her residency. She didn't want to wait in the union hall with everybody else until her name got to the top of the list. She wanted to find a fast-forward button for her career and hold it down until it skipped over all the years of working hard and paying dues and zipped her straight to the executive suite.

"The fast-forward button she found was Gordon St. James, and she pushed it hard."

Now Jennifer spared herself a look at her client, and he was cued for it.

"But no, she says he was the aggressor," she said, while her client's abject slump shouted out the lie. "He forced her into the relationship, he threatened her job security, and she feared she'd be fired if she didn't submit. That submission took her to dozens of dinners at the finest restaurants in the city. That submission netted her a pair of diamond earrings and weekly flower deliveries. Does this sound like sexual harassment, or a love affair?

"Cynthia Lehmann says she feared for her job security if she didn't submit." Jennifer's voice went bitter. "Ladies and gentlemen, the only 'submission' she made was when she submitted her application for the vice-presidency.

"Gordon St. James was having a love affair, but it turns out Cynthia Lehmann wasn't. She was in his bed for one reason and one reason only, and that was to get the job she wanted. But Mr. St. James still had a company to run, and he had to make the choice that was best for the company. He chose the best candidate for the job, and it wasn't Cynthia Lehmann.

"She pushed the fast-forward button, but it didn't work. It didn't get her where she wanted to be. So what did she do next? She broke off the affair, she resigned from the company, and she went looking for another fast-forward button at Plex Systems. Oh, no more sex this time. She had a new weapon. Now she had Intellitech's customer list.

"Ms. Lehmann signed an agreement when she went to work for Intellitech—a covenant, they call it, it's that binding—that she wouldn't go to work for a competitive business for two years after leaving the company. She didn't wait two weeks.

"She wants you to release her from her covenant. 'Don't hold me to it,' she's asking you. 'I was the victim in this sordid little story.'

"But it's time for her to stop playing victim and start taking responsibility for her actions. She signed the covenant of her own free will; nobody forced her. She climbed into bed with Gordon St. James for reasons all her own; nobody forced her. She left the company because her ambitions were thwarted; nobody forced her.

"Don't let her play the role of victim any longer. Make her stand accountable for her own actions. I ask you to return your verdict for Intellitech."

The jury filed out for their deliberations at eleven-thirty, and Dan left the courtroom immediately after. There was no point in waiting for the verdict; he knew she'd won. And there was no point in staying to offer her congratulations, because he would've strangled on the words.

In the middle of her closing argument, it finally came to him that she was describing herself. The fast-forward button she'd pushed—the one that didn't work the way she wanted and sent her jumping across town to the competition—was him.

5

JUDGMENT WAS ANNOUNCED THE NEXT DAY WHILE JENNY LAY FLAT on her back, her knees raised and her heels cupped in cold metal stirrups. "Slight case of pregnancy," the doctor said.

Through the third-story window she watched thunderclouds scuttle across the sky, invading the spring afternoon like airborne insects. Her first day off in almost ninety days, and it was going to rain.

"Thought so," she replied.

After she was dressed, they sat down together in his office to calculate dates, he consulting his calendar and Jenny hers, as if they were adversaries scheduling a deposition. There was little guesswork involved. She could count on two hands the number of times she and Dan had been together, and they'd all been during a two-week span in late January. End of October, then, they agreed.

The nurse handed her a packet on the way out, advertising brochures for infant formula and pamphlets from abortion counseling agencies. All the bases were covered here—a true full-service obstetrical practice.

Outside, storm clouds billowed like black smoke across the sky. The temperature had plunged twenty degrees during her hour in the clinic, and a sudden gust of wind whipped at her skirt as she hurried to her car. She was barely inside before the skies opened and the rain poured out.

Three months along, she thought, staring blindly at the sheets of water that sluiced over the windshield. Ridiculously late for a pregnancy test these days, when a woman could have a blue-stick positive almost before she rolled out of bed. Embarrassingly late for someone who'd always been first in her class. Well, obviously she wasn't so smart anymore. A twenty-seven-year-old lawyer and she'd made a mistake most sixteen-year-olds knew how to avoid.

She started the engine and turned on the wipers and watched them carve two arcs of clear glass through the rain before another cascade obscured her vision again. Leslie was in Hawaii on her honeymoon and wouldn't welcome this news from Jenny now, if ever. Who else could she call? Certainly not her mother, who had strong morals and a weak heart, and not her sister, who would feel compelled to tell her mother. And somehow all the bosom friends and soulmates of her youth had become Christmas-card and cocktail-party acquaintances; there was not one she could call for solace.

She pulled out of the parking lot and onto the highway that led her to the expressway a mile away. The traffic was making no allowance for the weather. She pulled on the headlights and kept to the right-hand lane, but cars streaked past her at seventy miles an hour, and tractor-trailers sent up flumes of rainwater from their tires that drenched Jenny's car in moments of sheer panicked blindness.

She wondered if this might be her punishment—not for sleeping with Dan, she would never regret that—but for her more recent sins. She repeated to herself like a litany that she wasn't the jury, it wasn't her job to decide who was lying and who was telling the truth. She was an advocate. She *advocated* her client's position. The jurors knew that; they knew they were supposed to decide which position was correct. If they decided wrong, it shouldn't be on her conscience.

But every time she closed her eyes she could see Cynthia Lehmann's face at the moment the verdict was announced. There couldn't be any clearer evidence: she'd been screwed, twice.

Tears flooded her eyes and it was hard to know who they were for, Cynthia Lehmann, or herself, or the blameless child whose heart beat beneath hers. But in the end she knew what caused the tears, and when she saw a truck stop ahead, she exited and parked and dashed through the pelting raindrops into a telephone booth on the edge of the lot.

"Mr. Casella's office," his secretary announced.

Jenny gripped tight on the phone. "Hi, Betty," she said, fighting to hold her voice steady. "This is Jennifer Lodge. Is he in, please?"

There was a pause. "Oh, hello. Yes, hold on a moment."

Betty's voice was cool. Jenny had heard gossip swirling to the effect that Ken Stively had stolen away the Tramco business from Foster, Bell, and that Jenny helped him do it. If she had, she hadn't known it at the time; she'd assumed Tramco was his to take.

She waited for Dan to pick up and wondered whether she should blurt out the news at once, or suggest a meeting and build up to it more gradually. She supposed it would make a difference if she knew what reaction she wanted from him, but she didn't yet know what her own reaction was, and wouldn't, not until she heard the sound of his voice.

A small green sports car pulled up next to hers in the lot, and through the driving rain Jenny could see the driver sitting motionless behind the wheel. It looked like he was watching her. She turned her back to him, and clutched the phone close to her ear.

Betty's voice came back finally. "I'm sorry, Miss Lodge. He's with someone."

Jenny's balance pitched, and she pressed her back against the booth to keep from falling. Dan had *refused* to take her call. If he were really with someone, Betty would have known that when she first answered, as she always did. But maybe she meant something different—Dan was *with someone,* as in involved, dating, living together.

"Would you like to leave a message?" Betty asked.

Yes, please tell him his pathetic ex-lover finds herself unexpectedly pregnant and wonders if he'd drop his current lover and come hold her hand. "No. No message," she said.

The phone dropped from her hand and swung crazily on the end of the cord before she managed to grab it and hook it into the cradle. When she turned around, the driver of the sports car had his car phone to his ear, and was now unmistakably staring at her.

She ran to her car, dove behind the wheel, and hit the lock button. Rivulets of rain coursed down her face and from her hair, down her shoulders and onto her lap. She started the engine and cast a quick glance to the side. The driver hadn't moved from his car. She took a deep, shaky breath and headed back onto the expressway.

The rain had the wind behind it now, and a deep rumble of thunder sounded five seconds before a streak of lightning split the sky. Jenny clenched the wheel so tightly her hands went numb. Another storm replayed in her mind, and another desperate drive home, Dan's voice saying, "I'll never make it," and her own murmur echoing, "Please come in."

She shook her head against those memories and checked the traffic around her. Looming in the rear-view mirror was a small green car.

She turned on the radio and tried to ignore it, but a minute later it was still there, following steadily two car lengths behind.

Jenny pressed her foot down and swung into the passing lane without signaling. Now it was her tires that sent up flumes of water, but she pushed the car faster, passing two, three, then four cars before she pulled abruptly into the right lane again.

Her eyes shot up to the mirror as the green car cut in close behind her.

A sob tore out of her, but she bit her lip and watched the road. A car ahead slowed down and peeled off an exit ramp to the right. The green car was following close, less than one length behind her. A truck passed them both on the left, sluicing water over her windshield, then over his, and in his moment of blindness, she wrenched her wheel to the right and lurched over the shoulder and across the grass until she hit the bottom of the ramp. She threw a wild look back to the highway, in time to see the green car hit its brakes, but too late to make the exit.

She sobbed loudly, her terror unabated by her escape. She turned right at the bottom of the ramp, then made an immediate left, and a mile later, a right onto a narrow country road, and it was only when there wasn't a car in sight that she started to feel a moment's relief.

And then she realized she didn't know where she was.

Woods stood on both sides of the road, and as far as she could tell through the pouring rain, nothing but deeper woods lay ahead. She slowed the car and swung it around.

But the road was too narrow, and the shoulders too soft. The right front wheel sank into the mud, and when she tried to pull it back onto the road, the rear wheel slid into the mud as well. She threw the car into reverse and tried to back up, but the tires only spun. She turned the steering wheel sharply to the left, then the right, but everything she did seemed only to dig her in deeper.

The effort of holding back the panic was finally too much. She collapsed over the wheel and sobbed, out of control. She was lost, she was pregnant and unloved, maybe she was being followed—or worse, maybe she'd imagined the whole thing. The rain hit the roof and hood of the car in a deafening drumbeat, and Jenny cried loudly and without restraint as she hadn't cried since childhood.

A horn tooted beside her.

She swallowed a scream and whipped her head around. Pulled alongside was a white Volvo station wagon, and the man behind the wheel was lowering his window.

Jenny ran her sleeve over her face and lowered her own window a crack. The man was barely visible through the downpour, but she could make out fair hair and a smile. He said something that was drowned out by the rain, and Jenny shook her head at him. He held up a phone with one hand and cupped his mouth with the other. "Would you like me to call a tow truck?" he yelled again.

She nodded emphatically. "Yes. Thank you!"

He closed his window and she hers, and she watched him punch the numbers into the phone and speak into the mouthpiece. A minute later, he lowered his window again, and she did the same, all the way down this time, leaning back to avoid the spray of water that splashed into the car.

"They said it'll be half an hour or so," he shouted.

She nodded. "Thanks!"

"I'd better wait here," he yelled. "Make sure they don't forget about you."

136

"No, that's not necessary—" she began, but his window had already closed.

She realized her engine was still running, and she switched off the ignition. The roar was less deafening now, and her panic started to subside. She dried her eyes and leaned her head back. The world might be full of loss and menace, but there was still the unexpected kindness of strangers to give her hope.

The half-hour passed. The rain finally began to slacken, and the sky brightened a shade. Jenny glanced over at the Volvo. The man's face was visible now. She could see that he was passing the time by reading a newspaper. When he turned a page, she could see that he was Scott Sterling.

6

ASTONISHED, SHE TURNED HER EYES FRONT, BUT HE CAUGHT THE tail end of her glance and smiled at her briefly before returning to his paper. An instant later his forehead creased, and he lowered the paper and stared at her. He put down his window again, and Jenny did the same.

"It just hit me," he said in an apologetic tone. "You won't remember, but we met once before, last winter. I'm—"

"Scott Sterling," she said.

His smile was luminous, as if she'd given him a long-awaited gift. "And you're the lawyer who's a ballerina. Or the ballerina who's a lawyer."

"Actually I'm not a ballerina anymore."

"What d'you know?" he laughed. "I'm not a lawyer anymore."

There was an awkward pause, filled finally by Scott. "The new haircut threw me off, I guess. But I like it." Jenny lifted a self-conscious hand to her hair, but he'd already turned to point toward the road. "Funny meeting you here."

Her glance followed his gesture and took in the road, the cars, the mud, and the rain, and suddenly her good fortune struck her. "Lucky thing for me you came along," she said.

"Not lucky yet," he replied. "The tow truck should have been here by now. Let me try them again."

He spoke into his phone and turned back to Jenny when he hung up. "On their way, they say."

"Really, you don't need to stay," Jenny said.

"It's no trouble."

"But I don't want to take your time—"

He cut her off. "One thing I have plenty of is time."

She didn't know what to say. Her gaze drifted away.

"So, how's life at Foster, Bell?" he asked, pulling her back.

"I'm not there anymore."

His face registered surprise. "How come?"

Jenny gave a little shrug. "I made a stupid mistake."

"Hey, what d'you know? Me, too."

Her eyes met his, and she felt again the spark of kinship she'd felt the first time she saw him, on a January night in a crowded conference room.

He crooked his elbow over the window and leaned a little closer. "Are you practicing somewhere else?"

"Yes, at Jackson, Rieders."

"Good firm. I wish I could bounce back from my mistake that well."

"My mistake's still waiting to catch up with me."

"What d'you know?" he said again, laughing this time. "Mine, too."

Disbarment, conviction, prison—sobering thoughts all dissipated by the gentle wash of his laughter.

"Tell me if you'd rather not talk about it," Jenny began. "But how's the case going?"

"Which one? There's four, you know." As he spoke, a gust of wind drove the rain against his face, and he pulled his head in, sputtering and laughing. "Hey, how 'bout continuing this conversation in one car or the other?"

Jenny hesitated only a second. "I'll come around," she said. She climbed out of her car and jogged around the rear of his. It was a working family car, cluttered with the debris of parents and children, home and lawn. A child's safety seat was still strapped into the back, and she remembered the little girl with the sun-kissed face. He leaned over the passenger seat to hold the door open for her, and she slid in beside him. He wore khakis and a cotton sweater and Docksiders on his feet, the uniform of any professional man on his day off.

"Now we can talk a little easier," he said, but if anything he looked more uneasy.

"Four cases, you said?"

"Yeah. First there's the disciplinary board case, and that's going just fine. They'll have me disbarred in no time."

"Oh, Scott, I'm sorry."

"You know what's funny about that case? They keep asking if I was under the influence of alcohol or drugs at the time. Because if I were, there's programs to help and I might get off with a suspension. But there's no program for my kind of problem."

Jenny glanced at him uncertainly.

"Go ahead. You can ask."

"Okay. What *is* your kind of problem?"

"I wanted to be thought well of," he said. "Too much, I guess."

She nodded and thought she understood. She remembered her own schoolgirl days, with her arm waving wildly in the air for the teacher's attention, desperately hoping for the chance to answer and please and impress. Twenty years later, her behavior with Dan Casella had scarcely been different. What was it Dan once said of Scott? He craved approval like a junkie. The words fit her just as well.

Scott turned and stared vacantly through the windshield. "Then there's Uncle Curt's civil suit for damages against me and Harding & McMann," he said. "I don't keep up with that one too much. All my money's going to my criminal lawyer."

"Who's that?"

"Bill Lawson."

Jenny knew the name and the reputation. Lawson was the kind of high-priced white-collar crime defense lawyer who specialized in making deals with the government. No one could remember when he last took a case to trial. "How's that going?" she asked.

He shook his head. "I don't really keep up with that one, either. I just ask Bill to give me enough warning when I'm indicted so I can get my shaving gear packed before the cops come for me."

Jenny could hardly conceal her shudder.

"And finally there's the custody case."

"Your little girl?"

"My ex-little girl, if Val has her way. Apparently if I'm unfit to practice law, I'm automatically unfit to be a father."

"I'm so sorry," Jenny said, and the words sounded even weaker with repetition. He seemed so vulnerable, and so endearing. Quiet, safe, and eager to please—the kind of man she thought didn't exist anymore.

He turned to face her and shook his head with a gentle smile. "Don't be," he said. "I was the one who did what I did. I wasn't anybody's victim. It would be easy to claim I was, but I'm not going to play it that way. I have to shoulder the responsibility for what I did, and I will. And who knows? Maybe in the end it'll turn out to be the best thing I ever did. A real character-builder, Father would say."

He was joking at the end, but his words came to her in a sudden sober burst of understanding, and she knew that everything her erstwhile kindred spirit was saying was even more true of herself. In that instant, she made her decision, and once it was made, she felt elated, relieved of a thousand burdens. And she knew that through all of her life, she would never regret the choice she made in that second of clarity.

"Well, it's about time," he said as the tow truck chugged into view.

Scott moved his car out of the way, and they both climbed out and stood watching from the roadside as the driver hooked the chains to the frame of Jenny's car.

Something fluttered on the grass beside them, a bird pitching its weight crazily as it tried to limp for cover. Scott ran to it and crouched to the ground. When he stood, the bird was flapping in his hands.

"It's got a broken wing." He smoothed its pearl-gray feathers and crooned softly until the bird went still.

Jenny peered into his hands. "What is it?"

"A dove. The storm must have driven it into a tree or something." He moved his fingers gently under the wing. "You know what? I think I can fix this."

She followed him to the tailgate of his car and swung it open for him. He placed the bird softly onto a folded blanket. Its good wing fluttered briefly, but he stroked its feathers until it tucked its beak into its breast and went quiet in the makeshift nest.

"I've got tape, but I need something hard for a splint," he said. "Got any Popsicle sticks?"

Jenny shook her head and tried to think of a substitute. "Emery boards?"

"Perfect."

Her car had been successfully extracted from the ditch, and she paid the driver and retrieved her purse.

"It feels like a clean break," Scott said when he finished binding the emery boards to the wing with masking tape. "She oughta heal okay."

"She?"

"I'm her doctor now. We know these things."

Jenny laughed. "What's the course of treatment, Doctor?"

"I'd like to take her home, and feed her to keep her strength up until she can fly again." He chewed his lip, but finally shook his head. "I can't do it. I'm living with my parents now. And the last thing Father wants is another wounded bird coming home to roost."

Jenny felt another pang of pity for him, but this time she had something better to say than "I'm sorry."

"I'll take her home with me if you tell me what to do."

They settled the dove in her blanket in a box on the back seat in Jenny's car, and after Scott had given her all the care and feeding instructions he could think of, she got behind the wheel.

"I don't know how to thank you for your help today," she said as he leaned on her door. "You were a real lifesaver."

He nodded at the bird in the back. "Now you're the lifesaver."

She reached to pull the door shut, but he blocked it with a sheepish smile. "I'm so embarrassed," he said. "I've forgotten your name."

"Jennifer Lodge," she replied.

"Jenny," he said.

7

IT WAS ALMOST TEN O'CLOCK WHEN JENNY STEPPED INTO THE OFFICE elevator Monday morning, and never before had she come to work so late. But this was the first day of life after Intellitech, and she supposed she'd earned it. People called out greetings to her as she walked down the corridor to her office. Her new-associate anonymity was over. Somewhere in the bowels of the firm, Bill Moran might be throwing darts at her picture, but it was he who was anonymous now. Her star was up and rising.

On her desk sat a floral arrangement with a card offering the firm's congratulations. Beside it was a vase holding a dozen red roses from Gordon St. James, which she promptly carried out to her secretary's station.

"Thanks," Marilyn said. "Here. This memo just came for you."

It was from Art Lessin. Apparently she'd earned more than the right to arrive late. She was reprieved from the RTC project; from now on, she could choose her own cases. She intended to choose carefully, and none too soon. The best lawyers in town couldn't count on more than one big win a year. She'd had hers, and by her reckoning, a year was exactly what she needed.

The phone rang and she picked up.

"Aloha!"

"Leslie! You're back?"

"With a deep suntan and a big happy smile."

"Was it wonderful?"

"Oooh," Leslie said, swooning. "Beyond my wildest dreams."

"And of course you toured all the museums and took lots of photos of historical sites?"

"But of course." She giggled.

"Can you come over and show me your souvenirs?" Jenny asked. "What about Sunday brunch?"

"Oh, we'd love to!" Leslie's voice went coy. "Hey, is it all right if we bring someone with us?"

"Who?"

"Oh, I don't know. Maybe a friend of Bruce's."

"Sure. Eleven o'clock?"

"See ya then."

Marilyn was waiting in the doorway when she hung up. "Mr. Boenning would like you to join him in the conference room. He wants you to meet a client of his."

"What for?"

"To show you off, of course," Marilyn said. "You have to expect this sort of thing now."

She led her to a conference room down the hall, and Walt Boenning threw the door open at her knock. He was white-haired and mustachioed, and so portly he blocked the person behind him.

"Ah, Jennifer. Thank you for coming. I'd like you to meet—"

A woman rose from the table behind him, an elegant blonde in a pink Chanel suit. "Hello, I'm Cassie vonBerg."

"I'm handling a small matter for Mrs. vonBerg," Boenning said.

"He means my divorce," the woman said, wrinkling her classic nose. "Though he's too gallant to say so."

"Cassie's mother was a long-time client of mine," Boenning said by way of explanation.

"How do you do?" Jenny said, reaching around Boenning to shake hands.

"Thank you for seeing me on this impromptu basis," she said, holding out a smooth white hand. "I was just telling Walter how much I admired the way you handled that case for Gordon St. James."

"Let's sit down, shall we?" Boenning said.

The woman bent her legs and effortlessly folded herself into a chair, a movement so innately graceful that even Jenny's twenty years of ballet wouldn't have helped her duplicate it.

"You followed the trial?" Jenny asked as she took a seat across from her. Boenning settled into the chair at the head of the table, but it was clear he was to be a spectator to this meeting.

"Followed it? I devoured it! I was terribly impressed. So much so that it's you I want for my own case."

Jenny threw a confused look toward Boenning. "Your divorce?"

Boenning harrumphed. "No, not that."

"My other case," Cassie said. "I've been robbed of two million dollars. Or at least my mother's trust fund has."

The names and circumstances tumbled through Jenny's brain

and landed in the only place possible. She leaned back abruptly in her chair.

"You're Catherine Chapman."

She inclined her head.

The niece of Curtis Mason and the victim of Scott Sterling, all wrapped up in the lawsuit of Dan Casella. Jenny felt as if the world were closing in on her.

"I'm afraid I can't help you, Mrs. vonBerg," she said. "I have a conflict of interest."

"What's this?" Boenning snapped.

"Before coming to this firm, I was with Foster, Bell, & McNeil, counsel for Harding & McMann, and I worked briefly on this very case."

"That's not a conflict," Cassie said. "It just gives you a head start on the facts."

"You want me to sue a party that was once my client."

A trace of a smile appeared on Cassie's face. "You misunderstand me. I want you to sue Curtis Mason."

"Ah." Jenny remembered Mason barking at Dan, "Who's gonna sue me for breach of trust? Reese? Catherine? Not on your life." And she remembered Reese Chapman murmuring, "Curt's always looked after Catherine's interests. I'm sure he will this time, too." Neither of them had counted on Cassie to look after herself.

"Curtis was in on the theft, I know it," Cassie said. "I want him to repay the two million dollars, and I want him removed as trustee. He never should have been named in the first place."

"Why not?"

Cassie's spine went straight as she leaned into the table. "The trust has the single largest holding of Macoal stock. My uncle's personal fortune is all tied up in Macoal. Anything that happens to my stock directly affects his own net worth. So whose interest is he watching out for, his or mine?"

"Your mother must have known that."

"She knew. But she should have known *better*. And she had a perfectly good alternative. My father's a stock-market genius."

Jenny remembered Reese Chapman as a rakish ne'er-do-well, an image hard to reconcile with his daughter's description. "Then why didn't she name him?"

Cassie waved a dismissive hand through the air. "They had a

flawed marriage," she said. "And Mother turned it into a grudge match. But I don't have that problem. So what do you say?"

"I may have another conflict," Jenny said. "I'm acquainted with Scott Sterling."

"Lord, who isn't?" Cassie declared. "I've known him myself from the time I could walk. Or at least ride. That's why I know Curtis had to be behind this thing. Scott never could have pulled this off on his own." She folded her hands together and placed them before her on the table. "So. Will you handle it for me?"

Jenny stood up and braced her arms against the back of her chair. Boenning was watching her, and she could see impatience starting to simmer.

"I'd be happy to represent you, Mrs. vonBerg," she said finally. "But I think it would be a mistake at this juncture to sue Curtis Mason."

Cassie's features remained as smooth as the silken strands in her chignon, but her gray eyes clouded.

"There's already litigation pending between Mason and Harding & McMann," Jenny explained. "The strength of your case will be colored by the result of that one. For one thing, Mason may be absolved; that obviously weakens your position."

"And if he's not?" she flared.

"If he's not," Jenny said, "he'd be well advised to resign on his own. His refusal would make your case against him."

Understanding spread over Cassie's classic features, and she nodded slowly.

"I'll get copies of the pleadings and deposition transcripts," Jenny said. "And I'll monitor the trial. Then we can decide our strategy."

Boenning looked doubtful, and Jenny imagined he was calculating how much they'd lose in fees by monitoring a suit instead of bringing one.

"Cassie?" he prompted her.

"Do it," she said to Jenny.

"I'll open the file," Boenning said.

8

JENNY WAS UPSTAIRS SUNDAY MORNING WHEN THE DOG STARTED barking at a truck as it rumbled up the lane from Coventry Road. She raised the window sash and leaned out to scold him. By now he should have been used to the traffic passing by the carriage house. Since warm weather arrived, construction crews had swarmed like termites over the hillside of the old estate. But this was a white panel truck and it pulled into the courtyard. The passenger door swung open, and Leslie hopped out.

"Hello! What's with the truck?" Jenny called.

Leslie cocked her head back to see from under the brim of a big straw hat. "Hi!" she said, her arm shooting up in a wave.

Bruce climbed out of the driver's side. "We thought we'd load up the armoire while we're here," he yelled.

"Great! Let yourselves in. I'll be right down."

To no great surprise, Jenny found Leslie and Bruce downstairs, holding Scott Sterling between them and looking like two cats that swallowed the same canary.

"Hello, Scott, good to see you," Jenny said.

"Hi, Jenny, how have you been?"

Leslie's face fell. "You two *know* each other?"

"Sure," Jenny said. "We're fellow ornithologists."

"Speaking of which, how's our patient?" Scott asked.

"Come on, see for yourself."

She left Leslie and Bruce standing in bewilderment, and beckoned Scott into the storage bay. Once the door was closed behind them, they burst out laughing. "You didn't let on to them?" she asked.

"Nope. Not after I realized you hadn't."

"That makes us co-conspirators."

The dog pushed his way through the door behind them, and Scott dropped to one knee on the floor. "Who's this guy?" he asked fondly, hooking an elbow around his neck.

"I call him Sam."

"Hey, Sam," he said softly. The dog turned up adoring eyes and licked his face.

"You've got a real way with animals," Jenny observed.

Scott shrugged as he rose. "I just love 'em, that's all."

Jenny led him to the wooden crate she'd rigged up as a dove-cote. The dove cooed softly as Scott leaned over the top. "She looks good. Great job on the nest." He reached in, and the bird hopped onto his wrist without a second's hesitation.

"Wow," she said admiringly.

"It's not me, it's this place. I think she feels safe here." His glance took in the crate, the storeroom, the whole house.

"I think it's you. You should make house calls, Doctor."

Scott looked at her. "Maybe I should." Their eyes held for a moment before he lowered the dove back into the crate.

Jenny tilted her head back toward the house. "Should we go back and end their frantic wondering?"

He wagged his eyebrows mischievously. "Not until we fix our cover story. How's this? We met on a bird-watching trip in the Colorado Rockies—"

"And we spotted a bald eagle carrying this helpless dove up to its aerie—"

"On top of Pikes Peak! And you and I volunteered to try and save it. So we put on rappelling ropes—"

"And scaled the mountainside. And it started to snow, and still we climbed, until our hands were numb and bleeding—"

"And we reached the nest, where the eagle was just about to sink his fangs into the dove—"

"Do eagles have fangs?" Jenny interrupted.

"No, but Bruce and Leslie won't know that."

She laughed, delighted, and tucked her arm into Scott's as they went back into the house.

After brunch, Bruce and Scott got started loading the armoire, and Leslie pulled Jenny up the stairs for some girl talk. They sprawled together on Jenny's bed like the old days and Leslie regaled her with tales of endless white sand beaches and island music and a gorgeous tropical sarong she discovered in a little shop that was now making a hundred for her winter resort line.

When she ran out of stories, she asked Jenny, "So anything new with you? How's that case going?"

"It's over," Jenny said without elaboration.

Leslie squinted at her. "What's different about you?"

"What d'you mean?"

"Something's different," she said, and now her tone was one of full-blown suspicion.

"Well, I do have some news."

Leslie gestured with her palms up. "So? Give."

"I'm pregnant."

Leslie's eyes and mouth turned into three perfect circles. "Oh my God, Jenny!" she said, bouncing off the bed. "Does he know?"

"Why is that the first question out of your mouth?"

"Oh my God, you haven't told him!"

"It's none of his business."

"But he's responsible—"

"I'm responsible!"

"All right, all right," Leslie said, holding her arms up in surrender as she flopped onto the bed. "End of discussion. But at least let me go with you. When are you—?"

Jenny got up and stood before her dresser. "Actually," she said, "I've decided to keep it."

The silence swelled behind her. When Jenny turned around, Leslie was frozen on the bed. The first part of her to move was her head and it turned from side to side, slowly at first, then faster and more emphatic.

"No," she said. "No! You can't do this to yourself! You're only twenty-seven. You don't even have a biological clock yet. There's no reason to ruin your life forever."

"If I don't have this baby, it'll ruin my life forever."

"That's ridiculous!"

"Leslie, I had a once-in-a-lifetime love affair and it had an unhappy ending, a horribly unhappy ending. But don't you see? If I have an abortion, the ending becomes a tragedy. It'll be an unhappiness I'll never be able to reverse."

"You think having an illegitimate baby makes for a happy ending? It doesn't work that way, Jenny!"

"It will," Jenny insisted. "I'll make it work that way. I'll turn my unhappy love affair into the best thing that ever happened to me."

Leslie's mouth went tight. "When?"

"Late October."

Leslie did the math and scowled. "So you're already into the second trimester. It's basically too late for me to talk you out of this."

"Basically." Jenny turned back to the mirror and picked up her hairbrush.

Leslie shook her head helplessly until she had a new thought. "If you're having it, then you *have* to tell him."

"I don't." Jenny pulled the brush through her hair with short, angry strokes.

"It's like you're stealing it from him."

Jenny's reflection went white. That was exactly what she was doing, as surely as if she stole up on Dan in his sleep and snipped off a lock of his hair. But if it was a crime, she was convinced it was a justifiable one. He might have had the power to break her heart, but she would not give him the power to wreak an irreversible tragedy in her life.

Leslie stood up. "We'd better get going. Bruce promised to have the truck back by noon."

Jenny followed her downstairs, miserable. Either too much had been said between them or not enough, but it was clear that this was the end of their talking for now, and maybe for a long time to come.

The men had the armoire loaded into the back of the truck and were slamming the doors shut when they came out into the courtyard. Leslie pulled Bruce aside and spoke to him in a low voice. Bruce nodded.

"Ready to shove off?" he called to Scott.

"Already?"

Scott looked to Jenny, and she shook her head at him.

"Thanks for a great brunch," Bruce called as he and Leslie climbed into the truck.

Scott took Jenny's hand. "Thanks for having me," he said. "You don't know how much I needed to get out of my parents' house and spend some time with some friendly faces."

"Is it awful for you there?" she asked softly.

He shrugged. "My father doesn't speak. He won't turn me out, but he won't speak to me, either."

The horn sounded from the truck, but Jenny held Scott's hand a moment longer. "When are you going to make that house call, Doctor?"

His face lit up. "Tomorrow night?"

"It's a date."

He climbed into the truck as Bruce started the engine.

"I almost forgot," Leslie said, leaning over him. "I have a lead on a new housemate for you. One of the guys at work has a sister—"

"Thanks anyway," Jenny said. "I've decided to go it alone."

Leslie's mouth went tight. "I think you're making a big mistake."

She pulled her head back in and the truck turned out of the courtyard. Only Scott Sterling waved good-bye.

9

"HE WAS LIKE A SON TO ME!"

Curtis Mason's testimony was delivered in thundering declarations, each one punctuated with an exclamation point. He sat three feet from Dan, the two men separated only by the polished mahogany surface of the conference table. The court reporter was at the head of the table with her machine set up on a tripod beside her. Beside Mason was Robert Perlman.

Dan's first look at Perlman when he arrived that morning confirmed that he was right to schedule the deposition to begin first thing Monday morning. Word had it Perlman was partying too much these days, and he carried his weekend hangover into the room with him.

But beside Perlman sat his new associate Jerry Shuster, and he wasn't missing a thing. Notes were flying from Shuster to Perlman, and Perlman was taking each one seriously. Dan took Shuster seriously, too. He was an Army reservist whose unit was called up during the Gulf War. He'd seen some combat in the retaking of Kuwait, and he'd lost an arm in the process. When he returned to Philadelphia, Perlman wasted no time in hiring him away from his previous firm. Although he was only a third-year associate, he'd have a courtroom presence worth years of actual experience.

Dan wished he had an associate beside him, a backup to catch any shots he might miss. He couldn't afford any mistakes in this case.

His star in the Foster, Bell constellation had slipped since he lost the Tramco business. It was more than the ordinary client development failure. Too many of his partners scratched their heads over Jennifer's role in the whole mess and wondered whether Dan was to blame. His reputation needed some fast redemption, and a win in this case was the shortest route there.

"How was Scott Sterling like a son to you?"

"I watched him grow up. I took to him. He was an engaging young man. He was always eager to learn and willing to work hard." Mason gave a sudden snort. " 'Course, we now know it was all chicanery. He was setting me up from the start."

"What was the start?"

Dan had been asking such open-ended questions all day. He had an unbridled witness in Mason, a rare find. Every good lawyer prepared his client before a deposition, and the drill was always the same: answer truthfully, but answer only the question being asked; never volunteer, never elaborate. Perlman must have gone over the same instructions with Mason, but Mason had a runaway mouth and would not be reined in. Although this meant Dan had to sit through Mason's self-serving speeches and would end up with a transcript three times longer than necessary, it also meant that sooner or later, Mason was going to say too much.

"I guess the start was Ed and Margie's party last year. May, it must have been. Out at their farm in Chester Springs."

"Was Scott there?"

"Yeah. He tracked me down in the billiard room. Told me how sorry he was to hear about Doody's death. The sneaking little bastard! But I didn't see through it. He'd always been a polite boy. Polite! He was a first-class charmer.

"He got to talking about his career. Told me he was up for partner soon at Harding & McMann. Told me he was in estates, which I hadn't heard before. I thought he would've gone into corporate work, what with Ed at Phoenix Pharmaceuticals. It must have driven Ed crazy, his only boy practicing the kind of law where you hand-hold old ladies all day!

"I noticed the way Ed was acting toward Scotty—cut him cold a couple of times. And Scotty! Looked like he was stabbed in the

151

gut every time! It was always that way between them. There was no love lost there, let me tell you!

"Call me a soft-hearted fool, but I felt sorry for the boy, what with his divorce and all. Before I knew it, I was asking him if he'd like to handle Doody's trust."

"You already had counsel for the trust?"

"Sure, Dickinson Barlow. He does my own estate-planning work."

"What did you tell him about transferring the trust to Scott Sterling?"

Shuster saw where the question was headed and knew there wasn't time to scribble out a note. He leaned over and started to whisper to Perlman. But at the same moment, Mason began talking.

"I told him I wanted somebody to do what he wouldn't do. Handle the day-to-day management of the funds, deal with the broker, write out the checks."

"Dickinson Barlow wasn't willing to handle the day-to-day management of the trust, is that correct?"

"Objection," Perlman said in a rush to speak this time before Mason did. "Attorney-client privilege; instruct not to answer."

"He answered the last one, Bob; privilege is waived," Dan said, and when Shuster shook his head at him, Perlman let it go. "Read the question back to Mr. Mason, will you, Beverly?"

She pulled out her stenographic tape and read the question in the flat, inflectionless voice used by all good reporters to demonstrate their neutrality. Mason listened with his eyes shuttered, suspecting a trap but not hearing one.

"No, he wasn't," he answered.

"And you weren't willing to handle the day-to-day management of the trust, is that correct?"

"Christ, I don't have time for that kind of nonsense."

"Scott Sterling *was* willing to handle the day-to-day management of the trust, is that correct?"

"Of course he was!" Mason shouted. "That was how he planned to steal the money!"

Another self-serving speech followed, and at the end of it, Dan announced a break.

*   *   *

Perlman was more alert when the deposition resumed, and Dan guessed that he'd splashed some cold water on his face. He also guessed that he'd woodshedded his client during the break, because Mason was scowling furiously when he took his seat again.

"Were all the trust assets held in the account at Connolly and Company?"

"Right."

"Did those assets include shares in Macoal Corporation?"

"Yes."

"In the summer of 1994, did any single shareholder have a larger holding in Macoal Corporation than the Elizabeth Mason Chapman Testamentary Trust?"

"No."

"Did the trust assets also include other securities?"

"Yes."

"And some cash, correct?"

"Correct."

"Did the Connolly account offer check-writing privileges against the cash balance?"

"Yes."

"Could checks also be written against the cash value of marketable securities held in the account?"

"Right, but what you'd be doing there is borrowing against the securities. You run up margin interest every time you do that."

"Then borrowing against the securities was something you wanted to avoid?"

Mason gave him a pained look. "Mr. Casella, Doody's trust was worth ten million dollars. We only paid twenty thousand a month to Reese, and usually less than that to Catherine. There was no reason in hell to be borrowing money and running up interest charges."

"How was the money paid out to Mr. Chapman and his daughter?"

"By check, of course."

"Drawn on the Connolly account, is that right?"

"Right."

"Before May of last year, who had physical possession of the Connolly and Company checks?"

Mason gave him a wary look. "I did."

"When did you turn them over to Scott Sterling?"

Mason looked at Perlman, but got no signals back. "I don't know," he said, shrugging. "Sometime that summer."

"The summer of 1994?"

"Right."

"What instructions did you give to Scott Sterling about the checks?"

It was the first open-ended question since the break, and Mason was waiting for it. "Look," he said. "I know what you're trying to do here! You're trying to say I breached my fiduciary duty because I delegated check-writing to Scott."

Perlman laid a restraining hand on his arm, but Mason shook him off. "Listen to me. I ran a Fortune 500 company for fifteen years, and I didn't do it by sticking my fingers into every pot we had boiling. I did it by delegating! I had assistants and vice-presidents and managers to do the detail work. We wouldn't have been able to acquire Zenco Gas if my desk was all cluttered up with details. We wouldn't have been able to fight off Jack Stengel's hostile takeover bid if I had to do all the detail work myself.

"Doody knew that was the way I operated. She knew I'd delegate the detail work if she named me trustee. She named me anyway. So you're just whistling, Casella; there's nothing there!"

Dan repeated, "What instructions did you give to Scott Sterling about the checks?"

Mason's eyes bulged, and Perlman laid another restraining hand on his arm.

"All right," Mason said, blowing out his breath in exasperation. "I told him to pay the bills. The CPA, Harding & McMann, Reese's twenty thousand, whatever Catherine needed."

"Did you make Sterling a signatory on the account?"

"I authorized him to sign the checks, of course."

"What name did you authorize him to sign, Mr. Mason?"

"My own."

Dan switched gears. "Did you also authorize Scott Sterling to handle certain securities trades in the trust?"

"Sure. A certain amount of securities had to be bought and sold to generate the cash to make disbursements."

"The broker would buy and sell stocks in the trust account on Sterling's say-so?"

"They needed a trading authorization for their files. So I signed one."

Dan pulled out a document. "Let's mark this as D-21," he said to the reporter.

Mason squinted across the table, trying to read it upside down. When it was labeled with an exhibit sticker, Dan handed it to Perlman, and Mason whipped it out of his lawyer's hands to read it first.

"Is D-21 a copy of the trading authorization you signed?" Dan asked.

"It is."

"Mr. Mason, I'm curious about the typewritten clause added to the bottom of the printed form, the one that begins 'Provided that.' You see that clause?"

"Sure. 'Provided that Sterling shall have no authority to trade with respect to any shares of Macoal Corporation.' "

"Whose idea was it to add that clause?"

"Mine, of course. Majority control of Macoal is critical to my entire family. I wasn't about to risk that."

The deposition broke again at three, and Dan flipped through his telephone messages. The auditor had called at two and wanted to come over immediately to show him something. He pushed the intercom. "Betty, call Larry Biggs back and tell him to stop by at four-thirty if he can make it quick. I have to leave at five to catch Tony's game."

His first question after the break was, "Why'd you record your telephone conversations with Sterling?"

Mason smiled faintly and squared his shoulders. He was ready for this one. "Pure serendipity. I taped the calls on our answering machine so that I could play them back for Dorrie later."

"Why?"

"Scotty was like a son to her, too, remember. She was pleased at how well he was doing for us. But she didn't want to pick up the extension and have him think we were all breathing down his neck. So I recorded the calls and she listened to the tape afterward."

155

"Why didn't you erase each recording after Mrs. Mason listened to it?"

"There's the serendipity," Mason said. "I never could figure out how to run that damn machine. I thought I was rewinding the reel each time, but it turns out I was advancing it, so all the calls were saved."

"How'd you happen to discover that stroke of luck?"

Mason heard the sarcasm, but decided to ignore it. "After this whole mess broke, I was thinking over all the lies he spun, and I wondered if any of them might still be on the tape. So I went back and played it, and, by God, there they were!"

"You have three separate residences, is that right, Mr. Mason?"

"Right."

"Which one had the answering machine?"

Mason gave a little start. "This one," he said. "In Devon."

Dan saw Shuster's pen move. At least one of the calls on the tape was placed from Maine. Added to that was the fact that Mason was in Florida when the news broke and flew home on the same day Perlman announced the existence of the recordings.

"Who decided how much income Catherine should receive in any given month?"

"I did." Mason leaned back and laced his fingers over his chest. He knew there was only an hour or so left to go for the day, and with the end in sight, he was willing to relax.

"So every month you called Sterling and told him the amount for Catherine's check?"

"No. He told me what she asked for, and I said yea or nay."

"Before or after the checks were written?"

"Well, how would I know that?" Mason said impatiently.

"So you didn't know whether Sterling had already written the check to Catherine or not?"

"That would seem to follow logically."

"Yes or no, Mr. Mason."

"No."

"And you didn't know whether Sterling was following your yea or nay in the amounts for Catherine's checks, did you?"

"Of course I knew."

Dan hesitated before he asked how because he knew what would follow: "I trusted Scott—he was like a son to me. I believed him; he

156

worked for a reputable law firm." It was the same refrain Mason had chanted all day, and Dan wasn't sure he wanted to hear it again.

"How did you know?" he asked anyway.

"Well, it was right on the goddamned account statements that Connolly spit out to me month after month. I could see perfectly well how much money Catherine was getting."

Shuster's breath sucked in with a little hiss.

In a flat voice Dan asked, "You were receiving monthly statements from Connolly and Company on the trust account?"

"Sure." Mason shrugged and glanced again at his watch.

Alone in his office at the end of the day, Dan put a damper on his own excitement. There was always the chance Mason was remembering wrong. Sterling said the trust statements came to him, addressed to Curtis Mason, care of Scott Sterling. Mason might have been thinking of his personal account statements. *One way to find out,* he thought, and he picked up the phone and dialed Brian Kearney at Connolly and Company.

"Brian," he said when he got past the sales assistant. "Quick question. Maybe you can just pull up your screen and tell me: where'd the account statements go for the Chapman Trust account?"

"Hold on. Yeah, here it is: Curtis Mason, Trustee, care of Scott Sterling, Harding & McMann, et cetera. Guess you knew that, huh?"

"I heard a rumor."

"Then there's a duplicate flag," Kearney said.

"What?"

"The account was flagged to get duplicate statements. Another set went to Curtis Mason, Trustee, One Gladding Lane, Devon."

Dan sat up straight. "Since when?"

"Let's see. Flag was put on the same time Sterling's name was added. June 1994."

"There's records to back you up on this, Brian?"

"You bet."

The intercom buzzed when Dan hung up, and Betty's voice came into the room. "Mr. Biggs is here."

"Take him into the conference room. And Betty? Sit in with us. I might need you to take notes."

Larry Biggs was younger than Dan, almost completely bald, and one of the top forensic accountants in the city. He had his spreadsheets open on the conference table when Dan entered the room.

"Hey, Larry, what's new?"

"This bank account, for starters," Biggs said, his fingers walking over the papers.

"What's that?"

"You know how we've been tracing back all the deposits into Sterling's account at Savers Bank?"

"Yeah, sure, to confirm how much of the money came from the trust and how much was legitimately his own."

"Well, we traced back a check deposit that came in around December, 1993. It led to another account, on a bank in Atlantic City."

"So?" Dan said. But already his eyes had found the path of the spreadsheets, and he braced himself against what Biggs was about to say next.

"That account turned out to be Sterling's, too. And it shows—"

"Cash deposits," Dan said, his finger tracing the amounts in the columns. "More than ten thousand dollars a pop. Totaling—what's it come to, Larry?"

"A hundred and twenty thousand dollars," the accountant said. "In untraceable cash."

Dan straightened slowly and looked at the accountant, then at Betty. "This doesn't leave this room," he said.

10

JENNY CAME HOME EARLY FROM AN EASY DAY AT THE OFFICE AND still she was exhausted. It was a deep, stuporous fatigue that made her long to curl up someplace small and sleep for the rest of her life. "Your body's talking to you," the doctor said. The problem was Jenny was too tired to talk back.

Scott's car was in the courtyard, and despite the long day, it put a little lift in her step to know he was home. Pink and white impatiens bloomed in the beds that flanked the front steps, and new brass locks shone on the door. Although the old carriage house had only a few months left to live, Scott was keeping the place up as if it would last forever. It might be foolish and impractical and short-sighted, like throwing money away, but his spirit lifted hers.

"Hello?" she called. The smell of roasting chicken filled the house, and a vase of fresh-cut peonies was on the table. She drew in a deep, contented breath. Letting Scott have Leslie's old room was the smartest move she'd made in a long time.

She heard a bubble of laughter outside and turned to see Scott and the dog wrestling like bear cubs in the backyard. He carried on like a little boy with that dog, and it brought a smile to her lips to see them. She stepped outside onto the crumbling brick patio. The dove was perched nearby on the old dogwood tree. Her wing had healed; she could fly away whenever she liked. She liked to stay.

"Hi!" Scott rolled to his feet and brushed off his pants. "How was your day?"

"Fine, and I'm glad you're home. I have the *pro se* papers ready for you to sign."

Instantly his brightness dimmed. "Doesn't *pro se* mean I'm supposed to do it myself?"

"Oh, hush, and come inside."

She opened her briefcase on the table and spread them out: Answer of Defendant Scott M. Sterling to Plaintiffs' Complaint; Response of Defendant Scott M. Sterling to Plaintiffs' Motion to Compel Discovery; Response of Defendant Scott M. Sterling to Plaintiffs' Motion for Accelerated Trial. All bore a signature line for Scott M. Sterling, Pro Se.

He sat down and started to read. "You sure you won't get in trouble for this?"

"I'm not representing you. I'm just helping out a friend."

"Maybe I shouldn't file anything at all." He dropped his head into his hand and kneaded his brow. "Let Uncle Curt take a default judgment against me. I don't have any assets left for him to execute against."

"*Scott*—" Sometimes Jenny was amazed at his naïveté. "A judgment can be kept alive forever. Mason could seize any property you come into in the future—your trust distribution when you're thirty-five, for instance."

"So?"

"Scott," she said firmly. "If you won't think of yourself, at least think about your little girl."

The dog sidled up next to him and thrust his nose into his lap. He patted him absently. "Maybe you're right," he said.

"Here's where you sign." She pointed to the last page of each document.

"Initial each page, too?"

"No, silly," she laughed. "These aren't wills. Now, take them to the clerk's office tomorrow. You know where to go? Federal courthouse, Sixth and Market, second floor."

"What's this one?" he asked when he came to the bottom of the stack.

"Perlman's moved for an early trial date. This is a brief in opposition."

"But I don't want to oppose it. The sooner this is over with, the better."

"Your lawyer thinks the DA's waiting until the civil case is over to charge you. The longer you delay the trial, the longer you're a free man."

"Does that matter?"

She was tired of his endless self-flagellation. "It matters to me," she snapped.

Wordlessly, he signed the final page.

They ate dinner together on the patio as dusk was settling over the hillside and lights were glowing inside the construction trailers. The framing was complete on two houses, and they rose like skeletons in silhouette against the fading sky. Jenny hated to see the progress that was made each day. The closer the Estates at Dundee approached occupancy, the sooner her own occupancy of the carriage house would end.

"Have you thought about where you're going to live?" Scott asked, reading her thoughts.

She shook her head. "I have so many plans to make, I don't know where to start."

He watched her as she ate her chicken. "Have you talked to Leslie lately?"

"No, why?"

"I don't know; I thought maybe this was a time you could use a friend."

She wondered what he meant, and a second later realized it. She sagged back in her chair. "You *know?*" she exclaimed.

He nodded with a grimace.

"How?"

"You said you made a mistake that was waiting to catch up with you, and this is the only one I could imagine you making. I've seen other signs since then. I've been through this, remember."

Jenny got up and walked to the edge of the patio. The meadow grasses had been mown to stubble. The landscape was changing so fast she couldn't keep up with it anymore.

Scott said, "I know Leslie hasn't been around much—"

"She doesn't approve of my decision."

"Which is?"

"To have it and keep it and raise it."

A breeze blew across the meadow, and the dogwood shivered and dropped its blossoms like snowfall on the bricks. Scott came up behind her and put his arms around her shoulders. He swayed gently, and she swayed with him, like the two of them were drifting alone on the sea.

"You're amazing," he said softly.

She turned around in his arms. "You don't think it's stupid?"

The dove glided across the patio, and with a flapping of its wings, lit on the table to pick at the remains of their dinner.

"What could be stupid about having a baby? It's the most wonderful thing in the world."

Jenny looked up into the brightness of his eyes and saw herself reflected there. They were like two wounded doves, she and Scott—soiled ones, too—both waiting for the next storm to buffet them where it would.

"You're wrong about one thing," she said.

"What's that?"

"I don't need a friend." She slipped her arms around his back and leaned her head on his chest. "I've got one."

11

"GET A MOVE ON," DAN CALLED FROM THE HALLWAY. "WE'RE gonna be late for dinner."

"I'm coming!" Tony hollered back.

He came out of his room wearing oversized jeans slung low on his hips, a T-shirt worn inside out, and hightop sneakers with the laces dragging. Dan grimaced but held his tongue. One of the things he'd learned these past few months was to choose his fights carefully. In the bigger scheme of things, it didn't much matter what Tony wore to their mother's except maybe a pleasant expression, and all signs were positive there.

They drove out of the dim underground garage and into the bright light of a beautiful afternoon, past the elaborate spring-flowering gardens of Washington Square, then into the concrete city south of South, where the passage of seasons was marked only by the changes in the cardboard cutouts in the rowhouse windows.

"Been a long time since we've been here," Dan remarked as he parked the car and they started the two-block walk.

Tony took a quick look at his reflection in a storefront window and made an invisible adjustment to his backward baseball cap. "Yeah, I guess."

Except for a couple on-the-fly drop-bys, they hadn't been back at all, not since January. At some point, Tony had stopped pestering for visits home; Dan wondered about that, but decided to let well enough alone.

Mike diMaio opened the door at Dan's knock.

"You moved in or what, diMaio?"

"Hey, I'm sitting right beside the door. I'm supposed to make your mother run all the way out from the kitchen?"

Teresa came up behind him. "Don't pay any attention to him, Michael. He's just making a fuss so nobody will notice he's fifteen minutes late." She gave Dan a sharp frown.

"It's Tony's fault," Dan said. "He had trouble coordinating his outfit. Right, Tony?"

"You guys fight without me. I'm outta here. Mom?" he hollered.

"Back here, baby!" Mary called from the kitchen.

"You two chat," Teresa said and followed Tony into the kitchen.

Dan and Mike eyed each other. "I'd ask you to sit down," Mike said. "But it ain't my house."

"Have a seat, Mike."

Mike took a seat on the sofa, avoiding the La-Z-Boy seat of honor even before Dan claimed it. "Kid looks good," he said.

"He's doing great," Dan said. "He aced his midterms. He'll end up the year with a B-plus—maybe even an A-minus—average."

"Glad to hear it. Keeping regular hours, is he?"

Dan bristled. "Yeah, and he's not associating with any known felons. Who made you his probation officer, diMaio?"

Mike raised his palms in a gesture of surrender. "Okay, okay. Forget I asked."

Teresa came out with a beer for each of them, and settled cozily beside Mike on the sofa.

"You get the Mason transcripts I sent over?" Dan asked.

"Yeah, thanks. Inneresting reading."

"Interesting experience. I've never had a witness run off at the mouth like Mason. Some of his answers went two pages long. Perlman was apoplectic."

"Your boy Scotty—Mason makes him sound like a snake charmer."

"That's about right," Dan said. "Scott's a charmer, and Mason's a snake."

Mike shrugged. "He tells a convincing story."

Disagreement was a way of life for Dan—his livelihood depended upon it—but he didn't expect to encounter it in his own living room. "Convincing to you, maybe," he said. "You know why? Because Mason's thinking just like a cop."

Mike laughed. "How's that? Poor and tired?"

"What's the first thing you do when you got a suspect dead to rights?"

Mike shook his head at Teresa, refusing to rise to the bait.

"I'll tell you what," Dan said. "You dust off all your old unsolved files and stick him with everything else at the same time. He's guilty of one; you figure the jury'll buy the others, too."

Mike shook his head again and this time rolled his eyes.

"So here we have Sterling," Dan said. "Caught dead to rights with his hand in the trust cookie jar. Over here we have Mason reeling from one bad investment after another. Why not pin it all on Scotty?"

Mike considered the argument for a minute, then leaned forward, his elbows on his knees. "I'll tell you why. Because I buy this father-son business."

"What's that?" Teresa asked.

"Mason says they were like father and son," Mike explained. "He doesn't have any kids, and Scotty and his old man got no use for each other. Mason and Scotty sort of latched onto each other."

"That's only according to Mason," Dan cut in. "And it's a convenient excuse for why he'd swallow something no one in his right mind could believe."

"If this guy was like a son to him, he must really feel betrayed," Teresa said. Mike's arm went around her shoulders, and she smiled and snuggled close.

Dan gave up the argument. He sat back and took a pull on his beer.

"Speaking of Scotty," Mike said. "Looks like his old man tossed him out. I hear he's shacked up with his girlfriend somewhere out on the Main Line."

"Where?"

"Radnor, I think."

"Dinner's on the table," Mary called out. "Come and sit down."

"Find out the address for me, will you?" Dan asked as they went into the dining room. "Lose the hat," he said to Tony.

Mike and Teresa held hands at the table after the dinner plates were cleared. They kept them clasped together down low between their chairs, but Dan could still see and it irritated him, though he couldn't figure out why. For years, he'd been hoping Teresa would meet a nice guy, and now she had. Overnight, she was a happy woman.

"So, Tony," she said, sparkling over dessert. "Tell us about lacrosse."

Even Tony seemed lit by Teresa's new glow. "We're four and one for the season," he declared, elbows on the table. "Tomorrow we go up against the division champs from last year, and they're four and one, too. But we've won by bigger margins, so we got a real good shot at taking the title. Best shot ever, coach says."

Dan gave him a nudge. "Tell 'em who's leading the division in goals scored so far this season."

"Me," Tony said with an embarrassed grin.

"Tony, that's wonderful!" Teresa said, and Mary leaned over to give him a smothering squeeze.

"When I was in school, lacrosse was a girls' sport," Mike said. "Boys played baseball."

"It's a drag compared to lacrosse," Tony said. "All you do is stand around. In lacrosse, it's constant motion."

"Come on," Mike needled. "Baseball's a great sport. If you know what you're doing."

"I suppose you do," Dan shot across the table.

Teresa groaned.

"As a matter of fact," Mike said.

Dan set his jaw. "Tony, go up and find your ball and bat."

"What—are we gonna face off?" Mike laughed.

"A friendly little contest," Dan said. "Down at Paulie's lot on the corner."

"All right!" Tony crowed, and he charged up the stairs.

Dan and Mike stared at each other, their mouths twitching from the effort of holding back their grins. Teresa rolled her eyes.

"Hey," Tony shouted, his voice reverberating in the stairwell. "Who painted up here? It looks great!"

Teresa smiled. "Michael did it. He installed a new light fixture up there, too."

"What a difference it makes!" Mary said.

Mike shrugged.

Dan felt a stab of something he was stunned to realize was jealousy. That was it—his whole problem with Mike diMaio, the last guy in the world he'd expect to be jealous of.

Tony came down more slowly than he'd gone up, and he stopped at the foot of the stairs. "Who's been in my room?"

Dan looked up at him. The pitch of his voice was different, like strings strung too tight.

"Me," Mary said, staring down at her plate. "Spring cleaning."

Tony stood at the bottom of the staircase, watching the toe of his sneaker work a whorl into the rug. Dan looked from Tony's white face to his mother's red face and knew she'd found something.

Abruptly, she got up from the table and carried her plate out to the kitchen.

"Where's your gear?" Dan asked him.

"Couldn't find a ball."

"Well, run down to Paulie's and look around. There's usually a few caught in the weeds."

"Okay."

He turned and went out the front door.

"Mom, come sit down," Teresa hollered to the kitchen. "Leave the dishes for later."

"I will. Just a minute or two," Mary called back.

It had to be pornography—Dan was sure of it—and he couldn't think of any reason to embarrass his mother by confronting her about it. Or Tony, for that matter.

"Teresa, honey," Mike whispered. "I got a little business to discuss with Dan. Would you mind—?"

"Of course not," she said, beaming at him. "Never mind, Mom," she called again, sliding back from the table. "I'm coming to help."

"What?" Dan said. "If you're asking me for her hand in marriage, the answer's no."

Mike jerked his head toward the living room, and Dan followed him there, irritated at the secrecy.

"I'm not supposed to be telling you this," Mike began.

"Then don't."

"The criminal case against Sterling went front burner," he said. "We got orders to put it together and charge him before the end of the summer."

Dan stared at him. "Damn! The earliest we can get the civil case tried is September. And the last thing I need is Sterling on the stand in manacles and an orange jumpsuit."

"I know."

"There's a helluva lot more to this than meets the eye. Until I get Mason on cross, nobody can be sure—"

"Mason's the reason for the front burner. He says he's getting death threats."

Dan stared at him and laughed. "Get out—"

"Two threats by telephone," Mike cut in. "Male voice, heavily muffled. 'Drop the lawsuit and resign as trustee or you're a dead man.' "

"Jesus Christ," Dan said, still laughing. "Death threats in a breach of trust case? What's next? Revoke the codicil or we'll break your legs?"

"All we know is what he tells us," Mike said. "He came in with Perlman, shaking like a leaf and mad as hell. We offered to put a tap on his line, but he refused—breach of privacy, he said. But we did put a tracer on. He claims he got a second call, same voice, same message, Thursday night."

"Don't tell me. You traced it right to Sterling."

"Phone booth in Camden."

"Gimme a break," Dan said, disgusted. "Can't you see what he's up to?"

"Captain's taking it seriously. Remember that business with the dog? The last thing we need is for Mason to buy it while we're playin' with ourselves."

Dan paced to the front window. Through the sheers he could see Tony leaning against the house on the corner, loitering long enough to say he'd been to Paulie's and back.

"Sterling's gonna plead guilty. You know it," Dan said.

"Maybe."

"His guilty plea's admissible against Harding & McMann in the civil case. It's as good as a confession."

"It's outta my hands."

Dan blew out his breath. Crises were a way of life for him, too, and solving them his livelihood. He'd have to find a way to push the civil trial date up and get it over with before Sterling was charged in the criminal case.

"Thanks for the scoop, Mike." He started for the kitchen. "Hey, Teresa, hang up your dish towel. There's an ugly-looking guy in the living room wants to see you."

Teresa scowled at him as she hurried past. Dan snatched the towel from her and took it with him into the kitchen.

Mary stood at the sink with her arms plunged to the elbows in soapsuds. She had problems with her lower back, and she was standing with her shoulders hunched and her spine rolled in a posture that spoke of pain. "Mom, sit down," Dan said. "I'll finish up."

"Ha," she said, keeping her back to him. "What do you know about washing dishes, Mr. Cardboard Take-out?"

"No fair. We've been having real meals. Stuff even you would eat."

"Well, good," she said. "He's a growing boy, you know. You gotta feed him right. I remember when you were his age. I couldn't keep you full from one meal to the next. You used to stand there with the refrigerator door open and chug down a quart of milk without coming up for air."

Dan took her by the shoulders and turned her away from the sink. She gave him a startled look, then dropped her eyes and busied herself with wiping the suds from her hands.

"Mom, what'd you find in Tony's room?"

She took a deep breath, and it caught and shook on a sob. "Danny, I don't know what—! He's a good boy, I know he is, and he's doin' so good with you. I know there's nothing wrong—"

"Mom, tell me."

She went to the drawer beside the silverware drawer, the one they called the junk drawer when they were kids, where they kept their shoelaces and kite string and loose hardware. She reached to the back and pulled out an envelope.

Dan felt instant relief. His worst fear was that she'd found another weapon, a companion piece to the .38 he'd disposed of in January. But it was nothing but smutty pictures, and he was sorry he'd brought it up.

"There's a loose floorboard under his bed," Mary said. "I stepped on one end and the other end snapped up. And this was underneath." She held the envelope out to Dan.

"I'll talk to him about it, Mom," he said, reaching for it. "But don't you worry. It's normal, it really doesn't—"

The envelope didn't feel right in his hand. He opened it and blinked at the unexpected flash of green.

"More than two thousand dollars," she whispered.

Tony knew he knew. His sneakers dragged out of the elevator and down the hallway to the apartment door, and he took a deep breath as Dan turned the key. He knew as well as Dan did that the moment had arrived.

Dan swung the door in and grabbed Tony by the collar in the same arc. He slammed him against the wall and kicked the door shut behind him. Tony's head snapped from the force, and his eyes watered, but he didn't speak. He knew.

"There's only two ways a fourteen-year-old kid comes into money like that," Dan ground out, his voice cracking as it forced between his teeth. "Selling drugs, or selling his body. So which is it, Tony? Are you the neighborhood pusher? Or are you letting old queers blow you?"

"Neither," Tony gasped.

"What then? Did you steal it?"

"No! I swear!"

Dan hit him, an open hand across the face, and Tony started to sink down the wall. Dan grabbed his shirtfront and pulled him up, his face inches away. "Tell me, goddamn it! Where'd you get the money?"

Tony struggled to catch his breath through the tears that were spilling from his eyes. "Guns," he choked. "I sold guns."

Dan felt his heart stop.

"But I didn't steal them!" Tony rushed to say, as though it made a difference. "This guy—he found a couple cases that got left behind on a loading dock. He filed down the serial numbers, and me and a couple other guys sold them, and he split the money with us."

"Who'd you sell them to?" Dan whispered.

"Kids at school."

"How many?"

Tony shrugged. "Ten or twelve. Maybe fifteen."

Dan grabbed him with both hands on the back of his neck. His worst fear had been that Tony was peddling Baggies full of marijuana. He'd take that in a heartbeat now. The gun he'd taken from him in January wasn't a one-time fluke; it was Tony's stock in trade.

"Do you have any idea how stupid that was?" he shouted. "Guns kill people! Some kid at school gets pissed at his buddy one day, and instead of socking him in the mouth, he pulls out the gun you sold him and blows his brains out. And then blows his own brains out when he realizes what he's done. Two kids dead, all so you can have a stash of money in your room."

"Nobody would do that," Tony said, going white. "I mean, kids just wanna have protection, you know?"

Dan always knew Tony was a street punk, but now he knew he was the worst kind of street punk—the kind that hustled and cheated and made money off the weaknesses of others. Dan's efforts to mold him into prep-school boy, honor student, star athlete—they were pathetic.

"It's all been an act with you, hasn't it?" he said bitterly. "The good grades, the sports, the all-American boy routine. Big joke on me, right?"

"That's all stuff you wanted," Tony said. "I never pretended to be anything I wasn't."

"You had a shot," Dan said, not hearing him. "More of a shot than anybody ever gave me. And you blew it."

"Yeah, well, maybe I'm not you," Tony cried. "Ever think of that?"

But he was, that was the problem. Tony was everything Dan really was—scratch the surface of Dan, find Tony simmering underneath. That was the danger, that was what he had to expunge.

"Who's the guy who gave you the guns?" Dan said, giving Tony a shake. "What's his name? Where's he live?"

Tony shook his head. "I don't know. I never knew."

"Then where'd you find him?"

"He found me! When he wanted me, he found me."

"You're lying!"

"I'm not!"

Dan jerked his hands away from Tony and thrust them deep into his pockets, afraid of what he might do next. He moved away fast, to the windows on the far side of the room, the ones that looked out on South Philadelphia. Somewhere out there was the man responsible for this, the man who turned his little brother from schoolboy punk into a major felon.

Tony stood where he'd left him, his back flat against the wall, tears streaking his face. Dan wheeled on him. "You tell me who he is or you're off the team!"

Tony's face went whiter still before he buried it in his hands.

Division play-offs started tomorrow; there was no way Tony would forfeit the right to play. Dan waited, smelling victory as pungent as he'd smelled it a hundred times in empty courtrooms waiting for juries to return.

But this time his nose was off. When Tony's hands came away, his face was blank. His armor was back in place, and Dan knew in that instant that all he'd worked for and won with Tony these last few months was gone.

The phone rang, and Tony walked past it and into his room. Dan crossed the room and picked it up.

"Dan, it's Mike."

He felt a lurch of panic, that Mike knew everything and was coming for Tony. "Yeah, what?" he said.

"I got that address you wanted."

"What are you talking about, diMaio?"

"I get you out of bed or what?" Mike complained. "You asked me to find out where Sterling's shacked up. I found out. You want it or not?"

"Sorry." Dan's free hand went to the back of his neck and tried to rub some of the weariness out of it. "I forgot. What'd you find out?"

"Three thirty-nine Coventry Road, Radnor. It's some kind of old barn in the middle of a new housing development. Hey, you there?"

"Yeah," Dan said after a stunned silent moment. "Yeah, thanks, Mike."

He hung up and stared at the phone. The pressure he'd felt building exploded at last, and he wrenched the phone from its outlet and smashed it into the wall.

12

SCOTT WAS IN THE KITCHEN IN HIS BOXER SHORTS WHEN JENNY CAME downstairs the next morning. He gave a whistle at her appearance, and she sent him a grateful smile. She was wearing a cream-colored Duppioni silk dress that hung loosely from her shoulders. Her abdomen bowed out in a curve now, and there was an unmistakable hardness below the soft layer of skin and fat. Today marked the halfway point of her pregnancy and her first foray into maternity clothes. She'd already disclosed her condition to the people who needed to know, but after today everybody else would know, too.

"Morning," Scott said and kissed her on the cheek, a dry peck, harmless. The outline of an erection showed through his shorts. Jenny looked away. It didn't mean anything—even the most platonic of friends must occasionally suffer from morning erections.

The phone rang, and Jenny picked up.

"Is Scott there?"

It was a man's voice, a voice of authority that she was afraid might come from *the* authorities. "Who's calling, please?"

Scott looked over with an anxious frown.

Jenny's eyes went wide at the answer and she held the phone out with a choke in her throat. "Scott, it's your father."

He jumped for the phone. "Father?"

She hurried upstairs to give him some privacy, and as she left, she felt a swell of happiness for him. Cut off as he was from his former friends and colleagues, not to mention his little girl in Florida, an estrangement from his parents was more than he should have to bear.

When she came down with her briefcase, he was still on the phone. "Okay," she heard him murmur. "That sounds good." She gave him a little wave on her way out the front door.

An hour later, she was at her desk with a cup of decaf. She turned on her computer terminal and went online with the courthouse to check the docket in the Harding & McMann case. So far, she'd been able to monitor the litigation without having to reveal her role to either side, to a large extent simply by reading the papers the parties filed with the court. But most pretrial proceedings were conducted without any kind of public filing, and the parties alone had access to the papers. Having Scott Sterling as her housemate had proved to be a godsend. He was one of the parties, at least nominally so, and usually once a week a manila envelope full of papers from Perlman's office, or Casella's, was delivered to his parents' house and forwarded by them to Coventry Road.

The computer docket showed the titles of all the papers that were logged into the court file. Jenny was relieved to see that Scott had finally gotten to the courthouse to file his own pleadings. He was weeks late, but there they were: his answer to the complaint; his response to the discovery motion; and his brief in response to Perlman's motion for accelerated trial.

But something else appeared: Joinder of Defendant Harding &

McMann in Plaintiff's Motion for Accelerated Trial. This was a surprise. One of the things Dan taught her was press for an early trial when you're plaintiff, drag your feet when you're not. She wondered what could have happened to change his thinking.

Whatever it was, he got his wish. The last item on the docket was the court's scheduling order, and Jenny bit her lip when she saw it. Trial would begin August 7.

Time was running out for Scott. By September 5, he could be indicted in the criminal case; by September 6, he'd plead guilty.

But it was good news for Cassie vonBerg, who could hardly wait for her own day in court.

Jenny slumped back in her chair while her thoughts warred with each other. She'd been so careful in her first meeting with Cassie to disclose her prior connection with the case, yet since then, she'd become best friends with its principal actor and never breathed a word about it. None of the rules of professional conduct seemed to fit this situation; it wasn't a true conflict of interest, but there was no doubt she felt conflicted.

Marilyn buzzed her on the intercom. "Mrs. vonBerg is here," she announced. "In conference room 33C."

Jenny looked at her watch. Right on time. Whatever illusions she might have harbored that Cassie was nothing more than a socialite had been quickly dispelled. She actively monitored her own business affairs, and however she might spend her evenings, she spent her days with lawyers, accountants, brokers, and appraisers. She'd shown a keen interest in the Harding & McMann litigation and an eagerness to participate. It was a standing date now between them, these Monday-morning briefings.

Cassie was paging through the bound volume of a deposition transcript when Jenny joined her in the conference room. She looked up with a scowl over her half-lens glasses.

"Is that directed at me?" Jenny exclaimed.

"No," Cassie laughed. "I've just been skimming my dear uncle's testimony again. This business about Macoal being his lifeblood and he wouldn't dare risk my stock—it's an outrage!"

Jenny took a seat opposite her. "It's exactly what you said about why he shouldn't be trustee. He all but admits that he's not an independent fiduciary when it comes to your shares of Macoal."

"So that helps us, right?"

173

"You bet."

Cassie let the transcript fall shut and peered at Jenny before she pulled off her glasses. "My stars, you're looking well," she drawled.

Jenny murmured her thanks and slid some documents across the table, but Cassie wasn't through with the subject.

"Forgive me if I'm prying," she said carefully, "but are you pregnant?"

Jenny raised her eyes and braced herself. "Yes."

"When is this happening, may I ask?"

"End of October. Which won't in any way interfere with the H&M trial because the latest word is it'll start August seventh. And if we decide to go ahead and sue Mason for breach of trust, that'll be in September, long before—"

Cassie was holding up both hands. "Jenny, stop!" She laughed. "I trust you to keep all this under control. I only asked because I wanted to congratulate you!"

Jenny gave an embarrassed smile. "Sorry. I guess you can tell I'm just a bit defensive on the subject."

"Because you're doing it alone?" she asked and Jenny nodded. "Don't be defensive. You don't have to explain anything to anybody."

"You don't work for this law firm."

Cassie pulled herself erect into a bearing of pure haughtiness. "No. This law firm works for me. And I won't abide it if they don't treat you well."

Jenny was amazed, and then by degrees overwhelmed. "Cassie, that's so generous of you."

"Not at all. I'm being completely selfish. I need you on this project, and in fact, I have a new one for you."

"Please don't say your divorce."

"No, Walter has that in good hands. This project concerns Macoal."

"How so?"

"Sooner or later I'm going to be the biggest shareholder of that company—preferably sooner. I want to know how things stand. I want to know what they're doing before they do it. I want to know where the money's going and what the opportunities are."

Jenny nodded. "We've got people in the corporate department

who specialize in this kind of thing. John Cushman comes to mind, and maybe Vanessa Gold—"

"I know, I've met them," Cassie cut in. "But you don't understand. I don't want someone in your firm. I want you."

Jenny was at once flattered and fainthearted. "This is out of my league. I'm a litigator, Cassie. You need someone with the expertise—"

"You can hire any expertise you need, carte blanche. What matters to me is that I can trust you. Come on, Jenny, say yes. This'll be good for both of us."

Jenny stopped listening when she heard the words *carte blanche.* A world of possibilities went spinning through her mind. She hesitated only a moment. "I'll do it."

It took her the rest of the day to tap into all her intelligence sources and run the number to ground, but early that evening she was dialing the phone and praying the office hadn't closed for the night—or for that matter, closed for good, since her sources told her the business was failing.

The line picked up. "Lehmann Consulting." The voice was brisk, professional, and unmistakably Cynthia Lehmann's.

"Ms. Lehmann, please."

"Speaking."

"Oh, I'm glad I caught you at this hour. I want to hire you to do some consulting work."

The woman's voice came out on an enthusiastic upbeat. "Well, that's fine. What kind of work do you have in mind?"

"A financial and operational analysis of Macoal Corporation."

A suspicious silence was growing as Jenny spoke. "Who is this?" she asked sharply.

"Jennifer Lodge."

There was an explosion of breath over the line. "How dare you—"

"As I said, I want to hire you."

"*You* want to hire *me*," she repeated.

"On behalf of my client."

"Who is . . . ?"

"Catherine Chapman vonBerg, beneficial owner of the largest holding of Macoal stock."

There was another silence while Cynthia digested that information.

"What is this?" she asked finally. "Some kind of payoff? Conscience-cleansing, maybe?"

"Absolutely," Jenny said. "But make no mistake, this is a difficult project. You won't get any inside information. Your research has to be drawn from what's publicly available, and whatever else you can pick up discreetly. The job calls for someone with imagination and resourcefulness. I hoped that might be you."

The silence continued.

"Cassie vonBerg wants to know as much as she can about Macoal. She'll be running the company someday."

"She will?" Cynthia said, and Jenny could tell that possibilities were reeling through her mind.

"I want you to report directly to me," Jenny said. "But anything that passes muster with me goes to Cassie with your name on the cover."

"I'll be expensive," she warned.

"I'll be watching."

Jenny's conscience tweaked her as she left her office for the parking garage that evening. There were probably a hundred people in town who could do a better job than Cynthia Lehmann—her expertise was in banking operations, not energy conglomerates.

Jenny circled up the concrete ramp in search of her car. The air was hot and heavy and smelled of leaking motor oil and gasoline fumes, and she began to feel sick with self-reproach. She'd acted out of pure selfishness in hiring Cynthia, to assuage her own guilt over the Intellitech case, but if Cynthia failed to perform, it was Cassie who would suffer.

Her car appeared ahead of her as a dusty blue gleam in the shadows of the garage. The scuff of footsteps sounded on the ramp below, and she fished for her keys and stepped up her pace until she was at the driver's door. She had the key in the lock when a voice spoke.

"Jennifer."

She whirled around with a muffled cry.

Dan Casella stood beside her, hardly more than a shadow himself in the half-light of the garage. He was in shirtsleeves against the heat, with his tie pulled loose.

She fell back against the car, her heart pounding. "What are you doing here?"

He stepped closer, and the light revealed him. His face was drawn, and deep circles hung under his eyes. "We need to talk," he said.

"About what?" Jenny's hands were shaking so badly her keys rattled, and she clenched them together.

Dan moved close enough to breathe the same air and laid his hands over hers, holding them until they stilled. An engine started up with a roar, and a fragment of conversation echoed from another level, as distant as the other side of the world.

"Jennifer," he whispered and bent his head to hers.

Jenny's breath caught on a doubt in her throat, but an instant later her lips were opening to his. His taste and his smell and the feel of his body under her fingers—they all stormed her at once. As if in a trance, she pressed closer and her hands stole up to his shoulders. She felt weak in his arms, so weak that it took a moment for her to remember her resolve. "Never again," she'd vowed to herself, and with an effort, she pushed against his shoulders and broke free.

"What do we have to talk about?" she said, gasping to catch her breath.

The trance was broken. Dan raised his head and gripped her arms tightly. "Jennifer, what the hell do you think you're doing?"

Her mind raced wildly over a hundred possible wrongs, from representing Catherine Chapman to having his baby, but he couldn't know about any of them. "What do you mean?" she asked, her face full of guilty fear.

"Scott Sterling," he spat out. "What in God's name are you doing with him?"

This was something else he couldn't know about. "Are you spying on me?" she exclaimed.

"I wasn't, until you started shacking up with the guy I am spying on. What's going on? Are you still taking in strays, or are you actually involved with him?"

"None of your business! I don't work for you anymore."

"Are you crazy or just stupid? Scott Sterling is a big-league felon, and you let him move right in on you."

"Felon?" Jenny repeated. "You always said he was Mason's victim, not vice versa."

"There's a lot you don't know."

"Like what?"

"Like he's gotten mysterious infusions of money into his bank account over the past five years. A hundred and twenty thousand dollars in untraceable cash."

"What's that got to do with Mason?"

"It's a pattern, that's all. I'll tell you what does have to do with Mason. He's been getting death threats."

"From Scott?" Jenny blurted, and laughed out loud.

His eyes went dark and his fingers squeezed her arms. He pushed her back against the door of the car, and pressed his body full length against her as he crushed his mouth over hers.

She could read his intent in the force of his body. He was out to defeat her with his hands and his lips and his groin. He was trying to control her as surely as when he sought to tuck her out of sight at Lassiter & Conway. She shook her head, but he pushed closer, and his erection pressed against her belly. She planted her hands on his chest and pushed until the seal of their lips was broken.

"Let me go!"

He dropped his hands and took a step back, but there was no contrition on his face. "Get rid of him," he said.

Jenny lifted her chin. "No, I won't."

"For God's sake!" Dan shouted, and his voice echoed eerily through the concrete building. "Does his pedigree mean so much to you that you don't care that he's a thief and a liar?"

Jenny's eyes narrowed, furious. "His 'pedigree' doesn't mean a thing to me!"

"Then what the hell is his hold on you?"

"We're having a baby!"

The words were out. Dan's eyes went wide, and dropped to the curve of her abdomen under the maternity dress. When he looked up again, the pain in his eyes was boundless. "You're pregnant?"

"Yes," Jenny said, her voice strangling.

"When?" he said in an expulsion of breath.

"December," she blurted, adding two months, and she could see him doing the math, too, and the pain in his eyes went deeper. "So you see, I'm hardly going to get rid of Scott just because you don't like the looks of his bank records."

"Jennifer!" The anguish in his voice would have melted her resolve if he hadn't spoken further. "Are you so fucked up you don't know what you're doing?"

Her mouth went tight. She opened the door and slid behind the wheel.

He grabbed the door and braced it open. "You said you loved me," he rasped.

"My mistake," she hurled back, and wrenched the door shut.

13

THE HEAT WAS SWELTERING IN JENNY'S BEDROOM THAT NIGHT, AND outside her open window a full moon glared like a streetlamp. Her sheets were twisted and damp with perspiration, and she tossed between wakefulness and feverish dreams through the night.

She'd replayed the scene with Dan a hundred times in her mind, and it only grew worse with repetition. She'd meant to keep the truth from him, but never to lie to him about it. Now he believed she and Scott were lovers, and had been for months. Now he believed his own baby was the child of a man he despised. Now she couldn't tell him the truth if she wanted to; he'd be suspicious, or hurt, or furious.

No lie ever went unpaid for—she believed that firmly—and if Dan ever found out the truth, there would be a heavy price for her to pay. A second's impulse created the lie, but the lie created a life of its own, and now there was nothing she could do to stop it.

She flopped over on the bed and tried to forget the hours she'd spent in it with Dan, but those scenes replayed in her mind, too, and there was only one thing she could do to stop them.

The clock read four-thirty. She staggered out of bed more exhausted than when she'd climbed into it, and pulled on shorts and a T-shirt and went downstairs.

A cigarette glowed orange on the patio, and after a second,

Jenny could see Scott behind it. He sat with the dog at his side, both of them gazing at the moon.

"What are you doing out here?" she asked as she opened the door.

He started. "Oh, Jenny. Sorry, did I wake you?"

She wandered out beside him. "No, I couldn't sleep."

"Me neither." He took a drag on the cigarette.

"I never knew you smoked."

With something like surprise, he looked at the cigarette in his hand and dropped it to the patio, then ground it out. "Not since college," he said. "But all my bad habits seem to be coming back."

"None that I've noticed," Jenny said. "Except maybe generosity and thoughtfulness. Nasty habits, those."

He gave a little laugh. The moon was setting and the sky was turning a muddy gray with the hint of the sun behind it.

"Been out here long?"

"About every night," he admitted.

"Oh, Scott," she sighed. "I wish I could tell you everything'll be all right."

"I wish it, too."

A long silence passed between them, full of regrets and sorrows that, if not shared, ran a parallel course. There was comfort there, sitting together as the night slowly reached its end.

"Let's go for a walk," Scott said suddenly.

"In the dark?"

"We can watch the sun come up from the top of the hill."

"Oh, Scott, I don't—"

"Come on! It'll be fun." He added softly, "Who knows when we'll get another chance?"

Jenny looked up at him and her heart pinched at the thought of this golden sunshine boy growing pale somewhere in a dim cell. "All right," she said.

They walked up the hill through the woods and the sounds of birds stirring awake in their nests filled the morning. At the clearing on the top, they stopped and faced east, and within minutes the sun appeared as a little orange arc on the horizon. They watched it inch up, growing bolder and brighter and streaking the sky with gold and amethyst. The morning light washed over the open hillside, revealing pink surveyors' flags and half-dug foundations gaping like craters in the earth. Backhoes were parked at another home site, their necks folded to the ground like grazing robotic dinosaurs.

The old Dundee mansion had once looked out over this hillside. It was gone now, and the rubble cleared away, but the pattern of grass still marked the outline of the old house, like police chalk lines around a murder victim. Scott walked slowly inside the lines and turned to Jenny with a wistful smile. "I remember this place in its heyday."

"You came here?"

"Lots of times. The Dundees used to throw big parties when I was a kid. Limousines used to line up along the lane, and there was always an orchestra playing somewhere, and waiters threading through the crowds with trays of canapés." He stopped and gazed out over the hillside. "It's gone now, all of it."

Jenny knew the story of the estate. The taxes and maintenance and upkeep got to be too much, even for people like the Dundees, and so the estate had bowed to the bulldozers. But as Scott stood there, a solitary figure inside the ghostly confines of the old mansion, she could almost imagine that some romantic tragedy had befallen this house and its people. She moved beside him and laid her hand on his.

He stirred from his reverie and tucked her hand inside the crook of his arm, a gesture she found charmingly old-fashioned. "Come on. I want to show you something."

Green meadows rolled down the other side of the hill. Jenny had never gone this way, but Scott led her swishing through the tall grasses wet with dew. They came to a path through a stand of oak trees, the vestiges of an ancient forest cleared for farmland a hundred years before. The limbs met and touched overhead, and the light of the dawn went dim.

"I always felt like I was coming into church when we rode this part of the trail," Scott said. "We'd all stop talking, right at this point, and just listen to the woods, all the way to the barn."

Somewhere there was a honeysuckle vine sending out a fragrance of intoxicating sweetness. "You used to ride here?" she asked.

"All the time. The Dundees hosted most of the hunt club events."

"Look, I knew I smelled honeysuckle," Jenny said, pointing, and Scott waded through the brush in that direction. He came back with a sprig and arranged it in the pocket of her T-shirt. "There. A corsage for the dance."

She laughed and bent her nose to the blossoms.

"Come on," he said, and pulled her by the hand.

The double row of trees ended, and here the path was bounded by post-and-board fences once painted white, and now a blistered and weather-beaten gray. Clumps of day lilies sprouted under the bottom rail, and clematis climbed the posts. Jenny and Scott followed the fences a hundred yards around a curve to a long tin-roofed stable behind a fifty-year-old boxwood hedge.

"I never knew this was here," she exclaimed.

Scott folded his arms on the top rail of the fence. "I wasn't sure it still was. It's been twenty years since the Dundees moved their horses to Chadds Ford. Come on, let's look inside." He stepped on the bottom rail and vaulted over the fence.

"Do you still ride?" Jenny asked, climbing more carefully after him.

"No, I had a bad fall when I was about twelve." He led the way to the stable block and opened the hasps on the Dutch doors. "Father made me give it up after that."

The light was faint inside the stable. He hit the switch inside the door, but nothing happened. He propped the door open, and enough light penetrated to show an empty tack room to the left and a dozen box stalls stretching ahead.

"Smell that," Scott said with an exaggerated sniff. "Twenty years and you can still smell horses."

"All good things endure?" she joked, but he didn't seem to hear her. He walked ahead through the corridor. A loft ran under the roof rafters along the rear, and she heard the hay rustling overhead and the unmistakable skittering of rodents.

He stopped at one of the stalls and stared into it. Jenny tried to picture him as a twelve-year-old boy, booted and hatted, maybe saddling a fine-muscled horse in this stall. She imagined him untroubled, unashamed, worried about nothing more than the next horse show.

182

He lifted his head and gazed around the complex, then turned back to the empty stall. "This is it," he said suddenly. "This is my nightmare place."

"What do you mean?"

"I've been having the same dream, night after night." He spoke in a low voice, and Jenny drew closer to hear him. "I'm in a stable. It's dark and somebody's pushing me down the row. I'm in manure up to my ankles. I squint hard to see through the darkness, and slowly, small white circles take shape in each of the stalls. They're eyes, watching me as I'm herded past. I squint harder, and I can see faces behind the eyes. They aren't horses, they're men. I start to run, but my feet won't move through the manure, and suddenly all the stall doors open at once, and all these men come out at me, and—"

"What?" Jenny whispered.

Scott blew out his breath. "That's when you save me, Jenny."

She groped for his hand and grasped it.

"Ha! Doesn't take Freud to figure out the symbolism in that one!"

"Ssssh," she said, squeezing his hand.

He shook his head helplessly. "It's the waiting that's driving me crazy. It's been almost six months! If I stole a five-hundred-dollar car, I'd be in jail within twenty-four hours. I steal two million dollars, and here I am. Go figger."

"You didn't steal it," she reminded him.

But he didn't hear her. He turned to her with tears in his eyes. "When does a man reach the point where he can't live with his own stupidity anymore?"

"No, Scott, don't say that. Things will work out somehow, you'll see."

She put her arms around him, and a moment later, his own arms squeezed around her. Her honeysuckle corsage smashed between them, and gave off a fragrance even headier than before.

"Oh, Jenny," he groaned, and pressed his mouth to hers.

This kiss was no dry peck, and Jenny's arms went slack with surprise.

"I love you," he breathed.

She fell back against the stall door, stunned. "Scott, I—"

"I know." He touched the side of her face, hesitantly, as if she might evaporate. "You're still in love with him, aren't you?"

"I don't mean to be. It's just—" She struggled to find the words. "I haven't learned how to fall out of love. When I fall in love, I stay there."

His fingers laced into the strands of her hair and pulled through them in long, ponderous strokes. "I wish I could fall with you, and stay there forever," he whispered. "I know it's too much to hope for, but—"

"No, Scott, it's not. I hope for it, too."

His face was suddenly radiant. He pulled her to him and brushed her lips lightly with his. "That's all the hope I need. I can get through this now, I know I can."

He reached into his pocket, and came out with a glint of light in his palm. "For a while there, I thought it wasn't working." It was the antique pocket watch etched with the prancing horse. He tossed it in the air and caught it with a grin. "But it's still my good-luck piece."

14

IT SEEMED A HUNDRED YEARS SINCE DAN LAST MADE THE DRIVE from Center City to Radnor, and as he turned onto Coventry Road, nothing looked familiar. It was winter then, and Jennifer was his for the taking. Now it was the middle of a heat wave, and she belonged to Scott Sterling. The grounds around her house had been covered with snow, but now they were lush and flowering and as fertile as she'd proved to be with Sterling.

Watery waves of heat oscillated up from the cobblestones as Dan stood at the door and knocked. Jennifer opened it. He had expected she might, but still wasn't prepared for the shock of seeing her again on that doorstep where they used to cling to each other. She held the door cracked an unwelcoming two feet, her body blocking the opening. Even with his eyes held carefully on her face he could see the swell of pregnancy stretching the cotton knit of her shirt.

"Hello, Jennifer. I'm here to see Scott."

"I know. He told me," she said, her voice as unwelcoming as her stance.

"And that's why you're home in the middle of a workday."

"You shouldn't be meeting with him."

"I cleared it with his lawyer. And I cleared it with Scott. So what's going on, Jennifer? Are you representing him now?"

"There's no point in preparing his testimony. You know he can't testify."

"I'd like to hear him say that."

"You could have gotten that much on the telephone and saved yourself a trip out here."

"I always enjoyed the trip out here," Dan said, but when Jennifer flushed, he regretted the snipe.

Scott's face appeared behind hers. "Jenny, what are you doing? Let him in."

Jennifer turned away, and Scott threw the door open. He was wearing nothing but a pair of blue jeans and a shirt he was still buttoning, as if he'd just risen from a quick tumble in Jennifer's brass bed.

"Sorry," Scott said. "She's a little too protective of me sometimes. Come on in."

Jennifer walked stiff-backed into the living room, and Scott ushered Dan in after her and waved him into a chair like it was his own. "How about some coffee?" he said. "There's a fresh pot on."

"Thanks," Dan said, thinking only that it would buy him another minute alone with Jennifer.

"I'll have a cup, too," Scott said.

Jennifer left for the kitchen. Dan snapped open his briefcase and did a slow count to ten as he pretended to search for his papers. He was as annoyed with himself as he was with Scott's proprietary attitude toward Jennifer. He was here on business, not to claim back a woman who was already lost to him.

"We go to trial Monday," Dan said.

"Yeah, I know."

Jennifer returned with a mug for each of them. She sat down on the other side of the room, her arms folded tightly below her breasts, above the sloping curve of her abdomen. She'd grown her hair longer again and wore it a little softer. Sunlight streamed through the open window behind her and circled her in a hazy aureole. Dan took a sip of his coffee. Black, one sugar. She'd remembered.

"I hear Perlman served you with a trial subpoena."

Scott nodded. "I wasn't planning on coming to the trial, but I guess he wants to make sure I testify."

"Wrong," Dan said. "The last thing he wants is for you to testify."

"Huh?" Scott said, and out of the corner of his eye, Dan could see Jennifer shared his confusion.

"Perlman's counting on you to take the Fifth. He needs the adverse inference instruction."

Scott still didn't understand, but Jennifer did, and she explained it to him. "If you refuse to answer on grounds of self-incrimination, the judge will instruct the jury that your answer would have been adverse to your interests. And to your employer's."

Scott looked from Jennifer back to Dan. "So H&M gets screwed if I take the Fifth?"

"You got it."

"Jesus." He took a long gulp of his coffee and shook his head.

"There's nothing else he can do," Jennifer insisted. "Not until the criminal case is resolved. And we haven't heard anything about that."

Dan noted the *we* and rankled at it. "You won't be hearing anything. Not until the civil case is over."

"How do you know?"

"I got the DA to agree not to indict until then."

Jennifer's eyes opened wide. "How'd you do that?"

"I showed him exactly what I'm about to show Scott." Dan laid the exhibits in two stacks on the coffee table. "These are the Connolly account statements. These"—Dan placed his palm down on the first stack—"are the statements Mason got on his personal account. And these"—his hand shifted to the second stack—"are the statements he got on the trust account."

Jennifer's arms unfolded.

"Hold up," Scott said. "The trust account statements came to me, not Uncle Curt."

"So you thought," Dan said. "But the account was flagged for duplicate statements. They went out to both of you like clockwork every month."

"But that can't be! He never said— What does Uncle Curt say about this?"

"He says he never looked at them. He counted on you for that."

"Yeah, okay," Scott said. "I guess that could've been."

But Jennifer was doubtful. "It's hard to believe he never looked at *any* of them."

"He didn't take a whole lot of interest in the trust," Scott reminded her.

"But he was interested in one asset of the trust, wasn't he?" Dan pressed.

"The Macoal stock," Jennifer said.

Dan picked up one of the statements and handed it to Scott. "Here's the trust account statement for November. Mason's copy went out around December fifth. On December seventh, he called Brian Kearney."

Scott's head came up. "Uncle Curt called Kearney direct?"

"That's right. And not only does Kearney have it recorded in his phone log, but he remembers it clearly, because Mason was ranting about the value shown for the Macoal stock."

Scott's eyes were moving over the pages until he found it. "I remember that. Macoal did a stock split in November. There was some confusion about the per share price."

"He questioned Kearney about it down to the penny," Dan said. "He had the statement in front of him when he called. Kearney will swear to it."

"Maybe he did," Scott said. "But I don't see—"

"Look at the next transaction," Dan cued him. "Right below the Macoal entry."

Scott saw it and went still.

"What is it?" Jennifer asked.

"Check number two-thirty-three," he read slowly. "Payee, cash. Amount, $249,875."

"Is that one of—"

"Yeah. That's one of my forgeries."

"So he saw it," she said.

Scott shook his head, unconvinced.

"Look," Dan cut in. "He's questioning pennies on the entry

right above that. You think he's going to skip past a check for a quarter of a million dollars?"

"Maybe he thought it was a legitimate disbursement. This doesn't show where it went."

Dan picked up another statement. "Take a look at this," he said. "Mason's personal statement for the same month. Sent out the same day."

"Does the deposit show?" Jennifer asked.

"Credit, local check," Dan read. "Amount, $249,875."

Scott was still shaking his head.

"Listen to this." Dan reached into his briefcase again and pulled out a cassette player. The tape was already in place, advanced to the right index. He hit the play button.

"Scotty, my boy."

Scott blanched at the sound of Mason's hearty voice, but Jennifer leaned forward, her eyes bright.

"I just got my statement from Connolly."

"Looks good, doesn't it?" Scott's voice said.

"Good? Son, I've never seen results like this. Two hundred forty-nine thousand, eight seventy-five. Outstanding!"

Dan turned the tape off. The room was suddenly so quiet he could hear birds singing outside.

"I don't get it," Scott said finally.

"You showed all this to the DA?" Jennifer turned to Scott. "Don't you see, Scott? They think Mason might've known. Maybe they'll think you're innocent!"

It was exactly what Dan wanted Scott to hear, but it stabbed him to hear it in Jennifer's hopeful voice. She wanted Scott to be cleared. She wanted him free from the threat of prison and safely ensconced here with her where they could wait for their baby together. Dan remembered how he and Jennifer played house one weekend. Now she was here with Scott, living it.

Scott was staring blindly out the open window. "I have to think about this," he said at last.

Dan stood to go. Scott got up and showed him to the door, but Jennifer didn't move. Dan gave one last glance back. She sat bathed in sunlight, her expression lost in a haze.

"If you decide to testify," Dan said, "I'd like to have a session with you to go over the facts."

"Let me sleep on it. I'll let you know tomorrow. No, tomorrow's Saturday—"

"I'll be in the office," Dan said. "Call me there."

15

IT WAS FOUR O'CLOCK BEFORE DAN'S PHONE RANG SATURDAY AFternoon. He dove for it across his desk, but it was only the security guard downstairs in the lobby.

"Mr. Casella, you got visitors," he said. "Michael diMaio and— whosit? Teresa—you'll know, she says."

"Yeah, I know; send them up."

He could hear their happy, animated voices as they got off the elevator and came down the corridor. On their way to a big Saturday-night date, he guessed, and on the spur of the moment he decided to make a date of his own. He scratched a note to himself on a message pad. "Call Lisa."

When he got up from his desk, they were standing in the doorway, all smiles and expectancy. "Hey, what's all the—?"

The question died on his lips. Mike was in his best suit and Teresa in a blue chiffon dress he'd never seen before. She held out her left hand. A ring shone on her finger.

"Jesus Christ," he said.

"Well, that's a fine way to greet the engagement of your only sister." Teresa came toward him with her arms open.

"You're getting married?"

"No, we're engaged to go steady," she said, slapping his shoulder.

"What's Mom gonna say?"

"Right now her and my old man are on their second bottle of champagne," Mike said. "Havin' the time of their lives."

Dan looked from Mike to Teresa. She nodded vigorously, her eyes glowing. He burst out laughing and hugged her tight. "You son of a bitch," he said, pounding Mike on the back as they pumped hands. "I knew I couldn't trust you the minute I laid eyes on you. When's this gonna happen?"

"Saturday before Christmas," Teresa said. She held onto his elbows and searched his face. "You are happy for me, aren't you, Danny?"

He hugged her again. "I'm happier for diMaio," he grumbled. "He's getting the better end of this bargain. Come on, sit down and tell me your plans." He pulled out a chair and Teresa took it with a smile that showed she was grateful for more than the chair. "Are you taking a honeymoon?"

"Just a short one," Mike said. "And no, we ain't tellin' you where."

"Mom wants us to live in the house," Teresa said as Dan perched on the edge of his desk. "Michael has a nice place, but we think we ought to stay with Mom. The neighborhood's changed a lot since you left, you know. We don't think she should be alone."

Dan glanced away. Once again, Mike was doing his job for him. He started off painting the stairway, and now he was taking over as the man of the house.

"I think it's a great idea," he said.

Mike and Teresa smiled at each other and reached out to clasp hands. "There's something else," she said. "It's about Tony."

Dan's features went tight. He walked around his desk and sat down. "What about him?"

"He oughta come home now."

"No."

"Dan, come on," Mike said. "You gave it a good shot. It didn't work. Send him back home."

"Have you forgotten?" Dan said, looking only at Teresa. "The punch in the face?" The gun, he meant to add, but would not say it in front of Mike.

"Michael can handle it," she said.

The implication was clear. Mike could do a better job of raising his little brother than he could. "No," he said again.

"Danny, you can see he's miserable."

"Oh, so now I'm supposed to be making him happy?"

"He failed three classes this last marking period!"

"And he's going to summer school to make them up. See—I got it under control."

"Danny," she said in a softer voice that signaled a new tack. "You're starting a big trial Monday. You're gonna be working around the clock. You don't need the aggravation. Let him come home."

"No."

Mike spoke up. "You just can't stand the idea of losin', can ya, Casella?"

"Michael—"

Dan fought down his anger. "Look," he said, struggling to find a voice of reason. "You two are gonna be newlyweds. You deserve to come home to a happy household at the end of the day. Let it ride."

Teresa sighed and turned to reach for Mike's hand again. "All right."

"But remember," Mike cut in, not giving up so easily, "if there's any trouble, you can always send him home."

Teresa stood up. "Now," she said, sparkling again. "Come out with us. Have a drink to celebrate."

"Sorry." Dan shook his head with what he hoped passed for regret. "I'm waiting for a phone call."

"Oh, come on," she pouted.

"From Sterling?" Mike guessed, and when Dan nodded, he said, "We'll give you a rain check. But let me know what he has to say."

"Yeah, I'll call you."

He put them on the elevator, still in high spirits, and when he returned to his office, his note to himself stared up from his desktop. "Call Lisa." He scratched off Lisa and penciled in Elaine, then scratched off Elaine and tried to remember the name of the woman Ed O'Reilly introduced him to a couple of weeks back. Finally, he picked up the phone and dialed his own apartment.

"Yeah," Tony answered.

"It's me."

"Yeah," he said again. It was almost three months since the cash turned up under his floorboard, and his armor hadn't slipped an inch since then.

"Teresa and Mike got engaged today."

"Yeah, they called me."

"They did?" Dan was annoyed, whether because Tony got the news first or because they were speaking to Tony without his knowledge, he didn't know. "Did they have anything else to say?"

"Like what?"

"Nothing. Well, I'll be home in an hour or so."

Tony greeted the announcement with complete silence. There was a time during the three or four good months they'd had together that he would have thrown out a dinner request and badgered for a video or maybe a movie out. Now he went to great silent lengths to show there was nothing he wanted at all. The irony was that the less Tony wanted from Dan, the more Dan wanted from him—some company at the end of the day, a few laughs, the easy affection they'd once shared. Sometimes it was all Dan could do to remind himself that it was Tony's fault those things were lost, and not his.

The red light blinked on Dan's other line and gave him an excuse to end the silent standoff. "Tony, I got another call." He hit the other button. "Dan Casella."

"This is Jennifer Lodge."

The use of her last name carried a message as clear as her cool, distant voice. Dan answered in the same tone. "Hello, Jennifer."

"Scott thought it over, and he talked to his lawyer, and he's decided against testifying." The words came in a rush, clearly rehearsed and maybe even scripted.

"Why are you the one telling me?"

"He feels bad about it," she said, faltering now, this part spontaneous. "He's—I don't know—ashamed, I guess."

Dan scribbled on the notepad, obliterating the names of the women he'd jotted there. "Seems like you'd want to avoid talking to me even more than he would."

"I don't have anything to be ashamed of!" The anger flared in her voice.

He pulled off his glasses and rubbed his eyes. "That's more than I can say for myself."

She didn't respond. He wished she were seated across the desk from him where he could read her feelings on her face. Maybe her silence meant she was relenting, or that she was yearning for him with all the fervor of her old crush. Or maybe it meant the same as Tony's silence, that there was nothing she wanted from Dan anymore.

There was no point in speculating. She belonged to Sterling now, and Dan had no one but himself to blame. He had thrown them together; he had forced Jennifer to sit in this same chair and dial Sterling's number. "He'll talk to you," he'd insisted over her protests. What he didn't know was that Sterling wouldn't stop at talking.

"Give Scott a message for me," he said finally. "He'd better think again about testifying or the only time he'll see his baby it'll be through a glass panel, and I don't mean the one at the hospital."

Her breath sucked in sharply before she hung up.

He worked late into the night, all thoughts of making a date forgotten. He carried his papers into the conference room down the hall and spread them out over the twelve-foot table. But midway through the night, he found himself staring blindly at the plate-glass window.

This was the conference room where he and Jennifer worked the night of the blizzard. He was on a high that night as the defenses and strategies started to crystallize in his thoughts. And when he turned and read Jennifer's feelings for him in her face, he went higher still. But her feelings turned out to be as portable as Ken Stively's billings, and she'd picked them up and carried them away, far away from Dan.

The TV and the lights in the living room were on when Dan arrived home late that night. The cool white mixed with the eerie blue and cast silver shadows over Tony where he lay sleeping on the sofa. Dan started to speak, but went to switch off the TV first. When Tony stirred but didn't wake, Dan changed his mind about speaking and sank into the chair beside him.

He was asleep when Dan left in the morning and asleep when he got home at night. Dan had no idea how he was spending his days or what was going on in his life beyond the fact that he left the building and returned to it at the appointed times every day. He didn't know who his friends were but suspected there were none. His skin should have been an August bronze by now, but instead it was a pasty white, and he'd lost most of the muscle tone he'd built up during spring sports. He'd flunked three classes even though he had a high B average three weeks before the end of the marking period; his teachers said he couldn't have done any worse if he were *trying* to fail.

For the first time Dan noticed the line of dark fuzz on Tony's upper lip. Jeez, when had that started? If the kid had any kind of father figure in his life, he'd be shaving by now.

He got up and found a blanket in the linen closet and then spread it over the boy and tucked it in around his shoulders. Tony mumbled and moved his head on the arm of the sofa, but still he didn't wake.

He needed friends, fresh air, and a steady male influence in his life. He had friends at his old school, the run of the neighborhood, and Mike diMaio in the family, and that combination beat anything Dan could offer. Mike's accusation was right on target. It was only Dan's refusal to admit defeat that kept him from sending Tony back home where he belonged.

Summer school was almost over. He'd take Tony home at the end of it, and chalk up one more failure on his chart of human relationships.

PART 3
TRIAL

1

THE HEAT WAVE ENDED SUNDAY NIGHT WITH A FLASH OF LIGHTNING and a roar of thunder a heartbeat behind. The rain was still pounding on the pavement in the morning when Jenny's cab pulled up to the courthouse. A palette of golf umbrellas swirled on the sidewalk, one Crayola color blurring into the next through the raindrops on the window. The white van of a local TV news team was parked in front of the cab, and a camera crew was setting up at the courthouse doors. Some politician or mob figure was probably being sentenced today. Jenny wondered if the cameras would be trained on Scott that way when the day of his sentencing arrived. From the look on his face at breakfast, it could have been today.

She went to the tenth floor and cracked open the door to Judge Steuben's courtroom with a lump of dread forming in her throat. A middle-aged woman was filling water pitchers on the counsel tables, and she looked up at Jenny's entrance.

"Are you here on the Mason case?" she asked.

"Yes."

"Come on back. The judge is seeing all counsel in chambers."

"No, I'm only a spectator."

The woman disappeared through the door behind the bench. A hush rose up through the room and Jenny's gaze followed it to the ceiling twenty feet above. The courtroom seemed vast and still, like the sanctuary of a church. Centered at a penitent distance before the bench was the lectern at which the lawyers were required to stand to speak, and behind the lectern stood the two counsel tables. As attorney for the defendant, Dan would be relegated to the table farthest from the jury box and witness stand, on the right. Jenny took a seat on the left.

The rear doors of the courtroom opened with a crash, and two men entered, wheeling dollies of document boxes before them. An officious young woman charged past them and pointed out their path to the defendant's counsel table. Jenny recognized her as a Foster, Bell paralegal, apparently Dan's latest. The boxes were unloaded and opened and ordered. The men left, but the performance was repeated with a different cast five minutes later when Robert Perlman's documents arrived.

A dark, stocky man came in and planted himself in the middle of the first row. When the doors opened next, Curtis Mason strode in with a scowl on his face. The first man stood up at his approach. "Detective," Mason said, without breaking stride. In his wake followed a tall, thick-shouldered black man.

"Who you got here?" the detective asked him.

"My bodyguard," Mason shot out as he took his seat at Perlman's table. "Since the police don't seem to be able to protect me."

The detective deadpanned, "You ain't dead yet that I noticed, Mr. Mason."

Mason's only response was an irritated twist of his shoulders.

Charlie Duncan arrived a few minutes later. His eyes darted toward Mason, but when no greeting was extended, he hurried to his seat and sat alone.

The supporting cast was assembled—the parties, the paralegals, a bodyguard, a detective, and Jenny. It was time for the principal players to appear, but long minutes stretched by with no sign of them.

Jenny began to nurse a hope that they would never arrive. Maybe the case was being settled in chambers: Mason would resign and repay the money; Scott would be forgiven and forgotten; she would never have to face Dan again. But it was a useless imagining. Mason would never cede control; Scott would have to have his day of reckoning; and someday, inevitably, so would she.

The door to chambers finally opened. Robert Perlman emerged first, his head bowed deep in conversation with a young man who had an empty sleeve pinned up on his suit coat. He extended a broad smile to Mason before he reached him and dipped his head for a huddle.

Dan came through the door last, and Jennifer was the first and only one he saw. He felt a burst of joy at the sight of her, and dead on the heels of that feeling, a gut-tightening anger at himself. Charlie Duncan was waiting for him to deliver some reassurance, and he went to speak with him first.

"How'd it go back there?" Duncan whispered.

"No surprises."

"What about the tapes?"

"They're coming in."

Duncan's shoulders slumped. He couldn't be persuaded that this evidence would end up working for them. He heard only one thing on the tapes, and that was a Harding & McMann associate lying through his teeth.

Dan slid into the bench beside Mike diMaio and nodded toward the black man. "Who's the muscle?"

"Mason's bodyguard."

Dan gave Perlman's back a calculating look. The ploy would backfire when Scott Sterling finally put in his appearance. The jury might buy a lot of things about Scott, but they'd never believe he was a physical threat to Mason.

"Seems I'm not doing my job," Mike said.

"Since you're just sitting here, I'd have to agree."

"Hey, I'm lookin' for you and Bobby to put my case together for me." Mike dropped his voice and gestured to the back of the courtroom with his chin. "Who's the girl hopin' nobody'll notice her?"

Dan's face went tight. "She used to work for me."

"What's she doin' here now?"

"I don't know."

He stood and turned. Jennifer's eyes grew wide as he approached her, and it made him angrier yet. Her face used to light up at the sight of him, but now there was nothing there but fear and loathing.

"What are you doing here, Jennifer?"

"I'm a spectator in a public courtroom."

"You're here for him, aren't you? You're representing him."

She shook her head, refusing to answer.

"Maybe if I'd knocked you up, you'd give *me* this kind of stupid, blind loyalty," he said, disgusted.

"You're stupid and blind enough all on your own," she fired back.

"All rise," the bailiff called.

Dan stared hard at her before he spun on his heel and stalked to counsel table.

"The Honorable Gerald Steuben, presiding."

The judge emerged from behind the bench. He was a recent appointee, younger than most, who tried to dispel his reputation as political hack with frequent displays of his own petulant brilliance. He took his seat with an attitude of permanent annoyance at all who would waste the court's time by calling upon it.

His law clerk rose from his seat below the bench and whispered up to him. A piece of paper followed the whisper.

"Where's Scott Sterling?" the judge barked.

Perlman stood. "Your Honor, he's under subpoena and on call."

"Well, that would be fine if he were only a witness, Mr. Perlman, but he also happens to be a party to this action. Who's representing him?"

"He's appeared *pro se,* Your Honor," Dan said, on his feet.

"That's right," the judge said, thumbing through the case pleadings. "He filed an answer to the complaint. He even filed a joinder in the motion for an accelerated trial date. And now he doesn't show up for trial?"

The judge peered down at the woman who'd filled the water pitchers earlier. "Call him and tell him he's got thirty minutes to appear or we start without him." She whispered something up to him, and the judge spoke again to the courtroom. "Anybody know his phone number?"

Dan stood up and recited it from memory, and Jenny's heart welled up inside her as the deputy dialed the phone.

"No answer," she reported after a moment.

The judge's eyes wandered the courtroom before he shrugged. "Then I suppose we won't have the pleasure of his company until you activate your subpoena, Mr. Perlman. All right—let's get the panel and get this jury picked. And quickly, gentlemen," he said, frowning down at both counsel tables. "I want openings right after lunch and the first witness sworn by three o'clock."

The court recessed, and the lawyers began to move their chairs to the other side of the tables to *voir dire* the jury panel.

Jenny left the courtroom and went into an empty attorney conference room in the corridor outside. Something puzzled her. The judge said Scott had joined in the motion for accelerated trial, but she knew he'd done just the opposite, because she prepared the response and watched him sign it. She opened her briefcase and flipped through her copy of the case filings. There. In June, Perlman filed a motion to advance the trial date. Ten days later, Dan joined in the motion. The next pleading in the file was Scott's brief in response to the motion.

The first sentence of the document read: "Defendant Scott Sterling joins in plaintiffs' motion for an accelerated trial."

Jenny read it again. The brief was produced on a high-quality laser printer, but with a different typeface from the one at Jenny's office. She flipped to the last page. There was Scott's signature. If it was a forgery, it was as good as his own.

She sat back in her chair. She didn't understand. Then suddenly, she did, and she felt a fresh ache for Scott. It was only to placate her that he'd given in and signed her opposition papers. Somehow he'd found a computer and put together his own papers and filed them instead. He said he wanted this case over with, and he was as good as his word.

2

DAN DIDN'T NOTICE WHEN JENNY RETURNED TO THE COURTROOM IN the afternoon. By then, his focus had only three poles: the jury, the judge, and opposing counsel, in descending order of attention.

The jury was selected and in the box. Five men, three women; six whites, two blacks. One accountant, one a retiree with an active trading account, and three blue-collar workers who'd never believe anyone could be too busy to bother with a ten-million-dollar trust fund. He would have felt reasonably satisfied with the composite except that Perlman seemed equally satisfied, which only showed nobody knew how these facts would play to a jury.

Steuben gave a good neutral summary of the case to the panel at the start, and turned *voir dire* over to counsel after making only a few inconsequential inquiries of his own. He saved his testiness for moments when the jury was out of the room. He was irritated that the case hadn't settled. Like a lot of judges, he thought juries were useful only in accident cases, and was loath to send them out with a complicated commercial case. Capitalizing on that irritation, Dan laid out all the settlement bidding back in chambers. Perlman's counter was weak, and for the moment at least, Steuben was channeling his irritation in Perlman's direction.

But it would take more than a testy young judge to make Perlman cave. Dan wondered if he'd spent the weekend in a steambath, sweating every drop of alcohol out of his pores and even a few pounds off his gut. Whatever, he was in top form today. And his associate with the military bearing and the empty sleeve—the jurors couldn't keep their eyes off him.

"Mr. Perlman, you may open," Steuben said.

Perlman stood and walked to the lectern, where it had been moved to face the jury box.

"This case is about trust," he began, without any of the usual preliminaries. "Trust: a firm belief in the honesty and integrity of another person."

He planted his elbows on the podium and leaned forward. "Faith," he said, punctuating the word. "Reliance. That's what Webster tells us it means, and that's what the evidence will show you.

"Who are the people you trust? Your family, maybe your clergyman, your lawyer if you ever have need of one.

"Curtis Mason needed one. He had a sister, Elizabeth, affectionately called Doody, his only sister, who passed away last year. It was a hard loss for him to take. And a hard burden came with it. You see, Doody left a sizable estate—ten million dollars in trust for her daughter—and she wanted Mr. Mason to manage it. It's a complicated business, taking care of that kind of money. There are taxes and stocks and bonds and all kinds of things to worry about. So Mr. Mason did what any prudent man would do. He lined up some professional help. He hired an accountant. He hired a stockbroker. And he hired a lawyer. A whole firm of lawyers, in fact— Harding & McMann."

Dan kept his eyes on the jury, but in his peripheral vision, he saw Perlman turn to fix a baleful stare at the defense.

"Mr. Mason put his sister's money in the custody and keeping of Harding & McMann. Ladies and gentlemen, you'll be hearing a lot from my friends across the aisle about what a fine and reputable law firm Harding & McMann is. Well, we don't disagree with that at all. Why else would Mr. Mason entrust them with the care of all his dear sister's earthly assets? Of course they were a fine and reputable firm! He *trusted* them to do a good job. An honest job."

Perlman shifted his weight from one foot to the other, then forward and back. Like Dan, he was accustomed to moving freely during opening speeches, and he found the lectern confining. Dan knew he'd feel the same way, but it gave a shiftiness to Perlman's opening that he intended to avoid. He made a mental note to himself. He'd copy Jerry Shuster's ramrod posture if he had to, but he'd stand still.

"For a time it went smoothly," Perlman went on. "Harding & McMann did everything the way they were supposed to. They earned his trust, and he gave it to them. He gave them more day-to-day control over the trust assets. Deal with the accountant. Deal with the broker. Pay the bills and make the payments to Doody's heirs. This is what he trusted Harding & McMann to do, and to do honestly.

"Like the proverbial camel's nose, Harding & McMann inched farther and farther into the tent of his goodwill—so far that he decided to trust them with some of his own private funds as well. 'We'll invest this for you,' they told him. 'We'll make it grow.'

"And once again, Harding & McMann delivered. They invested Mr. Mason's money. They doubled it, then tripled it. He was thrilled. Well, who of us wouldn't be?

"But ladies and gentlemen, it *wasn't* real. One day last winter, Mr. Mason found out there were no investment profits. There never were. Harding & McMann lost his money, every red cent of it.

"All right, that happens; there're no guaranties in the stock market. *But they lied to him.* They deceived him into thinking he'd earned a fortune in trading profits. And just how did they do that? They put two million dollars into his account. Two million dollars that he thought he'd earned in the market.

"And where did it come from? From his dead sister's trust, that's where! Two million dollars, stolen outright from the trust they were supposed to be safeguarding! Trust? They betrayed his trust in every way imaginable."

It was another ten minutes before Perlman sat down, and the name Scott Sterling never once escaped his lips. Dan knew his game. A judgment against Sterling was worthless. Perlman had to impute Sterling's liability to H&M to score any real victory. Eventually, the evidence would show that Sterling was the only one who took the money, Sterling was the only one who lied, but meanwhile the seed was planted—it was the firm's fault and the firm's financial responsibility.

Jenny took careful notes during Perlman's opening, but her pen faltered as he sat down. An expectant hush swelled through the courtroom. The jurors' heads turned toward Dan, and when he had their complete attention, he rose and moved to the lectern.

His voice was almost startling when he finally spoke.

"This case *is* about trust. It *is* about faith and reliance in the honesty of another. But, ladies and gentlemen, ask yourselves, 'Just who was it that Curtis Mason trusted? Or did he trust anybody at all?'

"You won't hear any evidence that Curtis Mason trusted Harding & McMann. Harding & McMann meant nothing to him. It's a law firm like five or six others in town, no better or worse. With one difference only—Scott Sterling."

A few quizzical looks passed through the jury box. They'd heard that name when the judge explained the case in the morning, and during jury selection they'd been asked if they were acquainted with anyone on a long list of names that included Scott Sterling's. But the recollection was faint now.

"Remember that name," Dan said. "It's the one Mr. Perlman forgot to mention to you. Scott Sterling—the only reason Mr. Mason ever brought his business to Harding & McMann. It's the name that's at the core of this whole case.

"Scott Sterling. Mr. Mason knew his family before he was born. He went to school with his father; he was a constant part of his life all the years he was growing up. Scott called him Uncle Curt. Mr. Mason called him son."

An elderly woman dressed in gray cocked her head at that, her interest piqued.

"Mr. Mason had another law firm handle his own affairs. He still does. He had half a dozen other firms handle the legal work for his company, Macoal Corporation. Harding & McMann was never one of them. Its reputation as a fine law firm never appealed to him before last year. Mr. Mason didn't bring the trust to Harding & McMann. He brought it to Scott Sterling, his surrogate son."

Jenny's pen and notepad were forgotten. Dan stood motionless in front of the lectern, his voice his only instrument. Or perhaps it was a weapon, because each time he uttered the name Scott Sterling she felt as if she'd been stabbed.

"He didn't place any trust or confidence in Harding & McMann. He didn't even deal with Harding & McMann beyond the person of Scott Sterling. All of his contacts were with Scott and Scott alone.

"So when Mr. Perlman tells you that Harding & McMann solicited the trust business or offered to handle investments for Mr. Mason or lied to him about his trading profits or stole two million dollars from the trust, you have to substitute Scott Sterling's name for Harding & McMann's every time."

Dan heard a snort behind him; Perlman was doing some posturing for the jury.

"If Mr. Mason trusted anybody," he went on, "he trusted Scott Sterling, not Harding & McMann.

"But you heard me say 'if—*if* Mr. Mason trusted anybody.' Because the evidence will show that he didn't trust Scott Sterling either. He doubted everything Scott told him, so much so that he secretly tape-recorded their telephone conversations."

Eyebrows went up among the jurors, and Dan knew Charlie Duncan was probably cringing behind him.

"That's right," he said. "And as you listen to the evidence, and especially as you listen to the tapes, ask yourself this question: why would Mr. Mason secretly tape-record this young man who was like a son to him, the one he trusted so deeply? The answer is, he didn't trust him. Not as far as he could throw him.

"But I told you this case is about trust, and it is. I'm talking about the trust that Elizabeth Mason Chapman placed in her brother when she named him the trustee of her assets. I'm talking about the trust that her daughter Catherine placed in her uncle that he would take care of her inheritance. The faith and reliance they both had that he would put the trust's interests ahead of his own personal interests.

"That's the trust that's been violated here. Because one way or another, Mr. Mason allowed two million dollars to flow out of the trust and into his own personal account. Two million dollars of his dead sister's estate, and of his niece's inheritance. He put his own personal interests ahead of them both. And to this day, ladies and gentlemen, he refuses to give it up. He wants you to hold Harding & McMann responsible. He wants you to blame a law firm he never even dealt with for his own failure to honestly safeguard the trust.

"Trust *was* betrayed here—the trust Mrs. Chapman placed in her brother when she put him in charge of the money for her daughter Catherine; the trust Catherine placed in her uncle that he would manage her money and look out for her best interests. Betrayed, both of them. And ladies and gentlemen, it was the worst kind of betrayal, because they were betrayed by someone they loved."

Dan let another full beat of silence fill the courtroom before he turned and walked away from the podium. His eyes touched on Jenny before he sat down. She realized she'd been holding her breath and wondered for how long.

5

"PLAINTIFF CALLS TUCKER PODSWORTH, AS ON CROSS, YOUR Honor."

Podsworth took the oath, looking greatly put out about it, and when he sat down in the witness chair, it was with a ruffling of his arms and shoulders, like a chicken cross at being called to the nest.

In response to Perlman's questions, he confirmed that he was a partner in Harding & McMann and the chairman of its estates department. He acknowledged that until January of this year, Scott Sterling was an associate in his department. For the jury's benefit, he explained that a partner was an owner of the firm, while an associate was merely an employee. He confirmed that Sterling reported to him.

He went on to acknowledge Sterling's acquisition of the Chapman trust business, and he identified Sterling's memorandum to him setting out the scope of the engagement. He admitted that Sterling later opened a file for Curtis Mason that had something to do with securities advice. He confirmed that he, Podsworth, acted as billing attorney for both matters.

Finally, in excruciating detail, Perlman led him through his discovery of Sterling's check forgery and his ultimate confession.

Dan reminded himself yet again never to underestimate Bob Perlman. It was a smart move for him to call Podsworth first instead of the more obvious choice of Mason. He killed three birds with one witness. He got a succinct explanation of Sterling's scheme, he proved that the firm was at least administratively involved in the whole affair, and worst of all, he established Podsworth as the personification of H&M—pompous, stuffy, and arrogant—the last candidate Dan would have elected.

Dan had no delusions that he might humanize Podsworth on direct, but there were a few points he might score.

"Before Sterling brought in the Mason business," he asked, "was Curtis Mason ever a client of the firm?"

"No," Podsworth intoned, no friendlier to his own lawyer than he was to the opposition.

"Was any other member of the Mason family ever a client of the firm?"

"No."

"Was Mr. Mason's company, Macoal Corporation, ever a client of the firm?"

"No."

"Are you acquainted with Mr. Mason personally?"

"Oh, yes, indeed."

"For how long?"

"Years."

"How many?"

Podsworth stroked his chin. "At least twenty, I should say."

"How did you first become acquainted?"

"Good Lord, I don't remember. Probably at a social function of some kind."

"Have you attended many social functions together?"

"A great many."

"Do you share many of the same friends?"

"Yes, indeed."

"Do you and Mr. Mason belong to any of the same clubs?"

"We do."

"Name some."

"The Merion Cricket Club. The Overbrook Golf Club. The Union League. Let's see—"

"That's enough, thank you."

First point scored. Podsworth might be a snooty son of a bitch, but so was Mason.

"Was Mr. Mason aware of the fact that you're a lawyer specializing in trusts and estates?"

"Of course. We discussed it on numerous occasions."

"Did you ever attempt to solicit him as a client?"

"Not in so many words," Podsworth answered with great offense. "That would have been crass. But I certainly let him know of my expertise and availability."

"But despite your twenty years' personal acquaintance and his knowledge of your expertise and availability, Mr. Mason was never a client of Harding & McMann until Scott Sterling brought him in. Is that correct?"

"Correct."

Second point scored.

The third also came easily. Scott Sterling was the only one at H&M, lawyer or paralegal, to perform any services on either the Chapman Trust or the Mason Investment Advice file. As billing attorney, Podsworth regularly received computer printouts detailing the services performed and by whom. Sterling's was the only name ever to appear.

"How were the bills submitted to Mr. Mason?"

"I mailed them to him."

"Did you write transmittal letters?"

"Of course." Indignantly.

The letters were marked and identified.

"Mr. Podsworth, I notice that each of these letters, D-3 through D-6, closes with the same language. Is that correct?"

"Yes."

"Read the closing paragraph to the jury."

Looking much aggrieved, Podsworth fished his reading glasses out of his breast pocket and perched them on his nose. " 'If you have any questions or comments about any of these services or the fees being charged for them, kindly do not hesitate to contact me.' "

"Did Mr. Mason ever contact you with a question or comment about his bills?"

"Never."

"Did Mr. Mason ever contact you with a question or comment about the services being performed for him by Scott Sterling?"

"Well—he never contacted me, but we did discuss the subject on one occasion."

"What was that occasion?"

"It was last December at a holiday affair hosted by a mutual friend of ours."

"What discussion did you have with him?"

"Oh, we talked about a great many things. But in particular, I asked him if Scott was keeping him satisfied."

"What was his response?"

" 'Beyond my wildest dreams,' he said."

Perlman would not let him step down from the stand with that last remark still ringing in the jurors' ears. He moved up to the lectern for recross.

"Take a look at Exhibit D-2, if you will."

Podsworth fumbled with the papers before him until he found it.

"Those are the time diaries for the Mason Investment Advice file, correct?"

"Correct."

"All the services were performed by Scott Sterling, correct?"

"Yes."

"And a description of the services performed on any given day is set out on D-2, is that right?"

"Yes."

"Read through those descriptions, would you, Mr. Podsworth?"

His feathers ruffling again, Podsworth pulled his glasses back on. "Well, the first entry reads 'phone client re securities advice.' "

"And the next entry?" Perlman prodded.

" 'Phone client re securities advice.' "

"In fact," Perlman said, his voice going into a dramatic up-swing, "isn't that how every single entry reads?"

Podsworth slowly and laboriously flipped through the pages of the exhibit. Finally, he lifted his head. "No," he said smugly.

Following along, Dan saw the entry. He clenched his jaw, hoping against odds that Podsworth wouldn't reveal himself for the ass he was. But Perlman was confident he would. "I suppose you're referring to the single entry on the third page that reads 'Meeting with client re securities advice'?" he said, dripping sarcasm.

"Correct." A few eyes rolled in the jury box.

"Rather a general description, isn't it?"

Podsworth shrugged. "A bit."

"Did you ever once go to Sterling and ask him what it was specifically he was doing to advise Mr. Mason on securities matters?"

"No," Podsworth admitted. But then he redeemed himself. "Every entry involved a communication with Mr. Mason himself. I assumed he knew what Sterling was doing, and if he didn't, he'd contact me, as I invited him to do."

"No further questions," Perlman said stiffly, conveying with his voice and posture what an unworthy witness he considered Podsworth to be.

"Through with this witness, Mr. Perlman?" the judge asked. Perlman nodded. "Then we'll adjourn until tomorrow."

4

SCOTT WAS WAITING AT THE DOOR WHEN JENNY GOT HOME THAT night. Over sandwiches and salad, she recounted the openings and Podsworth's testimony, while Scott listened with his fists clenched and his knuckles white.

The phone rang as he was clearing the plates, and Jenny picked up.

"Is Scott there?" asked the voice she now recognized as Edgar Sterling's. She mouthed "your father" across the room. He nodded and ran to the phone upstairs, and she hung up when she heard him say "Hi." His father's calls were coming with more and more frequency, and Jenny hoped this meant a reconciliation was underway.

She finished clearing the table and washed the dishes. She wanted to go upstairs and change but hated to intrude on Scott's privacy. Instead, she poured herself a glass of lemonade and went outside.

The rain had ended during the day, but the grass was still wet, so she sat on the patio and watched the twilight fall. The lights in the construction trailers glowed like constant sentinels on the hillside. Crickets were chirping in the meadow, and the harder Jenny listened, the louder their song swelled, until her ears rang with it and it was all she could hear.

She felt as if she'd been cast in a play, in two or three different roles, none of them true to herself. She sat all day in the courtroom pretending to be a neutral trial observer. She came home and pretended something else with Scott. She lied to Dan, and she withheld the truth from Cassie vonBerg. The play had taken on a life of its own, until she couldn't remember where the exits were anymore.

But she did remember one.

She went inside for her purse and scribbled a quick note to Scott and left it on the counter.

Cassie vonBerg's house was in Gladwyne, on a hill overlooking the city. In an area known for three-story fieldstone colonials, it was a sprawling one level of white stucco and red-tiled roofs—a Mediterranean-style villa in the heart of Quaker country.

A dozen lights burned inside, but no one answered the doorbell. Jenny rang again and strained to listen for a footstep. Instead, she heard the crunch of gravel in the drive a second before the headlights of a car swept over her. The car stopped behind hers, and the lights dimmed.

It was a black Mercedes limousine. A uniformed chauffeur rose from behind the wheel and kept on rising. He was well over six feet tall and a third as wide across the shoulders, an imposing and improbable figure. He revolved slowly, and Jenny realized he was doing a reconnaissance of the premises when his eyes landed on her. The eyes were round and blue in an otherwise Asian face. He kept her fixed in sight as he opened the rear door of the car and spoke a few low words to its occupants.

"It's all right, Moi," a louder voice said, and a black-and-silver-haired man in a tuxedo emerged. The chauffeur stood at attention while the tuxedoed man trotted around to open the other rear

211

door. He reached in and his hand came out on the elbow of Cassie vonBerg.

She was wearing a long black column of silk, and her blond hair was piled high on her head, making her look impossibly tall and slim and rich. Jenny shrank back and folded her arms awkwardly over her stomach as they approached the door.

"Why, Jenny," Cassie drawled. "What a surprise."

"Forgive me for not calling ahead. I didn't mean to intrude. I'll call you tomorrow if it's convenient."

"Oh, don't rush off; I was hoping to hear from you tonight." She glided up the walk on the man's arm. "Jenny, this is Jack Stengel. Jack, this is my lawyer, Jennifer Lodge."

"A pleasure," he said, flashing perfect teeth as he shook her hand. His skin was bronzed, and his lips full.

"Care to join us for coffee, Jack?"

Jenny noticed the deft way she turned him into the third wheel, and so did he. "Not tonight, thanks. But I'll speak to you again soon."

"Wonderful."

"And as you're Cassie's lawyer," he said, turning to Jenny, "I certainly hope to see you again."

"Nice meeting you," she murmured.

He said good night and kissed Cassie on the cheek before he turned. "Moi," he called, but the chauffeur had anticipated him and was standing with the door already open.

"God, what perfect timing," Cassie said as the car backed out of the driveway.

"I'm so sorry—"

"No, I mean it. Your timing was perfect. Another ten minutes alone and we would have ended up in bed." Cassie unlocked the carved wooden door and swung it in.

"Is that *the* Jack Stengel? The corporate raider?"

"The same." Cassie pulled off her diamond earrings and dropped them on the console table in the hall. "Come on in."

She kicked off her shoes and led Jenny into the living room, an underfurnished room decorated in subtle shades of white. "What would you like to drink?"

"Nothing, thanks. Cassie, he tried to take over Macoal last year."

"I know," she laughed. "Isn't it great?"

"Isn't what great?"

She flopped on the sofa. "That he's courting *me*. He must think I've got a good shot of ousting Curtis from the trust. Otherwise, why waste his time chatting me up? I can't sell him any shares."

Jenny sat down on an ivory suede ottoman. "Is he still buying?"

"No, I don't think so." Cassie pulled some pins from her hair and shook it loose. "Not as long as Curtis controls the majority. But he dropped a lot of hints about our doing business together in the future. You heard him—since you're my lawyer, he hopes to see you again soon."

"Would you sell to him if you could?"

"Probably not. But who knows? Maybe we could join forces and take over somebody else!" She swung her legs up on the white damask sofa. "So—tell me. How did it go in court today?"

"A draw, I think," Jenny said. "Both sides scored some points. Casella's putting Mason on trial, no question about it, but Perlman's getting in some good licks against H&M."

"Scott Sterling's the wild card," Cassie said.

Jenny stood up and walked to the window, then to the fireplace. "There's something I have to tell you." A row of framed photographs lined the mantel, Cassie in her white debutante ballgown and later in her white wedding gown. "It's something I should have told you sooner." Another picture showed Reese Chapman clutching a horse's bridle in one hand and a trophy cup in the other, and Jenny stopped and studied it.

"Well," Cassie said, reclining on the sofa. "I'd say the suspense is killing me, but the truth is I'm afraid I'll fall asleep before you finally spit it out."

Jenny turned to face her. "I've engaged a consultant to do a financial analysis of Macoal—"

"That's fine, I told you—"

"She's a very talented woman, and I think we'll get first-rate work from her—"

"You don't have to justify—"

"And her name's Cynthia Lehmann."

Cassie's features were blank a moment before she remembered the name. "Ah. The woman from Gordon St. James's company."

Jenny nodded. "I hope you won't hold that against her. I mean, I think the circumstances—"

"You don't have to explain the circumstances. I followed the trial. It was perfectly obvious to me that St. James was lying through his teeth."

Jenny stared at her. "You knew that, and you still hired me?"

Cassie gave an unapologetic shrug. "I'm no better than any other client, I suppose. I wanted a lawyer who could be ruthless, as ruthless as Curtis. Integrity mattered less."

Jenny winced. The accusation stung, and more so because it was deserved. "I can't say I knew St. James was lying," she said. "But the truth is I didn't care. I only wanted to win. It was later I realized the price was too high."

"And that's why you hired Cynthia Lehmann."

"Small reparation." She gave a feeble smile. "So I guess I'm not so ruthless after all."

"I know that now," Cassie said. "And you know what? I'm finding that integrity matters more to me than I thought. And I'm glad I found a lawyer with a conscience."

Jenny looked away. She might have a conscience, but it was still unappeased. She took a deep breath to fortify herself for the next disclosure.

"There's something else, Cassie. Scott Sterling's a friend of mine." But she knew that disclosure wasn't full enough. "More than a friend. He's living with me."

Cassie swung her feet to the floor and stared at her. Jenny waited for her outburst. Now she'd be fired, as she deserved to be, and remorse and relief welled up in her at once.

"Jenny, do you think that's wise?"

"The point is, what do you think?"

"Well, I don't see that it's any of my business."

"Of course it is! He stole your money."

"Curtis stole my money. Scott Sterling was just the conduit. That's what I believe, and I thought you did, too."

Jenny sat down beside her with a sigh.

"Is he—?" Cassie pointed at Jenny's abdomen.

"No! It's nothing like that. We have mutual friends. We ran into each other last spring. He needed a place to live, I needed a housemate. One thing led to another—"

"Stop," Cassie said, holding up her hand. "You don't owe me any explanation. If you came here tonight and told me you were sleeping with my Uncle Curtis, then I'd worry about a conflict. But as it is, I'm only worried about you. I hate to say it, Jenny, but this sounds like the classic relationship without a future."

"You don't object if I continue to represent you?"

"I'd object if you didn't. And if you're telling me to mind my own business about your romantic complications, so be it."

"Cassie, thank you—"

"Do me one favor, though," she added.

"Of course."

"Find out everything you can about Jack Stengel."

"Already on my list."

5

COURT ADJOURNED AT FOUR-THIRTY ON WEDNESDAY, AND DAN WAS at his desk by five, as exhausted as he would be at midnight. It was always tiring to listen sharply and show no expression during your opponent's case, but he'd never found it as hard as in this trial. Perlman was putting his case on through Dan's own witnesses. First Tucker Podsworth, then Scott Sterling's former secretary, and for half of Tuesday and all day today, Charlie Duncan.

Poor Charlie. The jury would never understand that the slump in his shoulders and the anxious darting of his eyes came not from a lack of character and conscience, but from an overabundance of both. He'd already condemned himself and his firm by his own standards; the guilt he showed was the guilt he'd adjudged to himself. To make it worse, today was the day some of Charlie's partners finally decided to put in an appearance. Dan felt their gauging eyes on his back all day, and behind them, in the back of the courtroom, Jennifer, like a constant ache.

Stacks of mail and phone messages sat side by side on Dan's desktop, and he picked up the mail first and riffled through it without focusing. Perlman had scored some major points with Charlie. H&M had written policies and procedures for supervising the work of its associates but no mechanism for enforcing them. H&M had received twenty-three client complaints in the last three years that were serious enough to alert the malpractice carrier. Seven of those complaints involved alleged improprieties in the handling of client funds. At least two of those were determined to have some merit, but in neither case was the responsible lawyer fired or even reprimanded. In fact, in one case, the lawyer in question was elected a partner the following year.

That opened up another avenue of questions, and one that especially bothered Dan because he hadn't seen it coming.

"How long does it take for the typical associate to be elected to partnership at your firm?" Perlman had asked.

Charlie could have quibbled over *typical*, just as Dan could have objected, but both had let it pass. "Normally about eight years."

"So," Perlman had said, turning to the jury to make sure they were doing the math with him. "Scott Sterling would have been up for partner when—the end of this year?"

Charlie shifted in his seat, understandably butt-sore from sitting all day, but it looked bad. "That's right."

"Was he going to make it?"

"The election isn't until next month," Charlie had said. "We'll never know if he would've made it or not."

"Come on now, Mr. Duncan," Perlman had said. "You're not going to tell us that after eight years of service, it's a last-minute, spur-of-the-moment decision?"

"Well, no—"

"There must be some ongoing evaluations, some early indicators?"

"Yes, we do annual evaluations of our associates."

"So—how did it look for Scott Sterling?"

Charlie had hesitated. "He wasn't a likely candidate."

"Did you tell him so?"

"Yes."

Dan wasn't sure what the point was or even if there was one— after all, Sterling hadn't pocketed the two million—but it still bothered him that he hadn't seen it, that he hadn't even thought to ask Charlie about it.

It was eight o'clock when he got home, and Tony was sprawled on the couch watching rock videos. "Hi," Dan said.

"Hi." His eyes didn't move from the screen.

Dan pulled a beer out of the refrigerator and gave the bottle opener a hammered wrench that threw the cap over the counter and onto the dining table. He tipped the bottle back and took a long swallow. Tony didn't move.

"Don't you have any homework?"

"Duh."

"What's that supposed to mean?"

"Today was the last day."

He checked the calendar on the kitchen wall to confirm it. "Let's see the report card."

"It'll be mailed."

Dan took another swallow and wondered if he were lying. "Maybe I'd better call the school."

It was the kind of trap he liked to lay for an adverse witness. Watch his reaction, see if he looks nervous or blabs an excuse.

"Suit yourself," Tony said.

Dan pulled off his coat. His shirt was soaked with sweat, and he pulled that off, too. He switched off the TV and sat down bare-backed against the cool leather of an armchair. Tony watched him as if he were watching paint dry, not a drop of emotion showing.

"I've been thinking," he began. "Now that summer school's over, there's nothing tying you here anymore. You'd probably be better off back home."

Tony stared at him without expression for another minute before he barked a short laugh. "I knew it!"

"What?"

"I knew you'd ditch me the minute it got to be a drag."

"I got news for you—it's been a drag from the start."

Tony got up without another word and went to the kitchen. He pulled a bottle like Dan's out of the refrigerator.

"What do you think you're doing?"

"Celebrating." Tony raised the bottle high, like a toast. Gone was the neutral expression. He was sneering, trying his best to provoke a fight.

"Put it away, wise guy."

Tony popped off the cap and lifted the bottle.

"Goddamn it, I said put it away."

Tony tilted the bottle to his mouth.

Dan was out of his chair and in the kitchen before the first swallow was done. He grabbed the bottle with one hand and gave him a whack on the rump with the other.

Tony backed away, staring with hot, stung eyes.

"Go get your stuff together," Dan said.

He turned to the counter to mop up the spilled beer, and felt more exhausted than ever. Tony's footsteps sounded in the hall, but it took Dan a second to realize they were going the wrong way, and in that space of time, Tony had the door open and was bolting down the corridor.

"Hey, get back here!"

Dan lit out after him toward the stairwell. Tony was already one landing below, and Dan galloped down the stairs, his feet jarring hard on the concrete. He gained on the first flight, but at the next turn, Tony grabbed onto the pipe railing and vaulted himself over to the next landing, a maneuver Dan couldn't begin to copy. It was twenty stories to the ground and he fell behind a little on each one. By the time he reached the ground floor, the rear door was slamming shut.

Dan grabbed the knob and jerked, but the door didn't budge. He remembered then. It could only be opened with a key—the same key he gave Tony to get into the apartment. So much for his brilliant security plan. Tony had probably cracked it his second day in the building.

He fished for his own key in his pocket and burst through the door. Tony was heading north at a trot, and Dan took off after him at a dead-out run. The boy threw a look over his shoulder and went into a sprint, but Dan closed the gap enough to make a diving leap. He tackled him around the knees, and Tony came down hard on the pavement.

Dan's breath was knocked out of him, and in the time it took for him to get it back, a crowd gathered. Their voices rose in an angry swarm.

"Hey, get off him!"

"What d'you think you're—?"

"Stop it!"

"Somebody get a cop!"

Dan got his feet under him and pulled Tony up with a tight grip on his collar. "Are you all right—" he started to ask, but he could see the boy was crying.

"Let go of him!" a woman shrieked, and a chorus of voices joined her.

"Listen—" Dan began in a voice of reason to the crowd.

"Somebody help me!" Tony screamed. "This guy's after me! He locked me in his apartment, and he wouldn't let me get away!"

Dan's jaw dropped. "What the hell—?"

"Pervert!" someone bellowed.

His arms were wrenched from behind, and Tony sprang free.

"Hey!" Dan shouted, trying to shake loose the hot hands on his bare skin. He threw a look over his shoulder and saw two men behind him, each with a firm hold on an arm. "He's my brother! Come on, he's running away! I'm taking him home!"

"Save it for the cops," one of the men growled.

He waited for the resemblance to become apparent, but this time no one noticed.

"Tony!" Dan yelled. The crowd had grown to about twenty people, and the boy was already edging his way past them. "Don't go. We'll talk, okay?"

"Here comes a cop now," the other man said.

Dan suddenly realized how he must look, shirtless, tackling a teenage boy on the street. "Okay, okay," he said, fighting down his fury. "One of you grab the kid, and we'll talk this out, all right? Just don't let him get away."

Tony gave him one last look before he turned and broke into a run. At the end of the block, he rounded the corner and was gone before the cop shouldered his way through the crowd.

"What's this all about?"

"Go get my brother—"

"He's a pervert!" a woman yelled. "He was after that boy!"

"He's my brother. He was trying to run away, and now thanks to you fucking idiots, he's gone!"

With a final roar, Dan pulled himself free, but it was no use. Tony had too big a lead.

The security guard finally emerged from the building to confirm that Dan and the boy were brothers and lived together in twenty-oh-six. The cop shrugged, the crowd thinned, and the two men who'd let Tony get away disappeared.

"He'll be back by dark," the cop said.

He was trying to be helpful, but Dan aimed all of his fury at him.

"What the hell do you know about it? You got no idea what's going on with him, or where he's going, or what he's getting into!"

"You wanna file a report? Get the patrols out looking for him?"

Dan hesitated. A report meant that Mike could find out, and the family would have to know. "Nah. Never mind," he said.

He cruised the streets around the neighborhood, on foot and later in his car, sweeping wider and wider with each circle. Night was falling, and he peered through the dim half-light at everybody he passed. At the sight of any dark-haired figure over five two and under five ten, male or female, he slowed to a crawl. Cars behind him honked in annoyance.

He gave up on the neighborhood and drove to The Alexander School, hoping for a faint moment to find Tony shooting baskets on the court. A couple of boys were cradling lacrosse sticks and passing the ball back and forth to each other as they ran the length of the field. Neither one was Tony.

That was his mistake, making Tony quit sports. Or at least one of his mistakes. Smacking him on the butt might be another. Or leaving him alone too much. Or never talking to him about anything important. A hundred different mistakes could have caused him to bolt tonight.

But why tonight, when he was about to go home and escape from all of them? That's what he couldn't figure.

At eleven o'clock, after three hours of random searching, he thought of another place Tony might have gone—home to Gasker Avenue—in a fuck-you gesture to show he didn't need Dan to take him there. Dan turned south, but the last thing he could do was knock on his mother's door and ask if she'd seen Tony lately. He drove slowly past the house. If Tony were home, he'd probably be in his room. The windows were black, but that didn't mean anything. He could be asleep, or maybe downstairs catching up on all the news with the family.

The more he hoped for it, the more likely it seemed. But if it were true, somebody would've called to let him know. He pulled a screeching U-turn at the end of the block and raced north on Broad and east back to his own building.

But the message light on the answering machine was dark. No one had called.

He pressed his head against the wall, and picked up the phone to dial.

"Mike," he said as the call went through, "I need your help."

6

JENNY RETURNED TO HER OFFICE THURSDAY AFTER COURT ADjourned and sat down at the computer to organize her notes of the day's proceedings. Perlman had called his expert that morning, an accountant commissioned to trace the path the money took. From flow charts propped on an easel between the jury box and the witness stand, he followed the two million dollars from the trust account to Mason's account. Forging Mason's signature, Sterling wrote checks to cash drawn on the trust's brokerage account at Connolly and Company. He deposited those checks into his own bank account. He then wrote checks on his account payable to Mason and deposited them into Mason's account at Connolly. The checks he used for this last phase were blank counter checks with no name or account number inscribed on them; Sterling filled in his account number and signed them with a scrawl that could not be read as his name or anyone else's. This, the witness explained, was the circuitous route taken by Sterling to disguise the fact that money was moving out of the trust account and into Mason's account.

Two things bothered her about the day's proceedings, and one of them was Dan. Something was troubling him. He'd arrived later than usual, haggard and with none of the adrenaline-pumped vigor he normally brought into court. He'd huddled longer with Mike diMaio than with Charlie Duncan, then sat almost passively through the expert's testimony. His cross took less than half an hour.

The other thing that disturbed her was probably the same thing that was troubling Dan: something in the way the money moved didn't make sense.

Jenny leaned back to stare at her summary on the computer screen. The cursor blinked at her, four beats to the second, and still she stared. She pulled out her notes and checked them again, then flipped to her copy of the auditor's report and made the same check.

The realization hit Jenny, and with it, a thought so awful she would not even include it in her notes. Scott had gone to great lengths to conceal the fact that the funds deposited into Mason's account came from the trust account. Yet the amounts of each deposit matched to the penny the amounts of the checks drawn on the trust account.

If he were trying so hard to conceal the flow of money from the trust to Mason, why didn't he change the amounts of the check deposits to Mason?

"How goes the war?" spoke a voice, and Jenny looked up to see the rotund frame of Walter Boenning in the doorway.

"Oh, hi, Walt." Although lawyers of his generation were computer-illiterate, she immediately blanked her screen. "Well, it still goes. I'm sketching out my notes for Cassie vonBerg."

"She called me today to tell me how pleased she is with your work."

"How nice."

The compliment was doubly pleasing. Jenny had raised more than a few eyebrows when her pregnancy became evident. There'd been some grumbling among the older lawyers, but Walt was making it clear his voice was not among them.

"I think we can anticipate a lot of fees from this representation," he said. "The suit against Curtis Mason should be a major piece of litigation. And this open-ended research you're doing on Macoal— that could be a real cash cow."

Jenny lifted a shoulder in a noncommittal shrug.

"Well, keep up the good work," he said, his voice going into a hearty boom. "We want our relationship with this client to be well cemented."

"I'll do my best."

Marilyn appeared beside him in the doorway and Jenny looked to her expectantly, but it was her other boss she came for. "Mr. Boenning," she said hoarsely, "they're waiting for you."

Jenny gave her a quizzical look. Her eyes were rimmed red; something was wrong.

Boenning turned at once down the corridor, and Marilyn started to retreat to her desk.

Jenny rose from her chair. "Marilyn?"

Marilyn stopped without turning back and stood undecided a moment before she came back into Jenny's office and closed the door.

"What's wrong?"

"They're forcing him out!" she cried, and clapped both hands over her face.

"How can they do that? He's a partner."

"It's the new mandatory retirement," she choked out. "Mr. Boenning was supposed to be grandfathered out of it; he's been lobbying for votes, but he couldn't get enough. All these young partners." She gave a scornful sniff. "All they can think about is the size of their distribution check this year. They don't think back to who brought in the clients in the first place, and they don't think ahead to where the clients are going to come from down the road. Mr. Boenning devoted his life to this firm, and this is the thanks he gets!"

"Maybe he'll enjoy retirement," Jenny said. "Maybe it'll be good for him."

"Oh, no," Marilyn said, her red eyes going wide. "He'll never retire. He says he only feels alive when he's practicing law. If he tried to stop, he'd die within the year." Her voice turned ugly in bitterness. "A fat lot they care about that!"

"So what will he do?"

"He might start his own practice."

"Solo?" Jenny looked askance. A solo law practice had the well-deserved reputation as being the fastest route to bankruptcy, malpractice, or both.

"Maybe a small firm." Marilyn gave her a sly glance. "Maybe you'd go with him."

Jenny shook her head. "I've already switched firms once. I'm not doing it again." She had a sudden horrible thought. "Would you go with him?"

Marilyn dried her eyes and stood up. "Of course," she said, as if Jenny were foolish to ask.

233

*   *   *

Scott's father called again after dinner that night, and while they spoke, Jenny went outside to admire the flowers before the sun set. The roses had been plagued by Japanese beetles, and although she dusted them regularly, they were eaten through, the buds destroyed before they could even open.

She wandered through the grove to the meadows that were now half-acre lots bearing houses in varying stages of completion. The dirt-packed loop of road would soon be Canterbury Lane, the major thoroughfare into the subdivision. The houses were fieldstone and stucco, big and built to look bigger, with two-story entries that the realtor described as lawyer foyers. Another house had been sold since she'd last walked the loop, and the Sold sign was triumphantly displayed in the newly seeded lawn.

The glow of lamplight spilled from the carriage-house windows when she came back, and she could see Scott pacing in the living room with the phone to his ear. She dropped to the grass and leaned on one elbow to watch him. The house was like an open-air theater and Scott an actor in the spotlights. But the play was one Jenny couldn't seem to follow anymore. She gave up trying and lay flat on her back to watch the stars come out.

Miniature hands and feet stirred inside. Jenny smiled and spread her hands over her belly in an embryonic hug. It moved again, pressing a foot or maybe a buttock against the left side of Jenny's abdomen. She pressed her hand against the spot, and the movement came again, acknowledging her reply. Her hand moved to the right and pressed, and was rewarded by an answering kick over there. She laughed silently, but not to herself.

She no longer thought of the baby as a symbol of her broken heart or as contraband stolen from Dan. It was no longer Dan's baby, or even her own. It was simply itself, and she loved it completely, without a particle of concern that this love might also be unrequited.

Scott hung up the phone and started moving from window to window in search of her. She rose from the grass and brushed herself off and went inside. They stretched out in the living room for an hour of television, mindless entertainment but engaging enough that no sideline conversation was required. But after they

224

turned off the lights and started up the stairs for bed, the question Jenny had pent up all evening broke free.

"There's something I can't figure out," she said. "How come you made the deposits into Mason's account in the same amount as the checks drawn on the trust account? I mean, that would've been a road map for Mason if he were paying attention."

"I don't know," Scott said. "Maybe Casella was right. Maybe I did have a subconscious urge to get caught."

Jenny opened her bedroom door. The answer did not satisfy her, but she would not press further.

"No, I remember," he said suddenly. "It was because I didn't want a penny of that money sticking to me. If I wrote Uncle Curt's check for a smaller amount, then some of the trust money would still be in my account. And even if I made it up on the next check, there'd be interest to account for. So that's why. At least I think so. To tell the truth, it's hard to know what I was thinking when all that was going on."

Jenny nodded. There was nothing rational about what he did during those months; there was no reason to expect flawless precision in the way he did it.

He took her in his arms for a good-night kiss, one that had become routine and expected yet always ended with the same unspoken question.

"Good night," she whispered, and he gave a resigned smile, accepting the disappointment once again.

She closed the door behind her, and it was Dan's face she saw, and the words he spoke in her memory gave her something new and more awful to worry about. "He's gotten major infusions of cash into his bank account," he'd said. "Untraceable cash."

7

THE BUILDING SECURITY WAS ON ALERT, AND COPIES OF TONY'S LAST school picture were taped to the dash of fifty police squad cars. Dan went from the courthouse to his car Thursday afternoon and spent the night cruising every backwater he could think of. But by eleven o'clock, there was still no sign. It was more than twenty-four hours. The second night was starting, and God knew where Tony was going to spend it.

The car phone rang and Dan grabbed for it so fast the tire ran up over the curb. But it was only Mike, checking in.

Dan exploded. "Christ, Mike, what are your guys doing out there? How long does it take to find one kid?"

"About as long as he wants it to take, I'd say."

That could be forever.

"Listen, give it up for tonight," Mike was saying. "Our guys are watchin' for him, and you got another big day tomorrow."

"Yeah."

He parked in the garage and stopped at the security desk again in the lobby, but the answer was the same as always. "We'll keep our eyes peeled, Mr. Casella, don't you worry."

There was nothing more he could do. He went into his apartment, poured himself a drink, and settled in to greet oblivion.

Dan's head shattered at the explosive sound of the telephone. He'd nodded off with his head on the table beside it. He grabbed it and shouted, "Yeah!"

There was silence on the line, and during the span of it, all of his senses came alert.

"Tony?"

Another silence, then a catch of breath it took him a second to recognize as the uptake of a sob.

"Tony, where are you? Are you hurt?"

"No," he choked.

Dan went limp with relief. "Tell me where you are."

"I don't know," he whispered. "I'm in a house. It's in Manayunk, I think. I wanna leave, but they won't let me!"

Dan's relief ended abruptly. *Who*, he wanted to yell, but instead he said, "Where? Tony, where's the house?"

"I don't know! I think they said Manayunk. It's in a block of old rowhouses. The windows are all busted out, there's a bar across the street, but I don't know—"

"Tony, okay, take a breath." Dan got to his feet and stood straight and tense. "Look around you. Tell me what you see. Are you at a window?"

"No, I'm in a closet. I don't want them to hear—"

"What's the name of the bar? Try to remember."

Long moments passed with only the sound of Tony's labored breathing, until he burst out, "The Bullfrog! It's got a big green frog on the sign."

"I'll find it. You stay put, hear me? *I'll be there.*"

Dan dialed an operator and got a listing for the Bullfrog Tavern in Manayunk, then punched the number for the bar.

"We're closed," a gravelly voice informed him when he asked for the street address.

"I'm planning ahead," Dan said testily. "Just tell me where you are."

Grudgingly the address was imparted: 303 Mill Street.

Tony was alive, and Dan knew where he was. He repeated those two thoughts as he raced to the garage for his car. It was raining when he emerged from underground, and he switched on the wipers, but it was another two blocks before he remembered his headlights. He reached the expressway and floored the accelerator. The last thing he needed was to get pulled over now, with blood-shot eyes and liquor on his breath, but he pushed the car to seventy, then eighty.

He reached Manayunk in fifteen minutes and got off the highway and started to cruise the streets. But this wasn't his turf. It was an old working-class neighborhood crowded on a jumble of hills on the eastern banks of the Schuylkill River. Its main street had been gentrified, but at this hour, the trendy shops and restaurants were closed, and the BMWs had all dispersed to Center City or the suburbs.

It was hard to read the street signs through the rain, and he panicked when he realized it could take him all night to find Mill Street. He left the business district and steered away from the nicer neighborhoods. When he hit the worst part of town, he started looking for signs of life.

He found it. Three young toughs stood ducking raindrops under an overpass. They eyed the Jaguar as Dan pulled up to the curb next to them. He lowered the window, and when he held out a twenty-dollar bill, one of them swaggered up to the car.

"We ain't dealin', man," he said in a tone that invited further negotiation.

Dan added another twenty. "Point me to The Bullfrog on Mill Street."

"Ain't nothin' happenin' there," he cackled, reaching for the bills.

Dan snatched them back. "The directions."

"Right at the light. Down the hill till you can't go no farther; turn left," he said, and this time when he grabbed for the money, Dan released it.

He followed the directions, and in minutes he was there, on a block that held the ruins of an old mill on one side of the street and the grimy stone rowhouses once occupied by the millworkers on the other. The Bullfrog was at the end of the block. Dan parked in front of it and scanned the houses across the street.

The windows are busted out, Tony said, and one house fit the bill, a three-story house, one room wide, with broken panes and loose shutters and a front door, hanging from one hinge, that was only propped shut. A van with blacked-out windows was parked at the curb.

Dan grabbed the penlight from the glovebox and dashed through the rain to the porch. He strained to listen for sounds of life inside, but couldn't hear anything through the pounding of the rain on the porch roof. Carefully, he gripped the doorknob and lifted up and in at the same time. The one operating hinge gave a groan, and he froze, but the same roar of rainfall that kept him from hearing also kept him from being heard.

He stepped inside and switched on the penlight. The stairs climbed in front of him; to the right was a trash-strewn room with no furniture but a shredded mattress on the floor. He started up the stairs, and halfway up, he caught the sound of snoring. He followed it to a doorway and shielded the light just in time to keep it from shining on the two bodies that lay entangled on a mattress on the floor. One was male—not Tony—and one was female.

Across the hall was another room, and he moved to it with his hand cupped over the end of the light so that it cast only the faintest illumination, barely enough to stop him from tripping over the body that lay across the threshold. There were no mattresses here, but the floor was covered with bodies. One of them sat up.

Dan's heart was pounding in time with the rainfall, but he took away his hand and shone the light that way. Tony's white face loomed out of the darkness.

Dan turned the light to his own face and put his finger to his lips, then stepped over the body in the doorway and held a hand out. Tony grabbed tight with cold fingers and got to his feet.

"What the hell," a voice spoke, and the lights went on in the room.

A man leaned against the doorjamb, greasy-haired, with a straggly beard and vacant eyes Dan had seen before. The bodies on the floor stirred, and half a dozen teenaged boys sat up.

Tony made a noise in his throat, and Dan pushed him behind him.

"Tony, you goin' somewhere?" the man said.

Dan recognized the face from the mug shot—Joey Ricci, a small-time hood running a gang of boys like a modern-day Fagin. The female from his bed came up behind him; she was a pasty-skinned girl scarcely older than Tony.

"Sorry to wake you," Dan said. "We'll get out of here so you can all get back to sleep."

Ricci's vacant eyes fixed on Dan. He gave a signal, and the boys got to their feet and closed in a circle around them.

"Tony, Tony," Ricci said, still staring at Dan. "You let us down, man."

"Just let me go home, Joey," Tony pleaded.

"You know I can't do that. Wouldn't be fair to the other guys—would it, boys?—if I let you skip out owin' me money."

"What's this?" Dan cut in.

Ricci smirked. "Tony had some property of mine a while back. He owes me for it. Either he pays up or he works it off. That's the way it works around here, right, guys?"

The boys in the room were watching sharply. Something more than the dispute with Tony was going on here.

"I remember that property," Dan said. "I'm the one who ended up with it, so it's me who owes you for it. And you're right, I need to settle up."

Ricci thrust his chin out. "Five hundred bucks."

Dan shrugged. "Fair enough." He opened his wallet and pulled out a check.

"Dan—" Tony whispered.

"Sssh," Dan said and scribbled rapidly across the face of it. He handed it to Ricci and thrust his hands in his pockets.

Ricci's eyes flickered as he read it. He looked up at Dan, then stepped aside. "See?" he said to the boys. "All I ask is that I get what I'm entitled to." He gestured to Dan and Tony. "Go on, get out of here."

Dan grabbed Tony by the elbow, steered him past Ricci, down the stairs, and out door into the rain. Tony pulled free when he spotted the car, and he broke into a run for it.

Dan slid behind the wheel. "Are you all right?"

Tony turned his face to the window where rivulets of rainwater streamed down. "I wanna go home," he said raggedly.

The word was ambiguous under their circumstances, but now was not the time to debate it. Dan started the engine and pulled out of Mill Street with a spray of water gushing from the tires. He raced through the empty streets of Manayunk to the expressway ramp, where he stepped hard on the gas to merge with the traffic. It was three A.M. and still the traffic moved thick along the dark ribbon of highway.

Suddenly Dan threw on his right-turn signal and rocked to a stop on the shoulder of the highway. A car swerved around them with a wail of its horn, and he pushed the emergency flasher on.

Tony spun from the window. "What are you doing?"

"We're not going anywhere until I get some answers."

"I don't know anything."

Dan turned the ignition off.

"I can't tell you!"

He leaned back against the headrest.

Tony's eyes moved in all directions. The rain pounded on the roof of the car. To the left lay four lanes of highway, to the right a steep face of rock. The traffic rushed past, high-pitched, then low, in eerie Doppler effect.

"His name's Joey Ricci," he burst out. "He's the guy who gave us the guns."

"Start over."

"A guy at school, my old school, he knew Joey from the neighborhood," he said in a rush. "He took me to meet him. Joey said, 'You wanna make a few bucks?' I said, 'Sure.' I never thought about it—you know, what you said about guns?"

"Yeah, I know."

"I sold a bunch, like I told you. I was supposed to turn all the money over to Joey—he paid me out of it. But that last gun, the one you took—"

"I remember."

"The other day? I went back to the old hangout to look up some of the guys, and Joey was there, and he brought me out here and said I wasn't goin' anywhere. And as soon as I could, I called you."

"When you got mugged at school last winter," Dan said. "It was Ricci?"

"Don't tell Mike!" he blurted. "If Joey finds out, he'll *kill* me next time."

"He's going to jail, Tony; he won't be able to hurt you or anybody else. We have to tell Mike."

Tony set his jaw and turned to stare through the water sluicing over the windshield. He shook his head.

The traffic continued to stream past them. In a few more minutes, a cop might pull up with the lights on and demand some I.D.

Dan laid his hand on the back of the boy's neck and gave it a squeeze. "Tony," he said more softly, "I won't let him hurt you."

There was a long silence before, at last, Tony nodded.

His head sank back against the seat and his eyes closed as Dan dialed Mike's number, and by the time the call was done, he was half asleep.

"I'm sorry about the other day," he mumbled drowsily. "I wanted to make a scene, I guess."

"Forget it."

"I'll pay you back all the money you gave to Joey, I swear it."

Dan grinned, almost tempted to say "forget it" again. "I didn't give him any money."

"But—"

"I wrote him a little note is all."

Tony sat up, his eyes suddenly wide. "What'd it say?"

" 'I've got a beeper in my pocket that'll bring the cops here in ninety seconds. Or you can let us go right now.' "

The boy's eyes went wider yet, and it was a full minute before he said, "That's the coolest thing I ever heard."

"Listen," Dan said. "You gotta promise me you're through with him and his kind. No more running with that crowd, ever. You got that?"

"I promise," Tony said, and there was a yawn in his voice. "Let's just go home, okay?"

This time there was no ambiguity. Dan started the engine, and headed the car for home.

8

DAN WAS THE FIRST ONE IN THE COURTROOM FRIDAY MORNING. TWO hours of sleep felt like ten, and he was primed for battle today. "Morning, Bob," he called when Perlman came in with his client, and to Mason's obvious annoyance, Dan engaged Perlman in two minutes' worth of banter and gossip.

Mike arrived later and gave him a thumbs-up, and Dan crossed the room and ducked his head. "You found Ricci?" he whispered.

"State troopers picked him up in his van on the turnpike. We're throwing the book at him. Aggravated assault on Tony, statutory rape on the girl—he'll probably give up his supplier before noon. How's the kid?"

"He'll probably sleep till noon, but he's good. When this is all over—" Dan nodded toward the jury box. "We're gonna get away for a few days. Maybe go down to the shore."

"Good idea," Mike said.

Dan listened for a hint of criticism or at least reservation, but there was none, nor did Mike bring up the idea that Tony should come home now. Maybe last night's reconciliation with Tony meant the family was reconciled to the situation, too. He clapped Mike on the shoulder and returned to his seat.

The rear door opened and Brian Kearney came tentatively into the courtroom. He was an affable, Tom Sawyerish young man, with curly red hair and a smattering of freckles and a demeanor that would make any little old lady happy to turn her life savings over to him. Dan gave him a wave, but it was Jerry Shuster who strode to the door and led him to the plaintiff's side of the courtroom.

The next time the door opened, Jennifer Lodge came through. The sight of her was a cold reminder, and Dan felt it through the length of his body. For half a minute, he'd deluded himself into believing he had his personal problems licked, but seeing her again was enough to convince him that he hadn't even begun. It was driving him crazy, her abiding presence in the courtroom. The first day he might have chalked up to curiosity, maybe even the second, but now she'd given up a full work week. It was strong evidence of her devotion to Sterling, though he hardly required more: nothing could be stronger evidence than the baby she was carrying.

When the jury was in place, Jerry Shuster rose for the first time and called Kearney to the stand. Dan sent a sharp look across the aisle, but Bob Perlman was clear-eyed and straight-backed. Shuster wasn't pinch-hitting—this was a calculated move.

With military precision, Shuster established that Kearney was a registered representative of Connolly and Company and that he handled the separate accounts of Curtis Mason and Curtis Mason, Trustee. Kearney explained that the accounts in question were what Connolly called its X accounts—X standing for ECS, Extra Convenience and Service—which could hold both cash and securities and offered check-writing privileges.

Shuster handed up exhibits and did so with sufficient awkwardness that the jury would not forget that he was newly one-armed. Kearney identified the account-opening forms and the initial account statements. One of the statements was blown up on posterboard, and Shuster led Kearney through an explanation of each of the entries.

"Who made the investment decisions in these accounts?"

"Mr. Mason at first. Scott Sterling later on."

Copies of the trading authorizations were marked: P-62, authorizing Scott Sterling to trade in the trust account, and P-63, authorizing him to trade in Mason's personal account.

"Was any trading conducted in Mr. Mason's account after he gave Sterling the authorization?"

"I'll say," Kearney replied, and somebody on the jury tittered.

"Describe how it took place."

"Scott Sterling would call me and place the orders. He named the security and the number of shares and said buy or sell. Sometimes he said sell if it hits 97, or buy if it drops below 80. But mostly just buy a hundred, sell fifty, you know."

"Did he ever ask for your advice or recommendations?"

"He had his mind made up before he picked up the phone."

"Did you ever try to talk him out of a trade?"

"Yep. I mean, geez, I used to scratch my head sometimes, wondering if he was trying to lose money or something. But he'd say, 'Brian, I got a program here; I gotta stick to it.' "

"His program lost money, didn't it?"

"It sure did."

Shuster put a chart of the deposits into Mason's account on the easel. Kearney matched each line item with an entry on the account statements, and confirmed that each was a check deposit received into Mason's account.

"Were you reviewing the account statements on a regular basis?"

"On Mr. Mason's account, at least once a week, since the trading was so active."

"What did you think when you saw these checks coming into Mr. Mason's account?"

"I thought he was trying to shore up the account and hopefully turn around some of his losses."

"Did you know where these checks were coming from?"

"No. All that shows up on my screen is what you've got on that chart there."

"You didn't see the checks as they came into Mason's account?"

"No," Kearney said, and an explanation followed as to X account check-clearing procedures. "The clearing bank holds onto the checks, and its computer tells our computer what accounts to credit or debit," he summed up.

"So nobody ever got canceled checks back?"

"No."

"Mr. Kearney," Dan began when the jury was back in the box after the recess, "you say you tried to talk Sterling out of some of the trades he directed you to make?"

"Yes, I did."

"Because you pegged them as losers?"

"I sure did."

234

"Did you warn Mr. Mason?"

"No."

"Why not?"

"He was getting his account statements every month. He could see the losses as easy as me. He said he wanted to let Scott prove himself, and I figured this was his way of doing it."

"Wait a minute—back up. You said Mr. Mason was getting his account statements every month?"

"Sure."

"I thought Scott Sterling was getting them."

"He was getting duplicates. We put a duplicate flag on an account when you get a trading authorization in there."

The Connolly internal forms directing duplicate statements were marked. Dan picked up one of the monthly account statements from the stack already marked on the exhibit table.

"Let's take a look at December, for example. Do any trading losses appear on this statement?"

"Yep," Kearney answered and then pointed out the purchase of two thousand shares of Xenon on December 6 at ninety-eight, and their sale on December 20 at eighty-three, for a loss of thirty thousand dollars in the span of two weeks.

"Did Mr. Mason ever call you? To ask about these losses on his statement?"

"He called me, but not about any losses."

"What did he call about?"

"To challenge the value on the Macoal stock in the trust account."

"When was that?"

Kearney chewed his lip. "It was after the Macoal stock split—could I look at the trust statements?"

Dan handed him the stack of papers, and Kearney flipped through them until he found the one he wanted. "Yeah, here it is. Macoal did a split in November, and it showed up on the month-end statement. Mr. Mason didn't think we had the shares priced right, and he called me about it."

"How did Mr. Mason know how you priced them?"

"It was on this, here." The exhibit flapped in his hand.

"That's the November account statement for the trust?"

"Right."

"But wait a minute, didn't the trust statements go to Scott Sterling?"

"Yeah, and the duplicates went to Mr. Mason. There was a flag on this account, too."

"When Mr. Mason called you to question the Macoal share value, would he have received both the trust statement and his own?"

"Should have. I know for sure he had the trust statement, because he referred to it when we were haggling over the share prices."

"Let's take a closer look at the November statement for the trust account."

Dan turned around, and his eyes moved past Curtis Mason, who sat with his shoulders hunched, glowering. His paralegal pulled the cover off the posterboard blow-up of the statement and handed it to Dan to place on the easel.

"Is this the Macoal value you discussed with Mr. Mason?" he asked, pointing.

"That's it. And that's the entry he called me about."

"And what exactly was Mr. Mason's question?"

"We showed the shares priced after split at fifty and he thought it should have been forty-nine and a quarter."

"A difference of three-quarters of a penny."

"Correct."

"Take a look at the entry directly below that one."

Dan moved the sheet of transparent colored plastic to highlight the check entry on the next date.

"That shows a check written on the account," Kearney said.

"Payable to?" Dan prompted him as the pointer moved over the words.

"Cash."

"Amount?"

"$249,875."

"On the date this check was drawn, was there a cash balance of $249,875 in the trust account?"

"No."

"Then how was the check funded?"

"It was an automatic borrowing from Connolly using the securities in the account as collateral."

"Do you charge interest on the funds advanced?"

"Sure. That's margin interest, and it shows up here." He pointed to a box on the statement.

"Let me see if I understand this," Dan said, moving back to the easel. "As of November thirtieth, the trust account had paid more than ten thousand dollars in margin interest?"

"Yes."

"Did that set off any alarms in your shop?"

"Yeah, our compliance people picked it up. An account this size shouldn't be running this kind of interest."

Dan marked two new exhibits and handed up one.

"Yeah," Kearney said. "This is the form letter that our compliance department sent to Scott Sterling, advising him of the unusually high interest accruing, and inviting him to call to discuss how to avoid those charges."

"Did he call?"

"No," Kearney said, and snickered.

Dan handed up the next exhibit.

"Oh, yeah," Kearney said. "I forgot about this."

"What is it?"

"The same letter, only it went to Mr. Mason. Because of the duplicate flag on the account."

"Did Mr. Mason call to discuss how to avoid the margin interest charges in the trust account?"

"No."

"Did Mr. Mason ask you anything about the check for $249,875?"

"Nothing."

"Did he ever ask you anything about the check deposit for $249,875 that showed up in his account that same month?"

"No. He never did."

9

SCOTT PROWLED THROUGH THE HOUSE SATURDAY MORNING, PACING from window to window and peering out each as if he were expecting the U.S. marshal to have the place surrounded. Jenny watched him anxiously from the breakfast table. Last night, he'd received a call from Jerry Shuster, advising him that he would be summoned to appear at trial in compliance with his subpoena, probably as soon as Wednesday.

"Call Bill Lawson," she urged him, as she'd already urged him the night before.

"What's the point?" Scott said, turning from the window. "He knows I've been subpoenaed. He even gave me the magic language for taking the Fifth."

"The point is you might feel better if he's in the courtroom with you."

But Scott shook his head. "At a thousand bucks on his meter? I'll manage without." His gaze softened. "As long as you'll be there."

"I'll be there," she assured him.

She rose to clear the table, and he followed after her to the sink and wrapped his arms around her from behind. "I wish you didn't have to go to the office today."

"After being in court all week, I must have a foot-high stack of work piled up."

He rested his chin on the top of her head. "Do me a favor tomorrow, then?"

"What?"

"Go to church with me?"

She turned slowly out of his arms. In three months as housemates, he'd never mentioned church before. No—he did, once—on the bridle path to the stable, he whispered, "I always felt like I was coming into church."

"If you like," she said.

"I'd like it a lot."

Dan arrived early at his office Saturday morning and plunged into work. He'd promised Tony lunch out and an afternoon showing of *Die Hard 3*, and he had five hours of work to finish first. The paralegal had shepherded the movement of all the document boxes back from the courthouse, and now they were stacked around the perimeter of Dan's office. He found the box labeled "Witness Kits," and pulled out two three-ring binders, one marked "Curtis Mason" and one "Scott Sterling."

Mason would probably take the stand Monday morning. Perlman's direct examination would certainly consume a day, but on the remote chance that it didn't, Dan had to be ready to launch into his cross-examination. He was the kind of lawyer who worked without notes but never went into a courtroom without them. They were like the net under a trapeze; he performed better knowing they were there.

He sat at his desk and opened the Mason binder. Inside was a fifty-page synopsis of Mason's five-hundred-page deposition transcript, followed by copies of the key documents Dan expected to question him about. Still to go in the binder was his outline for the cross-examination, and it was that outline he had to complete today.

The two bound volumes of Mason's deposition lay before him on the desk, a hundred Post-Its flagging pages he needed to revisit. Beside them was a pile of exhibits and charts, and behind that was his tape player, already loaded with the cassette of Sterling's calls.

He picked up the Sterling binder and flipped through the few pages inside. There was no deposition summary, because he'd never given one. Bob Perlman had made some noises early in the case about serving Sterling with a deposition subpoena, but he didn't pursue the idea after Bill Lawson made it clear that Sterling would take the Fifth. There was an outline, one Dan had drafted weeks ago when he still hoped Sterling might testify, useless now.

Behind the last tab in the Sterling binder was a memorandum to the file, headed "What Really Happened"—Dan's extemporaneous musings on the case dictated on a long-ago night in January while the snow swirled outside and Jennifer gazed at him with the shine of tears in her eyes.

Abruptly, he shook his head. It was no good remembering that night. He gulped down his coffee, rolled up his sleeves, and got to work.

Two blocks away, Jenny was sorting through her own stack of documents. She'd requested a database search on Jack Stengel, and the results lay in a three-inch ream on top of her desk.

Much of it was old news. He'd gained notoriety in the eighties as a take-over artist, and there were a hundred newspaper accounts of the standard aftermath: factories closed, equipment sold, workers laid off in one-plant towns. Market analysts and social critics alike included Stengel's name in their list of people to blame for America's decline. Meanwhile, *Architectural Digest* and *Town & Country* paid homage to him and his lavish estates and glittering parties. The photographs captured him as Jenny had met him, tuxedoed and flashing a million-dollar smile.

Recent articles reported a change in his tactics. The eighties were over; he'd suffered some setbacks; a Democrat was in the White House. Stengel was scouting new opportunities, and all of them lay in the Pacific Rim. He'd hired a corps of Asian advisors—a lawyer, a financial analyst, even a cultural guide—and was participating in a dozen joint ventures with a dozen different Far Eastern companies. None of his recent activities fit with a current interest in Macoal.

But Macoal was still an attractive target, Jenny concluded after studying Cynthia Lehmann's preliminary report. Its stock was drastically undervalued, probably a deliberate maneuver designed to keep any renegade family members from selling, but it was also a strategy that made the company ripe for take-over.

At noon, Jenny left the office for lunch. She went to the Summerhouse, a gourmet cafeteria that served Evian with its cheeseburgers and was a favorite haunt of Center City workers who liked to lunch amid the hanging ferns and pretend they were further away than a half a block and thirty stories from the office.

She got in line with a tray and watched the man behind the counter slap her sandwich together, then paid the cashier and carried her tray to the condiment table.

Suddenly her pulse changed, and she knew before she looked up that Dan was near. Her gaze swept the restaurant until she found him in the sandwich line. The baby gave a kick, and Jenny shrank behind the soda machine. She could see only his back, but that was all she'd seen for a week, and she'd know him anywhere, even dressed in khakis and a sports shirt as he was today.

He bent his head to speak, and it was then Jenny saw the boy beside him.

Her eyes went wide. The resemblance was so strong she would have known him anywhere too, even without Dan beside him. He loaded his tray with two sandwiches and an order of fries, and trailed after Dan to the cash register, nibbling at his fries while Dan opened his wallet and peeled out the bills. She stood stunned, staring openly at this younger version of Dan while the baby flipped over in her womb.

Dan picked up his tray and turned from the cashier. He stopped when he saw her, and the boy nearly stumbled into his back.

"Hi."

It was the first friendly syllable she'd heard from him in months. "Hi," she echoed.

The boy came out from behind him with a question on his face. "Jennifer, this is my brother Tony. Tony, Jennifer Lodge."

"Your brother," she repeated.

"Jennifer used to work with me," Dan said.

The boy's gaze hadn't moved from her belly. "You a lawyer?" he asked, disbelieving.

Dan jabbed an elbow in his ribs. "Come join us," he said to Jenny.

She found herself nodding and following after them. They sorted out chairs, Jenny on one side and Dan and the boy on the other.

"Do you live in the area, Tony?" she asked.

His mouth was already full, and Dan answered for him. "He lives with me."

It was true, then. She'd been wrong about the make-believe brother, and maybe that wasn't all she'd been wrong about.

She couldn't form words to speak to Dan. She turned instead to Tony. "Where do you go to school?"

Tony answered himself this time, though still chewing. "Alexander."

"I went to Alexander!" She glanced at Dan and remembered the day he'd asked her opinion of the school. "Tell me," she said, leaning toward Tony, "is Miss Claybell still there?"

Tony laughed so abruptly he sputtered. "Did you have her? God, what an old walrus! What about Mr. Diehl? Did you have him?"

Jenny giggled. "Did you ever see them stand face to face in the hallway?" Tony hooted and pounded the table. She turned to Dan to explain. "Miss Claybell is built like the prow of a ship, with about a sixty-inch bustline. And Mr. Diehl—"

"—has a gut the diameter of the earth!"

"And when they stand together, they look like two pieces of a jigsaw puzzle fitting together!"

Dan smiled, but more at the sight of Jennifer and Tony laughing together than at the image of the two teachers. He'd imagined this scene once, the three of them sharing a meal together. Jennifer asked Tony about the new gym, and that topic led into school sports, good for another ten minutes of conversation while they ate. She was wearing a shapeless tent of a dress that exposed bare arms plumper than before, and her hair had grown out enough to pull back into the old familiar ponytail. She looked beautiful to him.

"How about some dessert?" Dan said after Tony wolfed down both sandwiches.

"Jennifer?" the boy asked, jumping to his feet. "You want anything?"

"My friends call me Jenny," she said. "And no thanks. I've had enough."

She watched him fall into line at the counter, and when she turned back to the table, Dan was watching her.

"I never knew that," he said.

"What?"

"That your friends call you Jenny. All this time I've been thinking of you as Jennifer."

Tears welled in her eyes, and she picked up her drink and turned to look across the cafeteria at Tony. "What a nice boy."

"He's all right."

"I thought you made him up," she whispered.

There was a beat of confused silence. "What?"

"When you said your life was complicated—" She broke off, still gazing across the restaurant but feeling Dan's eyes on her. "You remember, back in January? You said your time wasn't your own?"

"Yeah?"

"I thought—there was another woman."

"Oh, God, Jennifer." A second later he said, "Jenny."

She shook her head wordlessly. Tony hadn't reached the counter yet; they had a few more minutes, but there was nothing more she could think of to say.

"I'm sorry I lit into you in court the other day," he said. "It was just that—I don't know—"

"No, I'm the one who's sorry," she said, blinking away the tears as she turned back to him. "I lied to you. I'm not just a spectator.

I represent Catherine Chapman vonBerg. I'm gathering ammunition for a breach of trust suit against Mason."

Dan fell back in his chair. Tony was headed to the table with a dish of ice cream in his hands, and Dan couldn't think fast enough to know whether this was good news or bad. It meant she wasn't in court for Sterling's sake, but she wasn't there for Dan's, either. It meant Mason might be sued for breach of trust, but too late to do any good for H&M.

Tony started to sit down and Dan pulled the dish from him. "Why don't you get yourself some?" he said with a wink.

Tony heaved a put-upon sigh and turned back to the counter. "Has Scott gotten the call yet?"

"Last night," Jenny said. "From Jerry Shuster. He said they expect to call him Wednesday."

"Sounds right," Dan said.

"You're doing a great job," she said. "It makes me wish I were up there with you."

"I wish you were with me, too."

Her throat burned and she pushed back her chair and rose on unsteady feet. "I—I'd better get back to work."

Dan got up, too, and they were both standing beside the table when Tony returned.

"It was so nice meeting you," she said in a rush to Tony. "Dan, good to see you again."

She held out her hand and he took it and held it. "Keep in touch," he said before she finally pulled her hand free and turned to go.

Tony sat down and shoveled a spoonful of ice cream into his mouth. "Old girlfriend, huh?"

10

CURTIS MASON'S POSTURE HAD BETRAYED HIM ALL THROUGH THE first week of trial, and there was no disguising his anger and disgust by the time he placed his hand on the Bible Monday morning.

"Mr. Mason," Bob Perlman said when the preliminaries were done. "The jury has seen you exhibit some pretty strong emotions during this trial. Why is that?"

Smart move, Dan thought once more. *Get it out and over with.*

"I've never been anybody's patsy," Mason said. "I ran a major corporation. I employed two thousand people right here in the Philadelphia area. I went head to head with some of the craftiest players in the business and never came out on the short end of a deal."

"And now?"

"And now I've been made a fool of by a boy whose nose I used to wipe."

"That boy now being the man named Scott Sterling."

"That's him."

"Tell the jury how you know Scott Sterling."

In her back-row seat, Jenny stopped taking notes and listened closely. Scott never spoke of Mason, and yet he'd once called him uncle and craved his approval so much that all this had resulted. She wondered that Scott didn't feel his loss more, and guessed that there were simply too many other losses competing for his attention.

Mason told of his old friendship with Edgar Sterling, and that of their wives, the two childless couples seeking out each other's company over the years, the Masons' vicarious delight when Scott was born. They vacationed together at Bar Harbor every summer, and as the only youngster among them, Scott came in for a good share of everyone's attention, Mason's included.

When Scott was about twelve or thirteen, they developed a special relationship. By then, it was apparent that Scott and Edgar didn't get along. Edgar behaved as if Scott was a disappointment to him, but to Mason's eye, he was a fine lad. He sought out his Uncle Curt often for advice, conversation, sometimes just a moment's attention.

Scott wrote him long letters when he was away at school, full of the kinds of doubts and worries Mason imagined he'd never reveal to his father. Mason picked up the phone now and then, gave the boy a few pointers on how to get on in the real world. One of Scott's biggest doubts was how he'd do in the business career he was destined for, and Mason told him if he didn't want to go into

244

business he could always become a lawyer. Scott took that advice, finished law school, and was hired by H&M. He got busy with his own life, and Mason didn't hear as much from him, not until the spring of last year.

When Mason described the party at the Sterlings' country house in Chester Springs, Jenny could picture it as if she were there. Flaming torches lined the walks, tuxedoed waiters swept through the crowd with circular trays balanced on white-gloved hands, music played from an unseen orchestra, and a faint woodsy, horsy scent drifted out of the darkness beyond the circle of light. She could picture Scott, golden and charmed, smiling at the guests while trying to catch his father's eye for one second amid all the festivities.

Mason was in the billiard room, watching a game in progress and talking about the sailing that season. Scott came in to say hello, and offered his condolences on Doody's death. Mason asked about his practice, and Scott told him he was in estates, and working hard for his partnership election the next year.

That might have been the end of it, except that Edgar chose that moment to step into the room.

"Father!" Scotty called out. "I wanted to tell you about—"

But Edgar turned on his heel and walked out.

Scotty left soon afterward, but Mason couldn't forget the look on his face. It nagged at him for the next hour or so, and finally he went looking for Scott.

He found him alone on a garden bench, nursing a drink while he listened to the orchestra. Mason sat down beside him and told him about Doody's trust and asked him to handle it.

"Did he accept?"

"He did."

Mason recounted Scott's eagerness to take over the mundane tasks that cropped up in the trust, and Mason's growing reliance on him. Scott's role expanded little by little until Mason trusted him with virtually every aspect of the account.

"Did you give him the trust account checkbooks?"

"Yes, of course!" Mason declared. "He agreed to make the disbursements and pay the bills, and the easiest way to do that was to write a Connolly check. Well, it's no different from what a bank trust officer does, and that's what Scott was by this point, a trust officer."

"Did you make him a signatory on the account?"

"I guess that's the way you're supposed to do it," he admitted, grudgingly. "But it was just a piece of bureaucratic red tape as far as I was concerned. So I told him to go ahead and sign my name on the checks. It was no big deal. Saved me some time and trouble was all."

"Did you have any concerns about Sterling writing these checks?"

"If the bills didn't get paid, I would've heard about it. If Catherine or Reese didn't get their checks on time, I would've heard about it. So the answer's no, I wasn't concerned in the least. Scotty gave me no cause to worry. Everything he did only made me trust him more."

"And did you ultimately trust him with more?"

"Yes, I trusted him with my own personal trading account."

Although almost all of Mason's net worth was tied up in the family corporation, he did maintain a small trading account at Connolly. Scott had a real passion for the market, and from time to time Mason asked him his view of certain securities or strategies. The boy never gave an off-the-cuff response like a lot of market honchos who got by on gut instinct. He always said, "Let me look into that and run out some scenarios." The next day, he'd call back with an answer that sounded right on the money to Mason.

Scott began to sketch out some hypothetical portfolios showing how different strategies would have yielded bigger profits. One day Mason said, "How'd you like to do that for real, for me?" He liquidated the account, left a cash balance of a hundred thousand dollars, and signed a trading authorization in favor of Scott.

Judge Steuben cut Mason off and announced the lunch recess. The parties and their lawyers lingered long enough to allow the jurors to claim the first round of elevators, and Jenny remained even longer as she tried to condense a morning's testimony into five minutes of hastily scribbled notes.

Something puzzled her again. Scott was a stockmarket genius, Mason said—he loved to follow it, even just on paper. Scott made the same claim during his confession to H&M in January. Yet in their four months together, Jenny never once saw him pick up the *Wall Street Journal*. One more thing he wanted to forget, she supposed.

Trial resumed for the afternoon session with everyone back in their places and Curtis Mason on the witness stand. "You're still under oath," Steuben droned, a routine recitation, but Mason threw him a look of hot indignation.

"Tell the jury about the trades Sterling made in your Connolly account," Perlman prompted.

Scott directed the trades from that point on, Mason explained. He placed the orders with Kearney and usually called afterward to report what he'd done and why. He was very specific in those calls, always detailing the exact number of shares bought or sold, the exact price per share. Later when he started to close out positions, he read the profit figures to Mason over the telephone, again to the penny. The results were astounding.

It was true those results were not always reflected on the Connolly statements, but Scott explained that the brokerage was having computer problems. This was no great surprise to Mason, who'd had a few tangles with banks over their statement errors in the past. As far as that went, he'd tangled with Connolly over the Macoal per share values, and Kearney finally admitted their computer had made the goof. Scotty was keeping his own records, and Mason was confident he'd straighten everything out with Connolly.

"Did you ever have occasion to tape-record any of your conversations with Sterling?"

"I did, several of them."

"Why?"

"I was so proud of Scotty, I wanted my wife Dorrie to hear how well he was doing. She loved him, too, you realize. So I sometimes hit the Record button on our answering machine, and then I could play the conversation back later to Dorrie."

"Did you tell Scott Sterling you were recording him?"

"No. I didn't want to embarrass the boy. It would be like videotaping his first date or something."

"Did you record the conversations on your answering machine at your home in Devon?"

"Mostly, yes. But we also had a machine at our summer house up in Maine, and one of the conversations was taped there."

"How did you discover that the tapes still existed?"

"I flew home immediately after Mr. Casella's call, and after I finished talking to you that night, Bob, I sat staring at the telephone a while, trying to understand what in God's name had happened and remembering all the things Scott told me about my profits. Then I remembered the answering machine, and I wondered if any of those recordings might still be there. So I rewound it to the beginning and played it back. And sure enough, there they were."

"What about the conversation in Maine?"

"Yes, well, it occurred to me the same thing might have happened there. So I called the caretaker and told him to take out the cassette and FedEx it to me the next day."

"How many conversations in total are recorded?"

"Nine."

"Are those all the telephone conversations you had with him during this time period?"

"Oh, good Lord, no. But these were the only ones I recorded."

"Why not record them all?"

"Sometimes I wasn't at home, or I was at a different phone, not the one hooked up to the machine. Or sometimes I just forgot to push the right button. So I ended up with just these nine on tape."

"Mr. Mason, in a few minutes the jury will hear those tapes for themselves, but let me ask you this now. Did you record your conversations with Scott Sterling because you were suspicious of him?"

"No, of course not."

"Did you record them because you had any doubts about what he was telling you?"

"None at all. I was proud of a young man who was the closest thing I'd ever have to a son, and I wanted to share my joy with my wife, and that is all."

11

SCOTT'S VOICE FILLED THE COURTROOM AFTER THE MIDAFTERNOON recess. The tapes were played from start to finish, with everyone following from a written transcript of the nine separate conversations from September to January. The jurors' interest was pitched higher than any other point so far. They were clutching the first document they'd been permitted to see, and for the first time they were hearing the voice of Scott Sterling.

"I really want to do a good job for you, Uncle Curt."

"I know that, Scotty. I appreciate it."

"You don't know how much this matters to me. This is the first chance I've ever had to show what I can do, and I'll never forget who gave it to me."

His eager voice didn't slip once in any of the calls.

Perlman concluded his examination at the end of the day, and court adjourned. Jenny returned to her office to check her messages and to organize her notes. A brisk knock sounded on her door, and Jenny looked up to see Walter Boenning beaming at her.

"Thought I'd find you here," he said. "How's the trial going?"

"Mason testified today."

"Already?"

"At last," Jenny said. "He's been chomping at the bit all week."

But Boenning wasn't interested in the play-by-play. He had other news to impart. "I had dinner last night with Marvin Glasser."

The name meant nothing to Jenny, and she shook her head.

"You've never heard of him? He has an impressive Wall Street practice. Represents the big players all over the world. Including Jack Stengel."

Jenny's polite gaze went sharp. "How'd you happen to have dinner with him?"

"He called yesterday, said he'd be in town and we ought to get together."

"Why?"

"Stengel's been talking business with Catherine vonBerg, he

says. He understands we represent her and thought we ought to get to know each other."

Jenny leaned back in her chair, unconcerned for once with how her belly swelled before her. "Walt, I wouldn't advise Cassie to do any business with Jack Stengel."

"Why is that?"

"He's a looter and plunderer. He tears through these companies and doesn't leave anything standing behind him."

"He was hardly alone in that strategy. That's the way business was done in the last decade."

"I know, but—"

"Jennifer, we're Catherine's lawyers, not her business advisors," Boenning said. "She decides the deals, and we put them together."

"I know. But it's our duty to see that she makes an informed decision."

He nodded deliberatively. "Why don't you send me a memo if you see any clearcut danger signals? Then we can look into it together and decide what's best. How's that?"

The message was received. She was not to say anything negative to Cassie about Jack Stengel without Boenning's prior approval.

"I'll certainly do my duty," she said.

His eyes narrowed only a bit as he gave her a parting smile. If he'd received her message as well, he wasn't showing any signs of it.

Alone, she wondered why she'd even bothered sparring with him. His days in the firm were numbered; there was no reason for her to worry about him. But neither was there reason for him to care about what deals Cassie did with Stengel, because he wouldn't be in the firm to do them.

Unless he didn't intend to do them in the firm.

12

TUESDAY MARKED THE EIGHTH DAY OF TRIAL, AND FAMILIARITY WAS breeding expectation that the proceedings would continue as before. If something happened once, it was routine; if it happened twice, it was law. The jurors took the same seats every day, though Steuben did not require it; the lawyers and parties kept to their places as if they'd been assigned; the spectators were the same every day: the bodyguard, the detective, and Jenny.

So when the rear door to the courtroom opened after everyone but judge and jury was already in his appointed site, the heads whipped back like they were on pivots.

"What are you doing here?" Curtis Mason snapped.

It was Reese Chapman, blinking behind his glasses as he registered Mason's rancor. He wore a pale blue jacket over white trousers and whiter bucks, and he carried a leather satchel on a strap over his shoulder, altogether a different look from every navy blue–suited man in the room.

"Time to show the flag," I thought," he murmured, and pushed his hair off his forehead.

Mason shook his head disparagingly and turned away as the door to the jury room opened and the jurors marched single-file into the courtroom. Chapman moved into the row in front of Jenny, and he gave her a gentle smile before taking his seat.

"All rise," the deputy announced, and as Steuben took the bench and completed the preliminaries, Dan rose to the podium and waited. After a beat, Mason got up and returned to the witness stand.

"Let's go back to the night of the Sterlings' party in May of last year."

Mason sat with his legs crossed, his shoulders hunched, and his body angled a full ninety degrees away from Dan. "I wish I could go back," he snarled. "I wouldn't make the same mistake twice, I'll tell you that."

"You followed Scott out of the house and through the garden until you found him sitting on a bench, is that right?"

"Right."

"What did you say to him?"

"As I said," Mason grated, giving the jury the glare he meant for Dan, "I told him I was trustee of Doody's trust, and how would he like to handle it for me."

"What was his response?"

"As I said," Mason repeated, the words squeezed out through teeth clenched even tighter. "He accepted."

"What was his *first* response?"

Dan reached for the bound volume of Mason's deposition testimony, and Mason saw where he was headed.

"All right, he pretended to decline at first. He made it look good."

"What reason did he give for declining?"

"Wasn't Dickinson Barlow handling it already, he didn't want to cut him out, and so forth and so on."

"Dickinson Barlow *was* handling it, wasn't he?"

"Up to that point. Doody was barely cold, I might remind you."

"In fact, Mr. Barlow handles all your own estate work."

"He does."

"But you wanted a hands-on, day-to-day manager for your sister's trust."

"I wanted someone reliable."

"Read the question," Dan said, and the court reporter stopped and pulled out his tape and droned out the last question.

"Yes, all right," Mason replied this time.

"You considered the day-to-day management of the trust to be nonsense, didn't you, Mr. Mason?"

His face going deep red, Mason thundered, "I most certainly did not!"

"Approach the witness, Your Honor?" Dan said and handed Mason a copy of his deposition. "You remember I took your deposition last spring?"

"Yes."

"And there was a court reporter there taking down your testimony, and you swore to tell the truth, you remember that?"

"As I always do."

"Page two-forty-three," Dan said across the aisle to Perlman. "Mr. Mason, you remember I asked you, quote, And you weren't willing to handle the day-to-day management of the trust, unquote. Is that correct? And you replied, quote, Christ, I don't have time for that kind of nonsense, unquote. You remember that, Mr. Mason?"

"No."

"But you see it there in the transcript, don't you, and you see your own signature on the last page, attesting that the transcript is accurate, right?"

"I see it."

"So were you lying then, or are you lying now?"

"Objection!" Perlman called.

"Permissible impeachment, overruled."

"Neither time," Mason said. "By nonsense, I just meant more work than I had time for. I hire people to take care of things like that."

"And Scott Sterling was the one you chose to take care of the trust?"

"Right."

"And he turned you down."

"It was an act! He knew I'd insist."

"So Scott turned you down, but you insisted he do it."

Mason shook his head at the jury. "It wasn't like that."

"At any rate, you hired him to pay the bills and make the disbursements."

"Yes."

"You gave him the trust account checkbooks."

"That was the easiest way."

"Why did you give him a trading authorization in the trust account?"

"The trust was almost fully invested. From time to time, cash had to be generated to make the disbursements. That meant selling securities out of the account. I had to give him authority to do that."

Dan picked up the exhibit marked as P-62. "And you did that by signing this form."

"That's a standard Connolly form. They use it all the time."

"Is all of it a standard form?"

Mason took the document from him and scanned it. "Well, no. I added a clause."

"The one that reads 'Provided that Sterling shall have no authority to trade with respect to any shares of Macoal Corporation'?"

"That's it."

"You didn't want Scott selling off any shares of your family company, is that right?"

"Right."

"Because majority control of Macoal was critical to you?"

253

"It still is."

"And you weren't about to risk that."

"Of course not."

"But you were willing to risk everything else in the trust by turning it over to Scott?"

Mason sucked in his breath. "There was no risk as far as I knew. I trusted him completely."

"Then why carve out the Macoal shares?"

"I told you."

"Because you weren't willing to risk them?"

"Yes."

"So Scott Sterling must have presented some risk, right, Mr. Mason?"

"I was just being prudent! That's what a trustee is supposed to be!"

"But prudent as to only one asset in the trust? And coincidentally the only one that impacted on your own net worth?"

Mason set his jaw. "I was prudent as to everything in the trust, Mr. Casella."

"The trading authorization enabled Scott to sell enough securities to raise cash to make the trust disbursements, is that what you said earlier?"

"Yes."

"But it wasn't necessary to sell out positions. Cash could have been raised in the account by borrowing on margin from the brokerage house, isn't that right?"

"Sure, but those brokers charge an arm and leg on margin interest. There was a ten-million-dollar corpus in Doody's trust. There was no reason to run up double-digit interest."

From her seat in the back, Jenny sneaked a glance at Reese Chapman. He was listening impassively, his expression giving no clue that he understood a word of the dialogue, and Jenny thought once again of the improbability of Cassie's description of him as a stock market genius.

"So Scott wasn't authorized to borrow on margin?" Dan asked Mason.

"Certainly not."

"How'd you react when you got the monthly trust account statements and you saw the margin interest figures running up?"

"I never looked at that. That was Scott's job."

"How'd you react when you got the letter from Connolly and Company warning about the margin interest accrual?"

"Again, it was Scott's job to watch for those things."

"Let me see if I follow. It was Scott's job to catch himself doing something you hadn't authorized?"

"I didn't go into this assuming he'd make unauthorized transactions! I trusted him to do the right thing!"

The morning's testimony continued in that manner. The more Dan pressed Mason, the more fractious Mason became, and the more self-serving his speeches. Perlman rose to object a few times but gave up after it became apparent that Mason preferred to register his own objections in the guise of answering the questions. Mason's voice was growing hoarse by the end of the morning, and he gave the judge a grateful glance when at last the lunch recess was announced.

He descended from the witness stand, and Dan left the podium and tossed his notes onto counsel table. The lawyers and parties stood at attention as the jury began to file out of the courtroom. Reese Chapman gave Jenny a flustered look as she rose, and he hurried to his feet as well.

Mason and his lawyers and bodyguard walked out soon after the jury was gone, and Dan huddled a moment with Mike diMaio before he left with Charlie Duncan. Jenny sat down to finish her notes, and when she stood up again she saw that Chapman still lingered.

"Fascinating place, isn't it?" he said, his eyes sweeping through the room. "Just imagine the history this room is invested with. Oh, not this particular room, of course," he added when Jenny gave him a confused look. "I mean our whole Anglo-American system of justice. For good or evil, a lot of drama has been played out in courtrooms like this one. The idea of it truly gives one pause."

Jenny murmured vague words of agreement and decided to let him pause on his own. When she left, he was still in his seat, gazing in wonder around the room.

13

"LET ME ASK YOU THIS, MR. MASON," DAN began in the afternoon session. Everyone was back in his place but Reese Chapman, who probably decided he'd shown the flag enough. "If Scott alone was responsible for watching what went on in the trust account, why'd you study the November statement so carefully? And call the broker to complain about the Macoal share price?"

"I've been responsible for Macoal for most of my life. I wasn't about to abdicate that. But that's all I looked at in the trust. Scott was responsible for everything else."

"Including borrowing against the Macoal shares to raise cash?"

"I told you I didn't know about that."

"Let's look at that November statement."

The paralegal came forward with the posterboard blow-up and balanced it on the easel.

"Save yourself some time," Mason said. "I watched you do this routine with Kearney. The simple answer is I looked at the Macoal price and nothing else."

"You didn't look at the check entry for $249,875?" Dan pointed. "Directly below the Macoal entry?"

"I see it now," Mason said, lips stretched back tight. "But I'm telling you I didn't see it then."

"You homed in on three-quarters of a penny here, and missed a quarter of a million dollars right below it?"

"Believe what you want, Casella! I'm telling you I didn't see it."

Steuben picked up his gavel, but at a flick of Dan's eyes, he laid it down again.

"You did see an entry for the same amount on your personal account statement, didn't you?"

Mason squinted at him, not following.

"Let's take a look at that statement, for the month of November."

"Another blow-up was propped on the easel, and Mason's brow furrowed as he studied it.

"Credit, local check, $249,875," Dan read, highlighting the entry. "See that, Mr. Mason?"

"Yes."

"What did you think that was?"

"Just what Scott told me. Trading profits."

"Mr. Mason, you've traded in the stock market for thirty years. When did you ever see trading profits paid into an account by means of local check?"

"I never focused on it."

Dan turned to the bench. "Your Honor, I'd like to replay a portion of the tape we heard yesterday."

Perlman was on his feet. "What portion?"

"You played the whole thing yourself yesterday, Mr. Perlman," Steuben said. "You can hardly object to a partial replay today."

Dan nodded to his paralegal to switch on the machine. The voices came into the courtroom.

"Scotty, my boy. I just got my statement from Connolly."

"Looks good, doesn't it?"

"Good? Son, I've never seen results like this. Two hundred forty-nine thousand, eight seventy-five. Outstanding!"

The tape stopped and Dan fixed a level stare at Mason.

"I never put it together with the trust!" Mason declared. "What more can I tell you?"

Dan paused, turned some pages, looked at the jury, and back at the witness. "You can tell me why you secretly tape-recorded Scott Sterling."

"Good God!" Mason exploded. "I explained that! It was so Dorrie could listen. I didn't even know I still had the tapes until all this broke."

"You found out fast, though, didn't you? In less than twenty-four hours you managed to fly back from Florida, hire Mr. Perlman over there, and put your hands on these tapes. Oh, and get another one express-shipped down from Maine."

"I'd just been told my sister's trust was missing two million dollars and you people were looking to me to replace it. You're darn right I acted fast."

"Where'd the two million go? Anybody end up with it but you, Mr. Mason?"

"Your Honor." Perlman was on his feet, a pained expression on his face. "This badgering has gone on long enough. Now it's pure harassment."

"Sustained."

Dan turned a page in his notes, ready to move on.

But Mason wasn't willing to give up as easily. "I'll tell you where the two million went—into Scott Sterling's bank account, that's where! The only reason he moved it into my account later was to cover up his lies on my trading profits."

"Yeah, let's talk about those profits. Scott told you how much you were making?"

"To the penny."

"But his numbers didn't match up with the Connolly statements, did they?"

"Or vice versa."

"And his numbers didn't match up with the 1099 tax form you got from Connolly. The 1099 showed that you *lost* money in the Connolly account, didn't it?"

"I don't know; I never looked at it. I send all that stuff to my accountant."

"But Scott's numbers showed a profit—a two-thousand-percent return on your money in just three months—is that right?"

"I haven't done the math."

"Let's do it now."

Dan went to the chalkboard and scrawled out two million divided by a hundred thousand equals twenty equals two thousand percent. "Let's annualize that," he said, and scrawled out times four.

"Eight thousand percent a year," Dan said. He looked to the jury, people with passbook accounts paying two percent if they were lucky.

"That's what he told me," Mason insisted.

"You assumed the Connolly statements were wrong, because they didn't match up with Scott's numbers?"

"That's right."

"How'd you know?"

Mason turned and gave him a blank look. "What's that supposed to mean?"

"How'd you know they didn't match? You had Connolly's statement in front of you, but you didn't have any statements from Scott, did you?"

"No, but he told me—"

"Detailed numbers, to the penny, right?"

"Yes."

"How'd you remember those detailed numbers when you sat down to match them up with the statements?"

"Well, I—"

"You didn't keep any notes, you told us that already in your deposition. How do you know what numbers Scott told you? You don't have any statements, any notes, nothing—"

"For God's sake!" Mason screamed. "I had it on tape, didn't I?"

Dan let the silence grow long enough for Mason's words to echo. "So that was your record. Your secretly recorded and carefully preserved tape recordings."

"No!"

"No more questions."

14

SCOTT HAD THE NIGHTMARE AGAIN THAT NIGHT, THE SAME ONE AS always, but familiarity was not hardening him—he woke up in a cold sweat every time.

He came downstairs wearing a suit for the first time in months. Jenny pretended to wolf-whistle at him, but his smile was weak. His hand shook as he lifted his coffee cup.

"This is the day," he said.

"No, it's not," Jenny said. "Your day comes later. All you have to do today is get through it without damaging the criminal case. Do you have your cheat sheet?"

Scott reached into his breast pocket and pulled out the folded page. " 'I respectfully decline to answer on grounds that my answer may tend to incriminate me,' " he recited. "I'm really supposed to read this thing?"

"There's no reason to add to your stress by trying to memorize it."

"Will I be able to see you?"

"I'll be in my usual seat."

"Sit closer to the front today."

"Scott! You'll do fine. Now stop worrying."

He sat back like a sullen child and nibbled at his toast. "Tell me again what Uncle Curt said yesterday."

She'd relived it too many times already—once to Scott when she got home, again to Cassie over the telephone, and even to Walter Boenning, who put in an unexpected late-night call for an update. She got up and moved behind him to massage his shoulders. "Try to relax. Just read your answer and you'll be done by noon."

"I'll be done forever, that's what worries me."

Dan watched them walk into the courtroom like two scared kids being marched to a shotgun wedding. Mike leaned over the back of his chair. "What's she doin' with him?"

Dan glanced away. "They keep company."

"But I thought she usta work for you."

"How do you think they met?"

The judge's deputy entered from the front of the courtroom. "Gentlemen," she said once, and again, to be heard over the voices. "The judge wants to see counsel in his chambers before we begin this morning."

Steuben was at his desk in shirtsleeves when the three lawyers trooped in. He waved them into the chairs that formed a semicircle in front of him.

"Here it is Wednesday already," he said without preamble. "The eighth day of trial, and we're not even into the defense case yet. I've got a criminal case starting Monday, and I've got a preliminary injunction motion scheduled for Friday. So where are we? How much longer, Bob?"

"We call our last witness this morning," Perlman said with satisfaction.

"Sterling?"

"Right, and he'll be over before noon."

"You're sure he's going to take the Fifth?"

"His lawyer told me so again last night."

Steuben turned to Dan. "How long's the defense case?"

"I've got two witnesses. Both experts." One was an expert on law-firm management to testify that H&M enforced reasonable supervisory procedures over its associates. The other was a stockmarket expert to testify that nothing could have earned Mason the miraculous rate of return he was claiming.

"That's a day apiece," the judge complained.

"I would've been happy to start sooner," Dan said, baiting Perlman.

"It's your marathon crosses that slow things down," Perlman shot back.

Steuben stood and raised a hand to end the spat. "Let's just keep it moving, shall we, gentlemen?"

"Plaintiff calls Scott Sterling."

The jurors shifted in their seats, leaned forward, buzzed to one another. At last, the witness they'd been waiting for. Their necks craned in search of him, and when he stood up and started for the front of the room, their murmurs swelled. So handsome, so wholesome-looking. And that pretty pregnant girl they'd been wondering about? She must be his wife!

Perlman and Shuster made no effort to conceal their own curiosity. This was their first Sterling sighting, too. Beside them, Mason sat with hooded eyes.

Jenny watched Scott approach the witness stand and knew he felt the stares of everyone in the room. She remembered another time when he'd been the focus of so many watchers—in the H&M conference room in January. She was appalled then at how he seemed to preen under the unaccustomed attention, unaware of how much trouble he was in. He wasn't preening anymore.

"Do you swear to tell the truth, the whole truth, and nothing but the truth?"

"I do."

Perlman rose to the podium in a posture of righteousness. He worked from a written outline this time. Because he wouldn't be getting any answers, he could make his record only by asking the right questions.

"You are the Scott Sterling who was once employed at Harding & McMann?"

"That's me," Scott said, ducking his head toward the microphone.

"Isn't it true that you were fired from the firm last January?"

"Yes."

"Isn't it true that you were fired after confessing to the theft of two million dollars from the Elizabeth Mason Chapman Testamentary Trust?"

Scott's hand moved, and Jenny waited for him to pull the sheet of paper from his breast pocket. But instead his hand closed on the microphone to pull it closer to his mouth. "Yes, sir, I'm afraid that's true."

She bit her lip. Perlman stopped, his eyes frozen on the script Scott had failed to follow. For the first time in the entire trial, Dan broke form and whipped around to look at Jenny. She shook her head at him.

Judge Steuben sent a puzzled look at both counsel tables and leaned toward the witness stand. "Mr. Sterling, you may decline to answer questions that might incriminate you. You're aware of that?"

"Yes, sir. But I swore to tell the whole truth, and that's what I want to do."

The judge turned back to counsel and raised his eyebrows.

"A moment, please, Your Honor," Perlman said and left the podium to huddle with Shuster. Frantically, Jenny tried to catch Scott's eye, but when he finally looked her way, he only smiled.

Perlman returned to the podium with new vigor.

"So you admit that you stole the money from the trust?"

"I can't deny it," Scott said. "Maybe *stole* isn't the right word, though. I mean, I didn't keep any of it. It was all for Uncle Curt."

"It was all to conceal your lies to Mr. Mason, isn't that right?"

"Yes, sir. At least—it was all to conceal his trading losses. That was the important thing."

"Because if he saw those losses, he'd know you'd been lying to him about his profits, right?"

Scott started to nod, but caught himself and chewed his lip for a minute. "Well, I'm not sure. All I was thinking was that I couldn't let Uncle Curt see the losses."

Perlman gave the jury an exasperated look. "Well, why not?"

"Because that was the one thing he said over and over to me. 'Don't ever let me see any losses in this account. I don't care what else you do—just don't let me see any losses.' "

Perlman froze again as Mason barked something unintelligible to Shuster. Dan and Charlie Duncan went into a huddle at the same time. Scott was impassive, waiting for the next question.

"Your Honor, a sidebar conference?" Perlman asked.

Steuben nodded, unsurprised, and wheeled his chair to the far side of the bench. The court reporter lifted his machine and carried it to that side, away from the jury and the witness. The three lawyers grouped around him.

"Your Honor," Perlman whispered, "I was expecting him to take the Fifth."

"So you told me in chambers, Mr. Perlman," Steuben said. "But he didn't."

"This is unfair surprise," Perlman said. "I request a recess to allow me to take his deposition before this examination resumes."

"Plaintiff had his chance during discovery to take the deposition," Dan put in. "It was never scheduled."

"We knew he was taking the Fifth!"

"Looks like you knew wrong," the judge said.

"Your Honor, my case is built around him taking the privilege!"

"Mr. Perlman, I can hardly order him to refuse to testify."

"But I don't know what he's going to say! I have to take his deposition."

"Request denied, on two grounds: one, waiver; two, as I told you in chambers, I've got two other matters crowding up against the back of this one. There's no time for a recess."

"What am I supposed to do?"

"You've got a witness in the box. Examine him or let him go."

Perlman and Shuster stood whispering with their heads down another few minutes. Perlman returned to the podium and stared at Scott. He shook his head. "No further questions."

The jurors' eyes followed him back to counsel table. They were jolted, and annoyed.

"Mr. Casella?" Steuben said.

"I've got a few," Dan said, rising to his feet. "In fact, quite a few."

The jurors shifted in their seats, ready for the show to begin again.

He moved to the podium. "Tell the jury exactly what Mr. Mason said to you about losses in his account."

"Like I said," Scott said. "He didn't want to see any. He'd shut the account down if he ever saw a bad trade. I wasn't to let that happen."

"When did he tell you that?"

"When he first gave me the trading authorization. And maybe a half dozen times later over the next few months."

"Let's focus on those later times. What prompted him to bring up the subject of losses then?"

"I don't know," Scott said, shaking his head. "Nothing I could really put my finger on—"

"Think back, Mr. Sterling. Was there anything going on in the account on any of those occasions that would have prompted a discussion of trading losses?"

Scott shook his head helplessly.

"Let me hand you his account statements. Take a minute and flip through them; see if anything jars your recollection."

Scott gave an obedient nod and began to page through the documents. He hesitated on one page, went past it, then came back again. "Geez, I never noticed this before," he said.

"What's that?"

"One time when he really reamed me out about not wanting to see any losses? It was in November. I remember because when he called I thought he might be inviting me to Thanksgiving dinner. Instead, he just repeated all the things he'd said before about no losses better show up in his account."

Dan held his breath and asked the next question. "Were any trading losses reflected on the October account statement?"

"Yeah," Scott said, his head drooping. "I lost eighty-five thousand that month alone."

"Is that when you first told him there were problems with the Connolly computer?"

Jenny couldn't sit quietly any longer. She surged to her feet and drew Scott's eyes to her, along with the judge's and jury's. This time Scott shook his head at her, and with a small, firm gesture of his hand, waved her down into her seat.

"No," he said. "The first time that came up was the month before. And actually Uncle Curt said it to me."

"What did he say?"

"He said, 'This statement must be wrong, because I made money last month, right?' And I said, 'Right,' and he said, 'Connolly must have a screw-up in their computer. Get that straightened out.' "

"Did he say how?"

"Only that I should make sure the bottom line was right."

"Was this over the telephone?"

"Yes. Uncle Curt didn't like coming to my office. Almost all our conversations were on the phone."

"How often did you speak?"

"At least once a week."

"Over a period of how long?"

"Five months, about."

"Let's see," Dan said. "Every week for about five months? That would be about twenty conversations?"

Scott nodded. "At least."

"You're aware that Mr. Mason recorded nine of those conversations?"

Scott's chin trembled, and he took a breath to steady it. "I am now."

"But you're telling the jury there's about eleven conversations that were not taped?"

"That's right."

"And in one of those, Mr. Mason himself raised the idea of a computer glitch?"

"Objection, leading," Perlman said.

"This is cross-examination," Dan flared.

"Is it?" Perlman shot back.

"Overruled," Steuben said. "Answer the question."

"Yes, that's right," Scott said.

"Did you suspect Mr. Mason was recording your conversations?"

"No! I thought Uncle Curt trusted me! He always said he did."

"Did he ever say he was trusting you to take care of his sister's money?"

"Well, I do remember once he said he trusted me to do the right thing with the money in the trust."

"He did?" Dan sent a sharp look to Scott and shifted it to the jury box. "And what did you think he meant by that?"

"I don't know. To keep good accounts and stuff, I guess."

"But Connolly was doing that much, right?"

"Sure."

"When exactly did Mr. Mason tell you to do the right thing with the trust money?"

"I don't remember."

"What else did he say about the trust money?"

"Not that much, really."

Dan paused, waiting for inspiration that didn't come. He tried the same question again. "Try to remember everything he said to you about the money in the trust."

Scott squinted, and a long minute went by. "I remember once he talked about the size of the corpus. He said, 'All that money just sitting there idle until—'" Abruptly, Scott cut himself off.

"Until what?"

Scott squirmed in his seat, like a little boy forced to repeat a bad word. "Well, he said, 'Until that goddamned Reese Chapman dies.'"

A barely smothered roar sounded from the plaintiff's table.

"When did he say that? Was it the same time he said he didn't want to see any losses in his own account?"

"Yeah. Yeah, I think it was."

"Was it the same time he told you 'Make sure the bottom line is where it's supposed to be'?"

Scott's eyes suddenly went round. "I see what you're doing," he burst out. "But it wasn't like that. This whole thing was my idea, not Uncle Curt's!"

"Answer the question," Dan said, his voice rising. "Was it the same time Mr. Mason told you to make sure the bottom line of his own account was right, and that all the money in the trust was just sitting there until Mr. Chapman died, and that you should do the right thing with the trust money?"

"Yes, but he didn't mean it that way. He didn't mean he wanted me to do what I did!"

"Because it was all your own idea, right?"

"Yes!"

"And he never suspected a thing, right?"

"Right."

"Then why did he tape-record you?"

From the last row of the courtroom, Jenny could see Scott's eyes swimming in tears. She barely heard him whisper, "I don't know."

Dan sat down. "No further questions."

"Redirect, Mr. Perlman."

A long silence swelled up through the courtroom as Perlman sat and pondered. He stared at the witness box, and when Scott raised his sleeve to wipe the tears from his face, he rose to his feet.

"Nothing more."

"Next witness, then."

"Plaintiff rests, Your Honor."

"Defense ready, Mr. Casella?"

Dan had two witnesses a phone call away, and fifty pages of notes for their direct examinations. He had a portfolio case of stock performance charts, and he had Scott Sterling still weeping on the witness stand.

"Defense also rests, Your Honor."

Charlie Duncan gasped. Perlman turned and stared across the aisle.

"We'll take a short recess before closing arguments. Mr. Sterling, you are dismissed."

Scott climbed down from the witness box and started for the back of the courtroom. As he passed the plaintiff's table, Mason shot out of his chair and jabbed his finger into Scott's chest.

"I'll see you burn for this!" he screamed as the judge's gavel pounded and his lawyers tried to wrestle him into his seat. "I'll see you burn in hell!"

15

THE VICTORY PARTY AT HARDING & MCMANN BEGAN WITHIN AN hour after the jury came back. Dan accepted a glass of champagne but felt little cause for celebrating. He'd had barely a minute to savor the verdict before Mike diMaio clapped him on the back and said, "See, I knew you'd do my work for me. Now I can close my file."

"There's still a criminal case."

But Mike said, "Nah. We'd never get an indictment against Sterling. It's Mason oughtta go to jail."

Dan was flying blind when he cross-examined Sterling, but

somehow it played like they were reading from the same script. The jury was out thirty minutes, barely long enough to elect a foreman and take a show of hands around the table. Their verdict: Mason manipulated Sterling into making the transfers, and did it so masterfully Sterling still wasn't sure what happened.

Dan found Charlie Duncan in one of the conference rooms thrown open for the party. Already into his second bottle of champagne, Duncan was regaling his partners with an imitation of Perlman grappling with Mason at the end.

"I have to go," Dan said, taking him aside. "I'll talk to you later."

"You can't leave your own party!"

"This is your night, Charlie. Live it up."

Dan slumped against the wall of the elevator. He was accustomed to winning, but he'd lost enough cases in his career to know how defeat felt, and that's what it felt like today. He'd saved his client but ended up clearing Scott Sterling in the process. Now Sterling could get himself reinstated to the bar, open up his own practice with some underwriting from his old man, marry Jenny, and live happily ever after. All thanks to Dan.

He ought to be named best man and godfather both.

PART 4

JUDGMENT

1

A BLAST OF HOT AIR DROVE ACROSS THE HELIPAD AND SLAMMED into Jenny where she stood waiting. Her hair whipped around her face and her dress ballooned up until she had to turn and crouch against the force. Behind her was the Mercedes limousine and standing at attention beside it, Stengel's Amerasian chauffeur Moi, unmoved by the wind, and unmoving, like a Coldstream Guard.

The *whup-whup-whup* of blades sounded until the helicopter landed, and at last, the whine of the rotors ceased. The long graceful legs of Cassie vonBerg descended the stairs. Behind her, through the heat waves, appeared Jack Stengel.

Jenny finger-combed her hair as she waited for them at the edge of the tarmac. Stengel's arm was slipped comfortably around Cassie's waist. Cassie gave an exuberant wave.

"Hello, Jenny! Thanks for meeting me."

"A pleasure to see you again," Stengel said through his perfect smile, his hand outstretched six feet before he reached her.

"Mr. Stengel."

"Please. Call me Jack. We'll probably be seeing a lot of each other."

Cassie turned in Stengel's arms. "Jack, thanks so much for the lift."

"Prettiest hitchhiker I ever picked up." He bent his head to kiss her, and her fingers trailed along his back until they pulled apart. He gave a short wave to Jenny and strode across the tarmac to his limousine. The chauffeur dipped his head to speak with him, and they were still standing there when Jenny and Cassie drove out of the lot.

"What did he mean?" Jenny asked when they were on the road. "That we'll be seeing a lot of each other?"

"Oh, God," Cassie groaned happily, her head rolling back on the headrest. "He's got so many ideas, I hardly know where to start. First, Jack's putting together a consortium to develop offshore oil drilling in the Gulf of Tonkin."

"*Vietnam?*"

271

"Uh-huh. With Japanese partners. Jack has a bunch of them signed up as investors, and I could be in it with them."

"Using what for capital?"

"Well, for God's sake, I have ten million dollars."

"In trust," Jenny reminded her.

Cassie closed her eyes with a contented smile. "Not for long."

Macoal maintained a suburban office for Curtis Mason in his retirement, in one of five granite-and-glass buildings situated at haphazard angles in a manicured landscape. There was no door-man or security desk in the lobby, but a brass-lettered directory listed Mason's name among title insurance companies and CPA firms.

A throat cleared and Jenny turned to see Walter Boenning cross-ing the lobby. "Hello, ladies," he greeted them.

"Walt, what are you doing here?" Jenny asked.

"Catherine told me you were having this meeting today, and I thought I'd better join you." He fixed his full smile on Cassie. "Shall we?"

Cassie started up the sculptural staircase, but Jenny remained where she was and put a light restraining hand on Boenning's elbow.

"I don't think this is a good idea, Walt," she said in a low voice. "The last thing we want to do is get Mason's back up. If we go in there like gangbusters—"

Cassie turned back to see what the delay was, and was listening when Boenning cut Jenny off.

"I think I've had a bit more experience than you at dealing with men of Mason's stature." His courtly manners were still in evi-dence, but for the first time Jenny saw them for what they were: a smokescreen for the way he imposed his will on others.

He brushed past her up the stairs. Cassie was watching, so Jenny spoke coolly. "I recommend against this. If Mason feels cornered, he'll fight, and we'll be facing a couple years of litiga-tion. The only chance for his voluntary resignation is for me to do this alone."

Boenning continued up the staircase, ignoring her. Cassie looked at Jenny and shrugged; she didn't know who was right, or didn't care enough to fight about it. Tight-lipped, Jenny followed after them.

The reception area one flight up was hung with portraits of dead Masons. Cassie breezed past them without a glance and approached the desk where a gray-haired woman awaited them with an unwelcoming demeanor. The woman's mouth turned down when their names were given, and she disappeared at once into the inner office. A moment later she emerged, still frowning, and gestured them inside.

Mason rose behind his desk. An abstract sculpture chiseled from gleaming black anthracite stood on his desktop, homage to the origin of the family wealth.

"Cassie," he said, but his eyes were on Walter Boenning.

"Uncle Curtis." She came around the desk to peck him on the cheek. Though he inclined his head to receive it, he was seething. "This is Walter Boenning and Jennifer Lodge."

Boenning moved forward with his hand extended, but Mason turned away and pressed his intercom button. "Send him in," he snapped, and a side door opened and Robert Perlman stepped into the room.

"My lawyer, Bob Perlman. You see," he said, leering at Cassie, "I was prepared for this little stunt of yours."

"It's hardly a stunt." Cassie seated herself without waiting to be asked. "I'm a young woman with no business experience. I couldn't negotiate on my own with a veteran like you, Uncle Curtis."

"Negotiate what?" Perlman said. Everyone else took a seat, but he remained on his feet.

"Let's start with the fact that Mr. Mason has two million dollars of Catherine's money." Boenning leaned back in his chair and crossed his legs, a picture of casual confidence.

The cords in Mason's neck bulged out. "I had, you mean. Harding & McMann lost it, remember?"

"The jury thought otherwise," Boenning declared.

"There's still one point seven five million in your account," Jenny said.

Mason gave her no more than an irritated glance around the coal sculpture.

"We're taking an appeal," Perlman said. "That verdict won't stand."

"The trial was a fiasco," Mason grated. "Sterling was in cahoots with Casella—nothing could be clearer."

"We monitored the trial," Boenning said. "We reached a different conclusion. Our demand is that you immediately repay the money to the trust. If you win on appeal, you'll get that much back from Harding & McMann. But there's no reason for the trust to sit empty in the meantime."

"It's not empty," Mason retorted. "It's holding the biggest stake of Macoal stock around."

"That leads to the second demand," Boenning said. "Your immediate resignation as trustee."

Mason gave a snarl of a laugh, and wheeled his chair ninety degrees. The posture was familiar to Jenny; as in the witness box, he turned bodily away from anything that displeased him. She'd observed this about him, and other things as well. He could never admit to being wrong, and any suggestion that he'd breached his duties as trustee would only put him on the defensive. She'd planned so carefully how to avoid that reaction, and all for nothing. Between an arrogant superior and an indifferent client, her strategy was lost.

"Resign and pay the money, and we waive all claims," Boenning said. "Otherwise, we end up in court on a breach of trust suit."

Mason swung back and glared at Cassie. "I'll pay over the money. Period. But I'll never resign as long as the company shares are in the trust. No bank's trust department will look after that stock like I will."

"I'm not interested in a trust department, either," Cassie said. "I'm a big girl now, Uncle Curtis. I don't need a sitter anymore."

"You heard my offer, young lady. Take it or leave it."

"Then I have to leave it, I'm afraid."

She rose, and Boenning and Jenny stood with her.

"Hold on!" Mason's face went red. "You don't have a clue what you're in for if you sue me. You talk to Reese first. You'll find he has something to tell you."

"Tell me yourself if it's so important."

Mason hesitated and glanced at Perlman.

274

"I thought so," Cassie said scornfully. "Daddy and I have no secrets from each other. There's nothing you can tell me I don't already know."

"He's a screaming fag, did you know that?" Mason bellowed.

The room was suddenly full of noise and movement. Boenning wrenched the door open, Jenny shot a worried look to Cassie, Perlman was shouting for everyone to sit down, and in the midst of it all Cassie stood quietly. Slowly a smile formed on her classic features.

"If you mean he's gay, of course I know. But what's that got to do with my trust?"

"I'll tell you what," Mason snapped. "If you try to sue me, Reese's little secret won't be so secret anymore."

Cassie's eyebrows lifted. "Blackmail, Uncle Curtis? Are you looking to embarrass the family even more than you've already done?" Mason scowled furiously. "If I didn't already think you were unfit to manage my money, I would now." She turned to Boenning and Jenny. "I think we're done here. Shall we be off?"

Boenning held the door open.

"Wait," Mason said, on his feet behind his desk.

"As the saying goes," Cassie said, gliding through the door. "See you in court."

Together they descended the staircase to the lobby. Cassie pulled the pins out of her hair and shook it loose, and when they reached the car, she leaned against the hood and sighed.

"We'll have the complaint ready to file tomorrow," Boenning assured her.

But she shook her head. "Don't file it until you hear back from me. I have to talk to Daddy."

By the end of the day on Friday, Jenny had finished the complaint: *Catherine Chapman vonBerg v. Curtis Mason*. Breach of trust, self-dealing, failure to safeguard trust assets, fraud, every claim for relief Jenny could think of. *What, no antitrust conspiracy?* She remembered Dan baiting Perlman, and her heart pinched at the memory.

Marilyn hand-delivered the drafts between Jenny's office and Boenning's next door. Jenny was in his bad graces, thanks to her attempted mutiny yesterday. Nonetheless, the final draft came back with only one red-inked scrawl to mar it: "Fine."

The phone rang and Jenny picked up.

"Telegram for Ms. Jennifer Lodge," droned a man's voice.

"Speaking."

"Dinner eight tonight. Stop. Best restaurant in town. Stop."

Jenny rolled her eyes. "Hi, Scott."

"No, it says 'Signed, Scott.' And I'm supposed to wait for your reply."

Laughter spilled out of his voice. He was golden again, a different man from the one who dissolved on the witness stand two days before.

"I don't know, Scott."

"We have to celebrate. Come on!"

"I think you should lie low for a while. See how things turn out."

A dark tone of irritation crept into his voice. "Things have already turned out. You were there. Uncle Curt lost."

"Will you please stop calling him uncle?" Jenny snapped.

There was a silence on the other end of the line before he said, "Sorry."

She felt a stab of guilt. "No, I'm sorry."

"Please," he wheedled. "It doesn't have to be the *best* restaurant in town. Come on," he said when she didn't respond. "Don't rain on my parade."

She bit her lip. "Let's wait a little while, okay? Maybe next week. Any place you like."

"All right."

Her other line rang as soon as she hung up.

"Jenny, it's Cassie."

"What's the word?" she asked immediately. "Do we file or not?"

"Not. At least not yet. Daddy wants me to sit tight a little longer and see if Curtis doesn't weaken."

"Was he upset?"

Cassie sighed. "He feels so torn. He wants Curtis out for my sake, but he seems genuinely afraid of what he'll say. I don't understand it. It's the nineties, for God's sake, there's no stigma anymore. Besides, I'm the only one he cares about, and I've already told him it's fine with me. I don't understand," she said and sighed again. "But meanwhile, let's just wait, all right?"

"All right," Jenny said. Waiting seemed to be her principal occupation these days.

2

LATE MONDAY AFTERNOON, JENNY DROVE FROM THE OFFICE TO BRYN
Mawr Hospital. Scott wasn't there yet, and she was on edge as she
awaited her appointment. She'd been on edge for days, ever since
the trial ended, waiting for Mason's next move, and for Scott's. She
was waiting for Cassie vonBerg, too, who called again that morning only to say, "Not yet."

A technician with a clipboard beckoned her into the sonography
room, and she went behind the screen and changed into a hospital
gown. It would have been scant covering for her under any circumstances, but with her belly ballooning before her, there was no
hope of closing it in the back. She took a deep breath and sidled
into the examination room and didn't breathe again until she was
flat on her back on the table.

"So you're six months?" the woman asked, uninterested, only
making conversation while the preparations were underway.

"Thirty-one weeks." Jenny lay with her gown pushed up and
the drape pushed down. Her belly rose up like a Thanksgiving
turkey on a platter. Conversation held little appeal in this posture.

"Hard to wait, huh?"

Jenny gave a noncommittal murmur. It wasn't hard for her to
wait, because she wasn't nearly ready. Barely more than two
months left, and she didn't have a nursery or a house to put it in.
There were so many things to be done before the baby could be
born that she sometimes thought she'd have to pass on it altogether. Planning ahead more than a week at a time seemed an
impossibility, and she recognized Scott as the cause.

The door opened and he bounded in with a smile. "Made it," he
said, and he bent to kiss her first on the navel and then on the
mouth. "I've got the greatest news," he whispered, his lips grazing
on her ear.

Jenny felt exposed in his presence, and she tugged the drape a little higher. The procedure began, and he stepped out of the way and clasped her hand. He moved again when the image came into focus on the screen, and before she could crane her neck to see, he cried out, "There! I see it!"

An angry gorge of resentment rose in Jenny's throat. He didn't belong here; it wasn't his baby. She pushed him aside.

On the screen she saw a perfect, completely formed little baby. Tears spilled out over her cheeks, and her heart swelled so full she could barely breathe.

Scott squeezed her hand and exclaimed, "Jenny, it's beautiful!" The hospital staff smiled at his joy, despite having witnessed the same scene hundreds of times before. Scott was like that, contagious in his ebullience, but Jenny was immune to it now. She wanted Dan there, and wanted it so hard her heart ached.

"This is the best day of my life," Scott declared when the procedure was done. "Jenny, wait till you hear my news!"

But he had to wait to tell her because her bladder was bursting from all the water they'd forced her to drink and hold. Before she left the sanctity of the restroom, she splashed cold water on her tears, looked sternly at herself in the mirror, and reminded herself of Scott's thousand kindnesses, and of the long, lonely nights she would have suffered through without him. When she emerged at last, he stood waiting in the corridor and she gave him a bright smile.

"What news?" she asked immediately.

"My lawyer—Bill Lawson?—he met with the DA this morning, and that detective, you know—"

"DiMaio?"

"Right. Bill says they're closing the file on my case! It's over, and I'm in the clear!"

"Oh, Scott!"

"They said it looks like Uncle Curt manipulated me into what I did. Given that, and the fact that I didn't personally benefit, they're not charging me with anything!"

"Oh, Scott," she said again and took his hand happily as they left the hospital and started across the parking lot. "Will they go after Mason, do you think?"

"Nah. But Catherine has her civil remedies, and Uncle Curt has to resign from the trust."

"But he's not going to."

Scott's grin disappeared. He wheeled on her. "What?"

"We demanded his resignation Thursday. He turned us down flat."

He dropped her hand and reached to grab her arm. "Why didn't you tell me?"

"I—I don't know," she said, bewildered by his outburst.

But his thoughts had already raced ahead. "Listen," he said. "I've got an errand to run. You go on home, and I'll see you there later."

"Okay. I'll start dinner."

"I may not make it for dinner," he said, already heading for his car in the next row. "You go ahead and eat without me."

Jenny stared after him as he ran to his car and gunned it out of the parking lot.

There was a package on the doorstep when she arrived home, an eight-by-eleven padded mailer addressed to Scott. Packages had been arriving regularly with his legal papers, but this one held something hard and rectangular. Jenny put it in his room before she went to bed that night. She was asleep by the time he came home.

Cynthia Lehmann leapt out of a chair in the reception area when Jenny stepped off the elevator Tuesday morning. "You've got to see this," she said, and charged ahead to Jenny's office.

"What?"

Cynthia had her briefcase open and was pulling papers out onto Jenny's desk.

"There's been some funny trading activity in Macoal." Her long dark hair fell forward as she bent over the pages, and she flipped it back with an impatient toss of her head. "Look." Her index finger pointed through columns of dates and dollars. "Five hundred shares sold July tenth, another three hundred July thirtieth, two fifty on August eighth, and now another five hundred last week."

"Who's selling?"

"Word is it's some of the Mason cousins. There's gossip that Curt's reins are slipping."

"Who's buying?"

Cynthia whipped another paper out of her briefcase. "A dozen different corporations. And each one with an offshore charter."

Jenny met her gaze. "Stengel?"

"I've got one of the companies traced back to him, I'm sure of it."

Jenny's voice mail light was flashing, but she ignored it. "So he's making another raid," she said.

"It's got all the earmarks."

"What's the big attraction? Why's he so persistent?"

Cynthia shrugged and packed her papers back into her brief-case. "Because he was thwarted last year? Maybe he's turned it into a grudge match."

"Maybe." But Jenny didn't believe it. From everything she'd seen, money was Stengel's only motivator. "Thanks, Cynthia," she said. "Great work."

"Of course," Cynthia said with an unsmiling nod and left at once.

Jenny dialed into her voice mail. Two messages were waiting, the speakerphone announced. The first was from Walt Boenning early that morning, demanding to know if the complaint against Mason could be filed today.

The second came in Scott's cheerful voice. "Hi! Sorry about dinner last night. I forgot to ask my lawyer something, and I knew I'd be distracted until I talked to him. But it turned out to be nothing for us to worry about. So I'll see you at home tonight, okay?"

3

THE NEW ROAD, CANTERBURY LANE, WAS OPEN WHEN JENNY drove home from the office late that afternoon, and she took that route instead of the old road past the carriage house. A banner proclaimed the grand opening of the Estates at Dundee, and cascades of balloons floated from the brick pillars that marked the entrance. A family was already moving into the first house. Jenny watched a crib and highchair being unloaded in the drive-way, and thought how nice it would be to have another baby in the neighborhood, until she remembered that it wouldn't be her neighborhood much longer. The builder had served notice over the weekend: she had a month to vacate before the carriage house would come down.

Scott was at the door when she dragged herself, exhausted, from the car. "Bad day?" he asked, rubbing her shoulders.

"No, it just seemed endless."

"I've got a special evening planned," he said, eyes twinkling. "If you won't go out for a fine gourmet dinner, a fine gourmet dinner will come to you. Tell you what. Why don't you take a nap, then put on something pretty and come down?"

Jenny was happy to indulge him as far as the nap went. She trudged upstairs and lay wearily across the bed. She wondered about his special evening and hoped it meant something. Maybe he'd gotten a job, or maybe the final reconciliation with his father had come about. He'd been cleared, he was free, he could reclaim his life—and maybe so could she.

When she awoke, the windows were dark and a wonderful aroma was coming from downstairs. She felt a rush of fondness for Scott. A special occasion might be what they both needed. She showered and brushed her hair until it lay shining on her shoulders. When she slipped into a maternity dress of pale blue crepe, she felt nearly pretty.

Scott was at the stove when she came downstairs. The spoon froze in his hand. *"Très belle,"* he cried.

"Merci," she said, and dropped a mock curtsy.

"Allow me to show *mademoiselle* to her table." He snatched up a dish towel and folded it over his arm. "This way, *s'il vous plaît.*"

Puzzled, she followed his gesture to the door to the ballet studio. It was a room she'd neglected for months, and she couldn't imagine why Scott was leading her there now.

He threw the door open, and she gasped when she saw what he had done. The patio table was centered on the dance floor and set for dinner with a vase of red roses and tall white candles. Dozens more candles glowed in sparkling votives placed around the perimeter of the studio, and the reflections in the mirrors cast dazzling lights through the room.

"Scott, how beautiful! What a lot of trouble you've gone to."

"Never too much for you."

He pulled out her chair, poured her a club soda, and turned on the CD player. "I'll be right back."

A violin concerto flowed liquid through the valleys of the room, and the candles in the mirrors looked like a thousand bright white stars in the sky. Jenny sat alone and remembered another time when candles glowed like starlight in the mirrors and Dan made a bed of quilts on the floor.

She missed him, she longed for him. A few weeks before, she didn't know how she could bear his presence in the courtroom every day; now she didn't know how she could bear his absence.

Scott returned, wearing a blue blazer and carrying two china plates with the portions neatly arranged.

"Coquilles St. Jacques," he announced. "Steamed carrots, asparagus vinaigrette."

"What an ambitious menu! I'd never have the courage."

"I get all my courage from you," he said.

A soft breeze floated through the open windows. The trees outside in the grove stood in black silhouette against the deep blue sky. Jenny thought of the night she stood wrapped in Dan's arms while the snow fell and not a light penetrated through the trees; they could have been miles from anywhere, alone together.

"Jenny," Scott said.

She smiled up at him with overlit brightness.

"I've done a lot of thinking this week about where I go from here. I'm in the clear now. There's no more cloud over my name. In a year or two I'll get myself reinstated to the bar. I'll start a whole new life. And I want you to be a part of it."

She looked down at her plate.

"You know how much I love you," he said, leaning forward into the circle of candlelight on the table. "Think how happy we've been in these last few months. Now that the trouble's behind us, our life will be perfect. You've done so much for me, but now it's my turn to take care of you, and give the baby a name. Marry me, Jenny."

She put her hand over her mouth and held it there to keep from crying.

"Jenny?"

"Scott, I'm sorry; I can't."

"It was a good name, once," he said, stung.

"You know I don't care about things like that."

His face faded back from the candlelight. "What, then? You don't love me?" His tone was moving fast from sullen to angry.

"I do love you, Scott. It's just—"

His chair scraped back, and he passed through the shadows and reappeared in a glow of votive candles on the other side of the room.

"God, what a fool I've been!"

"No, Scott, it's not—"

"I should have known it was hopeless—meeting you in the middle of confessing I'm a liar and a thief. Talk about lousy first impressions." He let out a strangled laugh. "But I couldn't leave it alone. I had to go on making a fool of myself over you."

"You've never done that."

"Ha," he scoffed. "You think it was just a coincidence we met on the road during that rainstorm?"

Jenny's eyes went wide. "It wasn't?"

"And when I found out Bruce and Leslie were coming here for brunch, I had to come along. I had to see you again."

She shook her head, confused. "What do you mean about meeting me on the road—"

"And what's the first thing I find out?" he raged. "You're in love with somebody else. You're having his baby! But that's still not enough pain for me. I have to move in, and sleep across the hall with a permanent hard-on and make myself miserable over you twenty-four hours a day."

"Scott—"

"And after all that, after all I've suffered for you—you still don't trust me. You still don't believe I'm telling the truth!"

"Scott!" Jenny threw her napkin on her plate. "I'm the one who talked you into your own innocence, remember?"

"Talked me into it?" he sneered. "What, like I wasn't innocent to start with?"

"Were you?" she shot back.

"What's that supposed to mean?"

"A lot of pieces don't fit, Scott."

"Like what?"

He was speaking to her in a voice he'd never used before, but she'd swallowed her doubts for three months; this time she would not back down.

"You're supposed to have a passion for the stock market, but you never glance at the financial pages. You went to great lengths to cover your tracks on the transfers, but you matched the amounts of the checks to the penny, and you walked away from your desk with a forged check lying in plain sight for anybody to see. You signed the opposition to the accelerated trial motion, then scrapped it and joined in the motion without a word to me. You told me you were taking the Fifth, then you got on the stand and testified about things you never mentioned before. Like it was Mason's idea to blame the Connolly computer, and it was Mason who said to fix his bottom line and the trust money is just sitting there, all in the same conversation—and by the way, all these things he said in the telephone calls he didn't happen to tape!"

"You think he'd save the tapes where he incriminated himself? Is that what you think?"

Jenny took a deep breath and got to her feet. "The auditors said you couldn't have lost more money in Mason's account if you tried. I think you *did* try. I think this whole thing was some kind of scheme to set up Curtis Mason."

"For what?"

"I don't know. To disgrace him somehow."

"I'd steal two million dollars, lose my job, and risk a jail sentence just to embarrass Uncle Curt?" He let out an ugly laugh. "Come on!"

"There must have been more to it."

"Nobody got the money but him! I didn't benefit from any of it, remember? I didn't get a dime!"

"Except for the money in your other bank account," she said.

The violin concerto ended, and behind it, Jenny could hear the tree frogs screeching and the dog scratching at the studio door to come in.

Scott was staring at her. "What did you say?"

"A hundred and twenty thousand dollars in cash deposits to your bank account in Atlantic City."

"That's a lie!"

He spun around and snatched up a votive and hurled it against the wall.

Jenny screamed as the mirror burst into a spray of sparks and broken glass. He picked up another votive, and another, and smashed them all, each one hitting the mirror and exploding like a grenade, until all of them were broken.

The dog was barking frantically in the house. The only light left in the room came from the two candles burning on the table. Scott came closer. Jenny backed away, her hands clutched over her mouth to keep from screaming. He put his hand in the flames and brought it down until the candles were snuffed out and they stood in darkness.

She didn't breathe until she heard his footsteps cross the dance floor. A moment later the front door slammed. But it wasn't until she heard his car roar out of the courtyard that she was able to move again.

She shut the windows and latched them, then ran into the house. The dog was waiting, alert and agitated, and he followed her as she ran to the doors and pulled the chains on the locks. She grabbed the phone and punched in Leslie's number. It rang once, and again.

"Come on, answer the phone, please!"

Two more rings sounded before Bruce's voice. "Hello, you've reached Bruce and Leslie Maitland. We can't come to the phone right now, but please leave a message at the beep."

Jenny's brain spun trying to phrase her message. *Hello, Bruce? I'm afraid your friend Scott might hurt me, because he said some really nasty things and broke all my votives.* She shook her head and hung up without saying a word.

Later, upstairs in bed with the dog on the floor beside her, she knew she'd overreacted. Scott could never be a threat to her or anyone else. He'd be back soon, she was sure, brimming with apologies and explanations.

Jenny reached down for the dog's collar and waited for a sleep that was a long time coming.

4

Margaret Gallagher worked for Macoal for thirty years before Curtis Mason's retirement forced her into a kind of retirement with him. The salary was the same, the benefits were less, and the commute required a bus, a train, and a five-block hike, but there was never any doubt that she would go with him. For thirty years, she'd spent more waking hours with him than any other living soul. Their relationship had been through every decent permutation possible, and now they abided in a constant state of mutual irritation. He couldn't do without her, and she wouldn't do without him, and there they were. She knew all of his secrets and had never once been invited to his home.

The package that arrived at five-fifteen was one of those secrets, and one about which he'd been pestering her all day.

"Here it is," she announced, breezing into his office and placing it on the desk before him.

He scowled furiously at it and wheeled his chair a quarter-turn away.

"I thought you were waiting for it," Margaret said testily.

"I'll look at it later."

"It's after five. I won't wait."

"Go on, then," he snarled.

She returned to her desk and remained another half-hour. At five forty-five, she picked up her handbag and cracked open his office door. The envelope lay lacerated on the desk, and he was pouring over a sheaf of papers.

"I'll be going now, Mr. Mason."

"What?" he mumbled without looking up. "Oh. All right."

"Don't forget to lock up."

"Good night, Margaret."

Alone, Mason felt a sort of resignation. Not the resignation that snippy Catherine was looking for, of course, but one that he felt forced to accept just the same. Today he consolidated the balance in his Connolly account with another quarter of a million from hastily liquidated tax-free munis, and it was ready to be paid over to the trust account, just as soon as Perlman extracted the necessary releases. The trust would be whole again, but it still wasn't over.

What a nightmare. Democracy, capitalism, and the American justice system had always served him well, but no more. There was no way he'd subject himself to the fiasco of another trial. He still couldn't believe how his tape recordings, the coup de grâce of his evidence against Sterling, ended up backfiring on him. What an idiotic idea that turned out to be. But no wonder when he remembered whose idea it was—Reese Chapman, who boasted that he always recorded his broker—"Keeps him honest," he'd declared in that phony half-English accent of his. An idiotic idea from an idiotic fool, and more the fool Mason for listening to him.

His eyes roamed his office and landed on the framed *Business Week* feature, the one they did after he finished wiping the floor with Jack Stengel. A brilliant strategist, they called him, a dynamic leader. But the adjective he liked best, the one he'd most like to yellow-highlight, was *fearless.* They could put that on his tombstone and he'd die happy.

He wasn't afraid of Catherine's threat to sue him. Fear didn't enter into it. There was simply no way he could allow it to happen. The thought of Reese Chapman controlling the company—well, it was unthinkable. And that would be the certain result. No matter how much Catherine liked to style herself an independent young woman, she'd always done what her daddy told her.

Mason was nothing if not a pragmatist. He'd thought it through since last Thursday. The only way to call off Catherine was to buy off Reese Chapman. The package he'd waited for all day contained a list of all his holdings. A million dollars, he reckoned, was the price of Chapman's cooperation.

The only question was what he had to sell to raise it. Not as easy a question as it once was, not since he'd started buying up Macoal stock that summer. First there was the market price to meet, and every goddamned fourth cousin thought he was entitled to a premium over market. Then there were the lawyers' fees for setting up the dummy corporations and getting the offshore charters. The whole program was costing him through the nose. But it was unavoidable. The lid would come off the trust someday, and he had to have majority control before that happened.

This was all Doody's fault, and at the thought, he flushed with anger as hot as he had felt the day she waltzed home with that fairy on her arm. She was a good-natured, horse-faced woman everyone loved and felt sorry for. There was a place for such a woman in every family, but Doody refused to keep to it. Long after she should have abandoned her romantic longings, she took up with a man fifteen years her junior and without a penny to his name. Worse yet, he was obviously queer, at least to everyone but Doody. He should have told her, Mason thought for the thousandth time, and saved the family a lot of money and heartache. Or he should have backed her up the first time she told him she wanted to divorce Chapman. But by then, she held the controlling interest in Macoal, and he couldn't forgive her for it. "You made your bed; now lie in it," he told her. The words were spitting back at him now.

The door cracked open again. "What is it now, Margaret?" he growled.

She didn't answer, and he looked up, glaring. But that door remained closed. He wheeled his chair slowly around to the door to the connecting office.

"You've got a hell of a nerve," he said.

5

TIRES SQUEALED IN THE COURTYARD, AND THE DOG JUMPED UP FROM the floor and raced down the stairs. Jenny opened her eyes, but it was barely dawn and there was little light in the room. She stumbled out of bed and followed after him, her white cotton gown billowing behind her. The bell rang at the same time a pounding rattled the front door.

She came suddenly awake and froze beside the door.

"Jenny, it's me—let me in!"

"Dan?" She unhooked the chain and threw the door open.

"Where is he?" he shouted, brushing past her into the house. The dog thrust his nose at him but he ignored the inspection.

"Dan, what are you doing here?"

He made a quick circuit of the first floor and spun back and grabbed her by the shoulders. "Jenny, you have to tell me where Scott is!"

She stared at him. He was unshaven, and his hair uncombed, and she knew something horrible must have happened.

"I don't know. We had an argument last night, and he stormed out. Dan, what's going on?"

He tried to calm himself, and his grip on her shoulders eased a bit. "Jenny." Before he said more he pulled her close. "Curtis Mason was found dead last night. Murdered."

Later, she realized she must have fainted against him. The room was spinning and he was repeating her name urgently when she could see again. He hooked an arm under her knees and carried her to the couch.

"When?" she gasped. "How?"

"Shhh." He pulled a quilt from the back of the sofa and tucked it over her. "Lie still."

She watched through a haze as he went to the kitchen and returned with a glass of water.

"Here," he said, kneeling beside her. "Take a sip."

She did, and slowly the haze started to clear.

"Dan, tell me what happened."

He reached out and stroked her hair. "I don't know."

"You think Scott did it."

He nodded, grim-faced.

So did she, or she wouldn't have asked, and the horror hit her in a fresh wave that made her sink back against the cushions.

"Tell me what you know," she begged him, but something was wrong with her brain and she had to struggle to listen to his response.

Mason was found dead at his office last night, discovered on the floor behind his desk by the cleaning crew. He'd been struck two or more times on the head with some kind of heavy statuette. His skull was crushed.

"An abstract sculpture, in coal," she whispered.

"Yeah."

Images crowded into her mind, of Mason's scowling face cleaved in two, a hand gripping the sculpture and smashing it against his head, a hand snatching up votives and smashing them into the mirrors.

The dog gave a sudden bark as the doorbell sounded again, and Dan shot to his feet. Jenny struggled to sit up as he crossed the room and opened the door.

"Dan?"

"Mike."

She peered around the fireplace and saw Detective diMaio on the doorstep surrounded by half a dozen uniformed cops.

"What are you doin' here?"

"I'm getting Jenny the hell out before Sterling comes back."

"He's not here?"

"No."

"Well, he won't come back now. Not with three patrol cars parked outside. Lemme talk to her."

"No."

"We got a search warrant."

"Let me see it."

Dan started to argue with him about defects in the warrant, and joint inhabitants, and whose premises were whose. Jenny listened to him in a fog. She felt so cold. Her hands trembling, she clutched the quilt around her shoulders, then pushed her feet to the floor and went to the door.

"Go ahead and search, Detective," she said.

Dan sent them upstairs first, and when they were done there, he took Jenny to her room and put her to bed. He lay down on top of the covers beside her and wrapped his arms around her until she slept. "Don't leave me," she mumbled as she drifted into sleep.

"Never," he whispered.

The baby drummed a steady patter against his palms as he held her. He never knew they kicked so much; he wondered how she could sleep with such a commotion going on inside her. He wished it had never been conceived; he almost wished she'd aborted it and spared them all the complications that lay ahead. But the fact that she hadn't touched him deeply; it told him something about the kind of woman she was. Now, he knew, it was time to find out what kind of man he was.

Mike was waiting for him when he came downstairs. "Mind tellin' me how you heard about this?" he asked.

"Bob Perlman called me. Right after you finished with him."

He lifted his eyes to the ceiling. "She got any idea where Sterling is?"

"No. There was some kind of scene between them last night, and he left. That's all she knows."

Mike nodded once. "Yeah, I figgered. C'mere. You better see this."

He led Dan through the dining room to Jenny's ballet studio and hit the lights.

Dan blinked. Three walls of plate-glass mirror lay shattered on the dance floor. Crusted food sat on china plates on the table, wilted flowers drooped over them, and tiny stubs of burned-out candles were scattered through the shards of glass.

Dan remembered this room and the mirrors and the candles. It was a desecration for Sterling to have been there and destroyed it all.

He turned to Mike. "Are his clothes still here?"

"Yeah."

"Got an APB out on him?"

"What d'ya think?" Mike switched off the lights. "This looks bad for us, Dan," he said as he pulled the door shut. "Mason warned us he'd gotten death threats."

"Yeah. Where was the bodyguard?"

"Like you guessed, that was all for show. Mason was in his office alone with his secretary all day yesterday. She left about six. He wanted to stay awhile and go through some papers that came in that day. She didn't lock up."

"What about the lobby? Wasn't it locked?"

"Security guard made his rounds at six and swears he locked it."

"He could've been in the building by then."

Mike nodded. "We figure he hid somewhere till the secretary left, slipped into Mason's office, and hit him two or three times with the statue."

"Any prints?" Dan asked as they moved to chairs in the living room.

"Latex gloves."

"Premeditated, then."

"I'd say so."

A long silence passed before Dan asked, "Got any other suspects?"

"Perlman says there was a meeting on Thursday. Him, Mason, Chapman's daughter, and two of her lawyers—one of them your lady friend upstairs."

Dan's face went tight.

"Chapman's daughter tells Mason to resign from the trust, he refuses, and she threatens to sue him. He says, 'Do it, and I tell the world your old man's a queer.' She says, 'Be my guest.' Meeting's over. So I guess that puts Reese Chapman and Catherine vonBerg on our list."

"But Sterling's gotta be at the top of the list," Dan insisted.

Mike gave a noncommittal shrug.

"Come on," Dan said. "Mason got him to steal the trust money, got him fired, disbarred, his name's mud everywhere he goes. Then to top it off, Mason threatens to see him burn in hell."

"But why now?" Mike said mildly. "He was in the clear. We just told him Monday we were closin' our file."

"What about the statue? What's it look like?"

"Yea high." Mike held his hands apart about two feet. "With a marble base on it. Must weigh thirty pounds."

"Thirty pounds?" Dan pounced. "Easy enough for Sterling. But Chapman? Or the daughter?"

"Coulda hired somebody."

"Come on," Dan scoffed.

Mike squinted at him. "You seem awful anxious to pin this on Scotty. What's the story?"

Dan shook his head dismissively, but Mike's eyes traveled upward and he answered his own question. "Well, I'll give ya this much," he said. "Sterling had motive and means. The only question is opportunity. Jennifer Lodge can tell me about that. If you ever let me get to her."

Dan looked at his watch. "You want to come back in a couple hours?"

Mike looked at his own watch. "I'll wait."

When Jenny opened her eyes, the horror was still there. Curtis Mason was dead and Scott might have killed him. He'd left the house in a rampage, but had he lost all reason? His tantrum in the studio proved he was capable of violence, but on the level of murder? It didn't make any sense. He was in the clear; his troubles were over—at least until she rejected him and accused him of a major fraud. Could she have driven him to this? She rolled over with a groan of fresh horror.

Dan's scent lingered on the covers beside her.

He'd come to her. He'd known she needed him, and he'd come to her.

She could hear his voice, and she wanted to be with him above all else. She hurried into her clothes and went downstairs.

Dan got to his feet when he saw her. "Are you all right? You shouldn't have gotten out—"

"I'm fine. I'm Jenny Lodge," she said to the detective as he stood up. "You wanted to ask me some questions?"

"If you don't mind, miss."

Dan drew her to the couch beside him, and the detective sat down and flipped open a notepad. If he found anything strange in the way Dan's arm went around her shoulders, he didn't show it.

"How long's Scott Sterling been living here?"

"Since May."

"Continuously since then?"

"Yes."

"When did you last see him?"

"Last night. He left about nine o'clock."

"Did he say where he was going?"

"No."

"Did he say why he was leaving?"

Jenny looked down at her hands in her lap. "No. But we had a disagreement."

"Mind telling me about what?"

She hesitated. Was this the time to air her theory that Scott somehow defrauded the court to disgrace Mason? It was based on innuendo and happenstance and might bear no more relationship to the truth than the tale she had spun about Cynthia Lehmann. Never again would she do that to someone. Besides, the detective wanted facts, not her feverish imaginings.

"He asked me to marry him," she said in a low voice. "And I said no."

Dan's hand came over hers and held it.

"He make that mess?" The detective jerked his chin toward the studio.

Jenny bit her lip and nodded.

"Do you know where he was between six and seven o'clock last night?"

Jenny thought she heard wrong. "I'm sorry—between when and when?"

"Six and seven P.M."

She turned astonished eyes on Dan. "Is that when Mason was killed?" When he nodded, she whipped back to the detective. "Scott was here between six and seven! He was here all evening!"

"You were here with him?"

"Yes."

"The whole time?"

She could see the doubt in his eyes. "Yes! I came home from work about five-thirty, and I never left, and neither did he, not until nine o'clock."

Dan was staring at her.

"Dan, he couldn't have done it. He was here with me."

He nodded, but the uncertainty remained in his eyes.

"He was here," she repeated. "In this house with me. Do you think I'm *lying* about that?"

"It's only a twenty-minute drive from here to Mason's office," the detective said. "He could've been there and back before you realized he was gone."

Jenny paused. She'd slept for almost two hours Friday evening; Scott wouldn't even have had to hurry. But she remembered the lavish dinner—it must have taken him more than an hour to prepare. There was no way he could have made a forty-minute round trip, killed Mason, and cooked dinner, too, all in the space of an hour and a half.

"He was here the whole time," she insisted. "I know he was."

DiMaio shrugged and slipped his notepad into his breast pocket. "That's all I got for now. Will you be staying here for the time being?"

"Yes," Jenny said at the same moment Dan said, "No."

He turned to her. "Jenny, you can't stay here—"

"Dan, I have a dog and two cats to look after."

"But what if he comes back?"

294

"We got the house under surveillance," the detective spoke up.

"There," Jenny said.

"I can't let you stay here alone." Dan glanced at Mike and lowered his voice. "I'm staying with you."

Jenny's eyes shone with a sudden mist of tears. "Dan, really?"

"You forgetting something?" diMaio said.

Dan scowled. "No, I didn't forget him."

"Bring Tony, too," she said.

"Really?" he echoed.

"Please. I'd like that."

Mike diMaio stood up to go. "Then I guess I know where to find all of you," he said.

6

DAN LEFT FOR A FEW HOURS IN THE AFTERNOON TO PACK UP TONY and their things, and after he was gone, Jenny remembered Cassie. She dialed her house in Gladwyne, but there was no answer.

She called her office next. Marilyn dutifully read off her messages. There was no message from Cassie, but Walter Boenning was eager to speak with her.

"Jennifer, I've been hearing the most incredible rumors—"

"It's true, Walt," she said listlessly. "Curtis Mason was murdered."

She expected his next question to be who or how or even why, but instead it was, "What effect does this have on Cassie's claims for breach of trust?"

A man is dead, she wanted to scream, *what difference does it make?* But as dutifully as Marilyn she replied, "The claim for monetary losses survives against his estate. The claim for his removal as trustee is obviously moot."

"Is there a successor trustee?"

"None named, but Mason had a power of appointment. He may have named a successor in his own will. We won't know until it's read."

"I see, I see," Boenning said, trying his best to sound solemn while he purred with satisfaction. "So your work for Cassie must certainly continue."

"I think that's up to her, don't you?" Jenny replied.

She tried Cassie's number again, but again there was no answer.

She went upstairs. Scott's door stood open and she gazed into his room expecting a *frisson* of fear, but felt nothing but worry for him. From the window, she could see the unmarked car parked in the woods, the officers in it watching the house. Was he out there somewhere, afraid to come home?

She stripped the sheets off his bed and made it up fresh for Tony. Scott's suits still hung in the closet, and his clothes were folded in the dresser drawers. She emptied a drawer into a box to make room for Tony's clothes. The top of the dresser was strewn with the clutter of Scott's papers and loose change, and she swept it all into the box, too. His antique gold watch wasn't there. He must have had it in his pocket last night, a good-luck piece to see him through his marriage proposal.

She sank down on the foot of his bed with a sigh. People were always imagining the worst about Scott, and for a brief, horrible moment she'd been one of them. It was impossible now to believe Scott had done it; not only was he with her all evening, he simply wasn't capable of the act. But where was he? He must have heard about Mason's murder and realized he was a suspect. He needed to come forward and end the speculation. He was only making himself look bad by hiding. But she remembered Scott's conference-room confession last winter: he had a talent for making himself look bad.

There was another possibility, and it didn't occur to her until that second. She'd been so concerned with clearing Scott as a suspect that she never stopped to consider he might be another victim.

When the phone rang an hour later, she ran for it, certain it must be Cassie. "Hello?"

There was silence.

"Scott?" she cried.

"He's not there?" came Leslie's voice.

"Oh, Leslie," Jenny said and sagged into a chair. "No. No, he's not. Have you heard from him?"

"No. Bruce is a nervous wreck. The police were just here. Nobody knows where he is. Jenny—do you think he did it?"

"Leslie! Of course not. Besides, he was here with me last night."

"Then I don't get it. Where is he? Bruce called the Sterlings. They said they haven't heard from him in *months*."

"That's not true! Scott's been talking to his father on the phone almost every night."

"I don't get it," Leslie repeated. "But listen, you shouldn't be alone out there. I'll come get you."

Jenny felt tears in her eyes. They hadn't spoken since May, they'd parted on harsh terms, but the friendship still remained. "Leslie, thank you. But I'll be all right."

Another call came through as soon as they hung up, this one from Dan on his car phone. "Are you all right? Your line was busy."

Just the sound of his voice was a comfort to her. "It was my friend Leslie. Don't worry."

"Any word from Sterling?"

"No."

"Okay. We're getting off the expressway now. We'll be there in ten minutes."

"Good."

Ten more minutes and Dan would be home. Jenny wrapped her arms together and hugged herself. It was more than she'd ever let herself hope for, but it was happening. He was coming to her, moving in and bringing his little brother, just to be with her, and he didn't mind about Scott, he didn't mind about the baby—

Jenny clapped a hand to her mouth, stricken. Dan didn't *know* about the baby. He thought it was Scott's—she'd told him so, and for no reason except to hurt him. She'd wronged him, a thousand times more than she'd ever wronged anyone else, and still he was coming to her, unselfishly, believing she carried the child of a man he despised and coming anyway.

The lie had been a burden to her from the moment she uttered it, but now its weight was unbearable. She would have to tell him the truth at once, and consequences be damned. He might hate her for the pain she caused him; he might think it was a ploy to trap him. It was certain he would never trust her again. She remembered him lashing out at Mason on the witness stand: "Were you lying then, or are you lying now?" He could turn the same words on her.

297

But that was the price she'd have to pay. No lie ever went unpaid for, and tonight it was past time to settle her account.

7

DAN CAME BACK WITH TONY, TWO SUITCASES, A PIZZA, AND A VIDEO. Through the course of the evening, he watched Jenny's face full of dread, and blamed Scott Sterling for it. Innocent or not of Mason's murder, he was guilty of that look in Jenny's eyes, and someday Dan would see that he paid for it.

When the movie ended, he sent Jenny and Tony upstairs ahead of him and went outside. A cigarette end glowed in the darkness, and he followed it to the surveillance car. "Turning in?" the cop asked.

"Yeah. All quiet out here?"

"Like a tomb."

He circled around the back of the carriage house. The lights glowed upstairs, and he watched Jenny pass by her window, and later, Tony by his. The thought that Sterling might be out here somewhere, watching them, too, made him grit his teeth and circle the perimeter of the property three times, but not really in hopes of flushing anyone. It was a more primal urge, like he was marking his territory and staking his claim.

Man, woman, child, the eternal triangle. He felt it here tonight, though none of it was a perfect fit. Jenny wasn't quite his woman, not yet, and Tony wasn't his child—he was hardly even a child at all. But it felt right, the three of them here together, and even the fourth one on the way.

Dan had spent years avoiding commitment, but in that moment, gazing at the lights in the carriage house, he was ready to commit to it all. He'd be the man of this family, a husband to Jenny and a father figure to Tony, and a real father to the baby. There was still a presumption of legitimacy in Pennsylvania. He'd marry Jenny and the baby would be his in the eyes of the law, and Sterling would never dare show his face to claim otherwise.

He called the animals inside, locked the doors, front and back, and turned out the lights before he went upstairs. Tony was already in bed when he stopped at his door.

"Everything okay?" he asked him. "Did you unpack?"

"Yeah, Jenny emptied a drawer for me."

Dan wandered into the room. Enough light spilled in from the hall to show him evidence of recent occupation, and of the gender of the occupant. He glanced at the suits in the closet, and the shoes on the floor, and the Tom Clancy novel open on the nightstand. Had Jenny banished Sterling here, he wondered, and how long ago?

Tony was scrunched into sleeping position already; today had been the first day of soccer camp, and he had the luxury of physical exhaustion. Dan reached down and tousled his hair. "Good night."

" 'Night."

Jenny heard him cross the hall and took a deep breath as he tapped lightly on the door before he opened it. The lights were off, and there was nothing but the gleam of moonlight against the brass headboard to pierce the darkness of the room. She could see him framed in the doorway, but it took another moment for him to see her on the window seat. He took a step toward her and hesitated.

"I can bunk in with Tony if you'd like," he said.

"I wouldn't like that at all."

His smile flashed as he started across the room toward her.

"No, wait," she said. "I have something I have to tell you."

He stopped. "I have something to tell you first. I love you, Jenny."

For seven months she'd longed to hear those words, but in all of her fantasies, the last thing she would have said next was what she did. "No, wait. Let me finish."

He stood uncertainly in the middle of the room. The window was open behind her, and a breeze stirred the curtains. Outside the calls of birds and bugs swelled up into a chorus of the night.

"It's about Scott."

A tightness came into his expression. "No. Don't let him come between us anymore than he already has."

"He's never been between us. Scott's a friend—a good friend—but that's all he ever was. We were never lovers. It's not his baby."

The sob she was holding in escaped and she cried, "I lied to you, Dan; I'm sorry."

Her words seemed to come at him faster than his razor-sharp mind could process. He stared at her, uncomprehending.

"I lied about the date, too. It's due the end of October."

He took a sudden step back, as if he'd been pushed off-balance. His face disappeared into the shadows, and when his voice finally came, it was from far away.

"It's mine."

"Dan, I'm so sorry," Jenny cried.

He moved across the room, and when the light hit him, she saw the gleam of tears in his eyes.

"You had no right," he said hoarsely. "You had no right."

And then he was gone. Jenny sat with her arms wrapped tight, her hands clutching her shoulders, and silent tears streamed down her face as she listened to the sound of his feet on the stairs. This was the price of her lie, then, to lose him now, just when he'd come back to her. But it was too much. No matter how much she deserved it, it was more than she could bear.

Through her tears, she waited for the next inevitable sounds, the front door slamming and the roar of his car's engine in the courtyard, and when minutes passed and neither came, she drew in a ragged breath and made her way downstairs. The room was empty and dark, but a light shone from the studio, and Jenny followed it to the door.

Dan was there with broom and dustpan, cleaning up the littered remains of the room and dumping them into a trash can. He saw her in the doorway, but he didn't stop sweeping. The broom made a lonely swishing sound that resonated through the hollow space.

"It happened that night in your studio dressing room," he said suddenly.

"Yes," Jenny said.

He held the dustpan against the floor and swept a pile of glass into it. "Do you know what the sex is?"

"No. I'm doing it the old-fashioned way."

He turned to look at her as he poured the pan into the trash can. "Not quite," he bit out.

He moved across the room and swept up another pile of broken glass, and when he turned around, Jenny was beside him with the dustpan. She stooped and held it against the rubble, waiting. After a moment, he swept the shards into the dustpan, and she carried it to the trash can and dumped it in.

"Why?" he said suddenly. He was leaning against the broom ten feet away. "Just tell me why."

Jenny swallowed hard and stared at the floor. "I wanted to hurt you, the way you'd hurt me. I wanted you to think I was over you. I wanted to make you jealous, I guess."

"You could have just told me you were seeing somebody," he said dryly. "That would have done the trick on the jealousy part."

"And I was afraid—"

"Afraid of what?" he demanded.

"Of you!" she burst out. "After the way you tried to take control of me and my career, I didn't know what you'd do! I was afraid you'd try to make me have an abortion—"

The broom clattered to the floor as Dan crossed the distance between them and seized her by the shoulders. "I would never have done that," he said fiercely. "Jenny, I love you—"

"You didn't love me then," she said. "You told me you didn't!"

"Then I lied, too." He pulled her hard against him. "Oh, God, Jenny. Do you have any idea how it's eaten me up all these months, thinking the baby was Sterling's and wishing it was mine?"

She wrapped her arms around him, and they clung to each other, and her sobs wracked them both.

Later, he led her upstairs and pulled her onto the bed, and they held each other, wide-eyed, through the night. He laid his palm against her belly, and repeated in wonder, "It's mine." And she repeated the same litany, "I'm sorry, Dan; I'm so sorry."

The dim light of early dawn was creeping into the room when at last Dan propped himself up on his elbow and loomed over her, his face drawn and tired and full of love. "Marry me," he said.

Jenny shook her head. "No. Not like this—"

He pulled her shoulders from the mattress and crushed her in his arms. "You little fool," he whispered savagely. "I meant to marry you before I knew the baby was mine. The only question was whether you'd have me. And now that I know the truth, I won't take no for an answer to that question."

Jenny pushed back and searched his eyes, looking for the distrust she must have planted there. But she couldn't find it. She saw hurt and anger, still, and love and a fierce possessiveness, but nowhere in his eyes was there distrust.

No lie ever went unpaid for, she believed that still. But in that moment she knew she'd paid already, through endless months of self-imposed exile from the man she loved. It was more than she'd ever dared hope for, that she'd be free of the burden of her lie, that he'd be free of his resentment, that all their problems would lay behind them with nothing but happiness ahead.

But here was the evidence before her: Dan, in her bed, in her arms, staring at her with love in his eyes and whispering, "Do you have any idea how it's eaten me up all these months, thinking you were his and wishing you were mine?"

8

THEY DROVE TOGETHER INTO THE CITY THE NEXT MORNING, stopping first on the Parkway to drop Tony off at The Alexander School. Jenny had to get out at the curb to let Tony squeeze out from the back seat, and as he trotted off with his cleats strung over his shoulder, Dan was shaking his head ruefully.

"What?" Jenny asked, sliding awkwardly back into her seat.

"I just realized," he said gravely. "My days of driving a sports coupe are over."

She shot him a look but saw at once the twinkle in his eyes. "I guess a four-door sedan *would* be more practical."

"Sedan?" he said. "At the rate we're going, I'm thinking minivan."

He found an empty spot in front of her building and pulled into it. Any number of Jackson, Rieders lawyers could be walking past, but he didn't care. He leaned over and gave her a long and fervent kiss.

"Pick a date," he said when they parted.

"Anytime," she said, breathless. "Soon."

"It had better be soon," he said, smoothing his hands over her abdomen. "Or I'll never be able to carry you over the threshold."

She jabbed him and they tussled a minute before he stopped her with another kiss.

"Do you want to invite your family?"

She winced. "I haven't even told them I'm pregnant yet. I think I'd rather tell them we're married before I break that news to them."

"Good plan. I'll do the same."

"What about Tony?"

Now it was Dan who winced. "I don't know. I don't trust him not to blab, but I don't want him to think we're just shacking up, either." He pondered for a moment. "I think I'd better tell him."

"And let him come to the ceremony, too."

"Anybody else?"

"Just us."

"Okay, but I won't let you cheat me out of a honeymoon. Let's pick a date when we can get away for a week."

"Mmmm. Someplace cool."

"The mountains? Or the coast of Maine?"

"Either. Surprise me."

"You check your calendar; I'll check mine," he said. "Six o'clock okay for tonight?"

"Fine."

"I'll meet you at the garage and we'll pick up Tony for the trip home."

Home, Jenny thought, kissing him good-bye before she climbed out of the car. He called her house home, and it felt like it already.

She bought a newspaper in the lobby and scanned the front page on her way up in the elevator. A photograph of Curtis Mason appeared below the fold, not angry and scowling as she'd known him, but resolute and commanding, like the business leader he'd been.

She finished the article at her desk. There was a long recitation of his civic and charitable achievements, a brief description of the circumstances of his death, and passing mention of two events that left the reader to speculate: that he'd recently been involved in acrimonious litigation against Harding & McMann; and that last January his dog had been killed in an apparent random shooting. A memorial service would be conducted Friday afternoon at the Church of the Good Samaritan.

Jenny scanned her phone message slips and dialed into her voice mail recordings, but there was nothing from Cassie vonBerg. She called Cassie's house and again got no answer.

Too much time had passed since Mason's murder Tuesday evening; now Jenny was worried. She opened a drawer of her credenza and thumbed through all of the folders labeled *Mason v. Harding & McMann* until she found the note Cassie had once scrawled for her, of her father's address and telephone number in Haverford.

She punched in the number, and on the second ring, a woman answered in a crisp and proper British dialect. "Chapman residence."

"Hello. Is Mrs. vonBerg there by any chance?"

"She is not," the woman replied firmly.

"This is her attorney, Jennifer Lodge. I've been trying to reach her at her house in Gladwyne. It's very important that I speak with her, as soon as possible. Do you have any idea—?"

"Hold, please."

Jenny waited an interminable two minutes before the woman returned. "She's visiting in New York," she said. "You might ring her up at the Pierre."

Relieved and triumphant, Jenny got the number for the hotel and reached the desk.

"Catherine vonBerg, please."

After a moment the clerk replied, "Mrs. vonBerg checked out this morning."

Jenny hung up in despair.

But at last that afternoon Cassie called her, from a phone with the roar of voices behind it.

"Cassie! Where are you? I've been trying to reach you— Do you know—?"

"Yes, I know," she said, and the strain in her voice was audible even through the noise of the crowd. "I'm at Penn Station, about to board a Metroliner home. The police tracked me down this morning. They want me to come in and give a statement first thing tomorrow. Can you go with me, Jenny?"

"Yes, of course. Cassie, were you—"

"I was here Tuesday night," she said wearily. "At a benefit. I have a hundred witnesses."

Jenny blew her breath out. "Okay. Here's what you do. I'll call the police. We'll do the interview at your house, not at the station."

"I'll be staying with Daddy."

"At his house, then. I'll make the arrangements. Now, tell me everything about this benefit."

The rest of Jenny's day was consumed by telephone calls and faxes between her office and New York, and at the end of it, Dan called.

"Ready to go?" he said. "I'm parked on level three."

"Could you pick up Tony first and meet me out front?" Jenny asked. "I have one more phone call to make before I leave."

This call was a local one. She tracked down the number and dialed it before she could stop to reconsider.

"Mr. Sterling?" she said when a man answered.

"Yes."

"My name is Jennifer Lodge. I'm a friend of your son's and I—"

"Oh, yes, the police mentioned your name to me," he said, and went on in a voice she'd never heard before. "Have you heard from him? Do you have any idea where he might be?"

She'd never spoken to this man, not on any of the evenings she'd picked up the phone and passed it excitedly to Scott. She stammered, "N-no, sir. I was hoping you might have heard."

"Not a word. But of course, this is the last place he'd call."

"Yes, I see; thank you," she murmured and hung up. She put her hands to her face. Her skin was icy.

Dan noticed the moment he kissed her hello in the car. "Are you feeling all right?" he asked.

"Fine." She turned to smile at Tony over the seat. "How was soccer?"

"Great. Wore me out, though," he said and proved it by stretching out over the entire seat.

"Why are you so cold?" Dan asked, clutching her hand.

"I'm worn out, too, I guess."

"We'd better talk about your hours," he said and headed the car for home.

9

REESE CHAPMAN LIVED IN HAVERFORD, IN THE HEART OF THE MAIN Line, in a house that had been in the Chapman family for four generations. Jenny followed Cassie's directions off Lancaster Avenue and through a neighborhood where every house was a mansion and every yard a park. A pair of stone gates marked the turn. Jenny drove through them and up a drive toward a hill where a Gothic castle seemed to rise out of the ground. It was built of gray boulders, with arches and turrets and a massive front door that could have been the drawbridge for a moat.

Jenny parked between Cassie's white Mercedes and a classic MG in British racing green. Over the front door was a keystone and she had a glimpse of a coat of arms carved into its granite surface before the door was opened by a woman in a starched white apron over a black dress.

"Miss Lodge?" She spoke in a clipped English accent.

"Yes."

"This way, please."

She turned on rubber-soled feet and led Jenny into the house. A great vaulted ceiling rose overhead, and Jenny's heels rang over the slate floor past a curving staircase. On one wall hung an oversized oil painting of a young boy in a sailor suit, with chubby cheeks, golden curls, and a little rosebud mouth.

The housekeeper opened a door on a cavernous oak-paneled room lined with bookshelves fifteen feet high. A staircase on wheels was against one wall, and a desk stood in the middle of the room, a computer terminal sitting incongruously on top of it.

"I'll tell Miss Chapman you've arrived," she said and disappeared soundlessly into the hall.

Jenny wandered the room. This house was an archetype of decaying gentility. The upholstery on the settee was of a fine old tapestry, now faded and worn. Cracks zigzagged through the diamond-shaped panes of leaded glass, and through them Jenny could see a swimming pool edged with broken blue tiles. The trust paid Chapman twenty thousand a month, and it didn't look to be enough.

"Jenny." Cassie spoke from the doorway.

"Cassie! Are you all right?"

"I'm fine," she said, though she looked tired in her black linen dress. "It's Daddy I'm worried about."

"The police spoke with him already?"

"Yesterday. And Mrs. Hastings tells me he hasn't been himself since."

"Is he going to the service this afternoon?"

"I thought so, but now I'm not so sure."

"Maybe he'll feel better after this interview is over."

"I know I will," Cassie declared and flopped down on the settee.

Fifteen minutes later, at the appointed time, they heard the doorbell ring and waited for the inevitable knock on the library door. Jenny went to open it, and found a trio of men gawking at the vaulted ceiling outside—a tall bespectacled man, a hefty man with a gray brush cut, and Detective Mike diMaio. She gave him a surprised glance but turned to complete the introductions. The tall man was Delaware County Assistant District Attorney Barry Klein, and the hefty man was Detective Leary, Radnor Township Police Department.

Cassie waved them to their seats, and the three men perched awkwardly on Hepplewhite chairs while Jenny and Cassie remained on the settee.

Leary operated the tape recorder and Klein asked the questions, leading with the obvious choice. "Mrs. vonBerg, where were you Tuesday between six and seven P.M.?"

Cassie folded her hands in her lap, the picture of composure despite her weary face. "I was in New York, attending a cocktail benefit at the Metropolitan Museum of Art."

Jenny pulled some pages from her briefcase and handed them to Klein. "Gentlemen, this is a copy of the guest list for the reception. Mrs. vonBerg has checked off the names of everyone she recalls speaking with at the function. This," she said, pulling out another paper, "is the name and address of the photographer who was engaged for the occasion. He should have several shots of Mrs. vonBerg."

Klein read through the papers and handed them to Leary. A look passed between them; they were satisfied.

"Do you know where your father was about that time?" Klein asked next.

Cassie gave him a puzzled look. "I thought you spoke with Daddy yesterday."

"We did. But we want to know what you know."

"I only know what he told me. That he was here at home, and that his housekeeper was here, too—Mrs. Hastings. Haven't you spoken with her?"

Klein ignored her question. "Your father seems pretty rattled by all this, but we hear there was no love lost between him and Curtis Mason. Any idea why he'd be upset?"

Cassie's mouth went tight. "My mother's only brother was brutally murdered. Of course he's upset, whether there was love lost or not."

Leary cut in. "You got any idea of who might've wanted to see your uncle dead?"

"Hundreds of people," Cassie said. "Should I start inside the family or out?"

Klein snickered.

"Put it another way," Leary said, unamused. "If you had to guess, who would you say did it?"

"Scott Sterling. That's what everybody else thinks, isn't it?"

"If you have nothing else, gentlemen," Jenny said after a pause, "Mrs. vonBerg has a memorial service to attend this afternoon."

Leary switched off the machine, and they all got to their feet. Cassie remained in the library while Jenny ushered them to the door.

"Got a minute, Miss Lodge?" diMaio said as Klein and Leary stepped outside.

"Yes, Detective?"

"Call me Mike."

"Then I'm Jenny."

"Jenny. Seems like you're tangled up in this thing about every way possible."

"What do you mean?"

"Only that I'd like to know what you know."

She looked away. What did she know? That Scott failed to read the *Wall Street Journal* and spoke frequently with a man who was not his father? "I know the characters of the people involved," she said finally. "That's all."

Mike watched her with his kind eyes. He hadn't gotten his answer, but he wouldn't insult her by pressing the point. "You think Reese Chapman did it?"

"No," she said at once, and she anticipated the next question. "But neither did Scott. I'm sure of it."

He shook his head with a chuckle. "You're running me out of suspects, Jenny."

She gave a half-smile as he stepped outside and pulled the door closed behind him.

Cassie was waiting at the library door. "What do you think?" she said anxiously.

"You did fine," Jenny assured her.

"It's not me I'm worried about. That policeman was right about Daddy—his behavior's very strange. Jenny, maybe you could talk to him?"

She hesitated only a second. "I'll try."

Cassie turned at once and led her up the carved wooden staircase to the second floor and down a wide carpeted corridor. She stopped and tapped on a door. "Daddy?"

There was no answer. She cracked the door and peered inside, then swung it in.

The drapes were drawn and the room was in near darkness. Jenny could barely make out the dim figure sitting upright in a chair beside the bed.

"Daddy," Cassie said, and dropped to her knees in front of him. "This is my lawyer—the one we talked about?—Jennifer Lodge. She wants to update you on the police inquiries."

Chapman stared straight ahead while his hands twisted together in his lap.

"Hello, Mr. Chapman," Jenny began. "We've met before, you may remember, at Harding & McMann and again last week in the courtroom."

He gave no sign that he heard her. Cassie threw a stricken look up at her.

Jenny spoke on. "Your daughter just completed her statement to the police, and I can assure you they were completely satisfied that she was in New York at the time of—" She faltered a moment. "At all relevant times. And I gather your housekeeper has already vouched for your whereabouts. I don't believe there can be any question that you or Cassie was involved. The police are very much focused on their prime suspect, Scott Sterling, and he's—"

A strangling noise came from Chapman's throat.

"Daddy?" Cassie cried and clutched his hands.

Jenny drew closer, and in the faint light she could see that tears were streaming down his face.

"Cassie, I'm sorry," she gasped. "I didn't mean to—"

"It's nothing you said." Cassie rose up to kiss her father's cheek, then turned and beckoned Jenny out into the hall. "This is all he's been doing, ever since yesterday." She pulled the door closed and started for the stairs.

"Maybe you'd better call his doctor."

"I guess so. Oh, Jenny, I have the most awful feeling."

"What?"

"Daddy thinks I did it!"

"He couldn't possibly."

"He must. We know he didn't do it, but he's full of guilt and remorse anyway. No—it's more than that. It's like his heart's been broken. He must think he drove me to murder!"

"He couldn't believe that of you."

Cassie shook her head. "I don't know what to believe anymore. How could he?"

The housekeeper was waiting downstairs with Jenny's briefcase. She handed it to her wordlessly and turned to disappear once more until Cassie spoke.

"It looks like Daddy won't be going to the service, Mrs. Hastings. Would you mind staying until I get back? I have dinner plans, but I won't linger long."

"Certainly, Miss Chapman."

Cassie walked Jenny to her car, and her eyes landed on the little MG parked next to it. "Silly old deathtrap," she said, running her hand over it. "I've been trying for years to get Daddy into something safer, but he won't hear of it. 'She's a Thoroughbred,' he always says. 'You don't put a Thoroughbred down.' "

She turned away to watch a car sweep up the drive. It was a Mercedes limousine, and the moment it stopped, the driver emerged and snapped to attention beside the door.

Jenny felt a chill as she recognized the all-American body held tense with Oriental discipline. It was Moi, Stengel's genetically engineered factotum.

"Oh, how nice," Cassie murmured. "Jack sent his car for me."

"Is he in town?"

"Yes, he offered to go with me to the church. And God knows I'll need a friendly face in that crowd."

Jenny climbed into her car. "Where will you be staying?"

"You can reach me here."

"All right. And please, Cassie, call me if you need me."

"All right," Cassie murmured, her focus already shifted to Moi. "But I don't think I will."

10

UNDER ANY CIRCUMSTANCES, CURTIS MASON WOULD HAVE MERITED the equivalent of a state funeral. He was president emeritus of a major company; he sat on the board of trustees of two universities and three museums, the board of directors of five corporations, and the vestry of his church. He belonged to the Merion Cricket Club, the Overbrook Golf Club, and the Greater Philadelphia Chamber of Commerce, and if their respective memberships weren't enough, he was a Mason, too, and that was worth about two hundred cousins.

But he didn't die under any circumstances. He was murdered, brutally, and the throng of curiosity-seekers necessitated the police services of the two adjoining townships just to control the traffic into the overflow parking lots.

Dan was among them, and he supposed no better. He was there to appease his own curiosity, but more about himself than Mason.

He found his way inside and to a pew, where he waited for the service to begin. Something about Mason's murder shook him. At first he chalked it all up to Jenny and her distress, but it was more than that. As recently as ten days ago, he was grilling this man on the witness stand. Today he was dead. Somebody wrote once that the death of an enemy can affect you as much as the death of a friend. Maybe that was it.

Bob Perlman spotted him through the crowd, and Dan made room on the pew beside him. "Any news?" Perlman whispered.

Dan shook his head. Perlman probably thought Sterling did it—everybody did—but as long as Jenny provided the alibi, there was little Dan could say on the subject.

A few dozen folding chairs were added down both aisles, and another hundred outside under a tent with only a loudspeaker to look at, and when all the seats were filled, the widow was brought in, veiled in black, borne by two men and all but dragging her toes down the center aisle. The mourners rose and turned to watch her progress as if she were a bride.

The service began, and it was celebrated by the bishop. This was Dan's first time inside an Episcopal church, and he was startled at how similar the liturgy was to his own. He'd always thought a gulf as wide as the ocean separated his kind from Mason's, but it turned out they all read from the same pages on Sunday morning.

A former U.S. senator rose to deliver the first of the eulogies, and while he spoke, Dan came to realize what it really was that rattled him so much about Mason's murder. It was his own guilt. Something wasn't right about that trial. He couldn't identify it—the evidence was what it was. All he knew was that he'd had a hand in bringing down Curtis Mason, and that somehow something wasn't right.

11

TONY TURNED IN EARLY THAT NIGHT, AND DAN AND JENNY SAT UP together on the glider on the patio, arms wrapped around each other despite the heat. The night air was heavy and close, and heat lightning flashed in muted gleams in the starless sky. The dog circled restlessly, too hot to lie down and sleep; they could track him in the dark by the clatter of his claws on the brick floor.

"I told Tony about us on the drive home today," Dan said.

"About the baby, too?"

"Uh-huh."

"How'd he take it?"

"Well, I got four 'cools' and one 'totally cool,' so I'd say pretty well."

"Oh, good. I'm glad," she said.

"He's got a lot of rough edges, but he can be an engaging kid once in a while. I think, over time, you'd get along okay—"

"Dan, stop." She laughed, laying her hand on his shirt front. "I love him already."

"You do?"

"He reminds me of you. And you're not so hard to love, you know."

"Neither are you," he said and leaned over for a kiss. "But the question is, could you tolerate him on a daily basis for, say, the next four years?"

"Dan!" she exclaimed.

"I think it would be the best thing for him—" He stopped and shook his head. "No, that's not right. The truth is I want to have him with me. But not if you—"

"Of course I want him to live with us. I love having Tony around. And think of it this way," she added, her eyes twinkling. "We'll have a built-in baby-sitter."

Dan's smile faded.

"What?" she asked, watching him.

"Sorry." He gave a rueful shake of his head. "It still hits me like a sucker punch, sometimes, the idea that it's mine, that we're gonna be the actual parents of an actual baby. Thinking about things like baby-sitters—it throws me for a loop."

Her eyes filled with tears. "That's because you haven't had any time to get used to the idea. That's my fault, and I'm sorry."

"No, don't; we're past that." He laid his hand on her belly. "I just have to keep reminding myself it's real." At that moment, the baby kicked obligingly against his palm, and his expression went soft and warm as he leaned over to kiss her again.

She went upstairs while Dan locked up. Tony was still awake and halfway through Scott's Tom Clancy novel. "Good night," she called from the hall.

" 'Night," he answered absently. But a second later, he said, "Hey Jenny?"

"Hmmm?"

"I found some papers here. I thought I oughtta give them to you."

She came into the doorway as he pulled a stack of papers out of a drawer in the nightstand.

"Thanks," she said and took them from him.

She glanced at them as she crossed the hall. They were Scott's legal papers: letters from Bill Lawson; notices from the disciplinary board; the papers she'd drafted for him to file in the civil case, including the opposition to the accelerated trial motion that never found its way to court.

At the bottom of the stack was a sheaf of pages of the kind of slick-surfaced paper that used to come out of fax machines. Jenny was puzzled—nobody used that paper anymore—and she glanced at the first page.

MEMORANDUM

TO: FILE

FROM: DJC

RE: WHAT REALLY HAPPENED

Theory One: Just what it looks like. Sterling started playing the stock market for Mason, got in over his head, and couldn't stomach telling Mason the truth. So he lied—little lies at first. Harmless, he thought, forgotten as soon as he had a few good trades to compensate. But the good trades never came. The lie took on a life of its own. . . .

She blinked to clear her vision. This was Dan's strategic planning memo, dictated the night of the blizzard, confidential attorney work product that should never have left the confines of Foster, Bell, & McNeil and Harding & McMann. She couldn't think how Scott got a copy of it. Not from Dan—even if he'd had some motive for releasing it, it would have appeared on standard copier paper. This came either from an ancient fax machine, or something like a microfiche printer.

She flipped through the pages. Behind Dan's memo was another document: "Scott Sterling: Outline for Examination."

Despite the heat, she felt a chill come over her.

Dan's footsteps sounded on the stairs, and she hurried to slide the papers into a drawer.

He found her by the bed, staring at him with big eyes full of uncertainty. They'd been together two nights now, but the first night was spent awake and talking, and the second in exhausted sleep. He wondered if that look meant she was nervous that he might want more, or if it meant that it was time for more.

He doused the lights, and they rolled into bed together. All doubt vanished as she pressed herself close.

"God, I've missed you," he groaned.

He found her mouth, and his hands started the familiar roam over her body. But her shape was alien to him, and it made him stifle his urges—he had no business playing with the nipples of a pregnant woman. His erection was rock hard, and he rolled away from her to ease the discomfort.

She followed after and wrapped her fingers so tight around his penis, it jumped in her hand.

"Jenny, I don't know how—"

"Shhh," she said, and swung one leg over him. "I know how."

He slept soundly afterward, and Jenny clung to him and let her thoughts twist around the questions that plagued her. How did Scott get Dan's trial outline? Who was the man he spoke to every night and called "Father?" And what did any of this have to do with the trial that was somehow a plot against Mason?

She wished she could share her fears with Dan. But he would be quick to name Scott the murderer if he knew any of this, and once Scott's guilt was fixed in his mind, he'd marshal all the other evidence and build a case against him so strong, the truth would be lost in the tide. It was the same thing he'd done with Mason, though he didn't know it yet. And couldn't, not until she put all the pieces together.

12

JACK STENGEL POURED ANOTHER GLASS OF COGNAC AND HANDED IT
to Cassie before he picked up the phone again. She stretched her
long legs out before her and turned to gaze out the side window of
the limousine. Jack was barking orders at one of the young men at
his command center in New York. Sometimes it was hard for her
to reconcile the near-maniacal tyrant with the witty and urbane
man who'd been chastely squiring her about these past few
months. It gave her a sense of favored treatment, and she liked
that. She hadn't felt so sublimely spoiled since she was a little girl.

He was a godsend today, escorting her to the church and res-
cuing her from small talk with all the Masons. By the time they
finished dinner at the Striped Bass, she'd been able to put her
father's troubles out of her mind. For twenty minutes, they'd had
a wonderful discussion about the Macoal stock she would someday own. Jack made it clear that he coveted that stock, and even
clearer how much he admired her for wanting to hold on to it.

The heliport came in view, and Jack wound down his conversation with threats to resume it as soon as air-to-ground contact
was established. He pushed a button to disconnect, and turned to
take Cassie in his arms.

"You won't change your mind about tonight?" he asked.

"No, I can't leave Daddy alone."

"Then I won't postpone this trip any longer."

"Singapore?"

He nodded. "I'll get a flight out of New York first thing tomorrow."

The limousine slowed to a stop, and Moi climbed out to stand
beside the rear door. He was the only employee Jack didn't bark
orders at, but then he hardly needed to—Moi anticipated everything. Jack told an intriguing story of how he found him. It was in
Saigon in the early eighties, and Jack was at the airport waiting to
meet some government officials about oil exploration rights. A boy
so tall his head floated above the throng came darting through the
terminal with a pack of soldiers at his heels. Jack inquired of his
escort, and was told that the boy was of the *bui doi,* the dust of life.

The orphaned son of a local prostitute and presumably an American GI, he was called Moi, Vietnamese for "savage"; it was the only name he'd ever known. He'd beaten and robbed a French businessman and was now attempting to leave the country on stolen papers. The soldiers tackled him and brought him down, but after a few well-placed bribes, he was released to Jack. "Best driver I've ever had," Jack ended the story, though it was plain to Cassie that Moi was much more than that.

"How long will you be gone?" she asked.

"Four days, five at the most."

Cassie ran her fingers along the edge of his lapel. "A long time," she said. "Especially considering the plans we had for tonight."

He smiled. His lips were full for a man, a look she'd once thought unattractive, but now felt was deliciously sensuous.

"One of the advantages of my age and experience," he said, "is that I appreciate the rewards of patience." He bent his head and kissed her. "And eagerly await them," he breathed against her face.

Moi opened the door, and Jack picked up his attaché and was gone.

Alone, Cassie unpinned her hair and pulled off her earrings. She wished she'd had time to change before dinner. She was still wearing the black linen St. Laurent she wore to the memorial service, and it was horribly crushed by the day's wear. But a change of clothing would have necessitated a stop at her father's house. She wanted Jack to meet him, but not today, not like this. He would've refused to speak to Jack just as he'd refused all day to speak to her, or to his doctor or to his lawyer.

The limousine arrived at her father's house where the housekeeper was waiting with her bag in hand, anxious to be relieved. Her father used to have his housekeepers live in, but not lately. Cassie didn't know whether that was a symptom of romantic activity, or the lack thereof. His proclivities were something they never discussed or alluded to beyond a passing reference to his "situation." "Curt knows all about my situation," he'd told her. "He won't hesitate to make it public if it suits him."

"How is he, Mrs. Hastings?"

"Much improved," she reported. "He asked me to make him something special for his dinner. Luckily, I had a piece of tenderloin in the icebox. He ate it all, and enjoyed a nice glass of port afterward."

"Where is he now?"

"In bed, I believe. I heard the bath running earlier."

"Good night, then."

Cassie climbed the carved wooden staircase to the second floor. A lamp glowed in her old bedroom, and she saw that the bed had been made for her and the covers turned back. She dropped her earrings on the dresser and kicked off her shoes, but before she undressed, she went down the hall to say good night.

"Daddy?" she said, tapping on his door.

When there was no answer, she tapped again and swung the door in. His bed was also turned down, in a perfect fold still undisturbed.

"Daddy?" she called more loudly.

A sliver of light shone beneath the bathroom door. She crossed the room and knocked. "Daddy!" she shouted. "Daddy, are you in there?"

She pushed the door in and a scream froze in her throat. A lock of his hair fell over his forehead. His glasses slid down his nose, and his blood overflowed the tub.

13

A RINGING SPLINTERED THE NIGHT. DAN REACHED BLINDLY, BUT THE phone was on Jenny's side of the bed and she picked up first. A cry sounded over the line, and her body went tense against his.

"Cassie, what's wrong?"

He switched on the bedside lamp and watched Jenny's eyes widen and fill with tears as she listened. "Yes, of course. I'll be right there." She hung up and turned to Dan.

"Reese Chapman killed himself," she said and went into his arms.

"My God." He could feel her shaking, and he pulled her closer. But in the next instant, she broke away and swung out of bed.

"No, don't go over there," he said.

"She begged me to come."

"The last thing she needs now is her lawyer."

"She needs a friend, and I'm going."

He saw the set in her jaw and knew it was as pointless to talk her out of it as it was for her to go. He climbed out of bed and reached for his pants. "I'll drive you."

They hurried into their clothes and left the room together. Dan leaned into Tony's room across the hall. He lay asleep on his back, the sheet twisted around his waist, one arm flung so wide it hung suspended in the air. Dan hesitated, reluctant to leave him alone.

"There's a police car in the woods," Jenny said, reading his mind. "He'll be safe."

Dan stood a moment, torn, before he nodded and followed her down the stairs.

They raced over back roads through dark woods in near silence to Chapman's house. Jenny cleared her throat now and then to give monosyllabic directions. Her hands lay knotted in her lap, and her teeth kept catching on her lower lip to keep from crying. Dan cursed Reese Chapman—no, all the Chapmans, and the Masons, and at the top of the list, the Sterlings—for all their stupid battles over their stupid money that ended up spilling over and causing heartache to people like Jenny.

She pointed out the street. There was no need to search for the house, because it was marked by half a dozen police and emergency vehicles with their blue and red lights flashing. Dan parked in the driveway, and Jenny hurried to the front door.

Cassie must have been watching for her; she threw the door open and collapsed, sobbing, into her arms. Jenny held her and tried to murmur words of comfort. A green-shrouded gurney stood in the middle of the hall. Gently, she turned Cassie in the other direction and led her into the library. Cassie threw herself onto the settee, but she sobbed against its tapestry arm only a minute before she wiped her eyes dry and said, "Would you see if there's any vodka in there?"

Jenny followed the direction of her gaze to a liquor cabinet built into the bookcase. She splashed an ounce of vodka into a bar glass. Cassie threw it down her throat and held the glass out for a refill. Jenny brought it back and sat down beside Cassie as she drank it down.

"What can I do?" Jenny asked. "Is there anybody I should call?"

"Nobody." Cassie still wore the crushed black dress, and now ghoulish streaks of mascara circled her eyes. "There's nobody but Daddy and me. He was the last of the Chapmans, you know. Or I am, I mean. There's dozens of Masons, but I doubt they'll run to my side."

"Why not?"

"Think about it," she said bitterly. "Here's the proof that Daddy murdered Curtis. Why else would he kill himself?"

"Cassie, are they sure it was suicide?"

"He left a note," she drawled. " 'Darling Catherine, I wanted to help you, never to hurt you. Please forgive me.' Ha! He might as well have signed his confession in blood!" She burst into tears again.

Jenny stroked her shoulder helplessly.

"And here's the irony!" Cassie cried. "All this ridiculous fighting over removing Curtis as trustee? It was all for nothing, because the trust automatically terminates on Daddy's death. I own it free and clear now. Pretty funny, huh?"

She threw her head back and roared.

Jenny went to the front window and leaned her head against the leaded glass. She could see Dan at the street, and she longed to go to him.

A Mercedes limousine pulled up to the curb behind Dan's car. She backed away from the window when Jack Stengel leaped out.

His voice sounded in the hall, the words unclear but the tone unmistakably demanding. Cassie's head came up, and she was on her feet by the time he threw the door open.

"Oh, Jack," she wailed and fell against him.

"Cassie, I came back as soon as I got your message—"

Jenny turned away from their embrace, but in the leaded glass she could see the reflection of Cassie clinging to him and Stengel stroking her back and whispering assurances.

"Jack, will you do something for me?"

"Of course. Anything."

"Buy my Macoal stock. You still want it, don't you? I'll sell it to you, all of it, as soon as possible."

Jenny spun around. "Cassie, you don't know what you're saying—"

"Oh, yes, I do." She pulled away from Stengel, and the look in her eyes was ugly. "I know that my father and my uncle are dead because of that fucking stock, and I don't want any part of it!"

Stengel crossed his arms and leaned one shoulder against the bookcase. "Miss Lodge," he acknowledged her. "I didn't notice you there."

"Cassie, wait until you're sure," Jenny said. "You might decide you want the stock; you could end up running the company—"

"I am sure," Cassie said. "And if you won't handle it for me, Walter Boenning sure as hell will!" She took a step toward Stengel, but stumbled and caught herself on the arm of the settee. "You'll buy it from me, won't you, Jack?"

"If that's what you want, of course."

"Oh, God," Cassie groaned. "Would someone please help me to bed?"

Dan was leaning against the hood of his car when he saw Jenny come into the hall again. She skirted past the gurney and charged up to the knot of paramedics as they lingered over their paperwork. "Get this out of here, now," she ordered. "I'm taking Mrs. vonBerg upstairs, and I want this gone."

Dan straightened away from the car. In that instant, he recognized Jenny's second self, the proud, disdainful woman he'd glimpsed months ago on the dance floor, the one he knew he'd fall in love with next.

"Fancy meeting you here," Mike diMaio said, strolling up with his hands in his pockets.

Dan gave him a look of only mild surprise. "I could say the same thing about you. For a Philadelphia white-collar cop, you stray pretty far afield."

Mike rocked on the balls of his feet. "You figure it's just a coincidence these two guys buy it right after your trial?"

"I've given up trying to figure this one."

"Yeah, wish I could do the same."

They watched as two of the paramedics wheeled the gurney out of the house and over the lawn to load it into the ambulance.

"How are you calling it?" Dan asked him.

"The DA interrogated Chapman yesterday. His only alibi was his housekeeper's word, and he shook like a leaf the whole time.

Now he offs himself. The DA's gotta be thinkin' he fingered his man. A good suicide beats a confession any day, 'cause you can't get it quashed."

"Was it a good one?"

"The old boy showed a lot of class," Mike said. "He slit his wrists in the bathtub, like the Romans used to do. Only he did it fully dressed, just so's he wouldn't offend nobody."

Through the open door Dan saw Jenny in the hall again, this time with Chapman's daughter. Mike watched him watching her. "What's Jenny got to say about it?"

"She doesn't know anything. She's only here as a friend."

Mike shrugged. "Somethin' I should warn you about. Your mother and sister are awful curious about what's goin' on here, you packin' up the kid and all. They wanna meet this girl real bad."

Jenny crossed through the light in the hall and stood a moment in profile before she started up the stairs.

"I'd wait a while, though, I was you," he added.

Dan spun on him, looking for the smirk, and furious even when it wasn't there.

"That's my baby," he spat out.

Mike blinked and took a step backward.

"You lookin' for congratulations?" he said finally, disgusted. "Last I heard, it was nothin' to be proud of, knockin' up a nice girl."

Dan had forgotten what an old-world gentleman Mike could be. Suddenly the whole conversation was hilarious to him. He turned away, trying not to laugh, then turned back again. "And we're getting married," he declared.

Mike's face split into a grin, and he stuck out his hand at once. "Congratulations!"

Jenny watched them from a bedroom window upstairs and wondered at all the backslapping. Detective diMaio seemed a nice man, but he made her nervous, noticing all the things she noticed but no one else did. It was as if he were tracking her thoughts, and until she knew where they led, she didn't want anyone following.

As she watched, Stengel strode out to the limousine, and instantly his chauffeur was on his feet and holding a cellular phone out to him. Stengel turned away from the house to speak, and Moi stepped into position as if he were guarding his back.

"You should have known Daddy when he was young," Cassie mumbled from the bed.

Jenny crossed the room and pulled a chair up beside her. Cassie was lying in her slip, and the black silk looked harsh against the white bed linens. Jenny took a pink mohair afghan and tucked it over her shoulders.

"When I was a little girl—twenty years ago?—people used to stop and stare at him. He was master of the hunt, and the kids at the pony club flocked around him, all of them clamoring for his attention. He was like a Pied Piper. And so dashing! He'd ride into the yard, straight up in his stirrups, and he'd swing to the ground and pick me up and whirl me around and around and around."

Cassie's head turned from side to side on the pillow, as if she were whirling still.

"And the best part was that I was the only one who was his! I was the one he went home with at the end of the day. Oh, I could see why Mother fell in love with him. Even after I knew the truth, I could see why."

She mumbled in disjointed sentences for another few minutes before her head rolled on the pillow and her breathing became shallow and rhythmic.

"Cassie," Jenny whispered. She waited and whispered her name again.

"Is she asleep?"

Stengel lounged in the doorway, his black eyebrows lifted under his silver hair.

"No, she's drunk," Jenny said. "She was drunk before, too, when she offered you her stock. She'll think better of it in the morning."

"Following some sage legal counsel, no doubt?"

"No doubt," Jenny repeated tightly.

"All's fair," he said. "You wage your campaign, and I'll wage mine, and may the better one win."

Jenny brushed past him and down the stairs. When she stepped outside, she looked up at Cassie's window as Stengel's shadow crossed it. With a shudder of foreboding, she started to turn.

Suddenly she stopped. Engraved into the keystone over the door was a coat of arms with a rearing stallion and a flying dove. Her thoughts came in a jumble, and it made her head ache to try to sort through them. It made no sense, none of it.

Dan ran across the lawn, and Jenny went toward him. The blackness was sifting out of the sky as the gray fog of dawn rolled in from the east. She wanted nothing more than for them to hurry home to bed and hold each other tight for what remained of the night.

The ambulance driver started his engine, and she turned as it backed out of the driveway. Its headlights swept over Chapman's green MG, and in a sudden dizzying swirl, she remembered where she'd first seen it. In that moment, she heard Scott's voice echoing in her mind, *You think it was just a coincidence we met on the road during that rainstorm?*

"Oh, God," she groaned and buried her face against Dan's shoulder.

14

SHE SLEPT PAST NOON ON SATURDAY, AND COULD NOT ROUSE HER-self even when Dan whispered that he was taking Tony to the pool. She passed in and out of sleep, and her waking thoughts were as disjointed and incoherent as her dreams. A rearing stallion and a flying dove, on an ancient keystone and an antique pocket watch; a man on his car phone in a green sports car, hounding her off the highway onto a remote back road where no one could find her unless someone were giving him directions; Reese Chapman making an unexpected visit to the courtroom, and lingering after the lawyers departed; and a sheaf of papers in Scott's nightstand, printed from photographic negatives.

When Dan and Charlie Duncan first called Chapman in January, he said he didn't know who Scott Sterling was, and suggested they contact the trustee. But Cassie said she'd known Scott from the time she could ride. Scott went to all the hunt-club events, and Chapman was master of the hunt. They knew each other, then,

Scott and Chapman—they had for twenty years—but for some reason kept it secret.

Dan once said that his examination of Scott flowed like they were reading from the same script, and it turned out they were—a script written by Dan and stolen by Chapman and rehearsed with Scott in their nightly telephone conversations.

For good or evil, Chapman said to Jenny in court that day, a lot of drama was played out in courtrooms. He was there playing out one himself, and not for good. Dan's hard-won victory wasn't won at all; it was handed to him by Reese Chapman in some kind of unholy alliance with Scott.

She didn't know what to tell Dan. He already firmly believed that Scott was guilty of something, and she couldn't shed much light on what that was. She could tell him that Curtis Mason was Scott's victim, not vice versa, but only if public embarrassment were a crime. She could tell Dan that the trial was a sham and that he was nothing but a pawn in their scheme—but that was precisely what she could never do.

By late afternoon, she managed to drag herself from bed and down the stairs. She poured herself a glass of iced tea and held it against her cheek. It was too hot in the house. A ridiculous place to live, all told, freezing in the winter, broiling in the summer, leaking buckets of rain in the spring and fall. She should be glad to be rid of it.

The doorbell rang. "Who is it?" she asked at the chain.

"Mike diMaio," he called through the door. "And good for you for asking."

She pulled the door open. "Why's that?"

"They're pulling your surveillance," he said, and he turned on the doorstep to point to the unmarked car lurching out of its hiding place in the woods.

"Because Scott's not a suspect anymore," she said, her eyes following it.

"For the second time in a month, Scotty does everything wrong and still ends up in the clear."

"I'm afraid Dan's not here."

"I was hopin' we could talk," he said.

"Sure." She turned abruptly to compose herself. "Can I get you some iced tea, or something else cold to drink?"

"Tea sounds great."

She poured another glass, and handed it to him.

"Well, I'm glad about Scott," she said. "I knew he couldn't have done it. But to tell the truth, I can't believe Chapman did it either."

"He was a man with a lot of secrets."

"You mean because he was gay? But that doesn't—"

"That's not what he was," Mike said with an edge.

She gave him a sharp look. "I don't know what you mean."

He blew out his breath. "Look, this is all off the record—nobody wants it blabbed around—but we found a stash of kiddie porn in his house last night."

"Well—"

He held up a hand. "That's not all. He had that whole place wired for sound and video. There's a bunch of tapes of Chapman having sex with boys. He was what they call a chicken hawk."

"Oh, my God," Jenny blurted, her eyes going round. Chapman wasn't gay; he was a pedophiliac. Cassie had it all wrong.

He watched her closely as he spoke. "So here's the theory. Mason knew about his problem, and told him he'd ruin him if he didn't do what he was told. Mason told him to give up his right to fight the will, and Chapman did it, even though it cost him a third of the money. Mason told him to keep his mouth shut when two million dollars of the money ended up in Mason's own account, and Chapman kept his mouth shut. But there were limits to how much he'd take. When Mason wouldn't resign, Chapman snapped."

"But after all that, he kills himself?"

Mike shrugged. "Sometimes you don't know how hard it'll be to live with somethin' you did until you do it."

But Jenny was remembering Chapman yesterday morning, sitting alone with the drapes drawn, tears streaming down his face. It was more than guilt. It was as if his heart was broken. And that wasn't something you did to yourself; someone did it to you.

"I still got this feeling," Mike said, watching her, "that you know some missing pieces I don't."

She took a breath and turned to face him.

"This is what I know," she said. "Jack Stengel is involved somehow."

Mike cocked his head to one side. "Well, that's a new one. Run it past me."

"Last year, Stengel tried a hostile take-over of Macoal. Mason fought him off, and Stengel went away to lick his wounds. But this year, he resurfaced. He started to buy up blocks of Macoal stock. He started to wine and dine Catherine Chapman. One of two things had to happen for Stengel to get his hands on Catherine's stock: Mason had to be removed as trustee, or Chapman had to die. In one week, both those things happened. And last night, Cassie agreed to sell the stock to Stengel."

"I'll check it out," Mike said and drained his glass. "But unless Stengel *made* those two things happen, I'd say he's just a lucky guy."

She shook her head. "There's something there, I know it."

"I'd let it go, I was you. Under the circumstances."

His voice was suddenly gentle, and Jenny looked up at him in surprise.

He gave an apologetic shrug. "Hey, I know it's supposta be a secret, but I gotta say all the best to you and Dan."

"Thank you, Mike." She smiled.

"We're gonna be related, you know."

"I know. And I'm glad."

"When's the date?"

"Sometime in the next couple weeks. Dan's got a deposition schedule to work out first."

"Make it soon. I got trouble keepin' secrets." He carried his empty glass to the kitchen. "I better take off now. Tell the guys I said hi."

"I will. 'Bye, Mike."

Jenny stood at the window and watched him drive away. The sun hit the treetops in a glimmer of green-gold light, and a deer grazed serenely at the edge of the woods. It was hard to believe there was anything threatening out there, and if Mike was right, there wasn't.

She hoped he was right. They had enough to deal with, she and Dan. They had to find a house, plan their wedding and honeymoon, and prepare for the baby. It was more than enough. If Mike could be satisfied, so would she.

If only she knew where Scott was.

15

SUNDAY DAWNED HOT AND CLEAR AGAIN, AND JENNY'S THOUGHTS stayed with Cassie and the troubled man her father had been, all through the morning and afternoon, until at last she felt she had to call.

The housekeeper answered.

"Oh, Miss Lodge," she said. "Miss Chapman asked me to give you a message. She's gone away for a few weeks."

"Away?" Jenny said. "But what about her father—? The funeral?"

She left instructions, but the burial's to be private, and she can't even bear to be there herself, poor soul."

"But where has she gone?"

"To Mr. Stengel's beach house."

Jenny felt a flush of anger. Stengel was beginning his campaign already, and taking unfair advantage by whisking Cassie away to his private retreat.

"Where is Mr. Stengel's beach house?" She could spare a day to drive to the shore if she had to.

"In the Fiji Islands," Mrs. Hastings replied.

After dinner that night, Dan and Tony went out to play catch in the backyard. Jenny watched through the kitchen window while she washed the dishes. The dog kept racing between them and leaping into the air as if he were trying for an interception. The dove sat on a branch of the old dogwood tree as if she were watching, too.

Jenny remembered the dove's water dish, and filled a glass and took it into the storeroom, where she still liked to roost. Nothing stopped her from getting her own food and water, but Jenny coddled her still, and she seemed to like it.

She stood a moment in the musty half-light, remembering Scott reaching into the crate and the dove perching on his wrist without a moment's hesitation. A kind and gentle man she considered him then, and despite all she'd discovered since, that was still what she believed. She'd thought of herself and Scott as two wounded doves, but she knew now that Scott's wounds went deeper; she worried that they might be beyond cure. Why else wouldn't he come back?

She returned to the kitchen and stood at the sink, lost in her thoughts with her arms plunged to the elbows in soap suds. Dan saw her through the window. He left Tony rolling with the dog in the grass and came inside and wrapped his arms around her.

She didn't move, and he turned her around in the circle of his arms. "What's wrong?"

She looked up at him, at the face she loved, and wished she could tell him everything.

His eyes clouded. "You haven't heard from Scott?"

"No, it's just—I was just thinking—Dan, what would you do if you had a case where you won a courtroom victory, but not a moral one?"

He leaned back from her with a quizzical squint. "You're thinking about Gordon St. James, aren't you?"

She wasn't, but it rocked her to realize the extent to which that was also true.

"As long as you didn't knowingly suborn perjury, you shouldn't worry about it," Dan said. "You put on a case, the defense put on a case, and the jury decided where the truth fell."

"But what if the truth never really came out?"

He kissed her neck. "You were a new lawyer with your first jury trial. You'll call them better when you've had more experience."

She gazed at the face she always thought of as heartbreakingly handsome and knew it would break his heart to know the truth about Reese Chapman and Scott Sterling. She put her soapy hands on his T-shirt and pulled his mouth to hers.

A special-delivery letter arrived at Jenny's office on Tuesday afternoon. It was typed on stationery engraved with Cassie's Gladwyne address, but the airbill showed a foreign origin.

"Dear Jenny," Cassie wrote in an elegant longhand. "I've thought further about the sale of my Macoal stock and have concluded that my first instinct was the correct one. I wish to proceed at once with the transfer of all my shares to Jack Stengel. His attorneys will be contacting you to prepare the necessary papers. By copy of this letter, I am advising Walter Boenning of my desire to entrust this project to your good hands. Fondly, Catherine Chapman."

Stengel had won the game, before Jenny even got to play.

Mike diMaio called her on Wednesday. "I checked out the lead you gave me on Jack Stengel," he said. "Looks like you got some bad information."

"What?"

"He ain't the one buyin' up Macoal stock."

"Then who—?"

"Curtis Mason. His lawyer, Barlow, told us all about it. It was Mason's little insurance policy in case you got him kicked out of the trust."

"I don't understand."

"Like I said, Stengel just got lucky."

"He could still be behind it—"

"Come on, Jenny," he said. "You got better things than this to be thinkin' about."

Mike was right, she thought through the rest of the day. She had much better things to think about. The stock was Cassie's to do what she wanted with, and if she wanted to sell, it wasn't Jenny's place to object. Macoal stock was undervalued—Cassie might not realize a full profit—but that was her business, and how much difference did another half million or so make to her? During their long discussions about the company over the summer, Cassie voiced excitement about spearheading a new direction for Macoal, but Jenny could understand if that excitement had died. Cassie might want nothing more than a fresh start, far from Macoal, and a chest full of Stengel's cash could be her ticket there.

She resolved to follow Mike's advice, and let it go. But it would be easier if only she knew where Scott was.

An associate of Marvin Glasser's called Jenny a few days later, a young man named Josh Berman who announced he was to interface with her on the deal. His client had already agreed with hers on price. He'd be sending her a draft, she should mark it up and send it back, and meanwhile how did September 22 look for the closing?

She penciled it in and sent a note to Walt Boenning.

He appeared in her doorway that afternoon. "I want to congratulate you."

"On what?"

"On bringing in a major piece of business, of course. This could lead to big things."

"I don't see how. Cassie's withdrawing from the company. She'll probably turn her money over to an investment manager, and spend the rest of her life sunning herself on the Riviera."

"It could lead to something with Stengel," Boenning said pointedly. "He'll want Philadelphia counsel once he takes over Macoal. Do a good job on this transaction, a *fair* job, and we may see ourselves doing work for him in the future."

Jenny didn't respond. If Jack Stengel was the client Boenning wanted to take with him when he left the firm, he could be her guest.

16

DAN AND JENNY MET FOR LUNCH THE FOLLOWING WEDNESDAY AT the Summerhouse. He was waiting for her under the awning when she arrived breathless at the door, and he caught her up for a kiss. People streamed past them on the sidewalk and tossed smiles at each other at the sight of such an obviously expectant couple in love.

"Been waiting long?" Jenny asked as he swept her inside.

"About my whole life," he replied with a grin.

They ordered their sandwiches and carried their trays to a table in the back behind a lattice panel meant to simulate a gazebo. "How was the scrimmage this morning?" she asked as they took their seats.

"We won, but no thanks to Tony," Dan complained. "You should see him play. He's all aggression. Wherever the ball is, he's gotta be on top of it, and he doesn't pay attention to anything else. He probably missed two clear shots to a goal and never knew it."

"Let me guess," Jenny said. "He scored more times than anyone else."

"Yeah, but that's not the point—"

"The point is you're too hard on him, Dan."

Dan conceded with a shrug and took a bite of his sandwich. He wasn't wearing his glasses; it seemed he never wore them anymore.

"Enough small talk; this is a business lunch." He reached into his breast pocket.

"You got the discovery order?"

"Yep. The deposition schedule's set. Got your calendar?"

"Got it." Jenny pulled her pocket calendar out of her bag.

"How's the week of the eleventh?" he asked, flipping pages.

She shook her head. "I've got a summary judgment argument on the twelfth."

"I've got depositions in Buffalo the eighteenth through the twenty-second."

"That's okay. I've got the Macoal closing on the twenty-second."

"Clear the week after that?"

"Completely."

"Saturday, the twenty-third?" He chewed his lip. "That's cutting it kind of close."

"That still gives us five weeks until the baby comes," she said. "And it's the only way we'll get a honeymoon."

"That's it, then." Dan penciled it in. Suddenly he laughed. "Do you realize how ridiculous this is?"

"Yes, but nowhere near as ridiculous as it will be when we try to schedule the delivery of this baby."

"I'm throwing my calendar away when that happens."

He leaned over to kiss her, and when he pulled back, he had a glimpse of her calendar. "What's this?" he asked, pointing to a notation for the next night that read "Class, Bryn Mawr Hospital," with a line drawn through it.

"Oh." She flushed and closed the book. "That's the prepared childbirth class—you know, Lamaze?"

"Why's it crossed off?"

"I—" She cleared her throat. "You have to have a partner, so I dropped out."

His hand closed over hers. "Drop back in."

Her eyes shone as she looked up at him.

"Next item of business," he said and pulled some folded pages out of his breast pocket.

"What's that?"

"The realtor faxed me some listings he thinks we should take a look at."

Jenny gave a little sigh.

"Come on," he laughed. "We delay much longer, they'll be pulling that house down around us."

"I know," she said. "I just wish . . ." Her sentence trailed off.

"Listen. What d'you say we take a look at the new houses they're building there?"

"The Estates at Dundee? Oh, Dan, they're awfully expensive."

He teased her. "Hey, I'm marrying a rich lawyer. So, what d'you think?"

"I don't know. Maybe."

"But you can't get excited about it, huh?"

She gazed at him. She'd always felt a sadness about the new houses built on the ruins of the old estate, but surely none of that sadness could penetrate a house where she and Dan were together. "I can get excited about anything if you're there," she said.

His eyes lit up. "Hold that thought."

The meal ended, and they rose reluctantly and threaded their way through the tables toward the door.

A familiar squeal sounded, and Jenny spun around as a mop of black curls was launched toward her.

"Leslie!"

"Jenny! Oh, my God!" Leslie gave her a quick hug, then pushed her back. "Look at you!" she exclaimed, and already following her own command, her gaze fixed at Jenny's waistline.

"Leslie, it's so good to see you. How have you been?"

Leslie's gaze moved from Jenny to Dan, standing awkwardly beside them.

"Oh, I'm sorry," Jenny blurted. "Leslie, this is Dan Casella. Dan, my friend, Leslie Maitland."

They shook hands, and Leslie's eyes gleamed with curiosity as they moved from Dan to Jenny. "Please—come over and say hello to Bruce."

Bruce was on his feet by their table. The introductions were repeated, then Bruce turned pointedly to Jenny. "Have you heard anything from Scott?"

She shook her head. "You?"

"Nothing. And neither have his parents or his ex-wife."

"It doesn't make any sense," Leslie said. "He's not in trouble with anybody anymore. Why doesn't he come back?"

"I don't know." Suddenly Jenny was aware of Dan standing woodenly beside her. "We have to run," she said. "But listen, it was wonderful seeing you!"

"Let's get together soon," Leslie said and offered a final embrace before Jenny turned to go.

Outside, Dan took her hand but was silent as they started down the block, and she knew it was the mention of Scott Sterling that made him so.

"Do you have another hour free?" he asked when they reached the corner.

"I guess so. Why?"

"Let's go to City Hall right now and get the license."

She nodded, and they turned the corner.

17

THE STOCK SALE AGREEMENT ARRIVED FROM MARVIN GLASSER'S office at the end of the week, and the transaction was a complicated one. Cassie's stock was to be transferred first from the trust into a corporation wholly owned by her and created for the sole purpose of holding the stock for a minute before it was flipped into another corporation owned by Stengel's nominee, which would immediately sell it to yet a third newly formed corporation beneficially owned by Stengel and a group of his investors.

Jenny spent days with Cynthia Lehmann deciphering the mechanics of the transaction, and days more deciding how to restructure it to maximize the benefits to Cassie. Redlined drafts were exchanged by fax between her office and Glasser's. When she finally had the papers the way she wanted them, Jenny had them messengered to Cassie. She returned them with only one comment. Her name should now read Catherine M. Chapman; her divorce was final.

It was agreed that the closing would be conducted in Philadelphia, and Jenny reserved a conference room in her offices for all day on the twenty-second.

"We'd better get the papers on your system," Glasser's associate, Josh Berman, said to her during the week leading up to the closing. "There're always last-minute changes, and they'll have to be made on your end."

Three attempts were made Wednesday afternoon to transmit the documents by modem into the Jackson, Rieders computer system, but something went wrong each time.

"Listen," Jenny said as Berman writhed with frustration on the other end of the line. "Why don't you put everything on diskette and express-mail it to me?"

The diskette arrived in the morning's delivery on Thursday, the day before the closing. To be sure there were no compatibility problems, Jenny loaded it onto her PC and called up the directories.

Something was immediately wrong. According to her inventory, the closing called for twelve different documents, but the diskette held twenty. Some must be duplicates, or earlier drafts that should have been deleted.

Painstakingly, Jenny called up each document and read it word for word against the final hard copy. Everything matched until she came to the tenth document. It was an agreement of transfer for the correct number of shares of Macoal Corporation, as it was supposed to be, between Stengel's nominee corporation as buyer, as it was supposed to be, and M. Reese Chapman as seller.

It was a typo, Jenny thought at first, but the name M. Reese Chapman appeared throughout the document, even below the signature lines. She scanned back to the first page and stopped at the second recital clause. "Whereas, M. Reese Chapman was appointed Trustee of the Elizabeth Mason Chapman Trust on the _____ day of _____, 1995" . . .

The print blurred in Jenny's vision. Reese Chapman never was appointed trustee, and he never could have been the contemplated seller of the stock because he was already dead before the deal was struck.

Jenny exited from the document and returned to the directory to check the date of its creation. Among the neat row of dates all falling in September, it stood out clearly. January 9, 1995.

More than eight months ago. Before Scott's confession, before the scandal, before anything happened to rock the trust. In January, Curtis Mason was the trustee, and the last thing he would have done was sell the stock to Jack Stengel.

Jenny grabbed the phone and punched in the number of the house in Haverford. "Miss Chapman is not in at the moment," Mrs. Hastings said.

"This is her attorney, Jennifer Lodge. When do you expect her back?"

"Not until this evening."

Jenny bit her lip. "Do you know where I could reach her? It's very important I speak to her today."

"No, I'm sorry."

"Please ask her to call me as soon as possible. At the office or at home. It's urgent."

Jenny hung up and levered herself out of her chair, her back straining to counterbalance the weight of her abdomen. She went next door to Boenning's office and knocked briskly before she swung the door in.

Boenning was with Marilyn, both of them bent over a blueprint. "Oh, excuse me."

"What is it?" Boenning snapped.

It was a blueprint of the new office for his new firm. Boenning was leaving, and taking Marilyn with him and who knew who else. But of course Jenny knew who else. He was taking Cassie Chapman with him, too, or Jack Stengel, whoever proved to be the more lucrative client.

Her message died on her lips. "I—I just wanted to remind you about the closing tomorrow," she faltered.

"I'll be there," he said.

Jenny returned to her office and slipped Berman's diskette into her briefcase before she left for the night.

18

DAN WAS TAKING DEPOSITIONS IN BUFFALO, SO IT WAS JENNY WHO picked up Tony for the drive home after his game. It was another victory for Alexander, and Tony was full of the game, the team, and himself. A few smiles of encouragement, a couple really's and uh-huh's was all it took to keep him chattering all the way home.

She had half a hope that Dan's trip might finish early, that his car would be parked at the carriage house, and that he'd throw the door open at the sound of their approach. If those things had happened, she would have gone into his arms and told him everything from the beginning of time to the end of the world and wouldn't even stop for breath. But only Sam was there to welcome them home, and though he did it with a joyful bark, it did nothing to ease her mind.

She made chicken stir-fry for dinner, and Tony, admonished by Dan to make himself useful while he was gone, set to work chopping the vegetables. He did it comically, and a little recklessly, tossing a pepper in the air and spearing it on knifepoint on the way back down, and Jenny had to remind herself to give him the laughs he was working for.

But she couldn't keep the façade up through dinner, and eventually Tony noticed. "Anything wrong, Jenny?" he asked as he was clearing the table.

She forced a smile and shook her head. "I've just got things on my mind. Work things."

He nodded; this was old news. "I won't bug you," he said. "I'll just watch TV for a while."

He switched on MTV and sprawled on the couch. Jenny ran the water in the sink. A rock video came on with a hard jarring beat, and a headache started to pound in her temples.

"Tony, could you turn that down, please?" she said, but he couldn't hear her above the noise. She turned the tap to cold and splashed two handfuls of water on her face.

The dishes done, she pulled herself laboriously up the stairs and sank full-length across the bed. The music downstairs was crescendoing into an ear-splitting wail. Cassie was with Jack Stengel, she knew it, and that meant she might never return to her father's house tonight. Jenny might have no more than five minutes to buttonhole her in the morning, and when she tried to rehearse a five-minute speech that would persuade her that Stengel was out to defraud her, her head only ached worse.

The phone rang, and she sat up awkwardly to reach for it.

"Jenny."

"Dan!" she cried.

"Listen, I'm in a break; I've only got a minute. I just wanted to see how you're doing."

Only a minute, and she didn't know how she could explain to Cassie in five. "I was hoping you might make it home tonight." The rock music was shrieking, and she pressed the phone tight to her ear.

"I'm still hoping," he said. "My adversary wants to break now and resume in the morning. He's out of ideas, and he's counting on something occurring to him during the night. But I said we continue tonight until we're done. Everybody's supposed to be thinking it over now. If we can't agree, we're gonna call the judge and get a ruling."

"I'll keep my fingers crossed," she said. Maybe he could still make it home tonight; maybe he could persuade her she was imagining things and there was nothing to worry about.

"What's wrong, sweetheart? You sound a little down."

Something bright winked on the edge of the nightstand. She leaned over to peer at it. "I miss you," she said.

It was an antique pocket watch.

"I miss you, too."

Her hand came down and closed over it.

"Forty-eight hours from now, we'll be married and on our honeymoon," Dan said.

Scott had been here, today, in this room, and he left a message only she could read.

"That's all I can think about," she murmured.

The watch seemed to glow inside her fist; she could feel its engraving burn hot against her skin. A coat of arms with a rearing stallion in one quadrant and a dove in another.

"I love you, Jenny."

"I love you, too."

The music was pounding through the floor and into her skull. She hung up the phone and opened her hand to stare at the watch. She remembered where she'd last seen it, and knew that that was Scott's message—that was where he would be waiting for her.

She grabbed her car keys, slid her feet into her loafers, and hurried down the stairs. When she reached the bottom, the rock video ended, and in the abrupt silence, Tony turned to look at her with a question on his face.

"I have to go out," she said.

He nodded and turned back to the screen.

Jenny got into her car. From Coventry Road she made an immediate right onto Canterbury Lane and sped past all the new houses to the cul-de-sac at the top of the hill. She spun the wheel until the car pointed back the way she'd come, and stopped.

There was no car behind her, only a new homeowner watering his lawn and a late-working roofer on top of one of the unfinished houses.

She climbed out of the car and struck out across the meadow with the glare of the setting sun full in her face. When Scott had led her here before, the meadow was filled with wild timothy, knee-high but easy to walk through. Now, in September, it was waist-high in sun-dried brush and bramble, and every step was a struggle. Thorns tore at her hose and broke her skin, but she waded through until she came to the stand of old oak trees.

"I always felt like I was coming into church," he'd said, but now she knew that there was nothing righteous in the path he'd taken.

She followed the trail out of the woods and past the fenced meadows until the old stable came into sight. The heat and the exertion made her lightheaded, but she trudged on, across the dusty paddock and into the stable.

All the half-doors were closed in the stalls, and only tiny pinpoints of light penetrated through cracks and knotholes in the planks. She stood and breathed in the scent of horses until her eyes adjusted to the dimness, then she walked past the tack room and the ladder climbing to the loft overhead and down the length of the stable.

"Scott," she whispered.

A rustling sounded in one of the stalls to her right.

"Scott?" she said again, louder.

A shape rose, dark and silent in the shadows.

"Scott." Her voice shook, and she took a breath to steady it. "I brought you your good-luck piece." She held her hand toward him, palm up, the watch faintly glowing in the dim light.

He moved toward her and closed his hand over hers. "You got my message," he choked out. "You came."

He'd changed in the month he'd been gone. A brown beard covered part of his face and a sunburn the rest. His hair hung shaggy with a bandanna tied around his forehead like an Indian headband. He wore a tattered denim workshirt and jeans.

"I knew you'd come," he said and buried his face in her hair.

"Scott, I've come to take you back."

"I can't go back, Jenny; you know that."

"That's the only reason I'm here."

He tilted his head back. "If that were true, you would've brought Casella or diMaio with you."

"I couldn't. They don't know what I know."

He released her and stepped away, his old quirky grin twisting his face. "Ah, Jenny, you don't know anything, either."

He turned, and a long sliver of fading sun caught him in a second's light. The dull black metal of a gun showed above his belt.

She swallowed her gasp. "I know almost everything, Scott, and I know you'll only get yourself killed if you try to use that gun. Please, come with me."

He didn't seem to hear her. He went to the back of the stall and cracked open the top of the door to look out over the paddock to the hillside.

"You want to turn yourself in," she said. "That's why you sent for me."

"That's not why." He pulled the door closed and moved through the darkness beside her. "I just needed to know—is it true about Reese?"

"Yes. He killed himself."

He gave a low moan, and sank to his knees in the straw.

"Did he—did he say anything?" he whispered. "Or leave a note?"

"Only for Cassie. He didn't implicate you at all."

He put his hands over his face.

"Come back with me, please, Scott. The DA will make a deal with you if you confess, I know it."

He didn't hear her. He took his hands away and looked around the stall as if he didn't remember where he was. He got to his feet and looked both ways down the center corridor of the stable, and around the stall again.

"This is the place, isn't it?" Jenny guessed.

He turned and stared at her.

"This is where Reese used to bring you, when you were a twelve-year-old boy and he was master of the hunt."

His eyes went wild under the headband. "How do you know that? I never told, I never—"

"That's what Reese always said, isn't it? 'Don't ever tell.' "

"How do you know that?"

Jenny let her breath out slowly and lowered herself into the straw. "Oh, Scott, that's what men like him always tell their victims."

"No, you don't get it," he said. "He was *my* victim."

She reached for his hand and pulled him down beside her. "How was he your victim?"

"He had his eye on me, and I knew it, and I used it against him. I helped him untack one day. He said I had earned a special reward and he brought me back into this stall."

He looked around again. "It's smaller now," he said. "It's not the same."

"Scott, whatever happened here wasn't your fault."

"I was amazed when he opened his pants. You had to know what he was like then. He was like a god to us kids. All I could think was, I wonder why he's doing this, and what's in it for me. And I went ahead and let him fuck me."

Jenny squeezed his hand tightly.

"He cried afterward. I couldn't believe it. This god, the master of the hunt—crying! He said he was sorry, he couldn't help himself, and I mustn't ever breathe a word to anybody. He pulled out his wallet. His hands were shaking, but he started to peel off bills. They went flying around, drifting into the straw, and I dove after them and pocketed every single one. I didn't have any idea what his problem was. All I knew was instead of me craving his attention, he craved mine.

"I owned him after that."

Jenny remembered the twelve-year-old boy in the photograph, the boy who should have had nothing more to worry about than the next horse show, whose life was meant to be one of privilege and reward—all of it ruined because he'd caught the eye of a sick man.

"How did it end?" she asked.

"One day he was too rough; he hurt me and I needed a doctor. He made up a story for me to tell, that I was riding alone in the woods, and a strange man grabbed me off my horse and did this to me. Reese told me he'd take care of me the rest of my life if I'd only stick to that story. He gave me his father's watch and told me that was the sign of his sacred vow.

"I did everything like he said, but my old man didn't buy it. He knew something was going on, and he made me quit riding. I didn't see Reese anymore

"But whenever I wanted money, I called him, and he'd always get it to me somehow. He was afraid not to."

"No, it wasn't blackmail," Jenny said. "He did it because he loved you."

Scott shook his head, denying it.

"He protected you to the end," she said. "He never spoke your name. He just sat in a dark room with tears running down his face, like his heart was broken."

Scott shot to his feet. "It wasn't supposed to happen that way!" He cracked the door open and peered out at the yard again.

"Of course it wasn't," Jenny said. "That's why you have to come back. You have to explain that the plan was only to force Mason to resign from the trust so the stock could be sold to Stengel. And that it was Chapman's plan from the start."

Scott sagged into the straw beside her and propped his chin on his knees. "Reese had lots of plans. He told me to suck up to Uncle Curt; he'd be my ticket. But it didn't pan out—he never lifted a finger to help me. Reese's old bitch of a wife kept him on a tight allowance; he couldn't give me much, but he kept promising a big payoff when she died.

"Well, you know how that turned out—she as good as cut him out of the will."

A hundred and twenty thousand dollars in cash deposits, Jenny remembered, all of it spent, and meanwhile Scott's heiress wife divorced him and he was passed over for partner at Harding & McMann. By last summer, he needed cash more than ever. And Reese Chapman was willing to do anything to raise it for him; his obsessive love for Scott didn't die, even after the sexual attraction did.

"The trust was holding enough Macoal stock to give majority control—"

"And Stengel was willing to pay for that control," she said.

"He said he'd pay ten million for the stock. That's way above market, so Cassie'd get a good deal. And he said he'd pay Reese six million under the table for pulling it off, and half of that was mine."

"But the only way Chapman could pull it off," Jenny said, "was to get Mason ousted as trustee."

"We knew two things about Uncle Curt: he didn't want to be bothered with shitwork, and he was greedy."

"You convinced him to turn the trust over to you."

"That part was easy," Scott said. "The hard part was getting him to trust me with his own trading account. But Reese drew up phantom portfolios to show what he might have netted if he'd made the right picks, and Uncle Curt fell for it, hook, line, and sinker."

"And he really believed he was making money, didn't he? He never suspected the two million came from the trust."

"Of course not."

"Scott, how could you take such a risk? You confessed to grand larceny—you could have gone to prison!"

"As long as none of the money stuck to me, I'd never have to do time. I might lose my license, but big shit! I was gonna walk away with three million dollars! I'd never write another fucking will the rest of my life."

So that was Chapman's plan, Jenny realized. When Scott made his confession, Mason was caught in a clear conflict of interest. He should have resigned immediately. Chapman would have been named successor trustee, and the sale of the Macoal stock to Stengel would have closed in January, just as the draft contract contemplated.

"But Mason refused to resign," Jenny said.

"Reese had a contingency plan."

She knew that part, too, because Dan Casella was the center-piece of the contingency plan. The best defense for Harding & McMann was a good offense against Curtis Mason. Dan's fight to clear his client played right into Chapman's hands.

"It held us up," Scott said. "But as long as we got an accelerated trial, it was okay, because Stengel said he'd keep his offer open till year-end."

"But even after the trial, Mason refused to resign."

"Stupid son of a bitch!" he exploded. "After all that happened, after his dog was shot, after all the phone calls, the fucking idiot still wouldn't resign."

Jenny wasn't following. Mason's dog was killed the weekend of the blizzard, in a random shooting that had nothing to do with this. "What did you say about the dog?"

"I gave him fair warning."

Scott made the death threats, Scott shot the dog? "I don't understand—"

"Reese started holding out on me," he stormed on. "I didn't even know Uncle Curt refused to resign until you told me about it, that day at the hospital. He never told me."

Jenny remembered his outburst in the parking lot. She thought he was angry at her, but it was all for Chapman.

"I guess he wanted to protect you from what he was planning to do next."

"No, you don't get it. He lost his heart for it. He wasn't planning to do anything next."

"Scott, he was planning to kill Mason!"

There was silence. All she could see of him were his eyes, shining hard between his hair and beard.

"Ah, Jenny," he said finally. "I told you you didn't know anything."

She shook her head, so fast her vision blurred. "Scott, you were home that night, you were with me—you cooked dinner!"

He stared at her, his eyes empty. "You think only Chinese restaurants sell take-out?"

Jenny couldn't smother her gasp in time. Scott lunged at her, gripping her shoulders so hard she felt the imprint of his thumbs forming in a pattern of broken capillaries.

"I had to do it!" he shouted. "We went too far. I was hanging out to dry! What choice did I have?"

She was wrong—she lied for him, but she was wrong. He did leave the house that evening, he did go to Mason's office, and on the way home he stopped at a French restaurant and picked up the dinner she thought he'd spent hours preparing. He killed a man he called uncle, then came home to propose marriage to her.

Jenny fought down the scream in her throat. "You didn't have any other choice," she said. "It was the only way."

She put her arms around him. His grip relaxed and she leaned back in the straw and pulled his head to her breast and stroked his hair. He lay heavily against her, and his shoulders shook with silent sobs.

19

THE PINPOINTS OF LIGHT THROUGH THE PLANK WALLS SLOWLY WENT out, one by one, like candles snuffed. The night songs of crickets and tree frogs struck up outside, and an owl hooted off in the woods.

Scott's body lay heavily against Jenny. The butt of the gun pressed painfully against her, inches from her fingertips, but she couldn't use it, and he'd know she couldn't use it. There was no hope of maneuvering his capture, nor his surrender. The most she could hope for was her own escape. But it was half a mile to her car, over rough terrain, and she was in no shape for sprinting.

"Scott," she said softly and shifted her weight under him.

He rolled to his feet like a commando and jumped to the door to peer into the darkness.

"The police aren't looking for you, Scott. As far as they're concerned, Chapman did it, and you're completely in the clear. You've got nothing to worry about. From them or me."

He barked a laugh. "You think I've been hiding from the cops? Is that what you think?"

"Then who—?"

"Stengel. Or should I say Moi."

"The chauffeur?"

"Yeah, well, that's his day job."

"But why?"

"Stengel never planned on paying the six million. Reese knew that. And why should he? What were we gonna do, sue him? But Reese had it all figured. He had about three hours of Stengel on videotape, discussing all the details of the deal."

Jenny remembered Chapman's house, wired for sound and video, and she remembered the package that arrived for Scott, the padded mailer she'd left in his room and never saw again.

"He sent the tape to you, so you could blackmail Stengel?"

"I called him. I called him right after Uncle Curt died, and I told him, 'Look, we held up our end of the deal, and don't you even think about welching, because if you do, the cops and the FBI and the SEC are all gonna get a nice package of videocassettes in the mail.'

"He said, fine, no problem. But when I left your house that night, somebody was following me, and I lost him and doubled back, and it was Moi. He's been dogging me ever since."

"But he's just after the tape, right?"

"I'd say he's out to destroy whichever one he finds first."

"Then give him the tape! Where is it?"

"Someplace safe," he said, and grinned.

Jenny had to get out, she had to get away from him. She struggled to her feet.

"You can't go on hiding like this, Scott. If you won't turn yourself in, at least let me drive you somewhere."

He stared at her. "Would you take me to the airport?"

"Of course."

"Not Philadelphia," he said. "Newark?"

"If that's what you want."

"Okay."

Scott picked up a rucksack and slung it over his shoulder. He grabbed Jenny's hand and led her down the black corridor to the stable door.

Outside, the stars faintly lit their way as they hiked uphill through the meadow toward the grove. Jenny stumbled and gave a little cry of annoyance.

"Shhh!" Scott hissed, and in the downbeat of silence that followed, they heard something.

A millisecond later there was nothing. They glanced at each other, afraid to ask if the other heard it, too.

"Who did you tell?" Scott rasped. "Who else knows I'm here?"

"Nobody!" she whispered.

They froze again, straining against the great black wall of darkness to catch the sound they'd caught before. But when there was nothing, they moved on, keeping to the shadows of the trees and bushes as they made their way through the woods and across the meadow to the top of the hill. A gleam of sheetmetal shone in the starlight. "That's my car," she whispered over Scott's shoulder.

They started for it when the sound came again.

Scott dropped his bag and grabbed her hand and pulled her after him, in a freefalling run down the hill and through the weed-choked meadow to the woods. Jenny stumbled and caught herself against a tree trunk. When she looked back, a silhouette stood against the night sky.

"Come on!" Scott cried.

He pulled her after him back into the stable. Jenny couldn't catch her breath and couldn't see through the darkness. "Scott!" she gasped. "Scott, where are you?"

He grabbed her hand again and pulled her after him until they came to the ladder to the loft. He pushed her up until her hands and feet found the rungs and she could scramble the rest of the way on her own. She collapsed into the hay. Nothing but silence followed after her.

"Scott, where are you?" she whispered down the ladder.

"Shhh!" came a harsh response from the stall below.

She strained her ears, listening for the man outside. She tried to squint through the darkness, but it was too thick. On hands and knees, she felt her way to the back wall of the loft, then climbed to her feet and groped her way along the wall until she came to a wooden window. She pushed it open and enough starshine flowed in to light her way back to the edge of the loft.

Scott was in the stall below, standing with an eye pressed to the crack of the door. The gun was in his hand. She drew back from the edge of the loft, but at the same moment Scott leaned forward, his gun to the crack. She watched in horror as his body tensed and his hand jerked before she heard the roar of the report.

Jenny's arms flew over her head as she fell into the hay. Mice squeaked beneath her, and a bird whooshed by overhead on a flight line through the window.

Another shot sounded and she knew it wasn't Scott's gun an instant before she heard the bullet splintering the wall of the stable. Scott fired again and again, and the shots came back just as fast.

Jenny's ears roared. She clenched her fists against them and felt the tears on her face. The sulfurous smell of the powder burned acrid in her nose and throat. Dan's name was on her lips, but no one could hear it.

Then there was silence.

She leaned forward and looked down into the stall as Scott took aim and pulled the trigger again. There was no answering report this time. He squeezed the trigger once more. Nothing sounded but an empty click.

He backed away from the door, his head turning crazily in search of his canvas bag, the one he'd dropped at the top of the hill. He ran out of the stall and into the next, then the next, down the length of the stable, but there was nothing he could use for a weapon. There was nothing but moldy straw and the lingering scent of horses.

The door hinges groaned.

He was a shapeless shadow moving softly on the earthen floor. There was a sound, a faint scratching, then a flash of light on his face as he held up a match, and in that second, his round blue eyes shone. It was Stengel's steadfast disciple, Moi.

He tossed the match away from him, up to the loft and into the hay. It crackled as the flames caught and sent out a glow of light. Jenny shrank back from it, keeping to the darkness.

The shadow moved down the stable and crouched and spun soundlessly at the first stall until he saw it was empty, then moved on to the next.

The fire was spreading through the loft, and when Jenny looked back she saw the flames licking at the rafters of the roof.

She slipped off her shoes and moved down the row with the shadow, as soundless as he, twenty years of ballet training paying off with each silent step. When he looked up, she drew back, and when he moved forward, she glided along with him. She could see down into the stalls, and she saw Scott in the last one, his eyes gleaming wild in the dark as he smelled the smoke and knew what it meant.

Something ripped into the side of her foot, and she swallowed back a scream as the pain exploded and burned up her leg. She clutched at a roof truss to keep her balance, and gritting her teeth, forced herself to look down. Blood was spurting out of a gash on her foot and onto a metal prong half-buried in the hay. It was the tine of an old pitchfork.

She found the handle and pulled the pitchfork out of the hay. This was it, the weapon Scott was searching for. Up here, where he couldn't reach it and she couldn't get it to him.

Her foot was throbbing and she could feel the hot blood gushing out with every beat of her heart. But silently she lifted the pitchfork and moved to the edge of the loft.

The shadow was drawing closer to Scott. If she shouted a warning, Moi would kill them both. If she kept silent, he'd kill Scott and slowly and methodically search for her. And he'd find her, if the fire didn't kill her first.

One more stall until he reached Scott.

There was a roar as the roof caught fire, and suddenly the whole loft was ablaze. Smoke billowed through the rafters. Jenny's eyes stung and she fought not to cough, not to make a sound that would reveal where she was as she followed the shadow down the length of the stable to the stall where Scott was cowering.

The shadow went into a crouch, coiled, and spun, and in that instant, Jenny marked her target and hurled the pitchfork with all the force she had in her. It spun and wobbled and winked in the fire's glow, and she swayed on her feet, watching in horror as it seemed to float through the dead air in excruciating slow motion.

The shadow whipped around with his gun up a second before the pitchfork struck him on the neck and shoulder and knocked him to the ground. The gun flew out of his hand and skidded across the floor, and he rolled to his feet and lunged for it, but suddenly Scott was up and moving, too.

The blast reverberated against the wooden walls, and as a spray of blood splattered through the stable, Jenny screamed as loud as the roar. It was the last sound she heard. The fire in the loft went out, the stars faded into the night, and the world went black as she toppled into the hay.

20

THE CARRIAGE HOUSE WAS IN DARKNESS WHEN DAN PULLED INTO the courtyard, but he didn't expect anything different at one in the morning. The dog had learned to recognize the sound of his engine, and he trotted up without barking as Dan came into the house. That was some security, he supposed; at least they would be robbed only by burglars driving Jaguars. "Good boy," Dan said, and gave him a weary pat.

He was exhausted from a day spent playing games with his opponents and waiting to see who blinked first. It was a hell of a way for grown-ups to make a living. The teleconference with the judge turned into an hour-long harangue full of recriminations and grievances six months old. The judge complained that he felt like a marriage counselor trying to reconcile a couple who'd been fighting for thirty years. But however asinine the process, at the end of it Dan emerged the winner. The deposition resumed, but only briefly; he was right about his opponent running out of ideas. At eight-thirty, the deposition ended for good.

It was a good result for his client, but he knew the real reason he'd fought so hard: he wanted to get home to Jenny.

He left his bags in the hall and tiptoed up the rickety staircase. She sounded tired on the phone, so he wouldn't wake her; all he would do was slide into bed beside her and hold her for the rest of the night.

The starlight floated through the open window of their bedroom, gleaming against the brass headboard and over the empty bed.

"Jenny?"

He switched on the lights, then moved across the hall and hit the switch there, too. Tony buried his face into the pillow as light flooded the room.

"Tony, wake up," Dan said, rolling him onto his back. "Where's Jenny?"

Tony covered his eyes and mumbled something incoherent.

Dan pried his elbows away from his face and repeated, "Tony! Where's Jenny?"

Slowly he blinked himself awake. "I don't know," he said, his voice thick with sleep. "She went out after dinner and never came back."

Idiot, Dan cursed himself. Her car was gone and he hadn't even noticed.

"Where?" he said, shaking Tony before he drifted into sleep again. "Where did she go?"

"She didn't say," his voice faded.

Dan bolted back across the hall to search for a note. The bed was made, the dresser and nightstand clear, and not a sign of a note anywhere. He galloped downstairs and made the same search there. There was nothing—but of course there wouldn't be. She wasn't expecting him back tonight; she wouldn't have thought to leave him a note.

He picked up the phone and dialed her office—maybe she was working late on that closing she had tomorrow—and when he got her voice mail, he rationalized again: she was probably working in a conference room and had forgotten to forward her calls.

But he wasn't buying any of it.

He paced to the front window and tried to peer out into the darkness, but only his own panicked reflection came back.

Something had happened to her—he felt it suddenly with a certainty—and he lunged across the room to call Mike.

The phone rang before he reached it, and relief coursed through his veins like a drug. He grabbed the phone. "Hello?"

"Casella?"

It was a man's voice, speaking almost in a whisper but still somehow familiar.

"Yeah, who's this?"

"Jenny's been hurt."

The room started to spin. "Who is this?" Dan demanded, holding tight to the phone with both hands. "Where is she?"

"Bryn Mawr Hospital."

"Sterling? Sterling, is that you?"

The line went dead. Dan stared at the phone in his hands, then dropped it and ran for the door.

He parked in a tow-away zone at the emergency entrance, threw himself from the car, then ducked back to switch off the ignition. An ambulance was unloading at the curb, and he held the door open and scanned the face on the stretcher, but it was a corpulent old man with a grayish pallor. He elbowed his way through the crowd and charged up to a woman clad in pale blue nylon at the reception desk.

"Jennifer Lodge?" He realized he was shouting, and he lowered his voice and said her name again. "Is she here? Has she been admitted?"

The woman's eyes were down, and she gave no sign of having heard him. Her lips pursed, and her head swiveled to the woman at the file cabinet behind her. "Suze? That pregnant woman who was hemorrhaging? Where'd they take her?"

Hemorrhaging, he heard, and felt the blood drain out of his own body.

"The one that guy dropped off? Maternity," the other woman said.

He went numb, and so uncomprehending he almost couldn't remember the directions they gave him to the maternity ward. Hemorrhaging. Was her life in danger, or the baby's, and would Jenny survive either way?

He broke into a run out of the elevator and down the deserted corridor. A woman's moan sounded from behind one of the closed doors, and it built up to a wail and peaked into a scream.

"Sir?" sounded from somewhere, then, "*Sir!* You can't go down there."

He turned. A woman in a green scrub suit was running behind him.

"Jennifer Lodge!" he burst out.

The woman's steps slowed. "Are you the husband?"

He nodded.

"Come with me."

She led him through a set of double doors into another corridor, this one full of people and activity.

"Wait here. I'll get the doctor."

"I want to see Jenny," he called, but she disappeared into a curtained room.

A dozen people were milling, and Dan couldn't figure out who was who. It was all so different from a courtroom, where any fool could stumble in and tell in a minute who the players were. In court, everyone had their place, and they dressed for their parts. Here, no one stood still for thirty seconds, and they were all dressed in the same wrinkled blue and green cottons. Things were controlled and orderly in a courtroom, nothing like this chaotic scene.

A green-capped man with a full salt-and-pepper beard emerged from behind the curtain, and his eyes landed on Dan. "Mr.—" He consulted his clipboard. "Lodge?"

"Yeah." Dan almost leapt for him. "How is she? What happened?"

"She suffered an arterial hemorrhage from a laceration of the foot. Minor bronchial irritation due to smoke inhalation. Possible tetanus—the immune globulin was given intramuscularly as a prophylaxis. And shock, probably psychic as much as secondary to the trauma. We're still treating her for that."

Dan lost his wind all of a sudden, and he sagged back against the cold tile wall. "The baby—?"

"Still viable, heartbeat's regular so far. Is this her first pregnancy?"

Dan nodded. His throat was clogged, and he wasn't sure he could speak.

"Well, that improves the odds. The cervix'll be tight."

He was almost afraid to ask, "Odds of what?"

"The biggest danger now is that she'll go into labor."

"No, it's too soon—"

"We're doing what we can to hold it off. What *she* needs to do is get complete flat-on-her-back bed rest."

"Done," Dan said.

She was lying in a narrow bed with her feet elevated, in a narrow room marked Labor 3. Clear tubing ran into her nostrils, and a liquid was dripping from a plastic bag into the inside of her elbow. A wide band of flesh-colored elastic was stretched over her abdomen to hold an electronic monitor in place. Jagged lines traced a pattern of mountains and valleys on a portable screen beside the bed.

Dan pulled up a stool close to the bed. Her head was turned on the pillow, and the blue-veined lids were closed over her eyes. Her skin was pallid and clammy to his lips; her breath came in shallow draws.

"She'll come out of it soon," the nurse said when she saw the fear on his face. "You watch. In an hour she'll have her rosy cheeks back."

He did watch, intently, as if the force of his stare could will her awake, but his mind was racing as fast as his pulse. A laceration on her foot, the doctor said, smoke inhalation. Somehow Scott Sterling had been with her—he'd brought her to the hospital and stopped long enough only to make a phone call.

At last, Jenny's head rolled on the pillow, and she drew a deep breath.

"Jenny," he whispered, gripping her hand.

Her head rolled again, and her eyes fluttered open and took a moment to focus.

"Dan," she murmured.

A second later a shadow crossed her face, and her eyes opened wide. "The baby!" she moaned. "Oh, my God, the baby!"

She struggled to sit up and started to tear at the strap around her belly.

"No!" Dan said, grabbing her. "Jenny, no, the baby's fine!"

She twisted in his arms until he could make her meet his eyes. "Sweetheart, the baby's fine."

Slowly, she let herself sink back on the pillow. "Oh, Dan," she moaned. "I was so afraid—"

"Don't be. Everything's fine. You just need to get some rest."

Tears welled in her eyes and leaked out of the corners of her lashes. "You were right about Scott. You were right about every-thing!"

She told him the story from start to finish, as clear and cogent as if she were opening to a jury. He left her once, to call the police, but otherwise sat close and held her hand as she worked through all that happened.

And when she reached the part where she threw a pitchfork twenty feet and hit a target most able-bodied men couldn't have managed, let alone a woman eight months pregnant, he lifted her from the pillow and held her tightly in his arms. For a moment, he was reminded of her second self, but he knew now that they were all one: the sweet girl was the smart lawyer, and both of them were the strong and courageous woman who saved herself when no one else could, and he loved all of them so much it terrified him.

21

THE HOSPITAL BEGAN TO STIR AT SIX. A NURSE STOLE IN AND TURNED the blinds, and daylight filtered into the room. Jenny's eyes opened, and she glanced first at the monitor, where the baby's heartbeat registered strong and regular, then at Dan.

" 'Morning." He smiled.

"You look exhausted," she said.

He leaned over to kiss her. "I can't say the same for you. You're looking better already."

"I feel better already," she said. "Why don't you go home and get some sleep?"

He hesitated, his eyes moving over her and to the monitor.

"Don't worry," she said. "I'll—we'll be fine. I'll probably sleep most of the day."

"You sure?"

"Positive."

"Is there anything you need?" She shook her head. "Anyone I should call?"

"Oh! My office. Would you call Marilyn for me? She gets in about eight-thirty."

"You got it." He bent down and kissed her softly. "I love you."

Breakfast arrived after Dan left, and she nibbled at it and pushed it away. Later, a nurse bustled in and unhooked the IV and oxygen tubes and helped her to the bathroom. The doctor arrived a few minutes later and pronounced her and the baby to be doing fine.

She was so relieved she dozed for another two hours after he left.

Someone from administration came in with papers to sign, all the papers that should have been signed last night when Scott brought her in. These she couldn't push away, and she rose up on her elbows to read them.

The date was scrawled at the top of the page. September 22. She couldn't think why it rang familiar. Somebody's birthday? Not her wedding day, that was tomorrow. At least, it was supposed to be tomorrow. Now it might have to be postponed. Too bad, considering how much trouble they'd had scheduling it in the first place. Dan had his week of depositions in Buffalo to finish, and she had the Macoal closing—

The Macoal closing.

Jenny sat up and grabbed for the phone, and when she couldn't reach it she found the nurse's buzzer and held the button down until a flustered young woman ran into the room. "Get me that phone!" she shouted.

The woman pursed her lips and placed the phone gingerly on the tray table and wheeled the table over the bed. "No, wait," Jenny said as she started to leave. "What do you have to do to dial out?"

"The instructions are on the card beside—"

"Just tell me!"

She reached Marilyn first. Yes, Mr. Casella had called from his car; she'd given Mr. Boenning the news; they were all praying for her. No, don't worry, the closing would go ahead as scheduled; Mr. Boenning came himself to pick up her files.

"Put me through to Walt."

"He went out to meet Mr. Glasser for breakfast."

"Where?"

"He didn't say."

"Well, when will he be back?"

"Before ten, I imagine. They're both planning to come directly to the conference room. Mr. Glasser's associate is there already."

"Is Cassie Chapman there yet?"

"No, she left a message that she'll be arriving with Mr. Stengel at ten."

Jenny's eyes moved frantically through the tiny room. Walt and Cassie were flanked by Stengel and his lawyer. There was no way she could reach either of them before ten, and no way even then to guarantee speaking to them in privacy.

"Thank you, Marilyn," she said and hung up. She pushed the tray table out of the way, unhooked the fetal monitor, and swung her legs over the side of the bed. Her right foot was wrapped in yards of gauze and covered with an elastic bandage, but as she touched it to the floor, she found she could hobble on it as far as the closet. She pulled on her blood-streaked yellow dress, and found her left shoe and slid her foot into it.

The effort required simply to get dressed exhausted her. She couldn't do this alone. She shuffled back to the telephone and called Dan at home, but a recording announced that the line was experiencing a service interruption. Puzzled, she tried his car phone, but there was no answer there. She dialed his office next, expecting Betty to pick up, but instead it rang directly into his voice mail.

She hung up. There was no time for this: she had to stop the closing.

She staggered to the door and turned the corner, and plunged into the strong arms of Mike diMaio.

22

HE DROVE HER TO HER HOUSE AND WAITED IN THE LIVING ROOM while she went to her room to change. She pulled on her clothes and found Josh Berman's diskette in her briefcase and started downstairs with it.

Her steps faltered. A misplaced date on a computer diskette, a draft with the wrong name as seller—what kind of evidence was that against the forces of Jack Stengel? Reese Chapman knew it would take more than that to bring him down; that's why he videotaped him plotting his perfect crime. If only Scott had given her the tape, or told her where it was. But instead, he'd played cute: "It's somewhere safe," he said.

"Here it is," she said, handing the diskette to Mike.

Suddenly the word *safe* echoed in her mind. *It's this place,* he'd said when the dove perched on his wrist. *She feels safe here.*

Scott was here yesterday, in this house, and he left his pocket watch on the nightstand. Was that the only thing he left?

"Wait a minute," she said and hurried across the living room into the storeroom and to the back by the open window where the dove liked to roost. She lifted up the wooden crate that served as the dovecote.

Under it, mottled with droppings, lay a videotape.

Mike gave a low whistle behind her. "No tellin' what's on it, though," he said, picking it up. "I gotta get somebody to screen it while I'm with the judge."

"Can you get a warrant without it?"

"Do my best."

"Okay, then." Jenny headed for the front door. "Let's go."

"Hold on." Mike moved ahead of her and blocked the door. "That ain't such a good idea. You just got out of the hospital."

"Mike, I'm fine. The baby's fine. There's nothing to worry about."

"The doctor tell ya that?"

"Yes! Mike, I have to go. By the time you get there with a warrant, it could be too late. It could be too late already, if we don't get going."

He grimaced and stepped aside. "You gotta take it easy, though."

"I will."

Mike made her go over it all again during the drive to the city, and when she pulled a legal pad out of her briefcase, he started to dictate paragraphs for the probable cause affidavit. She edited liberally as they went.

He parked illegally in front of her building, and they went over the plan one more time. He would get the warrants and return with a backup unit as soon as possible. Meanwhile, she was to stay in her office and call Cassie out of the conference room and keep her out until after the arrest was made.

"That's all, understand?" Mike said. "If she won't leave, you just sit in your office and wait for me."

"Got it."

As she hobbled through the lobby, a pain squeezed through her pelvis and made her lean weakly against the wall of the elevator. But by the time the doors opened on her floor, it was gone.

Marilyn gasped as she limped past her on the way into her office. "Has Walt returned?" Jenny called.

"Yes. He's in 38C."

She sank into her desk chair and dialed the conference room.

"Boenning."

"Walt, who's in the room with you?"

"Jennifer, is that you?"

"Put Cassie on, please."

"We're all so sorry to hear of your accident—"

"Thank you, Walt. Please put Cassie on."

His voice was muffled when he spoke again, and she could picture him turning his back on the room and cupping his hand around the mouthpiece. "What's this all about?"

"You have to cancel the closing."

"Jennifer, are you sure you're feeling yourself—"

"Jack Stengel conspired with Reese Chapman to buy the stock out of the trust months ago, for ten million dollars plus a private bonus to Chapman of another six. Cassie's selling it to him for nine million. It's a fraud. You've got to stop it."

"Oh dear Lord," he said slowly. "I'll tell Catherine. We'll terminate this meeting at once."

It was a relief to be able to pass the baton to someone else. "Thank you, Walt," she said, and put down the phone with a sigh.

There. Nothing to do now but wait for Mike to appear with the warrants. Stengel might be gone by then, but he wouldn't get far. She could put her foot up and relax. She could call Dan.

She dialed his office, but again, could get only as far as his voice mail. He wasn't in his car, and when she tried the house, this time she got a service representative who said the apparent problem was a phone off the hook.

That was where he was, then, taking the nap she'd urged upon him. Just as well. By the time he awoke, she'd be safely ensconced in her hospital bed and all he would have missed were hours of worry.

She felt a little lightheaded, and it made her realize how foolish she'd been to refuse her breakfast. A drink of juice might help, and she rose with an effort and headed out of her office for the vending machines.

Marilyn was speaking in hushed tones on her phone, and she broke off at the sight of Jenny.

Jenny glanced through the open door to Boenning's office. He should have returned by now. "Where's Walt?"

Marilyn flushed and shook her head.

Jenny leaned over the side of her workstation, and Marilyn pressed a button and hung up, erasing the name displayed on her telephone console.

She'd been talking to Boenning. He was going ahead with the closing; he hadn't called it off at all.

Jenny went back into her office and dialed conference room 38C. The line rang six times without an answer.

They'd moved to another location. Jenny limped out into the corridor, and Marilyn's eyes tracked her. Her loyalties always lay first with Boenning—Jenny knew that from the start—and his instructions must have been to keep Jenny at bay until the deal was closed. Somewhere, he was proceeding with the stock sale.

She only hoped it was somewhere in this office.

"I'm not feeling well," Jenny said to her secretary. "I'll be in the ladies' room."

She started on the thirty-eighth floor. Conference room 38C was empty, as she'd suspected, and A and B were occupied by other groups of lawyers. She rode the elevator to 39 and repeated the search through all the conference rooms there, again without luck. She punched the button to call the elevator again, but when it took too long to come, she went to the stairs and pulled herself up by the handrail one step at a time until she arrived, panting, on the fortieth floor.

She felt again the clenching pain in the pit of her belly, and this one took her breath away. She sagged against the wall until it passed, then moved as fast as her body would let her to 40A. It was empty. She half ran to 40B, and when she jerked the door open, she found it in use for somebody's birthday party. "Sorry," she gasped, and stumbled on to 40C.

A hum of voices came from inside this conference room. No one answered at her knock, and she gripped the knob and swung the door in.

There they were, Cassie and Boenning on one side of the table, Stengel and two of his lawyers on the other. Boenning and the older of the two lawyers, undoubtedly Marvin Glasser, had their heads together at the near end of the table, and the younger lawyer, Josh Berman, was by himself, sorting through stacks of papers at the far end. At midpoint, Cassie leaned over the closing book, her reading glasses perched on the end of her nose. Across from her lounged Jack Stengel with nothing but a fountain pen on the table in front of him.

Boenning looked up in irritation when the door opened, and his annoyance grew when he saw it was Jenny.

"Excuse—excuse me," Jenny said, fighting to catch her breath. "Cassie, could I speak to you outside for a moment?"

Cassie's head came up. "Jenny, I thought—"

Boenning got to his feet. "Jennifer, I'll see you in the hall."

Jenny didn't spare him a glance. "Cassie, it's urgent."

Stengel tilted back in his chair, watching her with mild curiosity.

"What is this?" Glasser complained. "You know we have to be back in New York by three."

"Jenny, what's wrong?" Cassie pulled off her glasses, but didn't rise from her chair.

"Nothing's wrong." Boenning took Jenny's arm. "Jennifer's had an accident and hasn't given herself enough time to recover from it. I'll see she's taken care of. The rest of you, please carry on."

His fingers dug into her arm as he steered her toward the door. "Don't make me call security," he warned.

Jenny jabbed her elbow backward and caught him hard in the paunch. He dropped her arm with a yell, and she spun back into the room.

"Cassie, call off the sale. Stengel's been plotting for months to get Macoal away from you. He conspired with your father and Scott Sterling to try to force Mason to resign from the trust. Scott's confession, the trial—the whole thing was a sham to force Mason into resigning as trustee, so your father could sell the Macoal stock to Stengel."

"This is an outrage!" Glasser roared.

"I'll get security up here," Boenning said and grabbed the phone.

Cassie went very still.

361

"It's true," Jenny said. Another pain seized her, but she bit her lip against it and stood her ground.

Cassie turned to stare at Stengel. He met her eyes across the table and slowly, almost pitifully, shook his head.

"Yes!" Boenning was shouting into the phone. "I want an officer up here now! We have an intruder who must be escorted off the premises."

"Ask him." Jenny pointed to Josh Berman at the far end of the table. The young man went bright red under the sudden scrutiny. "Ask him why he drafted an agreement for your father to sell the stock to Stengel last January. Ask him why your father was described in the agreement as the trustee."

"That's a lie!" Glasser said.

"I can prove it. It's on the computer diskette he sent me yesterday. And you still have it on your hard drive back in New York, don't you?" she said, pointing again to the young lawyer.

The Adam's apple bobbed in Berman's throat. "I—I only did what Mr. Glasser told me to. I didn't know there was anything wrong—"

"Shut up!" Glasser shouted at him.

Cassie gazed across the table. "Jack?"

Stengel shook his head again. "Your father and I spoke once about the possibility of doing a deal if he were ever named successor trustee. I asked Marv to draw up some papers just in case. This is the way I do business."

Cassie turned a doubtful look on Jenny.

"Cassie," she pleaded, "he agreed to pay your father a six-million-dollar bonus to pull off the stock sale. But your father didn't trust him to keep up his end of the bargain. So he videotaped him discussing the whole thing."

Cassie shot a look at Stengel.

"Where's that goddamned security?" Boenning yelled and reached for the phone again.

"Scott tried to blackmail Stengel with the videotape, and Stengel sent Moi after him, to kill him."

"This is ridiculous!" Glasser thundered.

"I was there. Moi tried to kill him, but Scott shot him first. He's dead."

Jenny glanced at Stengel, but his expression didn't change. She turned back to Cassie.

"Your father had nothing to do with Mason's murder, Cassie. He killed himself only because he realized that Scott did it."

Cassie's face went white.

There was a knock on the door, and Boenning put the phone down in relief. "Yes, come in!" To Jenny he said, "Whatever they do with you, don't bother coming back to this office again."

Mike diMaio elbowed his way past him. "Police. Everybody stay where you are." Four uniformed police officers streamed in behind him, and pointing the way behind them was the building security officer.

Glasser shot out of his seat.

" 'Stay where you was,' he said," one of the cops muttered and pushed him back down.

"Jack Stengel, I got a warrant for your arrest," Mike said. "Everybody else, I got warrants to search this room, including all the briefcases and all the papers you got lyin' here on the table."

"On what charges?" Glasser demanded.

"Conspiracy to commit fraud, fraud, and felony murder."

Stengel still lounged in his chair. "This is a travesty," he said. "You don't have a particle of evidence against me."

"Lemme see," Mike said. "I got two dead bodies, a computer diskette, and—oh, yeah, a video starrin' Jack Stengel as himself."

At last Stengel's face changed. His lips drew into a wide, tight line across his face.

"Cuff him and read his rights," Mike said. "The rest of you gentlemen, your briefcases if you don't mind?"

23

CASSIE AND JENNY SAT TOGETHER AT THE CONFERENCE TABLE LONG after the room was cleared. Stengel was in custody; Glasser and Berman were being interrogated by the DA; Boenning pleaded illness and went home. From time to time, Cassie thought of another question, and Jenny answered it; otherwise they sat in silence.

The telephone rang and Jenny stirred herself to answer it.

"I thought you oughtta know," Mike said. "They picked up Sterling. Got your car back, too."

"Where did they find him?"

"Newark Airport, like you said."

She mourned him for a moment, but it wasn't him, it was never him. The spark of kinship was an artificial light, and it was extinguished now.

Another pain seized her. Less than two minutes apart, there was no mistaking it anymore.

"Do me a favor, Mike?"

"Anything."

"Find Dan and have him meet me at the hospital."

Cassie was at her elbow. "I'll drive you there," she whispered, and Jenny nodded her thanks.

"Okay," Mike was saying. "But it might take a coupla hours."

"Why? Where is he?"

"On his way back from Newark. He's the one that got Sterling."

24

A CHILL WIND BLEW THROUGH THE PARKING LOT AND SCUTTLED DRY leaves across Dan's path. The sky was a dull pewter gray, and the air was full of March uncertainty—in another minute, it could snow, or the clouds could blow away and the sun shine down on new green grass. He left his overcoat in the car; he remembered from past experience that prisons didn't come with cloakrooms.

He showed his papers at the gate and was waved through to the next gate, where a hand-held metal detector was run over his body. At the next door, there were forms to sign, and finally he was ushered into the attorneys' waiting room. It was Saturday, and the only other occupant of the room was a young black woman poring over a case reporter.

"Casella?" said a guard.

"Yeah," Dan said, and followed him down a long, unlit corridor lined with steel doors with small square windows at eyeball height.

The guard stopped at the fourth door, turned a key in the lock, and swung it in. "Wait here," he said.

The room was ten by ten, windowless, with cinder-block walls painted mustard yellow and an incandescent-light fixture in the ceiling. A metal table was plopped on the linoleum floor with vinyl-seated chairs on either side. The walls carried black scuff marks up to a height of about four feet. Dan wondered who climbed the walls more, the inmates or the lawyers put here to wait for them.

He sat down on the cracked vinyl seat and opened his briefcase. The papers inside were from a new libel case he was handling, but he spread them over the tabletop anyway, placebos for any guard who might peer in the window and grow suspicious.

"Why can't you give it a rest?" Mike had said when Dan asked him to make the arrangements.

Maybe after today he could. Maybe he'd stop feeling sick with guilt over the number he'd done on Mason. Maybe he'd be able to get through a night without Sterling lurking in the shadows of every dream.

The key sounded in the lock, metal grating on metal, and the door swung in. The prisoner ducked through the doorway and stopped and blinked as the light hit his eyes. He wore the regulation jumpsuit and had dirty blond hair hanging, unkempt, to his shoulders and a small brown goatee sprouting on his chin. He blinked once more, and a lopsided grin spread over his face.

"You got fifteen minutes," the guard said, and slammed the door shut.

"Since when are you my lawyer?"

His eyes were an overbright blue—drugs, Dan supposed, or maybe just craziness. He'd pictured him in prison long ago, but always in a minimum-security facility for white-collar criminals, housed between Ivan Boesky and Albert Nipon, doing some of the best estate-planning work of his career. Instead, he'd landed in maximum security with a ready-made reputation as a two-time killer.

"Since never," Dan said. "I want to ask you some questions."

Sterling came farther into the room. There was a swagger in his walk that was new since last year. He grabbed a chair and turned it backward.

"I'm done answering questions."

He straddled the chair and folded his arms over its back. Faint new lines traced like webs around his mouth and his eyes; whoever his old self was, he'd never look like him again.

"I think you owe me a couple of answers," Dan said, "after what you did to me."

"What *I* did to *you*," he sneered. "If it wasn't for you, I would've boarded my flight and I'd be on a beach somewhere right now."

That was one of the recurrent scenes in Dan's dreams. The terminal had been swarming with cops, but not one who could have recognized Sterling from the bar association photo they'd been wired. Maybe Dan wouldn't have recognized him either, but Sterling had given himself away—he bolted out of line when he saw Dan scanning the crowd at the gate. He took off, backward down an escalator and through the concourse, with a good enough lead that he would have made it if he hadn't slipped on a freshly mopped floor. Dan came down hard on him and didn't get up until the cops arrived.

"Besides," Sterling said now, shrugging, "I gave you another trial victory to notch on your belt—not to mention earning you some decent fees."

Dan's jaw clenched. "There was nothing decent about the fees or the victory. It was a fraud, and I don't like being made a part of it."

"So sue me," he said with an elaborate shrug.

"And I don't like what you did to Jenny."

The light dimmed a little in Sterling's eyes. He pulled a cigarette out of the chest pocket of his jumpsuit, clamped it in his mouth, and struck a match against the tabletop.

"She came out all right," he said with a deep inhalation. "I hear she landed Macoal as a client. Nothing for a third-year associate to complain about."

"You almost got her killed!"

Another elaborate shrug. "She survived."

Dan surged out of his chair and turned to the wall like he wanted to break it, second choice after Sterling's neck. A guard's head appeared in the square of glass, and Dan took a deep breath and swallowed down his rage. But he couldn't force himself to sit down again, across the table from Sterling. He stayed on his feet, his back pressed hard against the cinder blocks.

"Tell me this much," he said. "Why Jenny? What was her role supposed to be? That's what I still can't figure out."

"Role in what?"

"Some of it I got. Chapman told you his daughter hired Jenny, and you moved in with her so she could be your eyes and ears during the trial. But it was more than that, wasn't it? You knew about her and me. What was the idea? That I'd have more incentive to clear your name? Or was she supposed to steal my notes for you? Before Chapman did it himself."

Sterling took another drag on his cigarette and flicked the butt with two fingers into the corner of the room. He turned back to Dan and stared at him with his overbright eyes while a corner of his mouth lifted in a crooked smile.

"Is it so hard to believe I just plain fell in love with her?"

Dan couldn't speak. Sterling swung out of the chair and gave a sharp crack of his knuckles against the window. The key grated and the door opened. "We're all done here," he told the guard and disappeared down the long dark corridor.

25

SNOW CLOUDS HUNG LOW ALL THAT MORNING, BUT WHEN JENNY emerged from class at noon, they'd melted away and the sun shone brightly. She tossed her ballet bag into the trunk beside the collapsible stroller and got behind the wheel. By the time she reached Leslie's, it was so warm she and the baby were outside on a quilt on the grass.

"Hi! How was class?" Leslie called.

"My form stank," Jenny said with a big smile for Peter as she knelt on the quilt beside him. He was beginning to sit up unassisted, though Leslie still employed one hand for his backrest.

"I doubt anyone noticed," she said. "You're much too good for that class. Monsieur duBret would die if he knew you were slumming this way."

"I'm just happy to be dancing again. Was Peter a good boy today?" Jenny asked in a high-pitched voice that made him giggle until his jowls shook. He'd more than recovered from his prematurity, and was now cheerfully chubby.

"He was the best little boy in the world," Leslie declared, nuzzling his cheek and making him laugh louder. "In fact, I'd love to watch him this afternoon if you and Dan want to have some time alone."

"Thanks, but Dan's out of town today."

"Everything okay with you two?"

Jenny swung the baby up into the air to hide her face. Leslie's powers of observation were as sharp as ever.

"Great," she said, and it would have been true if only she didn't wake up so often to an empty pillow and find Dan brooding in the living room; if only when they held each other it didn't feel like some invisible force field were trying to pull them apart. If only Dan hadn't felt compelled to make his trip today.

"Give it some time," Leslie said. "You guys have been through a lot."

Jenny nodded, but it was six months already; she felt as if their life together was stalled and needed a push harder than time to get started again.

"Want to go shopping?" Leslie suggested. "I'll help you pick out some clothes for Peter."

"Thanks, but it's so nice out, I think I'll drive somewhere pretty and take Peter for a walk."

"Try Valley Forge."

"Good idea."

But Jenny had something else in mind, and she strapped the baby into his seat and pointed the car for Radnor. She hadn't been to the old Dundee place since Peter was born, exactly one hour after the service was concluded. It wasn't the wedding she'd dreamed of. The district justice had been peevish about being pulled from his courtroom in the middle of the afternoon session; Mike diMaio and Cassie Chapman were the most unlikely pair of wedding attendants she could imagine; and the doctor stuck his head under the drape while she was reciting her vows. But it had appeased Dan's old-fashioned need to be married before the baby was born. While she and Peter recuperated, Dan packed up the carriage house and found homes for the dog and cats, and when it was time to leave the hospital, he took them directly to his apartment.

The penthouse was spectacular, but it was never meant for a family of four. It was so confining during the winter that Tony started spending weekends with his mother. They should have moved out months ago, but this was one of the things that was stalled between them. At first, it was Jenny who couldn't muster any enthusiasm for house-hunting, but lately it was Dan. She'd been sliding brochures at him for weeks, but she couldn't seem to get his attention, any more than she could end his sleepless nights.

When she tried to talk to him about it, he only shrugged and said he had some demons to exorcise. But she knew his demons, and all of them were named Scott Sterling. Dan might have been the centerpiece of Chapman's scheme, but she was the one whose misplaced trust opened the door and let the demon into their lives.

She turned onto Coventry Road and drove to Canterbury Lane, where she parked at the stone pillars proclaiming the Estates at Dundee.

"Shall we go for a walk?" she sang out to Peter, and he gurgled an assent. She pulled the stroller out of the trunk, settled him into it, and set off up the hill.

An entire community had grown on the hillside. Crocuses bloomed in little circular beds around mailboxes, cars were parked in driveways, grapevine wreaths adorned front doors. The day's sunshine was drawing the inhabitants outside in probably the greatest numbers all year. Women were on their knees planting pansies along their front walks, men were raking the last winter debris from their lawns, children romped in the grass with their pets.

A new house was framed on the crest of the hill where the old manor house used to stand. Jenny remembered the dawn when Scott had stood within its ghostly outlines and reminisced about happier days. She'd imagined him as some kind of tragic hero, a good man suffering too much for a single mistake. She'd seen their lives running on parallel tracks and convinced herself that so long as he could endure, so could she.

Mike once said that Scott was able to deceive Curtis Mason so well because he told him exactly what he wanted to hear—a variation on the old adage, "You can't cheat an honest man." But Jenny had been deceived just as thoroughly, and by the same means. If only she'd been honest with herself, she never would have believed what he was telling her, no matter how badly she wanted to hear it.

Down the hill lay the woods, and beyond it, whatever was left of the ruins of the old carriage house. The builder had notified her of the demolition date last October in case she wanted to come and watch, but in the end she couldn't do it. Now, though—now she could go and look.

"Peter, let's run!" Jenny cried, and he gurgled on cue as she jogged down the hill and let him feel the wind on his cheeks.

The road through the woods was supposed to be plowed under and planted over by now. She was puzzled to find it paved and curbed the same as Canterbury Lane. Her steps slowed under the trees, and she grew more bewildered when the roof of the carriage house appeared through the branches.

It was still there. It was supposed to be demolished in October, but there it stood. Jenny pushed the stroller closer, and as it rolled into the cobblestone courtyard, the sound of hammering came from inside.

The house was still there, but it was different. The roof was covered with new cedar shingles, and second stories had been added to each of the garage wings, with dormers to match those in the central part of the house. The lower level still held a garage bay on the end of each wing, but the interior bays had been converted to living space and had French doors opening onto the courtyard. New muntined windows looked out all through the house, and a railed porch with a small gable roof over it marked the front door.

It was a vision Jenny couldn't fathom. The plan was to tear the carriage house down—that had always been the plan—yet here it stood, remodeled and renovated beyond belief. Or at least almost renovated, for a crew of carpenters was at work inside.

She unbuckled Peter from the stroller and carried him to the front door. "Hello?" she called, and a white-haired man looked up quizzically from the trim he was nailing into place around the window.

"I used to live here," she said. "I thought it was torn down."

"Some guy talked the contractor into selling it to him and fixing it up. You can look around if you want."

"Thanks."

She wandered inside. The rear wall was all windows looking onto a new brick patio. The central fireplace was missing, replaced by one at either end of the enormous room. The kitchen was gone, too, and a free-standing staircase rose like a piece of sculpture to the second floor.

"Kitchen's that way now," the carpenter said, pointing to the old storeroom. "And upstairs, there's five bedrooms."

"I can't believe it," Jenny said, her eyes moving through the beloved old house in amazement. It was the same space she remembered, but better, so much better.

Tires sounded on the cobblestones in the courtyard. "Here comes the owner now," the carpenter said, looking out the front door.

"I wonder if he'd sell it to me," she said, only half teasing.

"Wouldn't count on it," he said. "The way this guy's been watching over this project, I'd say they're gonna have to carry him out feet first."

She gave a final glance through the room and sighed. "I'd better be going, then."

She shifted the baby to her other hip and started out the front door, colliding with someone coming in.

"Excuse—" she started to say, then exclaimed, "Tony?"

His eyes opened wide and he spun on his heel. "I didn't tell her. I swear I didn't!"

Behind him stood Dan.

Jenny stared at him. "Dan, what are you—?" Then as realization struck, she gasped, "Dan—*you* did this?"

He took the baby from her and spoke softly to him before he gave a brief, uncertain nod. "I was hoping you might like it here. But if you don't, we'll sell it. I've had two good offers already."

"Like it?" Her voice started to choke, and she had to swallow back her tears before she could speak. "It's the most wonderful house I've ever seen."

"Can I hold Pete?" Tony asked, and Dan passed the baby to him. "Come on, little guy," he said. "I'll show you your room."

Dan's eyes went soft as he watched them go. Peter's tiny face was like an echo of Tony's. The resemblance was so apparent, Tony could see it himself; people routinely mistook them for brothers.

Jenny was blinking, trying hard to take in the room, and the house, and the emotions playing across Dan's face—all of it was too much.

"Have you seen this?" He pointed to the room across the courtyard, in the interior bay that had once been her ballet studio.

She shook her head.

"Come on."

She followed him across the cobblestones and through a pair of French doors, and froze on the doorstep.

Her ballet studio was still there, but better, astonishingly better. A gleaming hardwood floor stretched before her, from mirrored wall to mirrored wall. Barres were mounted on the mirrors, and clerestory windows lined the walls above the mirrors, letting in a wash of sunlight over the floor. A built-in cabinet held a CD player and a tape deck. Another cabinet held a sink and a tiny refrigerator.

She managed another step into the room, and rotated as if on a turntable. "Why did you do this?" she breathed.

"I think maybe just for this moment."

She revolved through the room, and her reflection and his moved panoramically across the walls. Memories flooded her mind, of all the events of this room, of nightly barre with Leslie, of making love with Dan, of Scott smashing votives into the glass. She could feel Leslie's effervescent presence still, and Dan was everywhere around her, but there was nothing of Scott here. He wasn't lurking in any of the shadows; there were no shadows in this room.

"Jenny." Dan spoke her name as if he were caressing a wild animal, in a voice full of love and wonder and wariness.

She looked up at him. This man for whom paths cleared had done more than clear a path for her—he'd made a home.

He opened his arms and she went into them, and as they held each other, the only force she could feel was the one that pulled them together.

"How was your trip?" she whispered, searching his face.

"It's over," he said, and kissed her.

They joined hands and wandered through every room of their house before they went outside to the patio where Tony was playing with the baby in the sun-dappled grass. A power saw started up inside with a whine, and at the sound, a bird whooshed out of the dogwood and disappeared over the treetops, beating its wings against the cloudless sky.